Magdalena's Song

Other Books by Pat Mestern:

Fiction:

Clara

Anna, Child of the Poor House

Rachael's Legacy

Nonfiction

Fergus, The Story of Fergus through the Years; Volumes I and II

Fergus, A Scottish Town by Birthright

So You Want to Hold a Festival: A-Z of Festival & Special Event Organization

Magdalena's Song

by

Pat Mattaini Mestern

Published by
High Country Publishers, Ltd
Boone, North Carolina

High Country Publishers, Ltd
197 New Market Center, #135
Boone, NC 28607
www.highcountrypublishers.com

This is a work of fiction. All names are fictitious.
Any resemblance to any person living or dead is coincidental.

Cover photographs by Ted Mestern
Cover design by Russell Kaufman-Pace
Typesetting by schuyler kaufman
Poetry fragment on p.42 from a poem by Elizabeth Akers Allen (1832-1911)

Library of Congress Cataloging in Publication Data

Mestern, Pat Mattaini.
Magdalena's song / Pat Mattaini Mestern.
p. cm.
ISBN 0-9713045-8-0
1. Labor unions—Organizing—Fiction. 2. Identity (Psychology)—Fiction. 3. Romanies—Fiction. 4. Ontario—Fiction. I. Title.
PR9199.3.M446 M34 2003
813'.54—dc21

2002013534

Manufactured in the United States of America
First Printing: March 2003

Acknowledgments

Seeds for *Magdalena's Song* were sown more than fifty years ago when a mysterious fellow, who liked to be called Count, stayed in the area for a while and spun tales of Eastern Europe and the Kumpania. These stories gave young ears magical moments in hard times.

Those seeds sprouted when I was introduced to a charming woman who recently celebrated her ninety-fifth birthday. I have promised to keep her true identity a secret, so I can only identify the lady by her gypsy name, Darnda. I owe Darnda a debt of gratitude for her assistance with the Romane language as she remembered it from her early years with the Kumpania. Darnda wishes to remind people that it was many years ago when she spoke the language, and spellings vary from country to country, familia to familia.

Seeds were watered with encouragement by my husband Ted and my mother, the late Edith Scott Mattaini. Without their unflagging support and belief in me, *Magdalena's Song* would have been a difficult book to complete.

Many thanks to Carolyn Howser for her excellent editing. Judith Geary must be given credit for doing such a professional job of bringing *Magdalena's Song* into print. Both Carolyn and Judith are a joy to work with and a pleasure to have as friends.

But for the vision of Barbara and Bob Ingalls of High Country Publishers, readers would not enjoy books such as *Magdalena's Song*. Thanks must be given for their dedication to publishing and unflagging belief in their authors.

A final nod to Dennis Danyluk who found himself in front of the camera playing a fiddle for the book's cover shot.

Last but definitely not least, my thanks to readers for caring enough about authors and writings to purchase this little tome.

Enjoy!

Dedicated to

Ossie Glen,

a *kindred spirit,*

whose friendship has been much respected and appreciated.

*It's a dark island we live on,
my grandmother Theresa used to say;
and I'd laugh because we were
nowhere near a lake or sea that might harbor
an island. It was later, not until well after
she had died, that I finally realized the true
depth and meaning of her statement. This
village, although pristine and pretty in its
exterior appearance, has a sinister, dark
interior that hides from passing
pleasure seekers, and only reveals itself to
those who dare to stop, stay and dig into its
pithy past.*

Pense Magdalena Aventi

Magdalena's Song

LULLABY OF AN INFANT CHIEF

O hush thee, my babie, thy sire was a knight,
Thy mother a lady, both lovely and bright;
The woods and the glens, from the towers which we see,
They all are belonging, dear babie, to thee.
O ho ro, i ri ri, cadul gu lo.
O ho ro, i ri ri, cadul gu lo.

O fear not the bugle, though loudly it blows,
It calls but the warders that guard thy repose;
Their bows would be bended, their blades would be red,
Ere the step of a foeman drew near to thy bed.
O ho ro, i ri ri, cadul gu lo.
O ho ro, i ri ri, cadul gu lo.

O hush thee, my babie, the time soon will come
When thy sleep shall be broken by trumpet and drum;
Then hush thee, my darling, take rest while you may,
For strife comes with manhood, and waking with day.
O ho ro, i ri ri, cadul gu lo.
O ho ro, i ri ri, cadul gu lo.

Sir Walter Scott
Guy Mannering
c. 1815

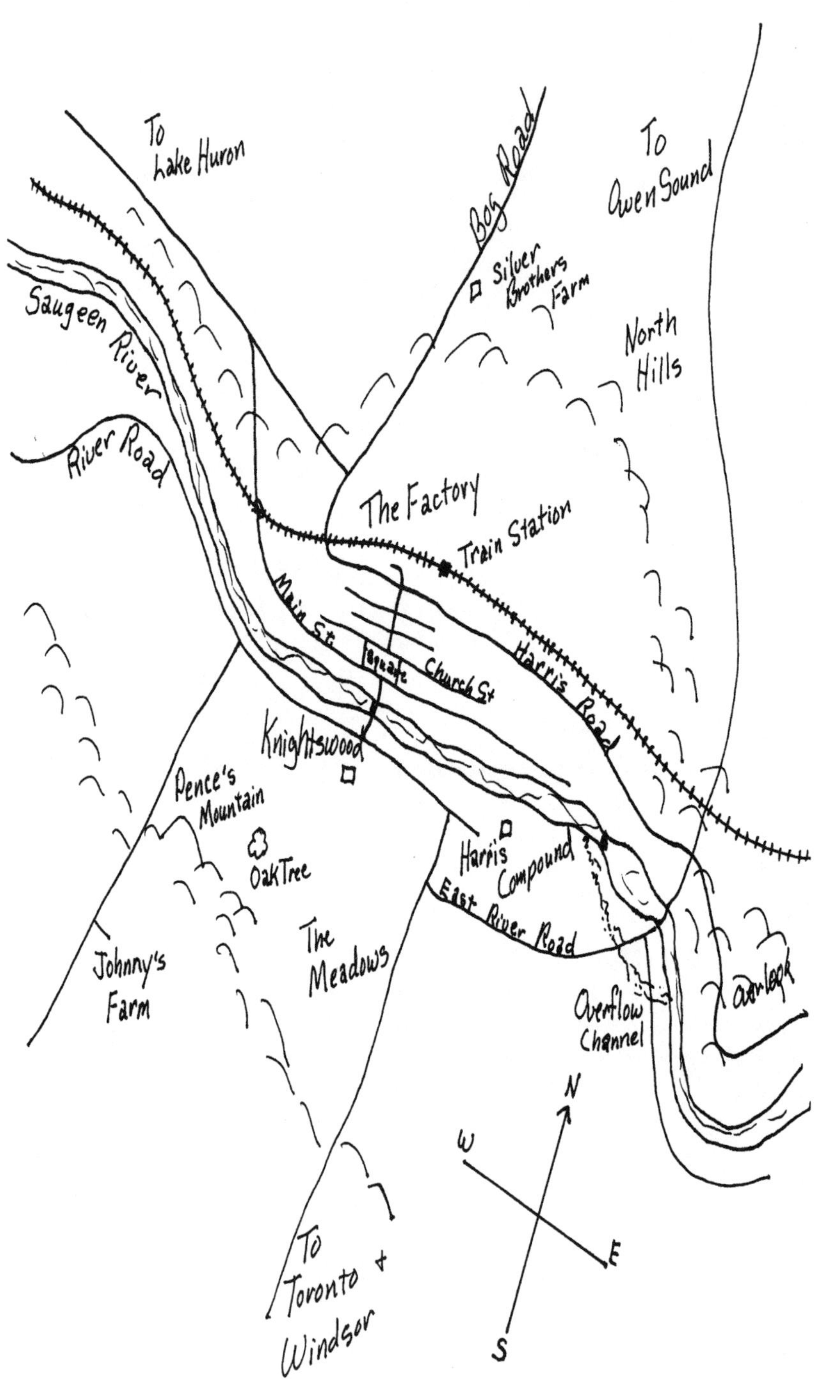
To
Lake Huron
Bog Road
To
Owen Sound
Silver
Brothers
Farm
North
Hills
Saugeen River
River Road
The Factory
Train Station
Main St
Square
Church St
Harris Road
Knightswood
Pence's
Mountain
OakTree
Harris
Compound
East River Road
Johnny's
Farm
The
Meadows
Overflow
Channel
overlook
N
W
E
S
To
Toronto +
Windsor

Foreword

The headwaters for most of the rivers that flow into the Great Lakes of Erie, Huron and Ontario are spawned in the high coun-try of southern Ontario where the majestic limestone spine of the Escarpment sweeps north from Niagara Falls to Tobermory on the Bruce Peninsula. Swamps, bogs and forests still line the upper tributaries of rivers such as the Saugeen, Grand, Credit, Nottawasaga and Humber. Small villages and towns nestle in valleys and on fertile bottom-land along the banks of these impressive river systems.

In particular, the Saugeen runs sparkling and clear through the counties of Grey and Bruce. Gathering waters from its tributaries, the North, Rocky, Beatty and South, the Saugeen courses through narrow rock-strewn channels before spilling onto a wide plain to complete its journey to the shores of Huron. Along the way it increases in volume with waters from artesian wells, peaty bogs and the Long Swamp.

It was to this part of Ontario that two young, wealthy gentlemen from the British Isles came during the early 1800s to establish new roots. They had been persuaded by rising estate prices in Britain and Scotland to raise their families in Upper Canada, where lands and labor were still cheap. It was their belief that by making such a move, they could ensure that future sons and daughters could ultimately own large tracts of land and continue to enjoy the lifestyle and amenities to which both families were accustomed. These men were yet to discover that Canada was a great *leveler* of race and class.

The two chose land along the Saugeen River, and by the mid-nineteenth century owned, between them, twelve thousand acres of beautiful valley, upland meadow and forest. They used their accumulated wealth to develop a model community, calling it Millbrook. The village's best acreage ran along the river valley, then over hill and dale on the north and south boundaries. In proper British fashion, the community was laid out around a square with main streets running parallel to the Saugeen. Water energy was harnessed by High Falls Dam, at the eastern edge of the village. With abundant water power and the availability of large quantities of wood, Millbrook was an ideal site for industry and commerce.

If the two founding families had been compatible, the future of Millbrook would have been greatly altered. As it was, the Anderson Clan belonged to the Free Scottish Kirk, and the Harris Family were strict Calvinists. By the end of a power struggle that lasted twenty-five years, Millbrook became the exclusive domain of the Harris family, while the Andersons withdrew to an impressive estate on the south boundary.

Although three generations of Harrises provided employment for villagers in their factory, their possessive and insular attitudes prevented the establishment of any new industry. In plain terms, Millbrook was a company town, and that company was J.P. Harris Ltd., manufacturer of quality housewares.

Millbrook's social life was dictated by the Harris family's frugal and religious attitudes. Dancing, smoking, drinking and other pleasurable pursuits were discouraged when one belonged to a church that retained the strictest of Calvinist rules. Indeed these activities were forbidden on pain of dismissal for anyone who worked for the Harris family. Although most people worshiped at the large, austere Memorial Church on the square, the first J.P. Harris had grudgingly let Irish Catholic farmers build, and worship at, a small church on Spring Street, several blocks north of Main.

Prospective villagers were put through a rigorous screening process before being allowed to purchase property. J.P. Harris II had allowed several Italian families to settle in the community, among them his gardener Antonio Inachio and Franco Adamo, a greengrocer. Greek culture was represented by the Kropolus family who purchased the China Inn from a disgruntled factory employee during a visit to England by J.P. Harris. The name China Inn, having been bestowed by the locals, had nothing to do with Chinese culture or food. The moniker referred to the fact that J.P. Harris II had insisted that good china be used for table service.

Although Harris's son J.P. the third had inherited his father's insularity, by 1947 cracks began to appear in his hold on Millbrook. He spent a lot of time away from the village. Harris was a traditionalist who believed a female's place was in the home. He dealt poorly with the influx of women doing factory work during the Second World War. The most unsettling circumstance, in the eyes of even the most diehard company men, was that he had begun to hang around Stanley David Compton, a shady, small-time land developer with a penchant for profanity and gambling.

The village of Millbrook was ripe for change. The war was over. People were restless, and personal relationships strained. Men had returned from the front physically tired and suffering from war-inflicted psychological problems. Jobs were few. Pay was low. Labor unions were forming across the country.

Perhaps the prophecy of Zizou, the matriarch of the Roma that paid the village a visit every spring and autumn, would come true. "The first builds; the second maintains; the third destroys. The first wine pressed is pure, the second is distilled and the third is putrid," Zizou whispered to those who would listen.

Chapter 1

September 25, 1947: afternoon

A broad grin broke across Daniel's craggy face as he stared at the naked child sitting on the roof of the barn. At first he couldn't believe what he was seeing, but the sheer exuberance of the comely girl made his heart soar alongside the white dove she was enticing to land on her outstretched hand.

Oh, to possess the uninhibited freedoms of childhood once again, Daniel thought. A bit ashamed, even in his amusement, that he'd so enjoyed seeing the girl in her nakedness, he turned his eyes to the house. Like flame to match, a flick of recognition passed through Daniel's mind, then subsided into his murky memory.

The view from the highway belied the actual size of the building. Expansive lawns and mature trees muted and softened its impact on the eye. The imposing two-story stone structure, with its gabled attics and wide, covered verandahs, was the epitome of Georgian architecture. Its verandah with inviting wicker chairs and large potted plants beckoned weary travelers. Lace curtains hung at windows open to catch fresh September breezes.

Halfway down the driveway, Daniel smelled baking bread and hot, spicy vinegar. His rumbling stomach reminded him that he hadn't eaten for over a day.

"I'm here to do a job so I may as well get on with it," he murmured. With suitcase in hand, he climbed the steps. Knocking on the front door took more courage than Daniel had anticipated.

"I'm coming," a female voice called from the interior. Footsteps clipped across wooden floors. Then she stood drying her hands on a large print apron, peering at the stranger before opening the screen door. Two large calico cats flew past Daniel's feet as she did.

"If you insist on running ahead of me, you'll get tramped on," the woman scolded the cats. "They do that all the time, trying to trip up an old lady." She now spoke directly to Daniel. "You must be Mr. Cudzinki. We held lunch because we thought you'd be hungry after the train ride."

Daniel smiled, bowed and extended his hand. He nodded, pleased with what he saw – comfortable body, a beautiful, time-caressed face with extraordinarily deep brown eyes and a ready, friendly smile.

In a voice with just the slightest hint of an East European accent, Daniel said, "It's my pleasure to meet you, Mrs. Inachio. I came in early, so took the opportunity to walk from the station, to stretch my legs. Unfortunately, I got carried away with the beauty of the area and extended my stroll past arrival time." Daniel bowed slightly. "You shouldn't have delayed lunch."

"It isn't a problem, Mr. Cudzinki. We serve a cold meal at noon on wash day. Nothing's spoiled or burned. Come in. I'll show you to your room. Theresa turned from the door. "By the way, it's *Miss* Inachio. "

Daniel stepped into the foyer, a space alive with color even after the sunlight outside. The impressive hall was more art gallery than private reception area. Oil paintings hung on walls. Statuary graced the newel post of a wide stairway that led to the second floor. High, ornate wooden arches supported a corniced ceiling. Beyond the arches a radio played, buoyed by a boisterous contralto voice.

In answer to his quizzical look and unspoken question, Theresa Inachio said, "Sharona loves to sing. You'll get used to it. Come on. I'll show you to your room."

Both walls in the stairwell were also hung with paintings. As Theresa led the way up the broad sweep of steps, Daniel stopped to give several closer scrutiny. One that depicted an early morning landscape caught his attention and again Daniel experienced a fleeting snip of recognition.

Theresa turned to see why Daniel had stopped climbing. "That work is by the former owner of the house. She loved to paint local landscapes. Pretty, aren't they?" Theresa pointed toward the second floor. "Your room's this way."

"Sorry," Daniel said. "I'm fascinated by . . . " His voice trailed off.

"I must confess that I was surprised to get your letter," Theresa said as she pulled herself up by the handrail. "My rooms are usually taken by travelers and salesmen who see the sign hanging out front. Sometimes people hear about the place from friends who've stayed. It's unusual for an individual to reserve by letter."

"I wanted to ensure you had a room available," Daniel said.

Theresa stopped and, running her fingers along the polished rail, turned to look at Daniel. "I was even more surprised to read that while here you're planning to look for some connection to the Anderson family."

Daniel cleared his throat. "A member of my family may have had such a connection."

"That's interesting," Theresa said. "Well, you're lucky you came to Millbrook now. A hydro crew is coming through mid-October and they've booked all of my rooms then."

They'd reached the top of the stairs before Daniel had nerve enough to ask, "What is that child doing on the roof of the barn?"

"You saw her."

"Yes. Stark naked and playing with a white dove."

"Dear bless me!" Theresa whirled and strode into the back hallway from the head of the stairs. "Pense," she shouted through an open window. "*Pense*! Get down at once and put your clothes on! I've told you countless times not sit on the roof in that state of undress."

Coming back to the head of the stairs, Theresa shouted, "Sharona. *Sharona*!" The singing stopped. "Pense is on the roof again and she's not got a stitch of clothing on her body." A screen door slammed.

"Apologies, Mr. Cudzinki. Pense is an unusual girl, I'm afraid, quite unimpressed by rules. You might meet her at lunch. I'd appreciate it if you'd just try to forget what you saw. I promise that she won't do it again while you're here. Thank God that we've no neighbors living near enough to see her in that state!"

"It didn't distress me, Miss Inachio, but I am curious as to why a child would sit God's cloth on a dangerously high roof."

Theresa's eyes were bright, her laugh a chesty trickle of energy. "The better to look over her mountain, Mr. Cudzinki, and she can't stand clothes. She loathes shoes. Don't we all?" She laughed again. "When you were a child, didn't you ever run naked and barefoot through long grass?"

Daniel grinned. "I admit that I did so on many occasions. But . . . isn't she frightened of heights?"

"No, she loves being up there. And fortunately, it's not a high barn." Theresa put her hand on Daniel's arm, "Your room's this way. I've put you in Mr. Anderson's former bedroom. It's spacious and overlooks the front lawn. Pense, Sharona and I have bedrooms off the back hallway. Needless to say, that area is off-limits for boarders. The bathroom's here." Theresa pointed toward a closed door. "It's shared with Johnny Wallace, Sharona, myself, and of course, other paying guests. There's an *occupied* sign on the back of the door. Hang it on the knob when you're using the facility."

"You said mountain, Miss Inachio. I didn't see any mountain nearby." Daniel followed behind Theresa along the upper front hall.

"That little issue doesn't faze Pense. For her, mountains materialize from molehills." Theresa opened the door to Daniel's room. "You've paid for the first week. The door locks but I can't find the key. You wouldn't need to lock your door anyway. I think you'll find everything you need in the room. Sheets are changed once a week. Ask Sharona or myself for clean towels."

She turned to face him squarely, her hands clasped in front of her. "Any questions?"

"I can't think of any at the moment."

"Well then, we'll eat in fifteen minutes in the kitchen. It's downstairs, to the left in the lower hall. The first room is the library and the second is the dining room. Go straight along the corridor, past the dining room, to the kitchen. Do you want me to call you in ten minutes?"

"That's not necessary," Daniel said. "I've got a watch." He fingered the timepiece in his pocket but thought better of showing it. "If I recall from our correspondence, lunch isn't included in the price."

"It is today." Theresa turned from the bedroom door and started for the stairs. "Ten minutes, then?"

Daniel closed his door gently and leaned against it.

Dordie, miri mort. The woman was like a clockwork toy, staying ahead of her would be a challenge. He surveyed his kingdom.

The tidy room looked comfortable enough. Pale green walls were hung with paintings – loons on a northern lake, a Scottish croft beside a loch, an autumn scene of river and hills. Once again, Daniel experienced a fleeting spark of recognition. A night table stood beside a bed covered with a colorful quilt. A large writing desk with a straight chair dominated a corner. An ornate chest of drawers with a mirror shared a wall with a built-in closet whose door could be locked. The nicest touch was a comfortable arm chair pulled up to a window overlooking the lawn. Beside it was a revolving book rack and reading lamp.

The handwritten card propped against the chest's mirror reinforced the house rules – $7.00 a week in advance – breakfast & supper, sheets & towels provided. No smoking, entertaining or drinking hard liquor allowed in the house.

Fair enough, thought Daniel. After all, it is a private residence. Mr. Anderson's books were surely still in the bookcase – Dwight's *Turkish Life in War Time*, Dana's *Muck Manual*, several of Abbot's *Pioneers and Patriots* series, Steinmetz's *SubtileBrains and Lissan Fingers.* What one would expect of a gentleman of his time. He pulled *Smalilou*, by Yoxall, from the rack. "Now here's a surprise." Perhaps there had been more to the old man than he recognized.

"May as well settle in." Daniel removed clothes from his suitcase and placed them in the chest's drawers. Not bad, he mused, for the sort of *shopping* he'd done to assure that he had a suitable wardrobe. He found it difficult to select the right size off a clothesline, when in a hurry and in the dark. Daniel was especially pleased with the suit that he'd won off a *gadjé*s back in a poker game, after he'd deemed it necessary to own one. A toothbrush, comb, clothes brush, straight razor and bar of soap were set out on the night table.

From pockets, Daniel produced an envelope of money – $143.27 at last count – the working mechanism of a pocket watch and a white linen handkerchief. Daniel tucked the handkerchief into the back left corner of the middle desk drawer. The watch went back into a pocket. The envelope of money went into the suitcase that was then locked in the closet. The closet key dropped into the same pocket as the watch. With a toothbrush in hand, Daniel went to tidy up for lunch.

Daniel descended the stairs with slow, deliberate steps. He stopped to admire the artwork again, taking the opportunity to rest his weary body. Glancing into the mirror at the foot of the stairs, Daniel smiled at the image. As long as a man with swarthy complexion, collar-length white hair and a trim figure looked back at him, he was satisfied.

At the kitchen door Daniel came face to face with Pense, a willowy slip whose thick brown hair hung loosely to her waist. This time, she was fully clothed.

Daniel's stomach churned as huge luminous green eyes matched him, stare for stare. His hand went to his pounding heart, and his breath came in audible gasps. My God, he thought, *it's her!* I was right. She's much younger, but it's definitely her.

As Pense dropped her gaze and stepped aside so Daniel could pass, a woman's voice scolded, "Don't you be late, Pense. Come home when you hear the six o'clock whistle."

Daniel felt a steadying hand on his arm.

Theresa was at his side. "Are you all right, Mr. Cudzinki? You've gone quite pale. Sit down – here, beside Sharona." She led him toward a chair at the kitchen table.

Daniel shook his head, looked around and then sat down heavily. "I . . . I'm fine. I've a . . . heart condition that sometimes puts me off a bit."

"Strong coffee, that's what's needed for a weak heart." Theresa grabbed the coffee pot from the cook stove and filled Daniel's cup. "Drink up."

Sipping the strong brew, Daniel was able to take a close look at the woman seated beside him. So this was Sharona.

Sharona, black hair in a neat bun at the back of her graceful neck, sat quietly taking in everything about Daniel's appearance.

Daniel felt uncomfortable under her gaze but met the challenge head-on. Inclining his head, he said, "I'm at a disadvantage. We haven't been formally introduced. You are?" Daniel offered his hand.

"Sharona Aventi."

"I hope that my little faint didn't alarm you. I'm inclined to take weak spells now and then. And I confess I haven't eaten in some time."

Sharona shook his hand but didn't answer. Instead she stared at him.

Bengalo daj. Daniel averted his eyes and turned his attention to the room with its wooden floor bleached from years of scrubbing. Tall glass-fronted cupboards lined one wall, the sink was in front of a window on another. A wood-burning cookstove dominated a corner. A tall flat-back pine cupboard stood against the third wall. Several rocking chairs were pulled up close to the stove. The kitchen table and chairs were in the centre of the room, handy to everything. Walls were painted buttercup yellow and again oil paintings hung in every available space. One painting in particular drew his eyes like iron to a magnet and set his heart racing again.

Theresa noticed Daniel was staring at the painting and said, "Startling, isn't it? The former owner liked bright colors. She painted that picture. I think that it tells the story very well."

"And what might that story be?" Daniel kept his voice low, trying to gain control of the second shock for the day.

"The silhouette is that of a man standing on the top of Pense's Mountain. He's playing a violin and the sun is setting behind him. That's why the picture's all gold and orange and black. She hung the painting in the kitchen so she could hear his music simply by looking at the picture."

"It surely does have impact."

"Magdalena used to say that hers was a wondrous house with all sorts of genius touches and comedic relief," Theresa said. "Looking at the picture, I'd have to agree. She entitled it *Silhouette.*"

"Magdalena." The name fell softly from Daniel's lips.

"Yes, Magdalena Anderson." Theresa placed a platter of cold roast beef on the table beside a plate of sliced bread. "Eat," she said. "We'll have no fainting around here."

"I've not been in many places where paintings were hung in the kitchen," Daniel said.

"It was a little eccentricity of Magdalena's and now of mine. The attic's full of paintings. Mr. Anderson collected fine art work and Magdalena was a good painter herself. There's no sense leaving them to rot so I hang the ones that appeal to me. There are only so many walls in a house so the kitchen gets its share. There are even a couple hanging in the pantry. Paintings are my windows on the world." Theresa pointed to several large canvases of English landscapes. "As depictions of the countryside in the Chelfont St. Peter area of England, these held sentimental value for Maggie and me. Another cup of coffee, Mr. Cudzinki?"

Sharona pushed the platter of meat closer to Daniel. *"Te den, xa, te maren, de-nash!"* She smiled at him as though expecting an answer.

"Sharona," Theresa said. "Mr. Cudzinki doesn't understand Romane. Don't confuse the man."

Sharona responded with a barrage of questions. "Doesn't he? Don't you speak Romane, Mr. Cudzinki? I've a feeling that you do and that I've met you before, in a different situation."

Easy does it, Daniel thought. Take it slow and easy. She's fishing. "I've not had the pleasure of your company before. You may have known someone who looked like me."

"Where'd you come from?"

"Windsor," Daniel said.

"You stayed at the Station Hotel. That was on the envelope you used when booking a room with us." Sharona gestured in Daniel's direction with her fork. "I meant what country are you from."

Daniel smiled. "Does it matter what country? I'm in Canada now."

Sharona asked the question again. "You've got the most peculiar accent." Her eyes on Daniel, Sharona listened carefully to his reply.

"I'd say that I'm speaking proper British English," Daniel said. "That could be considered peculiar, I suppose, the way people are fracturing the English language these days. Let's just say that I'm a displaced person, made homeless by the war."

"I'd say that you've lived in eastern Europe. I've heard that accent before. Why'd you choose to visit Millbrook? What's the nature of your visit?"

"I've some business in the area."

"What business?" Sharona wasn't letting up with her interrogation.

Daniel thought quickly. "Finance. Property."

"You'll be dealing with J.P. Harris, Ltd., then?" Theresa interrupted. It wasn't like Sharona to be so forward with boarders. She usually didn't have much to say to strangers. "Most travelers have business with Harris. He owns the only factory in Millbrook. Even if you don't, your paths will cross at some point during your visit. Harris will see to that."

"I overheard people talking about him on the train," Daniel said, glad that Theresa had changed the subject. He hadn't expected to be confronted on the first day. Daniel made a mental note not to let Sharona catch him so easily in a corner again. "And everywhere one looks in Millbrook, there's evidence that he's an important man. A sign on the factory says J.P. Harris, Ltd. I saw Harris Avenue, J.P. Harris Civic Square, J.P. Harris School."

"You're sharp," Sharona peered at him closely as if trying to pierce a disguise. "You've been here only four hours and you took note of such things?"

"It's so obvious," Daniel said. "His name's on everything."

Theresa cleared Daniel's empty plate from the table. "Harris likes it that way and people don't complain," she said. "Anyway, it wouldn't do any good if they did say something. They'd be talking into thin air. Nothing would change."

"It's that way, is it?"

"It's been that way for the last ninety-three years, Mr. Cudzinki." Theresa slid the plate into the waiting dishpan. "Let's talk about something a little more positive. Your letter said that you may have a connection to the Anderson family. I'm surprised because, frankly, I thought Magdalena was the end of the line."

Daniel cleared his throat, giving him time to think through his answer. He didn't want to lie. He wasn't ready to tell the truth. "My trip's for several reasons, one being to look for a connection. I believe that a member of the Anderson family was involved with mine. Let's just say that I'm here on business but also fitting a bit of family research into my stay."

"Well," Theresa said, "If I can help in any way, ask. There aren't many around here know more about Anderson family history than I do. They were a very closed-mouth group."

"I appreciate the offer." Daniel stood, then assisted Sharona to rise by holding her chair. May as well surprise the lady on her own turf, he thought.

Startled, Sharona smiled then thanked him for his courtesy.

"My pleasure." Daniel executed a slight bow. "Thank you for dinner . . . lunch, ladies. If you'll excuse me now, I'm going to walk down to Main Street. There are a few necessities I need to purchase, tooth powder being an important one."

"It's nice to see someone practice a few manners around here,"

Sharona said. "You wouldn't know there was a gentleman in the house by the way Johnny acts."

"You must be referring to the Johnny Wallace who was mentioned as living here."

"Why don't you go by the feed mill and introduce yourself," Theresa said. "He's loading oats this afternoon. Johnny's been curious about our new boarder all week. If you'd be so kind as to tell him not to be late for supper tonight." Theresa reached for the bread plate. "I forgot to tell you that breakfast and supper are served in the kitchen when there's nothing special to celebrate."

Daniel shook his head and laughed. "You people have peculiar word terminology. I'm used to English names for various meals. Here – breakfast is breakfast, dinner is lunch, high tea is supper."

"You lived in England long?" Theresa asked.

"I did," Daniel said. "It was a pleasant place to reside."

"Someone I knew very well lived in England," Theresa said. "But that was a long time ago. I used to dream about visiting England. . . . "

"Dreams do come true," Daniel said."You just have to believe enough to make them happen." He glanced toward the silhouetted picture.

"If only that were true, Mr. Cudzinki." Theresa's eyes sparkled.

Daniel's smile lit the room. "Oh you can believe me. If personal experience is testimony, dreams do become reality, wishes are fulfilled." Why did he have an overwhelming desire to tell this woman everything? The picture had loosened his tongue. Best to get back to solid ground. "As I don't wish to rattle any sabers on my first day in Millbrook, is there anything I should know before my little foray into the bowels of the village?"

Theresa laughed. "If you're late for a meal, don't use the excuse that you got lost. Streets are north and south; east and west roads follow the river. Just remember that it's a closed community. People won't be too friendly until they get to know you. There's one other thing, Mr. Cudzinki." Theresa went back to clearing the table, working around Daniel who was standing behind his chair, eyes again on *Silhouette*. "If you play cards, wait for an invitation before you barge into the Old Boys' Clubroom behind the garage. That club's not open to the general public. You have to live in the village awhile before you're invited."

"Advice taken, Theresa," Daniel said. "May I call you Theresa?"

"If I may call you Daniel."

"I'll answer to that name. If you hear me referred to as *Count*, don't let it bother you. It does slip out occasionally. I hold the title but none of the amenities that go with it."

Theresa's eyes mirrored her surprise. "You're a nobleman? A *Count*? As in *The Count Daniel Cudzinki*?"

Sharona turned from the sink to give Daniel a critical look. "It's difficult to live in the skin of a monkey," she said, "but to walk the stride of a lion. Is that not so, Mr. Cudzinki? Does the title not fit the man?"

She's sharp, Daniel thought. He smiled at both women. "It looks good on paper, ladies. In England I was known as The Count Daniel Vincent Cudzinki. Here, I prefer Daniel. I try not to use the word *Count*. Again if you'll excuse me, I'll go wreak some havoc on the village."

Daniel left the house and was well down the street before he realized that Sharona had rattled him so much with her questioning he forgot pocket-money. Daniel smiled. Sharona was one to watch. He'd have to be more careful around her. He couldn't let anyone derail his purpose for being in Millbrook. On the other hand, Theresa and Sharona could prove helpful. The advice about the Old Boys' Club was timely. He'd know soon enough whether or not he needed to breach its flimsy palisade.

Daniel cut quite a figure along his route. He bowed and tipped his hat to every woman he encountered, doing it impulsively, with little thought to consequences. Out of habit, he greeted the men that looked him in the eye and silently passed those who didn't. Some people turned and looked at his retreating figure, wondering what they'd done to deserve such a salutation. A few, after returning his greeting, wondered who the man wearing the odd-fitting suit might be.

By his own reckoning, Daniel's time in the village was going to be short. He knew that he couldn't waste too much in pleasurable pursuits. His first stop was Long's Jewelry Store. Lured by a display of gold watches, Daniel lingered at its window before entering the shop. The most worldly thing he missed was his gold, bejeweled pocket watch. It was the first *butji* he owned so many years ago. By its measured ticking, the minutes and hours bound him to *gadje* time.

Daniel ended his walk at the feed mill where he asked for Johnny Wallace. A short, barrel-chested man pointed toward the far end of the loading dock. "Name's Joe if you're askin'. Still is if you ain't. Ya cain't miss Johnny. He's the big un." Joe shifted a wad of chewing tobacco into his left cheek and spat in the direction of Daniel's shoes.

"I wouldn't do that again if I were you." Daniel waited until Joe retreated into the mill. Mark one against that *gadje*, he thought, sauntering down the platform toward a team of good-looking bay Clydesdales hitched to a farm wagon. Daniel ran a hand down one of the broad heads, letting it rest momentarily on the soft muzzle.

"You appreciate good horseflesh, do you?" a voice said.

Daniel looked around for the source of the deep, resonant voice. "I'm surprised in this day and age to see such a fine team."

"A lot of people are, but I like driving 'em. It's slow going but the best way to travel." A muscular giant of a man came round the side of the team, curly blond hair leaping from his head, piercing blue eyes on Daniel's face. A ham-sized hand reached to stroke a muzzle. "These fellows take their lead. They know how to get home. I just sit up there an' mull things over. I couldn't daydream and drive my Sunday motorcycle, could I?"

"I don't suppose you could," Daniel said. "You're Johnny Wallace." It was a statement, not a question.

"I am. An' who're you?" Johnny's eyes searched Daniel's face. "Have we crossed paths before?"

Ignoring Johnny's question, Daniel extended his hand. "Daniel Cudzinki at your service."

"Theresa's boarder." Johnny shook hands, matching strength for strength until he thought he'd better let go. "Yuh've got quite a grip for an old fellow. What's your name again?"

"The Count Daniel Vincent Cudzinki. I'm *Daniel* to most people."

"Formal name's sure a mouthful. How the hell did yuh come by that rack of words?"

"It's far too complicated a story to relate today," Daniel said. "Catch me when I've nothing better to do than reminisce. Theresa said I'd find you here. Said I should introduce myself because you were dying of curiosity about her new boarder."

"Theresa's a good woman." Johnny went back to his work.

"Look. When I'm finished loading I'm going to The China for a cup of coffee. Wanna join me?"

"You buying?"

"It's that way, is it?" Johnny said. "Okay, I'll buy."

"You don't happen to smoke and perhaps have some tooth powder in your back pocket too?" Daniel's grin was infectious. "Forgot my pocket money."

Johnny roared, pulled a hat from his pocket and slapped it on his head.

"Don't smoke myself," he said, "but I've a friend or two I can hit up for a cig or three. I'll meet you at the restaurant, over there – across the Square." Johnny pointed in the direction of the China Inn. "We call it 'The China'. Greeks by the name of Kropolus run it."

"I'll just skip across J.P. Harris Civic Square." Daniel smiled.

"As long as you don't skip across Harris's bow." Johnny took up the joke. "Look. I'll be fifteen minutes. Here's a dollar. I'll see you over there, okay?"

"You trust me with your money having only met me?"

"You won't get far if you take to the hills. And yuh can't get to Detroit on a buck."

Daniel laughed.

"Look," Johnny said, scuffling his feet in the dirt. "If you want work, I could use some help at the farm."

"Thanks, but I'm not sure how much time I have," Daniel said, then corrected himself. "What I mean is that I don't know how long I'll be staying in the village."

"No problem. I just thought if you're needing money I'd give you a job. I'll finish loading the wagon. If you're hassled at The China, tell 'em you're with Big John Wallace. They'll leave you alone."

"Why would anyone give me a problem?"

"There's been a lot of drifters through the village since the war. Someone might take exception to your accent, thinkin' you fought for the wrong side. An' if they take the notion you're Italian or German or Gypsy, they'll give you a really rough time. Harris doesn't like 'em so everyone has to hate them. Some of the men that fought in the war have some very bad memories of Krauts and I-ties too."

Daniel liked Johnny Wallace. He was a man who showed his colors and spoke his mind. It was secretive people that caused him problems. "I'm a survivor, Johnny. I've heard it all. Don't worry. I'll get on all right. I've a thick skin."

Johnny nodded. “Right, then. See you at The China.”

It didn’t take Daniel long to encounter his first two vigilantes. They were standing in front of the China Inn, a two-story wooden building that had obviously seen better days. *B. Chambers, Grocer,* the colored glass sign read over the front door. Windows were clean but bare of decoration except for a second yellow, blue and red wooden sign that stated, “China Inn – Good Food Cheap.”

Daniel expected unpleasantries when the pair didn’t step aside for him to pass. One was tall, thin and stoop-shouldered. Expensive clothes hung oddly on his spindly body. He was bald, had veiled, watery eyes and thin, colorless lips. A hawk-like nose sprouted from a sea of gray skin. Daniel immediately thought of a Cave Bat.

The second man, standing beside Cave Bat, was tall with flushed complexion and large pig-like nose. His eyes were steel-blue slits under bushy eyebrows. A fringe of wispy, dull brown hair ringed his bald head. His somber black suit was in keeping with Cave Bat’s but hung on broader shoulders. He resembled a circling buzzard, feelings under control, eyes always on the lookout for dead meat. An undertaker, Daniel was quick to surmise. Their eyes always gave them away. Undertakers looked at people as though they were constantly measuring them up for a coffin, always saying stupid things as they grazed the body.

“You the fellow that Johnson brought from the station?” Buzzard asked.

“No,” Daniel said. “I walked from the station and I haven’t yet had the pleasure of meeting a fellow by the name of Johnson.”

“You staying in town long?” Cave Bat asked.

“I don’t consider that anyone’s business but mine,” Daniel said. “Have I had a formal introduction to you two?”

His question was ignored as Buzzard continued. “You’re not from around here, are you?”

“Is this the Spanish Inquisition? Am I accused of a crime? Who’s Johnson?”

“It’s unusual for a stranger that hasn’t business with the factory to arrive midweek, especially one with a queer accent.”

“It’s nice of you to be concerned about me but it’s a free country. I didn’t see that the village was surrounded by barbed wire and armed guards,” Daniel said, his suspicions confirmed about Cave Bat. “Now, if you don’t mind, step aside and I’ll take my leave.”

"You a friend of John Wallace?" Buzzard nodded toward the feed mill. "You were talking to him a few minutes ago."

"I am," said Daniel. "Now if you'll excuse me." He was going to push through the pair but thought better of the idea and walked round them. There'll be time enough for a confrontation, Daniel thought. At the door of the China Inn he met two young women hurrying out.

"Excuse me." Daniel doffed his hat and pointed toward Cave Bat and Buzzard. "Can you tell me who those men might be?"

Both women took a look. "The one in the grey suit's J.P. Harris."

"And the one in black?" Daniel asked.

"He's Compton. He used to be an undertaker but's into land dealings now."

"Ah-ha! Thought so," Daniel said. "Thank you, ladies. To whom do I have the pleasure? Before you answer, could I ask you another question?"

By the time Johnny arrived, Daniel was seated in a back booth, a cup of coffee on the table, a smoke in his hand.

"Who'd you bum the cig from?" Johnny said, looking around the restaurant.

"One of the lovely ladies I met at the door after I crossed that bow we were talking about. Had a little run-in with Cave Bat and Buzzard, Harris and Compton to you. By the way, here's your buck. Coffee's on the house."

Mrs. Kropolus arrived with a fresh pot, warmed Daniel's drink and poured a cup for Johnny.

Johnny roared. "Yuh rustle free coffee off Mrs. K. Yuh try to pick up two strange women and yuh give the two most influential men in the village names that just happen to fit 'em like a second skin. Mind you, those names do have a nice ring to them. But don't use them too freely if you're lookin' for a job in any of Harris's businesses. Few people around here will appreciate the joke. The sun rises and sets on *The Factory*. Company men live an' breathe *The Factory*, eat an' sleep *The Factory*. And nothing escapes Harris."

Warming to the subject, Johnny doffed his hat. "The question is why that pair hangs around together? They've not much in common. Harris says that he doesn't gamble, drink, smoke, dance.

You know, all the pleasurable things. He doesn't know what he's missing, does he?" Johnny laughed. "Strong rumor has it that he must have *danced* once because he has a daughter. Compton indulges in 'em all, and more. The only things those two have in common are money and mayhem."

Johnny took a handful of cigarettes from his shirt pocket. "Here, I bummed a few smokes for yuh. This should keep you going for awhile. When I'm finished here, I'm headin' for the farm. Yuh wanna come?"

When Daniel shook his head, Johnny continued. "Then tell Theresa I'll be on time for supper tonight. I've got a bottle in my room. We'll talk some more this evening."

"Doesn't Theresa have a rule about drinking hard liquor in the house?" Daniel asked.

"Rule doesn't apply to Theresa's friends," Johnny said. "And besides, rules are made for breaking, aren't they?"

Mrs. Kropolus refilled Daniel's cup. "You ordering something?" she asked Johnny.

"Mrs. K, you were suckered by this fellow. You don't give me free coffee."

"He's an old friend of the family." She winked at Daniel.

"If you're going to get to your farm and unload before supper," Daniel said quickly, "you must drive like a bat out of hell, Johnny."

"Nah. Farm's just on the other side of Pense's Mountain. Land backs onto Theresa's property."

"That's the second time I've heard the word *mountain* and there's nothing in the area that resembles one."

"Mountains are where you put 'em," Johnny said, tipping his cup for the last of his coffee. "Valleys follow close behind. Pense thinks her hill is a mountain and who're we to argue? Look. I'll see you at supper time."

Chapter 2

September 26, 1947: morning

Daniel, his back to *Silhouette*, ate breakfast alone at the table in the sunny kitchen. From what he could gather from the con-versation, Johnny was in the barn, Pense was making beds and Sharona was in the garden.

"I apologize for being late." Daniel spooned chili sauce over his eggs. "The bed was so comfortable. I slept in."

Setting a platter of bacon and pancakes beside Daniel's plate, Theresa assured him that breakfast was flexible but supper was served at six o'clock sharp. "I don't hold supper for anyone," she said. "I like my evenings long and free."

"Great meal." Daniel helped himself to several pancakes.

Theresa passed a pitcher of maple syrup. "Betsy and the hens come in handy. Some people think we're stupid to keep a milk cow and laying hens in this day and age. Mind you, same people don't mind phoning to see if we have any extra to sell when they run short."

Theresa watched with amusement as Daniel ate. It was obvious that the man hadn't eaten much in recent days. For an old man he could sure pack the food away. She liked a fellow to have a hearty appetite.

Daniel cleared his throat with a long drink of Theresa's excellent coffee. "Sorry to break into your thoughts, but could you tell me a little about John Wallace? It was he that shouted in the middle of the night, wasn't it?"

"I apologize if he woke you, Mr. Cudzinki. You see, the war left him subject to terrible nightmares. We never know when he'll have one. I haven't taken any women boarders since he came back, and I'm very selective about the men that stay, too. Veterans will surely understand Johnny's outbursts. I took a chance with you, hoping that you'd be sympathetic to his problems."

"Please call me Daniel. Don't worry. I do understand his situation. The noise did startle me, but I soon realized what was happening. I heard you go to him and then he settled down."

"Yes. Well . . . ahh . . . ." Theresa tucked a few stray white hairs into the shell combs that held her bun. "Johnny's an intriguing fellow. He was a big, strong man even before he joined the army. He ran fast, talked quick and hammered anyone who crossed him up."

"He's an impressive lad," Daniel said, draining his cup. "Might you have more coffee, dear lady?"

Theresa retrieved the coffee pot from the stove, poured another cup for Daniel and one for herself. "Johnny's a good boy, but he has the devil in him. He's lithe as a cat, clever too. He quit high school and took every dirty job that came along to help his mother put food on the table."

"Does his family still live in Millbrook?" Daniel helped himself to the last pancake and smothered it with maple syrup, devoured it in four bites, and smiled as he politely dabbed his lips with his handkerchief.

Watching Daniel made her hungry, and Theresa moved the electric toaster from the cupboard to the table. She put a slice of bread on each rack, closed them, then plugged the toaster into an extension cord that led to a wall socket. "Necessity is the mother of invention," she said when Daniel smiled at her tactics. "To answer your questions about Johnny's family, his father was killed in an accident at the factory. He has two sisters, younger than himself. When his mother died during the war, Harris tossed them out of a company house. Word is that they went west to live with relatives. Johnny's tried but can't trace them."

"Go on," Daniel said.

Theresa flipped the bread and waited for it to brown on the back side. "When Johnny came back, he had his army pension and a little money inherited from his mother's estate. With it he bought land, one of the prettiest farms in the area, with a stream running through the property and rolling hills all round." She speared the toast with a fork, put one piece on her plate and passed the other to Daniel. "As there's a barn but no house, Johnny boards here. He plans to finish building his house this winter and move into it next spring."

"If you don't want more toast, you should pull the plug. You might trip over the cord," Daniel enjoyed this domesticity. "Why did Johnny buy a farm?"

"Why indeed?" Theresa spread strawberry jam on her toast then passed the jar to Daniel. "Johnny's an agitator. Harris won't give him a job. There's work in Toronto or Windsor but Johnny has obligations here. I think too that Johnny's fed up dealing with people. He wants peace and quiet. He has a few personal problems to sort out."

"What you're saying," Daniel said, "is that Johnny needs to bend his back to the land, to get his hands dirty. He's got to keep his body busy, to keep his mind at ease. I think that the land is Johnny's wife, his mentor and his master."

Theresa leaned forward at Daniel's nod, seeing a depth of perception in this man – a kinship, almost. "I'm not sure that Johnny has a master – but he did say that he'd never marry. He told me that during the war, he always slept with a knife at hand. The enemy sneaked up so quietly they could slit a man's throat before anyone knew they were in desert camp."

Theresa paused, unsure, but plunged on. No sense telling half the truth. "Johnny strangled a man after being startled. Told me that he was on top of the fellow and killed him before he knew what he was doing. Now he can't trust himself to share a bed, not even with Plumb Loco."

"It's a reflex reaction," Daniel said. "There are other men I knew who were like that. They were afraid to share a bed for fear they might strangle the woman. Was it friend or foe that Johnny killed?"

"Johnny didn't say and I didn't ask. Some things are better not discussed. It was hard enough for him to tell me in the first place. I think he was trying to explain about his . . . well, let's just leave it at that."

"Does he talk a lot about Africa?"

"No, he doesn't," Theresa said. "I have the feeling that the African tour of duty caused most of his problems."

"Poor man," Count said. "I gather that Plumb Loco is a dog. I heard a dog barking last night."

"That was Plumb Loco. Johnny left him on the back porch. Loco heard Johnny's screams and tried to get to him. Pense went out to calm him down."

"An admirable animal," Daniel said.

"Johnny found the poor thing by the side of the road. Loco had been beaten then left to die. Johnny nursed him back to health but the dog did lose one eye. Now that pooch is attached to the man, like paper to glue. No one bothers Johnny when Plumb Loco's around. He's not a people dog so Johnny often leaves him to guard the farm."

"Strange name," Daniel said. "Sounds like he lives up to it though."

"Sharona named him Plumb Loco and the name fits. He answers to Plumb, Loco, or both. Johnny shortened the name to Loco; said that Plumb was too fruity and the dog wasn't a fruitcake." Theresa chuckled at Johnny's joke. "Loco adores Johnny, loves Pense and tolerates Sharona and me. He'd never hurt us. Can't say the same for the person that beat him near to death. I figure he might get his revenge one day."

"You've been honest with me, Theresa." Daniel pushed his chair back from the table and stretched his long legs. "I appreciate your candor."

"You're an interesting person, Daniel. If you don't mind, I'm going to change the subject and ask a question or two. From the quantities you're eating, I'd say you've not been around food for a while."

Daniel hesitated before answering. "I'll be honest with you. In situations where there was no food, one doesn't think too much about eating. In some circumstances, food was an unattainable commodity, so was not a priority." He smiled. "I used to have a healthy appetite and it appears to have returned in spades, thanks to your good cooking. Now, then, did I tell you that I met two fascinating individuals yesterday?"

"Johnny told me you had a run-in with the sanctimonious bastards."

"My dear lady!"

"I didn't mean to offend you but I know them only too well. My advice is to stay clear of both."

"I don't intend to waltz with them." Daniel smiled. Personally, he'd enjoy a polka around them.

Sharona, arms full of garden produce, pushed the kitchen door open with her shoulder and closed it with her foot. "Morning, Daniel," she said. "Johnny's looking for you." She tipped tomatoes, carrots and a cabbage onto the kitchen table. "He's at the barn for another half-hour or so. Just don't sneak up on him because his dog's with him. Plumb'll be okay once he gets to know you. What he can't see with his one eye, he makes up for with his nose."

"Thanks, Sharona," Daniel said. "I'll go see if I can help him."

Theresa kept her eye on Daniel as he left the kitchen and headed to the barn. "Do you think he was a prisoner of war? He's been food-deprived for a while. He ate as much as three men this morning."

"Daniel's like the other people we've fed recently, Theresa, in that way. He's one of the lucky ones. He has money to pay for his lodging. I haven't sorted him out yet. I can't put my finger on it but that accent has a familiar ring about it. And what about the connection to the Andersons that he keeps alluding to?"

Theresa sighed. There'd been a score of tramps begging for meals at her door during the summer. She'd let some bed down in the carriage house, not having the heart to turn them away. She wasn't frightened of them because Johnny and Loco were always close by. Most were veterans, unemployed and battling their own personal devils. Some were refugees from Europe desperate for a better life, who'd immigrated to Canada. As long as Daniel paid board and behaved himself, he was welcome and would be made to feel at home. It was the least she could do for the old man. "How old do you think he is, Sharona?"

Sharona shrugged. "Seventy-five? Eighty? I honestly can't tell. He's got that timeless look and European manners. There's a graciousness about him that you don't find in many young men these days. You know what I mean. He's charming, but I sense cunning, too. There's a familiarity . . . I just can't put my finger on it. . . . "

"You're right," Theresa mused. "There's something familiar about his look. And I detect a craftiness that has brought him this far. He's got a bit of a silver tongue. I imagine that our lives will spark with him around. We'll have to be vigilant but I can't imagine Daniel doing anyone harm."

"Should I tell Johnny to keep an eye on him?"

"No. Johnny's very astute. He'll sort Daniel out soon enough."

Daniel found Johnny in the barnyard checking Betsy's back leg, Loco lying by his side. As soon as he saw movement, the big dog leapt to his feet to stand between Johnny and Daniel. A deep throaty growl alerted Johnny that someone was close by.

Johnny put a hand on the dog's head. "Settle down. Daniel's a friend." He called to Daniel, "Don't make any sudden moves. Approach slowly with your hands at your side. Don't pat him. Let him come to you if he wants to be a friend."

Daniel moved slowly toward Johnny, avoiding eye contact with Loco. "It's okay, Plumb Loco," he said softly. "You know that you and I are friends. You know I won't hurt you."

Loco stopped growling then walked stiff-legged toward Daniel. Daniel stood still. Loco stopped several times trying to catch the scent then circled Daniel once at a respectful distance. Satisfied, he turned and trotted back to Johnny's side.

"For God sakes!" Johnny said. "Loco didn't go for the jugular. He didn't bark. Didn't snap neither. You're a special one."

"I seem to have that effect on animals these days," Daniel said. "You want me to hold the cow's halter?"

"I'm almost finished. Betsy's touchy today. Loco nipped her pretty hard, not that she don't deserve it. Be careful round her hind quarters. She's got quite a kick. Give me five minutes and then we'll lead her to the upper meadow."

Daniel lounged against a fence and instinctively looked at the barn's roof.

"Lookin' for something?" Johnny asked.

"No. I was thinking the weather's going to cooperate today. It looks like the sun will shine."

Daniel and Johnny walked side by side down the tree-lined back lane, Johnny leading Betsy by her halter. "Better to lead rather than follow this cow. She's skittish around Loco. The pair has this love-hate thing goin' for them. He nips her heels, wants her to move quicker, an' she tries to kill him. I should'a left the dog at the farm. There's a bear living in the Long Swamp. Loco keeps it away from the barn." Johnny glanced toward Daniel. "You saw Pense on the roof yesterday, didn't yuh?"

"I didn't mean to . . . but yes, I did."

Johnny smiled. "There's another story. Pense'll accept yuh on her own terms and at her own pace. Don't push your friendship on her and don't think she's a child. Pense is much wiser than her young years."

"How old is she?"

"Thirteen, going on thirty." Johnny turned to face Daniel. "Don't take advantage of her, yuh hear? You shouldn't have seen her naked. If you so much as touch her or make rude comments, I'll – "

"Johnny, Johnny," soothed Daniel. "I'm a gentleman. I know my place. So far I've seen her two times, once on the roof and again for several minutes in Theresa's kitchen. I've no evil intentions toward Pense, toward any child for that matter. I asked her age because I'm curious. I mean, how many times does one see a naked child on the roof of a high barn enticing a white dove?"

As abruptly as he'd faced Daniel, Johnny turned away. He glanced toward a long swath of meadow at the bottom of the high hill that stretched west as far as the eye could see.

"That hill. That's Pense's Mountain." Johnny said. "It runs four miles west, follows the river valley. There's a spring by the boulders at the bottom that's so cold it rattles your teeth when you take a drink."

Loco barked and sniffed the wind. Johnny patted the big head then said, "Go, Loco. Off to the farm with you. Leave the deer alone, yuh hear?" Loco raced across the meadow toward the hill.

"So this is Pense's Mountain."

"The Gypsies camp down by the orchard and draw their water from the spring."

"Don't the villagers think it's unusual that the Cigany . . . the Roma, still come?"

"They've been coming for the past seventy-odd years – twice a year. They'll arrive soon for their autumn visit. They're not the kind yuh see roamin' around Europe. This group gave up horse-drawn wagons twenty years ago. They drive cars and trucks. They're supposed to be the descendants of Gypsies from Romania.

"Theresa gets into a hell of a lot of trouble for lettin' them camp on her land." Betsy balked and Johnny pulled hard on the halter to move her along. "She's not about to change the tradition. Villagers will tell yuh they steal chickens, gasoline, porch furniture. Rumors spread that babies will be ferreted away. When they're here, they tell fortunes, sharpen knives, sell baskets and trinkets, trade horses – and the villagers still come, whatever the gossip."

Johnny was warming to the subject. "You know. It's the same old story. Someone's different from yuh so you have to find a way to tear 'em down. Theresa's been through it, so she has something in common with the Roma. It doesn't matter that her family came here from Italy more than eighty years ago. Theresa was seen as on the wrong side durin' both wars. My mother used to say, memories are long-in-the-tooth. Prejudices die hard. You wait, Daniel. You won't be here long before —"

Daniel finished the sentence. "Before my accent catches up with me."

"Something like that. A lot of people from around here fought in both wars. First they'll be polite, then they'll begin to pick away at you. Exactly where did you serve durin' the war?"

"Underground," Daniel said. "Suffice to say, I was not on the wrong side. You might help me by getting the word out that I was . . . underground. I'd prefer not to say any more at the moment."

The answer satisfied Johnny. He removed the rope from Betsy's halter, slapped her on the back then closed the pasture gate. "Autumn's comin' early this year. There's a nip to the air and a haze on the hills. Maples are turning but the big oak is still a tad green. It's usually the first to bud in the spring an' the last to shed in the fall. Mark my word. We're due for an early winter and big snows."

Daniel let his eyes follow the contours of the hill. The uplands were wearing their trees like feathers in a bonnet. Majestic maples spread their leafy canopies in perfect symmetrical circles. Above them all loomed the ancient oak, the regal possessor of the hill. On a pinnacle of granite near the top, overlooking the valley, Daniel saw the young girl, legs dangling, hair tumbling in the wind, Loco by her side.

"Why is it that every time I look up I see an apparition of Pense?" Daniel asked, pointing to the brow of the hill.

Johnny, pushed his cap back and stared at the pinnacle. "Hell, man! She's at it again! She's up there where the whole world can see her, without a stitch of clothing covering her."

Daniel squinted into the morning sun. "At first glance it may appear she's naked but I do believe she's wearing tan colored pants and sweater. Why isn't she in school?"

"School's borin'. Theresa taught her to speak French and Italian. She knows her sums. Her English's good. She's on again, off again as far as school's concerned. Theresa teaches Pense." Johnny looked toward the hill again to reassure himself that Pense was wearing clothes. "She'll spend more time in class during the winter. School officials are always down Sharona's neck about attendance but they have to admit Pense's well educated. She passes every test with marks better than regular students."

"Why doesn't Sharona demand she attend classes?"

Johnny threw back his head and laughed. "My Sharona's as bad as Pense, given half a chance. She didn't have much schooling. Look, I'm going to ride the motorbike to the farm. If you take the path, over there, the one that winds back through the orchard, you'll come out in the vegetable garden near the carriage house."

Daniel followed the well-trodden path. He crossed through the orchard then took the cinder walkway among the espaliered grapes, knowing it would lead to the back of the house. Above him, an unseen force pushed a fast-scudding cloud in front of the sun, momentarily blocking its rays. Rivulets of wind tumbled through the vineyard. Sweeping by Daniel, a cool zephyr rattled the weather vane on the roof of the house. Shivering, Daniel glanced up and thought he saw a figure standing in one of the multi-paned attic windows. He strained to get a better look – more detail – but saw nothing.

Theresa sat on the kitchen steps, her back against the wooden railing. She was peeling pie apples, throwing the skins in a bucket at her feet. A saucy squirrel sat several feet away trying to pretend no one could see him. Theresa had watched Daniel walking through the orchard and thought that he looked tired. As he came closer to the porch, she called out, "September winds always catch me unprepared. They blow around the hills and rip along the valley. Feel like a rest and chat?"

"I sure do." Daniel settled on the step below Theresa and pulled an apple peel from the bucket.

"If you want to eat an apple, get one from the basket. Peels are for the chickens but you can toss that one toward that silly squirrel who's watching us from the laundry table."

Daniel threw a couple of peelings toward the squirrel, dug in the basket for a juicy MacIntosh, polished it on his sweater and took a bite.

"Saw you looking rather intently at the house," Theresa said. "It seems to hold a fascination for people who board with us."

"It's a beautiful home."

Theresa stabbed for another apple with her paring knife. "Joseph Anderson built it in 1852 when servants came cheap and families were large. He'd lots of servants but produced only one child, a daughter – Magdalena."

"And if I may be so bold as to ask, how did you come by the place?"

Theresa was straightforward with her answer, as the information was common knowledge around the village. "When Anderson died, his estate went to Magdalena. When she died in 1922, everything was left to me."

"And when you die," Daniel said, "I assume that everything will be left to Sharona or Pense." When Theresa didn't answer, Daniel continued, "That was personal, wasn't it? I apologize." He changed tack, threw the apple core toward the squirrel. "You've lived here a long time, haven't you?"

"I taught for one year at a country school then went to summer school to learn *how*. Came home to see my parents and never went back to teaching because Anderson hired me to be Magdalena's companion. Her parents didn't want her to live alone after they died. My father recommended that I take the job." The squirrel jumped from the table to the porch floor. Theresa set her knife aside to watch and said, "I've never regretted my decision to stay with Magdalena. We got on very well and she, a dear lady, did need a companion."

"It would make sense that the estate be left to you." Daniel dangled a long peel in front of him. Both sat quietly as the curious squirrel, its fat belly to the wood, sneaked across the porch until it was below the peel. It sat up and reached for the skin. Daniel let go and the squirrel dashed away, peel hanging from its mouth.

"Brazen little devil," Daniel said. "Curiosity has its rewards. As I was saying, who else did Magdalena have but yourself?"

Resuming her peeling, Theresa continued, "At first I was surprised that she'd left me everything. But when I thought about it, the decision made sense. After the split between the Harris family and her father, I'm sure that she didn't want Harris to get his hands on her property. Magdalena wanted someone who would love the house and its possessions like she did, and she had no family."

"Keeping the place up and Harris's hand off it is a bit of responsibility, isn't it?" Daniel said, taking another apple. Polishing it, he put it in his sweater pocket to eat later.

Theresa couldn't help but smile. "The property and house need money for upkeep so we take in boarders to help pay bills. I say that honestly, but, in reality, I like the company. Like the house, I'm an old lady that needs a bit of propping up and attention. Don't we all like to be surrounded by color and interesting people?"

"That we all could benefit from," Daniel said. "I understand that Magdalena died in the house."

"That she did and is buried under the oak on the hill. That's where she wanted to be laid to rest. There's a law that bodies must be buried in proper cemeteries. What village fathers don't know won't hurt them. A funeral service was held. The coffin went to the cemetery. Maggie went to the hill."

Daniel touched Theresa's arm. "You're going to wonder why I ask all these questions, aren't you?"

"That had crossed my mind, and I'm wondering why I answer you," Theresa said. "Either the wind's loosened my tongue or I'm so lonely that I'd talk to a total stranger."

"Trust," Daniel said. "You trust me."

"Maybe I crave someone that's my age to talk with. There aren't many villagers that visit me, you see. My world consists of my boarders and Johnny, Sharona and Pense." Theresa reached across her bowl to put her hand over Daniel's. "What I told you doesn't go any farther, you hear? Johnny's father did the burying. If I hear any rumors in the village, I'll know who told."

"My lips are sealed with the intrigue of forbidden knowledge." Daniel smiled.

"Good! Keep them that way. Now, can I be blunt with you and expect an honest answer?"

"Yes. Go ahead."

"Are you looking for a connection to the Anderson family because you want this property? Are you looking for a loophole in Magdalena's will? If so, you can pack your bag and leave immediately."

"I'm not here to take anything away from you. My mission is to give something back that's rightfully yours. Call it revenge speaking from beyond the grave. Trust me, Theresa."

"I can't do much more, can I? But if revenge can speak from the grave, can't love survive death?"

"Love does survive," Daniel said quietly, the subject touching something in his inner soul. "If a soul or spirit dwells somewhere in time, is it possible that it can travel forward or backward in that time? I mean life is time and time travels forward. Is it logical to think that it can travel backward too?"

Theresa was struck by the seriousness of Daniel's questions. "What I've always wondered," she said, "is that many more people see the past than the future. Is it because they know the past but not the future? They're so comfortable with the past that they see it and feel it."

"Are you saying that you believe that people can see ghosts?"

"Some people believe what they see in their mind's eye. I believe that there are such things as ghosts and that they can make themselves known when necessary. Perhaps they might regret some past deed they've done and come back to correct it."

"Possibly they've come back to bring a message or correct another's bad deed," Daniel said. "Maybe they didn't leave earth in the first place. Maybe they're trapped here."

"It's a possibility." Theresa prided herself on keeping an open mind. "'Backward, turn backward, O Time in your flight, Make me a child again just for tonight,'" she quoted from a favorite poem.

"'Backward, flow backward, O tide of the years! I am so weary of toil and of tears,'" Daniel said, his voice so low it was little more than a murmur. "What we all wouldn't change if given another chance."

Theresa glanced toward him to see if all was okay. The man looked . . .older . . . sad. He smiled warily when he realized he was being scrutinized.

"If you're interested, the attic's full of pictures, furniture, trunks of clothing. You're welcome to take a look, if you think it will help you find a link to the Anderson family."

"I'd like to look in the attic," Daniel said. "The stairs are just outside my bedroom, aren't they?"

"They are, but they're behind a locked door." Theresa wondered how Daniel knew the location of the steps. "You seem to have made yourself quite at home in Maggie's house, haven't you? You're familiar with its layout."

Daniel always was one to think on his feet. Knowing the fine line between fact and truth gave him a measure of leeway. "It's not particularly this house, Theresa. It's the architecture that I'm familiar with. Georgian style dictates that all rooms are placed in the same location on each floor." Daniel tossed his apple core in with the peels. So much vagueness swirling in his mind meant he couldn't risk the complete truth. "I'm used to the style. I've been in many of these buildings so that they all seem familiar."

"You know," Theresa said, "we could both do with lunch. I'll throw another cup of water in the soup pot. You don't need to pay for lunch. I feel that if you're related in some way to Magdalena, I should treat you as a guest, not a boarder."

"That's kind of you. By the way, is Sharona in the attic? I thought I saw her looking out the window." Daniel pointed up toward the third-story attic window.

"There's no one in the attic. Sharona's away with the car to do some shopping."

Strange, Daniel thought. I could have sworn there was someone looking out the attic window. He struggled to get up, then helped Theresa to her feet. "One more question. When did Sharona come to stay with you?"

Theresa wiped her hands on her apron, and surveyed Daniel's face, searching for signs of craftiness, pretense or evil.

"Oh, I know she's a Gypsy," Daniel said. "Sharona is one of the more common Roma names for a woman. And she has their distinctive features, the dark hair, the aquiline nose, the language. Johnny told me that the Roma come through twice a year. I could ask Sharona, I suppose."

"Although it's really none of your business," Theresa said, "if you must know Sharona's story, it's better you hear it from me. Fourteen years ago, when it came time for the Roma to leave after their autumn visit, Sharona stayed. Pense was born in January of the next year."

Theresa bent to pick up her bowl, apple basket and paring knife. Anticipating Daniel's next question, Theresa added that although Sharona and Pense were not blood-related to her, she considered them family.

Using a hand to shield his eyes against the harsh noon sun, Daniel looked across the orchard and down the valley. "If

I'm not mistaken, Pense is on her mountain waiting for her grandparents to arrive."

"And she'll settle down after they leave," Theresa said, "until next May when her vigil will begin again."

Daniel lifted the bucket of peels. "I'll not say anything to Sharona."

"I'd appreciate it if you didn't." Theresa took a handful of peels from the bucket and threw them on the lawn for the squirrel. "After you dump the peels, would you gather the eggs? Watch the rooster. There's nothing he likes better than to spur an ankle. Before you go, if we're telling secrets, you owe me one. Tell me, Daniel Cudzinki, and be honest. Did you suffer? Did you lose much during the war?"

"Yes," Daniel said after a long pause. "I suffered a great deal. I lost a lot. Ultimately I lost my life."

"Your life? I take it that means as in the style and way you lived in Europe?"

"My life," Daniel repeated, turning sad eyes toward Theresa. "But let's talk about you. What did you lose?"

"Young Millbrook men were killed in action. As for my relatives in Italy, some were in the Resistance. I understand they were shot. I know that some fought for Germany too. I haven't received any letters since the war. They may all be dead. I have no way of knowing."

"I wasn't particularly thinking of the last war," Daniel said. "We forget that we've been through several."

"Enough said." Theresa raised her hand to end the conversation. "It's too nice a day to talk about wars. They happened. I'd rather try to forget them. I don't know why I brought it up, Daniel. Something tells me the secrets you hide may be best left alone."

"Agreed," admitted Daniel. "Pense is the future. You're the present. I'm the past. And the past says you and I shouldn't discuss wars."

"As I'm as old as you we're both from times past."

"Not so," Daniel said. "You're only as old as you feel and today I feel . . . one hundred." He laughed at his private joke. "I'll go feed the chickens. You water the soup."

Chapter 3

September 27, 1947: morning

I see fate's fickle finger has put everyone in the kitchen at the same time for breakfast today," Theresa said, placing a bowl of applesauce on the table, then taking her seat beside Pense.

"It's more like hunger's hairy hand," Johnny said, fork in hand. "Wouldn't yuh say so, Sharona?" His eyes lingered on Sharona's back as she turned the potato cakes. As fast as she finished them, Daniel and Johnny pounced on the stack like hounds after a fox, smothering the golden cakes with butter and applesauce and wolfing them down.

"One would think that you two haven't eaten in months," Theresa said, making the rounds with the coffee pot. "Leave some for Sharona."

"For an old man, you eat a lot." Johnny poked his fork at Daniel.

"And for a young man, you talk too much. I've a weak spot for potato cakes that predates your birth. Leave me alone to eat."

Johnny jabbed Daniel with his elbow then smiled at Theresa. She'd cornered him last night, looking for some advice about the man. He'd told her not to worry. It appeared that for the moment she seemed to be enjoying the banter between the old fellow and himself.

Pense looked from one to the other but said nothing, which Theresa thought unusual because she was normally the most talkative person at the table.

"What's everyone up to today?" Sharona asked.

"I'm off to the farm but you'll see me at supper time."

"And you, Daniel?"

"Thought I'd go fishing." Daniel pushed his chair away from the table. "My compliments on an excellent breakfast, Sharona."

"Outlasted you, did I?" Johnny helped himself to another potato cake. "About this fishing, what'll you use for a pole and bait?"

"I don't need a pole. I'll talk nicely and the fish'll jump right into my arms."

Pense giggled then left the table and disappeared into the storeroom. She returned with a fishing rod and tackle box. "Here," she said offering both to Daniel. "Grandmother lets me use these. They're old but they work."

"Where did you get these?" Daniel glanced toward Theresa. He turned the rod slowly with trembling hands.

"They were part of the estate," Theresa said. "There's a closet full of fishing gear. Magdalena liked to fish so it must have belonged to her."

"That's an expensive pole," Johnny said. "And, I see by the way you're admirin' it that you appreciate good gear."

Gathering his wits about him, Daniel said, "It's one of the best." He glanced briefly at Pense who lowered her head. He cleared his throat. "I'll just get my sweater and then be off to the river."

Closing his bedroom door, Daniel sat in the rocking chair, right hand caressing the rod. How did she know? He gently rubbed the initials *YLD* carved into the wooden grip. Perhaps she didn't. Maybe it was simple impulse that made her give him the rod. Daniel closed his eyes and for a few minutes let the soothing action of the rocking chair ease his heart.

On his feet again Daniel ascertained that for the type of *fishing* he was going to pursue, he didn't need the rod and tackle box. He tucked the tackle box into the dresser drawer and stood the rod in a corner of the closet. Before leaving, he listened at the bedroom door to make sure no one was in the upper hall. Having told everyone he was going fishing, he didn't want to be seen leaving without the rod and tackle box.

In the village, Daniel walked east then veered left through a wooded area to walk along the south bank of the river toward High Falls Dam. One-half mile upriver, he found the Cascade, a man-made overflow channel that entered the river at right angles. Daniel picked his way down the dry, weed-choked depression then negotiated a rock-strewn channel to the river's edge. Sitting with a cigarette in his hand, back propped against a limestone ledge, he observed the riverscape while planning his next moves. It never ceased to impress him that nature's way of survival was by being constantly on the move.

Mud swallows swooped low over dark Saugeen waters toward steep cliffs on the opposite bank. Their acrobatics disturbed a mink that skittered away and disappeared into a rock crevice. A cardinal, a flash of red, landed in a nearby birch tree and called for his mate. Trees on the north bank were alive with grackles and starling, their incessant twittering muted by the sound of the high dam as it thundered thirty feet to the river bed, an eighth of a mile upriver. The dam's water no longer turned the mill's stones. When J.P. Harris bought the business, he shut the mill down as he wasn't in the habit of supporting land-rich, cash-poor farmers. The mill complex was turned into storage for finished products. The water's power now produced electricity for Harris's factory and home.

Returning to the path, Daniel rounded a cedar thicket then crossed a wooden bridge. As he had anticipated, he was challenged by a female voice. He'd smelled the smoke from her cigarette long before he saw or heard her.

"What are you doing on this property?"

"Ma'am?" Daniel stopped and looked to his right. A woman in her thirties stood twenty feet away, a cigarette in her hand. Daniel took a deep breath – too late to turn back now. The risks associated with contacting this woman had been calculated long before he arrived in Millbrook.

"You're trespassing."

Doffing his hat, Daniel stood at attention. "I'm enjoying a walk along a very pretty pathway toward a dam, I believe." He kept his voice low, giving full attention to his accent. "This is not private property."

"It is," she said, throwing the cigarette to the ground and grinding it with her heel.

"I didn't see any signs."

"We don't post signs. Everyone knows it's private."

"I'm not *everyone* and not from around here."

"That's no excuse, " said the woman, advancing toward him.

She stopped within three feet of him. She was almost as tall as he and had most striking blue eyes. Working to maintain his composure, Daniel said, "I haven't yet mastered the art of walking on water. So, unless you can tell me how to leave without swimming across the river or taking to the air, Miss Harris, there's no way I can obey. I have to tread the property to leave." As he spoke, Daniel made a mental note of her facial characteristics and her hand movements.

"Don't be clever," she said. "How do you know my name?"

"Sheer conjecture. The Harris compound backs onto this property. Who but a Harris would bar travel on a pathway that has always been common ground?"

"You're obviously new to the village."

"I just said so. I'm staying in the village while transacting some business."

"I heard. You're staying at Inachio's."

"I'm boarding at Theresa Inachio's." So, she knew about him. She knew he was staying at Theresa's. As he'd anticipated, gossip traveled quickly throughout the small community. She certainly hasn't learned to smother bread with honey, rather than slather it with lard, Daniel thought.

"What do you have to say for yourself?" Lillian lit another cigarette and blew smoke in Daniel's direction.

Smoke and mirrors, Daniel thought, standing his ground. "Harris has strung his hydro poles through a prime piece of public land. He should be congratulated on his ingenuity, but to get right to the point of this discussion, he stole the property." Daniel pointed in the direction of High Falls Dam. "I believe I'll go this way and continue my stroll to the dam."

"You're taking big chances."

"Well, life's full of chances, isn't it? In the future, I'll try not to get caught. If I do, I hope it's by you. I'm too old a man to deal with gardeners and nasty drivers, Lillian. It is Lillian, isn't it?"

"If you persist in trespassing, you'll be escorted off the property, thrown out of the village. Father can make that happen, you know."

"Idle threats, my dear," said Daniel. "You see, I know this is still public land, donated to the village by Joseph Anderson who owned the mills upstream. It was deeded with the proviso that if the village fathers didn't want it – ever – the land had to revert back to Anderson's estate or beneficiaries, which means that Theresa Inachio would own it."

Lillian's face darkened in fury. Daniel was getting the reaction he'd hoped for. "Either your father has grabbed the land for his own use, or the village fathers erroneously thought they could sell it. The simple truth is that they can't. If you want proof, I have it. Your family seems to have an outrageous penchant for privacy, whatever the scenario. Are you hiding something?"

Daniel didn't wait for an answer. Turning his back on Lillian, he walked toward the dam, leaving her to watch his retreating back. "Be damned," he said aloud. "She's a beauty! But she's certainly a product of Harris's upbringing. She's as tough as nails."

To reach his next objective, Daniel crossed the river by the road over the dam then went to one of the mill's lower doors, one he knew led to the former blacksmith shop. After consulting his watch, Daniel lounged against a wall, kicking stones with his boot. He didn't have to wait long. The door opened. A tall muscular fellow stepped out, asked several questions and beckoned for Daniel to follow him. In the dark, quiet corner of an office, they spoke.

"I'm pleased to meet you, Sebastian Temple."

"And I thought I'd never have the pleasure of laying eyes on you," replied the dark-haired man who appeared to be in his early forties. "To meet a legend is indeed an honor."

"I'm glad you feel that way," Daniel said. "You had no difficulty with the villagers?"

"Look at me, *Baro Shera.* How could they know anything?"

"It's true. You fit right in," Daniel said. "Did you have any trouble with Harris?"

"No, I gave the right answers and got the job. I've been here for the past six months, living in the mill. I'm on call twenty-four hours a day. If the power goes down, the factory goes down."

"Good man," Daniel said. "And thanks for the information on Lillian. I just ran into her in the park behind the house."

"Not a problem," Sebastian said. "My grandfather owed you a favor, and you were right. I landed the job because I knew about power generation and engines. My chances were also given a boost when the fellow that had the job left rather suddenly. Harris couldn't do anything but fire him after it was made public that the man was a gambler and womanizer."

"I feel sorry about that one," Daniel said. "He was a good fellow. But we can't dwell on deeds done. You've had time to look around? Do you perceive any problems?"

"None whatsoever. Just put out the word and give me one-half hour's lead time. The equipment's still operational. The south overflow channel has been neglected for the past forty years. It's overgrown but usable. Cattle are grazing it. Most people have forgotten about it, don't even know what the channel's for."

"Excellent! I won't risk being seen with you while I'm here. I don't want to jeopardize anything, but we'll keep in touch through The China. Leave a message if you need to see me. Have you heard where the Kumpania is now?"

"They're less than seventy miles away. Because of the old one, *Zizou,* they're taking it easy. Like in the old days, she's leading them, driving her wagon. I'd better get back to work. Harris is sending one of his tool men down to fix a screaming brake. He should be here in ten minutes or so. Take care, old man."

"You too," Daniel said, shaking Sebastian's hand. "You too."

Daniel walked quickly toward his next stop, the local garage. Damn! People calling me *old man* is getting to be a habit. At the back entrance to the shop, Daniel made himself comfortable on a seat that once belonged to a Model T. From it he had a good view of the Old Boys' Club, a windowless wooden one-story building badly in need of repairs.

"Do they still play poker in there?" Daniel asked a cigar-smoking mechanic who was tinkering with a '38 Chevy.

"Yeah," the mechanic said. "Don't know how they can stand the stinking hell-hole."

"How would a young man like you know what Hell smells like?"

"Just a saying, old man."

There it was again, that reference to an old man. "Ever see J.P. Harris go in to play?"

The mechanic's eyes narrowed. "You gotta be kidding." He threw a wrench to the ground. "But his driver's in there all the time, and so's Compton, that contriving skin'iver."

"Buzzard."

"Whoever." Mechanic laughed. "That's a good name for the beggar. Cheated me out of my family's farm up the road near Mildmay, he did."

"That'd be an interesting story. I've heard he's a cheater and a thief." Daniel checked his pockets for cigarettes. "How does one go about getting an invitation to play?" He nodded in the direction the Club.

"You don't. It's private."

"Nothing's locked when you find the key," Daniel said. "Can you spare a stogy?"

Mechanic pulled a cigar from his shirt pocket. "If you play poker, they might take you on, just to get your money. They've done that to a couple of traveling salesmen. Compton cleaned 'em right out." The mechanic leaned over the motor to reach a belt. "By the way, I heard you served in the underground during the war. I was in the tank corps. That's where I learned about engines."

"Horrible place to be . . . underground or in a tank."

"Someone had to do it. There'll be service-men that'll thank you for what you did. You know what I'm talkin' about. Think of the chances you had to take. You had to be clever to go underground."

"Or dead as a doornail," Daniel said smiling. "What's your name, son?"

"Edward MacTavish. Ed for short."

"Call me Daniel."

Daniel turned his face toward the warm sun and finished his cigar before leaving for his next stop, the newspaper office. There he spent several hours looking through old leather-bound journals and reading back issues of the paper. His last job for the morning was to steal some late-blooming flowers from a village garden before making his way to the oak tree on the hill.

Afternoon

Daniel was alive and life felt good. He shoved the fork into the dark loam of the potato patch and brought a clutch of earth apples to the surface so that Theresa, following behind, could gather them in a bushel basket. Where had he been that he'd missed the good earth, missed the act of working in it? The smell of fresh-dug soil was as ancient and primeval as man himself. Its aroma evoked memories for Daniel of crops sown and harvested. How often had he worked in the afternoon rays of a September sun, feeling its warmth on his back? How often had he felt the south wind dancing through his hair?

Every once in a while Daniel rested. As he leaned on the fork, his eyes always went to Magdalena's home. With the sun full on its flank, every hue of grey played across thick stone walls. Theresa's love for brilliance spilled into windows that beckoned with splashes of color and plants, all presented to a backdrop of filmy lace curtains. Windows on the second floor had been thrown open, a final airing, Sharona had said, before October's cold north winds swooped down the valley.

A clothesline, strung from the back porch to the carriage house, repeated the riot of color. It groaned under the weight of woolen blankets and feather-ticks.

Theresa, wiping her brow, noticed Daniel's preoccupation with the house."You're fascinated with the place, aren't you? You can't keep your eyes off it."

Daniel turned to Theresa and smiled. "I admit to having an interest in the property. Where did the name come from?"

"It was called Arrandale after Anderson's home in Scotland. Maggie changed the name to *Knightswood.* She wouldn't tell me why."

"The name meant something to her," Daniel said, his eyes on the attic window. "What do you call it, Theresa?"

"Home. Despite all the work and worry about the place, it's home."

Daniel went back to forking potatoes. "I'd say that this isn't good potato-growing soil," he said, picking up some of the dark loam and working it between his fingers. "Don't they need sandy soil?"

"It isn't," Theresa said, rubbing dirt off a spud with her hand. "We buy our winter's supply from a farm down the highway."

"You're lucky the property has enough land for gardens and orchards," Daniel said, forking a hill. "Growing your own keeps expenses down."

"My father Antonio Inachio was Anderson's gardener. Funny thing, he was Harris's gardener too. He acted as mediator between the two families, the only line of communication they had. Dad was a good negotiator. I think that's the only reason that Harris hired him."

Yes. A spark of recall held on the tip of conscious mind. I remember Antonio Inachio and his wife, Daniel thought, looking at his landlady. Just as I remember Theresa Letizia as a dark-haired newborn babe. "What happened to your father? Do you have any pictures of him?"

"Not a picture," Theresa said. "Dad died peacefully in his sleep in 1895. Mother passed away four years before him."

"Who helps you maintain all this?" Daniel extended his arms to indicate the extent of Theresa's property.

"Myself, Sharona, Johnny and Pense. They don't complain. They love the place as much as I do. I do what I can but at my age, that's not much. Is the digging too much for you, Daniel?"

"I'm enjoying it but I'm not about to dig for a living. One more hill should fill your basket. I have to do something to repay all your kindness. It's not often that a total stranger is treated with such courtesy and compassion."

"I think Sharona and I are good judges of character." Theresa pushed the basket along the row. "When we're wrong, Johnny rights the situation quick enough."

"I forgot about Johnny. Of course, he'd come to your assistance."

"If he didn't trust you, Daniel, he'd be hanging around the property now, waiting for you to err or slip up in some way. He's comfortable enough with you that he's gone out to the farm. By the way, don't forget we're celebrating his birthday tonight. We're eating in the dining room."

"He and I share the same birth week. My birthday's tomorrow."

Theresa touched Daniel's arm, smiled and said. "You should have mentioned that you were going to be celebrating a big day. We'll have two cakes tonight. And how many candles should we put on yours?"

"Please, no celebration," begged Daniel. "I'm past candles. Let this be Johnny's day, Theresa."

"Ancients like us shouldn't let a birthday go by without a celebration," Theresa said. "We never know how many we'll have left."

"Well, that's the truth," Daniel said. "This one could definitely be the last I'll ever celebrate."

Knightswood - supper

For all the celebratory atmosphere in the dining room, Daniel was uneasy. The gnawing in his stomach made Theresa's food sit uneasily, and distracted his thoughts. The source of his discomfort was a piece of furniture, an antique that whispered memories of a thousand days. Seated as he was at the round table, the antique was in his line of vision, it and Pense Aventi. To make matters worse, Pense spent a lot of time glancing toward him instead of paying attention to the conversation around the table.

Theresa and Sharona flanked either side with Johnny beside Theresa. Pense sat nearly opposite Daniel, her back to the wooden antique sideboard with its intricately carved crestboard.

"Daydreaming?" Sharona touched Daniel's arm to get his attention. "Are you enjoying your birthday? Would you like a slice of apple pie or chocolate cake?"

"Apple pie, please," Daniel said. "I forgot to thank you for taking me to Johnny's farm. The drive was just what I needed. Riding in cars is far more pleasurable than driving them. I never did get the hang of clutches and gears."

"Good land, isn't it?" Johnny was into his second helping of cake. Surprised and pleased that Sharona had driven Daniel over the hill to his property, Johnny had shown him all around the farm. "It's the highest bit of land and most productive two hundred acres in these parts."

Sharona handed Daniel his pie topped with a thick slice of cheddar cheese. "Daniel thinks Millbrook is located in one of the prettiest valleys in Ontario."

"And Harris owns most everything but the river and Theresa's property," Johnny said.

"Is Pense's Mountain part of Theresa's property?" Daniel asked.

"I own half of it," Theresa said. "Johnny's land backs onto it but Harris managed to buy a five-acre wedge before Anderson died. Unfortunately that wedge includes the pinnacle and oak tree."

"Theresa and I are the jam between the toad's toes." Johnny laughed and slapped the table, causing dishes and people to jump.

"That statement's more truth than fiction," Sharona said. "Considering the rumour that's going around now. Did you hear anything today, Johnny?"

"Nothing. Village fathers are closed-mouthed. No one's talking."

"A conspiracy of some sort?" Daniel asked.

"A suspicion is all," Johnny said. "Think hard. Soldiers come back from the war, get married an' have kids. They need housewares. Harris manufactures housewares. He has to expand and increase his line of products. Makes sense to build a new factory on this side of the river. He needs another rail line into the old factory. It'd be good business to run a spur from the junction, five miles south of the village on this side. Then he could service two factories. One problem. Theresa and I own most of the land on this side."

"Don't ruin a good meal with Harris talk," Theresa said. "A toast! Let's have some homemade wine. Pense, you get glasses out of the sideboard. Johnny, you open the bottle."

Pense, slid off her chair and ran her hand over the sideboard's ornate polished front doors, an action that sent shivers up Daniel's spine. She opened one, chose five crystal glasses and placed them on the table in front of Johnny.

Johnny laughed. "She thinks she's going to join us for a tipple."

"I'm old enough," Pense said.

"For milk." Johnny removed the cork from a bottle of sweet plum wine. "Theresa makes the best wine in the valley," he said, sniffing the cork.

"I imagine that Theresa makes the only wine in the valley," Daniel said

Johnny poured. Pense delivered a drink to each person saving the last for herself.

Daniel raised his glass high. "To your health, Johnny Wallace, and may you celebrate many more birthdays."

Johnny returned the salute. "To your good health, Daniel Cudzinki. It's a pleasure knowing yuh." Johnny emptied his glass and looked from Daniel to the sideboard. "As a birthday present, Sharona should tell you about that piece of furniture. You can't keep your eyes off it."

Uneasy, with sweat running down his back, Daniel reached for the wine decanter.

"Easy on that," Johnny said. "There's a real kick to Theresa's wine. Doesn't always happen after the first drink."

Sharona took up the story. "It's a gorgeous piece. Look at the cluster of hand-carved roses on the crestboard. They're perfect but for the middle rose that seems incomplete. The carvings were gilded at one time. You can still see bits of gold paint in the deeper grooves, see, there, next to the incomplete rose."

Sharona left the table and went to the sideboard, putting her fingers into an indentation in the middle of the rose. "It's deep," she said. "Whatever went here must have been beautiful. Look how the leaves are carved in such detail. And the petals. They look as though they folded around something." Sharona fingered the rose again. "We can't find any information on the piece. Antique dealers who stay here when they're picking the countryside don't know its value but they're always at Theresa to sell it."

Daniel spoke in a quiet, controlled voice. "It's a marriage board. Where I come from, the prospective groom makes such a piece for his intended bride. The custom died out nearly a century ago. It's one-of-a-kind and you rarely see such pieces on this side of the Atlantic."

"It's beautiful," Theresa said. "I'm not selling it. It's staying in the dining room. Really, the sideboard belongs to Pense. Pense, show Daniel what you found in one of the drawers."

Pense took an object from around her neck, secreted it in her hand and came to stand by Daniel. She dropped the object onto the table in front of him. "Here," she said. "A birthday present for you."

Daniel reached for a coin with a hole in the middle of it, strung on a gold chain. He turned the coin, reading its surface, feeling its texture.

"It's my good luck charm," Pense said.

"And it should still be." Daniel's voice was low, almost hoarse. "This is a very old coin, Pense. Are you sure you want to give it to me? Perhaps you should keep it, to bring you continued good luck."

"I found it nailed onto the back of one of the top drawers. Johnny put it on the chain."

"Pense!" Sharona said. "You told me that you'd never part with the coin."

"It's his now," said Pense. "It belongs to Mr. Cudzinki. It's his birthday present."

"Eighteen sixty-eight," murmured Daniel as he rubbed the coin between his fingers.

"The Irish nail a coin to the door frame of a new building as a good luck token. It's supposed to bring prosperity," Theresa said.

"This is the same theory," said Daniel. "The coin is supposed to bring good fortune to the marriage."

"Put it on," Pense said, still standing beside Daniel.

"Maybe Daniel doesn't want to wear it. Perhaps a pocket would suffice," Theresa said.

"I'll wear it," Daniel said. "If I put this in a pocket, I might." He pulled the chain over his head and slipped the coin under his collar where it lay warm against his skin. Smiling at Pense, he reached to touch her, then quickly pulled his hand back and put it on the table.

"It's a generous gift and a very kind gesture, Pense. Thank you. When I wear it, I'll think of you."

Pense hadn't left Daniel's side. "How did you celebrate your last birthday, Mr. Cudzinki? We held a big party for Johnny because it was the first birthday he celebrated after he got home from Europe."

"To tell the truth," Daniel said, "I can't remember the last time I celebrated my birthday. It must have been a very long time ago."

"Enough talk." Theresa rose from the table. "All of you, into the parlour. I'll bring the coffee. Pense, help me clean the table. Johnny, tune the radio to the late news."

"Another contraption I haven't gotten used to," muttered Daniel. "That and the telephone."

"Sounds like you're having trouble dealing with the twentieth century." Johnny pushed himself away from the table, then in a surprise move, held Sharona's chair. Sharona looked startled but said nothing.

Daniel smiled and winked at Sharona. "I can't keep up with new inventions. I'm a man of the old school who can't adjust to a world of gidgets and gadgets."

Pense, humming absentmindedly, had gone to the sideboard and was polishing it with her napkin. Daniel turned his attentions to the girl, transfixed by the tune.

"What's that song you're humming?" Sharona asked.

"It's something I heard," Pense said, fixing Daniel with a penetrating, confused look. "Do you know it?"

"It's music that was written a long time ago for a poem that was penned by Sir Walter Scott," Daniel said, his eyes searching Pense's face for a reaction. "Where did you hear it, Pense?"

"I don't know. It just came to me, Mr. Cudzinki, and I can't seem to get it out of my head."

Chapter 4

September 28: morning

Daniel had a lot of questions to ask Pense and he couldn't waste any more time waiting for her to come to him. They had to talk. He had to make the first move. Problem was, he was on the ground. She was on the roof of the barn. Fully clothed, she straddled the peak, facing the hill.

"Pense, come down so I can chat with you."

"No."

"Then I'll come to you," Daniel shouted. "I need to talk to you."

"You can climb up if you want to. I can't stop you."

"I'm not a spring chicken. I shouldn't be doing such things. It's a high roof. Come down."

"Heights never stopped you before."

"How do I get up there?"

"You'll find a way."

Daniel remembered seeing an old wooden ladder lying in the weeds at the side of the carriage house. Retrieving it, he leaned it against the wall of the barn. Daniel tested several rungs to see if they'd hold his weight. Silly man, he thought. You're being foolhardy in the extreme. You can't keep your balance on the ground let alone on a roof. But driven by the need to establish a rapport with Pense, Daniel climbed the ladder.

Wooden rungs bent under his weight. Halfway up, one snapped, sending his left foot crashing back down onto his right. It took several minutes for the pain to subside before he could continue the climb. Two cautious steps onto the slippery shingles and

Daniel realized anew the steep roof was no place for an old man. His mind's voice shouted *Besh! Besh,* you silly old fool, Sit down before you kill yourself.

With the wind on his back, Daniel climbed the slippery slope and straddled the peak, six feet away from Pense, folding his arms round his knees to keep his balance. Stupid old man, he thought. What goes up must come down. This might not work and you'll be stuck on the roof. Looking around he had to admit the view up and down the valley was magnificent and familiar.

Pense paid no attention to Daniel until he began to hum the tune. She turned around. Daniel hummed louder and sang a few words. That caused her to look at him, eyes expressive and a little frightened.

"Why are you singing that song again?"

"Again? It's just a song. Where did you first hear it?"

Pense studied Daniel's face. "I heard it once," she said. "That's all. I heard it once."

Daniel shifted his weight. The narrow ridge was uncomfortable and his old bones ached. "Why did you say heights never stopped me before? Why do you sit on the roof?" he asked, closely watching Pense's reaction to him. Was her aloofness because she was afraid of him – or afraid of herself? She was bold enough last night, but then there were other people in the dining room.

Pense turned the questions back on him. "Why did you bother climbing up?"

Daniel smiled. This girl will never be caught in a box, he thought. "I came to ask a few questions and share your beautiful view. That's why you sit up here, isn't it? To look at your mountain, your oak tree? To wait for someone?"

Pense took her eyes off Daniel, turned and looked toward her mountain. "Someday," she said, "I'll follow that mountain to wherever it leads. I'll go away from here and never come back."

"Isn't that a little drastic?" Daniel cleared his throat. "Why do you want to run away? This valley only leads to another that has the same problems from which you feel you must run."

Pense turned to him again. "I'm not running away from problems. I just want to see things, to follow . . . . " Her voice trailed off.

"I declare. Wanderlust has taken hold of your Gypsy heart.

Baby has outgrown her cradle. Commendable, I suppose, for a child your age to feel the urge to travel."

"I'm not a child."

"You're not an adult either," Daniel said. When Pense fixed him again with blazing eyes, they pierced his very soul. Daniel's heart pounded. He felt lightheaded. Magdalena's eyes, he thought. *My God, they're her eyes.*

Pense responded with a question. "Why'd you show up at Grandmother Theresa's?"

"Because . . . I was summoned. Because . . . I was asked." Daniel now didn't know how to proceed. He hoped she would be the one to explain to him.

"Who asked you to come to the village?"

"That's why I'm up here with you. I thought you'd know. Perhaps you did. Do you remember me, Pense? Do you remember seeing me before?"

Instead of answering, Pense stood and walked to the end of the roof where she sat with the abandon of a child, legs dangling over the edge. Heights held no terror for her.

"I'm not joining you over there," Daniel said. "If you're not going to talk to me, my climb has been in vain. I may as well leave. That might prove a challenge considering the condition the ladder's in. There must be an easier way down. How do you get onto the roof?" Daniel had difficulty standing. He waited a few minutes then carefully started to shuffle down the roof toward the broken ladder.

"No!" Pense called. "There's a new ladder on the other side of the barn, over where the doors to the threshing floor are, where it's not so high. It'll hold your weight. You'd better put the old ladder away so that when Theresa comes from church she won't know you were up here with me."

Daniel turned to face Pense."Why should I worry that anyone would find out I was on the roof with you?"

"For the same reason you should worry about asking me to go to the mountain with you. That was your next question, wasn't it? You want me to walk with you to the top of my mountain. You want me to go to the oak tree."

Daniel shivered. This was not a child speaking. This was an adult with a penchant for reading minds. He turned his back to Pense and the mountain.

"Are you going to take a walk with me? I really need to talk to you."

Pense didn't answer. Turning her back to Daniel, she looked to the mountain and began to sing, "O hush thee, my babie, thy sire was a knight, Thy mother a lady, both lovely and bright . . . ."

Daniel stood mesmerized. Was it the song, or Pense's voice, or just the giddiness of standing on the roof on a crisp autumn day? When she finished the song, he said, "*Schej*, that was nice."

"Mr. Cudzinki!" Pense called to him as he worked his way laboriously toward the edge. "I don't want to talk to you because you're a *mulani.* And I don't yet know the answers."

"My dear child. There's no need to be afraid of me. I wouldn't harm a hair on your head. If anything, I'd give my life for you. Deep down inside, you know that. In some ways, I am as frightened of you as you are of me."

"I promise to talk with you," Pense said. "But I need to think about some things that happened first."

"Please don't leave it too long. Come to me as soon as you're ready." Hanging on for dear life, Daniel climbed down the new ladder, then returned the broken one to the side of the carriage house and retreated to a bench in the vegetable garden from which he could see the barn's roof. He couldn't keep his eyes off Pense. She'd called him a ghost. She knew!

Pense suddenly let out a piercing whistle and raised an arm. A white dove flew over the barn, fluttered around her, then settled on her wrist. It was obvious that she'd expected the bird to appear.

How strange that the dove should be attracted to her, Daniel thought. He suddenly felt very tired, weighed down with the heaviness of years, with great, unrelenting, stalking age. He went inside for a nap.

Daniel roused himself from deep slumber, bewildered, neither here nor there, suspended somewhere between past and present. He was aware of the present, but unable to open his eyes to join it.

"Mr. Cudzinki? Daniel?" a voice said. "Are you all right?"

Daniel managed to wave a hand in the air, tried to struggle upright but fell back on the pillow. He tried again and this time was successful.

Sharona stood by the bed. The only light in the room wasfrom the open door.

"Child. How long did I sleep?"

"No matter how long," Sharona said, "as long as it did you some good."

"Traveling does tire an old man," Daniel said. "It's good to be back in the land of the living."

"You were traveling through the land of the dead?"

"Figuratively speaking. I slept through supper, didn't I? I'll wash and come downstairs."

"There's a plate of food for you in the warming oven. You looked awful when you came in from the garden. You staggered upstairs and Johnny said to let you sleep. He said you'd benefit from a good rest. When you didn't come down for supper, he checked on you. He said you were 'dead to the world', so we decided to let you sleep."

"I'm a bother." Daniel's guttural accent stuck in his parched throat. "Theresa's running a boarding house, not a convalescent home."

"Agreed," said Sharona. "But I've a feeling you're not our usual type of boarder. Theresa has a soft heart. Just don't take advantage of her too often." Sharona flipped the switch on the bedside lamp and looked closely at Daniel. Strange. He seemed to have aged.

"Is there something wrong?" Daniel asked.

"Not really," Sharona said. "Daniel, did you notice Johnny held my chair last night? That has to be the first time he's ever done that. Your manners are rubbing off on him."

"Well, it's nice to know I can be of some assistance around the house." Daniel managed a smile. "He's a good fellow, Sharona. His heart's in the right place."

"If only he'd allow someone to touch his heart," Sharona said. "You sure you're okay?"

"I'm fine."

"Don't rush. I'll see you downstairs."

Daniel staggered to his feet. He'd slept with his clothes on. Rooting in a pocket for the watch face, he squinted to read the time. If the hands were correct, he'd slept for nine hours. Daniel had almost slept his birthday away. The important thing was that he was alive and nearly through the day of his birth. He had marked September 28 as his first questionable milestone.

Chapter 5

Knightswood - September 29, 1947: morning

The sky began its liquid lament during the night, a steady rain that the earth absorbed as though it were an after-dinner li queur. The view from the kitchen window was fluid, with water dripping off trumpet vines and spilling over clogged eavestroughs.

Taking advantage of the stove's heat, Daniel sat at the kitchen table working on a crossword puzzle he'd cut from the weekly paper. And like the puzzle, he was fishing for the appropriate words that would allow him to delve further into Knightswood's past. Occasionally he glanced at *Silhouette* for inspiration. When he did, wild music played through his heart and soul. Daniel's chance came when Sharona mentioned that it would be a good day to sit by a fire and read. He pounced on her words.

"It's as good a day as any to do some Anderson research," he said. "You know, looking through old papers, diaries and account books can be rewarding. Business research extends to old manuscripts and historical books too. Did Joseph Anderson keep land documents, books of local interest? I'd like to see them if he did." Realizing he'd been a little too straightforward with his request, Daniel held his breath, waiting for an answer.

"Are you sure you won't come with us?" Theresa was filling a basket with eggs. "We're taking the car. It's not far to Mount Forest and there's plenty for you to see. The village has some nice stores. We won't be long. We'll be home before supper."

Daniel shook his head. "I don't think I'll go, Theresa. I'd rather read. If there's something I can do for you around the house, just tell me. I can do dishes and putter at odd jobs. I would like to do some reading. . . ."

"Give the stew an occasional stir," Theresa said, ignoring the bait. "There's enough for you and Johnny if he comes home for lunch. I can't think of anything else at the moment."

"And the family documents?" Daniel pressed for an answer.

Pense looked up from her breakfast. "He won't take anything, Grandmother." When both Sharona and Theresa turned to look at her, Pense said, "Mr. Cudzinki asked if he could look through some old records. Let him. He might find something interesting."

"Thanks for the vote of confidence." Daniel smiled at Pense.

"Well," Theresa said, "You have Pense's blessing, so away you go. Most of the old records are in the library. Joseph was a prodigious saver of papers. Journals in the bookshelves closest to the fireplace hold the oldest material. Personal papers are in the writing desk. The fire's laid in the hearth. Just strike a match to it." Theresa laughed, "If you find anything resembling gold or rare gems, I lay claim to them. I could use the money for new eavestroughing."

"If I find anything of interest, I'll be sure to show you," Daniel said. "You have to believe me, Theresa. I haven't any bad intentions. I just want to make a dreary day into a productive one."

"I've never had the time to go through everything," Theresa said. "I don't mind you looking but nothing leaves the house. I'd appreciate you showing me anything that's of interest to you."

The women left, giving Pense a ride to school on their way, and Daniel entered the dark, musty library. Leaving the door open, he felt for a wall switch, turning the overhead light off again after he'd switched on all the table lamps he found. Harsh light bothered Daniel's eyes. He then turned his attention to the fireplace. Opening the draft, he lit the kindling. Smoke curled lazily up the marble facade.

"Forgot," Daniel said "This one always had a stuck draft." Daniel jiggled the draft several times. Debris fell into the firebox. He repeated the action until the smoke curled back and found the chimney's draw. May as well get started, he thought, walking toward the desk.

Hours later, Theresa found Daniel surrounded by papers,

seated comfortably in an upholstered leather chair by the hearth. The cats slept peacefully among open account books in a chair opposite him. "Shame on you," she said. "You didn't eat lunch."

Daniel, startled by the voice, jumped. He hadn't heard Theresa come into the library. "Sorry. Johnny didn't come home, and I forgot all about eating. This is fascinating material. Joseph threw nothing away."

"I once promised myself that I'd read every book in this room," Theresa said, glancing around the bookcase-lined room. "I used to come to the estate with my father during the summer and Mr. Anderson gave me access to his books. That's how I got to know Magdalena. We used to read together, sitting on the front verandah."

"You do own some expensive volumes. If you're not interested in reading dull history, you should consider selling them to replace your leaking eavestrough." Daniel stretched his legs. "Have you ever seen legal papers pertaining to the hill?"

"No," Theresa said. "And I've seen all the documents held by the lawyer. Maggie and I didn't throw anything out. If they exist, they'll be here somewhere."

"Fascinating," Daniel said again, looking out a window to make sure it was still raining. "It's still a good day to see the attic. If you're game, I am."

"It'll be damp but we've enough time to go. I haven't been up there in ages. I bought new batteries for the flashlight, just in case you wanted to see it."

Daniel followed behind Theresa, climbing the stairs to the second floor. On the landing, he glanced in the mirror. Although a reflection looked back, there seemed a faintness to it. Was it his hair that was vanishing? His shoulders? Daniel rubbed his eyes and looked again. Indeed, there were subtle changes to the image.

"Are you coming?" Theresa called.

Hanging onto the railing, Daniel pulled himself up the stairs. He waited while she unlocked the attic door, then, holding a flashlight, climbed the dark, damp stairs ahead of her. At the head of the stairs, both shone their lights around the cavernous dark space.

"The third attic is over the back wing," Theresa said. "That's where Maggie used to spend her time. The second attic is beyond the tower room. Someone made an attempt to close the tower up. Johnny checked and said there was nothing behind the walls but mice and dead birds."

"My dear Theresa. There's not room to move in here." Daniel shone his light on stacks of paintings.

"Knightswood's attics are to furniture and paintings what its library is to books," Theresa said. "My parents' furniture is here. The Anderson furniture that I don't need downstairs is stored up here. Oh my! A bat! Shoo! Shoo!" Theresa flung her arms around, causing light to dance in fanciful patterns throughout the front attic.

Daniel was busy fighting his own personal demon, a piercing cold that wrapped around him and left him gasping for breath. It took several minutes for him to recover enough to continue the exploration. As the pair picked their way through the front attic, the chilling sensation followed Daniel. He tried shaking it off by giving a running commentary on the more interesting pieces of furniture, some from the eighteenth and early nineteenth centuries. The paintings were so many that he couldn't begin to do them justice.

"Anderson brought loads of furniture with him. He was Lord something-or-other in Scotland but never used the title here." Theresa buttoned her sweater. The attic was so cold she looked around to see if a window was open.

The third attic yielded a treasure of trunks. Daniel knelt to try one of the lids.

"If you can open them, you're welcome to go through their contents," Theresa said. "I forgot they were here. They belonged to Maggie." Shivering with the cold, Theresa decided a warm kitchen was better than a case of pneumonia. "I'm going to the kitchen. It's too cold and damp for me here. Are you coming?"

Daniel shook his head.

Theresa put her hand on Daniel's shoulder. Why, she thought, do I always have to touch Daniel to make a point? Did she feel compelled to have physical contact because of his age or her own heart's vulnerable nature? "Well, don't stay too long. You don't need to catch pneumonia at your age."

Daniel walked Theresa to the head of the stairs, then returned to the trunks in the third attic. His talent for picking locks made short work of the clasps. When the seal on the second trunk broke, fingers of cold raised the hair on the back of Daniel's neck. The turned-up collar of his sweater didn't protect him from the feeling that someone had thrown ice on his back.

Daniel sat on the floor, his music the rhythm of the rain and his heart. Carefully and methodically he sorted through the contents of two trunks. The first trunk held clothing and a box of trinkets that he set aside for Theresa.

The second! Oh, the second trunk made his heart soar. Beneath dainty nightgowns, beaded velvet slippers, frilly petticoats and lace bodices, Daniel found packets of letters tied with red ribbon . . . letters in a man's handwriting . . . letters in a woman's handwriting . . . letters from England . . . letters from Montreal. Thumbing through each bundle, Daniel set aside a number of envelopes for Theresa. The others, he tucked into his shirt, pressing them over his pounding heart.

Daniel tried to stand using the trunk for leverage and realized that his legs, from so much squatting, weren't solid under him. Again icy fingers struck, this time at his heart inflicting a searing deadly wound. Daniel gasped and prepared himself for the scream . . . the fall. But as fast as it struck, it fled, leaving Daniel on his knees, breathing heavily, bewildered and clutching his chest, looking for blood.

When Daniel appeared in the kitchen, he'd changed clothes and washed his hair. Setting the trinket box and envelopes on the table in front of Theresa, he said, "The letters are from friends of Magdalena Anderson, people who moved away. You might find them interesting. I found them in a trunk full of odds and ends. The second held what I would call trousseau items. Did Magdalena ever mention marriage to you?"

"She mentioned a man . . ." Theresa gazed at Daniel. Eyes met, and in a glance spoke what both hearts felt. Theresa saw anguish and agony as she looked at Daniel's's haggard face. Daniel felt pity and compassion when his eyes met hers. They both looked away, toward the window and falling rain.

Theresa broke the awkward silence. "You felt the unnatural cold, didn't you? I was making my bed when I felt a God-awful cold pass right through me, top to bottom. It felt like someone had walked over my grave. It seemed to come from above me, where I left you in the back attic. Did a window blow open?"

"There was no open window." Daniel cleared his throat, thinking again of the searing pain.

"You'd better sit down. I'll make a toddy for us. Johnny usually has some whiskey stashed in his room. You don't look well."

"I thought I was a goner in the attic." Daniel felt he had to be honest with Theresa. "I was sure that I suffered . . . a wound, not a heart attack, a wound."

"Well, you look like you've been through purgatory, at least. Off to the library with you. Throw a log on the fire. I'll bring us a drink. We'll look together for papers pertaining to the property and to Pense's Mountain."

Knightswood - late evening

Well after midnight, Daniel was awakened by shrieks of laughter coming from outside, beyond the back hall. Even though the area was off-limits, he ventured forth in his pajamas to investigate. From the reading nook's window he saw them . . . Theresa, Sharona, Pense, dancing round and round in the rain, their clothing stuck to their bodies, their hair matted to their heads.

"Of course, how could I forget!" Daniel laughed, hurried down the back stairway and out the kitchen door as fast as age and aching bones would allow.

"Can I join you?" He shouted from the porch steps.

Sharona laughed and held out her hand, breaking the line between herself and Theresa.

"Why, Daniel, only a Gypsy knows that if you dance in rain at night during the last day of the Roma summer, you will live to see your second century."

"It takes one to know one," Daniel said. "And I need all the help I can get." His laugh filled the night sky as he whirled around the circle like a madman in the downpour. The rain soaked him through and his pajamas clung to his frame, but he never felt so good! And as Daniel circled, memories surfaced of him as a young man. Arms up, fingers snapping to wild Gypsy music, he was whirling around the Kumpania's fire. As he danced, flames leapt and sparks flew on the wind. Then Magdalena's youthful face appeared in the flames.

"Eppah! Eppah!" Daniel shouted. "Victory!"

CHAPTER 6

Pense's Mountain - September 30, 1947: morning

Daniel and Theresa made an odd pair as they walked across the upper meadow toward Pense's Mountain. He was wearing rubber boots and a pair of Johnny's coveralls topped with an old jacket Theresa found in a closet. She wore Sharona's slacks, rubber boots and a barn coat. Pense's wardrobe had provided colorful knit caps.

Fires of autumn lay on the hills. They rose from the smoky mists and leapt in flaming tongues of color to the bluest of skies, filled with the whitest of clouds. Unlike the heat of fire, the air was cool like water, crisp and refreshing. Flocks of geese flew overhead, their plaintive cries answering the ancestral voice, whispering that, like the Gypsies, they must migrate.

The two made their way up the hill walking under canopies of golden maples and by scarlet bursts of hawthorn and sumac. Past the oak, they climbed to Pense's grey granite pinnacle. At the top, they sat in the lee of the wind, their backs to the rock.

"From here you can see up, down and across the valley," Theresa said. "And behind us, you can almost see Johnny's barn. I understand why Pense loves it so. She can look over Knightswood from up here. I wave a towel if I want her to come home. She can hear everything too – road traffic, train whistles, Betsy bawling in the upper pasture."

"I can understand why she sits here," Daniel said, his eyes on a black car moving slowly along the river road.

"Do you see the row of maples down by the back lane?"

Theresa pointed to a colorful line. "My property ends there. For Pense's sake, I do wish I owned this pinnacle."

"Exactly what does Harris own?"

"The heights and a bit of land by the old oak."

"Why would Anderson sell the hill? We didn't find any papers in the library that mentioned this piece of property changed hands. There were copies for other property transactions but not the hill."

Theresa shrugged. "I didn't think that Harris owned any land near Knightswood. But he told me six months ago that he has papers to prove it belongs to him."

"You've never seen the papers?"

"No."

"Do you think there's any truth to the rumor that he's going to expand the factory?"

"Look across the valley. What dominates the landscape? *The Factory.* Look west, down the valley toward the Long Swamp. What do you see?" Theresa indicated a flat, treed plain that lay several miles down the valley. "You've got bottom-land with a straight run toward Lake Huron. And this hill, it's full of sand and gravel for building. Expansion can mean a number of things, a new factory, spur lines for raw material to arrive and finished products to leave."

"You feel he's planning to push the village this way, to cross the river?"

"His plans are not so much to expand the village as to build a new factory. Johnny says that Compton's circling around again. He's the one that makes the land deals for Harris. That way, Harris keeps his hands clean and his mouth shut."

Daniel sat quietly, considering the mind of a mogul. "You're right. A rail line across the valley makes sense. And running a line down this side of the valley is the quickest route west. Damn, there's no end to him, is there? He wouldn't mind stripping beautiful land for his own financial gain."

"My thinking exactly." Theresa shifted her weight to give a better view of Daniel. There was something achingly familiar about the man's features – the high cheekbones, the Roman nose, rugged chin and shoulder-length hair.

"You are wondering who I am and what the real reason is that I'm in Millbrook," Daniel said, flashing a charming smile.

"Those questions have crossed my mind. There's a familiarity to your face. You mentioned that one of the reasons you were in Millbrook had something to do with finance?"

The truth would serve him now, Daniel thought, but how much and whose truth? He needed Theresa as an ally. "Partially true," he said. "I'm here on unfinished business. A long time ago, I promised myself to complete some unfinished tasks. And I promised someone close to me I'd fulfill a personal request."

"Does one of these situations involve J.P. Harris?"

"Harris is the unfinished business. Rather, his sins and the sins of his family are," Daniel said. "I'm sorry. I can't tell you more at the present time."

"We've common ground in our dislike for Harris. Age and wisdom conquer a lot," Theresa said. "I've lived around him a long time. You must let me know if I can help. How long have you been acquainted with him?"

Daniel, pretending he didn't hear the question, busied himself by removing his jacket and spreading it over his knees. While doing this, he kept his eyes on the black car now parked down by the crossroads. Two men got out to join a third standing near the automobile. Daniel's body was blocking Theresa's view of the crossroads so she wasn't aware of the situation. He didn't point the car out. Instead he turned toward her to find that she was examining every detail of his face.

"Why do you look so familiar?" Theresa asked.

"You've met people that look like me," Daniel said. "I'm Roma, a Gypsy. But you know, I'm not the one that you should worry about. Your enemy is Harris."

"*Enemy* might be too strong a word."

"For want of a better one," Daniel said. He swept his arms around to indicate the extent of Theresa's land holdings."Why hasn't Harris already gotten his hands on your property?"

"My parents and Maggie left me a bit of money. I can manage if I'm clever enough to handle it properly. And I do take in boarders."

"Clever?"

With pride, Theresa looked over her property – the big house, barn, carriage house, orchard, gardens, pastures, meadows and hill. "Yes, clever," she said. "You see, Daniel, I fill a niche. All those people the bank has turned down come to me for mortgages and loans." Like a fretful mother hen, Theresa reached to pull Daniel's hat over an exposed ear and went on to explain that most of those to whom she lent money worked for Harris. Because Harris influences the bank manager, she explained, those people he dislikes aren't approved for loans and mortgages. Theresa, arms crossed around her knees, sighed and said, "And do you know what? Until recently, no one faulted on a payment."

"And recently?" Daniel said.

"Several have lost their jobs and can't make regular payments," Theresa said. "They're good people. I'm not concerned. If I need money I can always sell some. . . . " She stopped mid-sentence, not wanting to hear herself admit that she might have to sell some of her precious paintings.

"Theresa, if Harris is the only employer in the village, where will these people find work? If they try to sell their homes, to whom will they sell? To another Harris employee who can't get a mortgage?"

"It's not your worry, Daniel. I shouldn't have said anything."

"If you don't collect mortgage payments, you can't pay your bills. If you don't pay your taxes, you lose the property. If you lose the property, you lose Pense's inheritance. Harris is squeezing you out. You can bet he'll buy everything you own. Think what a fine factory site Knightswood would make."

When she was worried, Theresa's left hand went to her mouth. It was there now as with eyes closed she thought through Daniel's logical reasoning. He had verbalized her unspoken thought during the past several months. "You believe there's a connection between the men losing their jobs, and the fact that I hold their mortgages?"

"There's a pattern," Daniel said. "Military men look for patterns. Look, Theresa!"

Wave after wave of blackbirds flew toward the hill, soared over the pinnacle, then swooped down to the cedar-lined banks of the Saugeen.

"They're going home. They're flocking for the journey," Theresa said, dark mood lifting.

Daniel kept his eye on the sky, then, whistling, he raised his left arm.

"It's the white dove, following the blackbirds!"

"Pense's companion," Daniel said. "I wonder if it would come to me."

The dove, hearing the whistle, circled above Daniel once. Then, changing direction, it fluttered toward the barn's roof.

"In some parts of Africa, there's a superstition about white doves," Daniel said. "If one sees a white dove, he believes that it has come for his spirit. The belief is that the dove will snatch the spirit from a dying person and fly as high as it can before releasing it. The spirit will either fall back to earth again to inhabit a new body . . . "

"Or? " Theresa said, watching the dove as it circled the barn before flying back to the pinnacle to circle Daniel. It then flew to the house and fluttered around the back attic window. Strange behavior for a bird, she thought.

"Or soar to the heavens," Daniel said, "as an accomplished and complete spirit, to live happily ever after, never to see earth again. The belief is that if the spirit falls back to earth, it will retain some of the knowledge of its previous life. That might explain Mozart, Strauss, Einstein."

"But it's a superstition."

"Truth lies in knowledge and in the depths of understanding," Daniel said with passion. "What one person believes, another may not. I must believe in reincarnation and life after death. I must believe in spirits and their ability to return to earth."

"What would cause the dove to release the spirit before it reaches heaven?"

Daniel gave serious thought to his answer. "Ah, you're assuming the spirit goes to a heaven. That might not be the case." He thought again. "Any number of things can interfere with a spirit's journey – a flock of birds, a woman's song, a cry of anguish, a baby's laugh. And what the spirit experiences on its passage back to earth is what influences its new life, or lives, for a spirit might be snatched then have its journey interrupted a number of times."

"I have to admit that's an interesting theory," Theresa said. "That might explain why some people believe making noise at a funeral will frighten the spirit back into the body."

Theresa thought about her Grandmother Cassolato who believed that one couldn't live on earth without leaving some thread-of-life behind when they died. Mama Cassolato said that the earth was layered with spirits and, in essence, we were living among them. On All Souls' Day she'd release songbirds in the hope they'd find the souls of deceased family members and take them to heaven.

"Too late to make noise at a funeral," Daniel said. "The dove snatches the spirit at the moment of death."

Using the rock for support, Daniel pulled himself up and, ever the gentleman, gave a hand to Theresa. "We should go back to the house. It isn't good that old people sit in one place for too long. We tend to seize up. Thanks for coming with me to Pense's Mountain."

"Thank you for the companionship. We're a real pair of idiots, Daniel. We threw caution to the wind last night just to prove we could tempt superstition. We perch on this cold granite rock today to tempt the Gods of Autumn."

As the pair made their way down the hill, Daniel turned occasionally to make sure Theresa was all right. When necessary, he gave her a hand over rough spots on the steep trail. They stopped briefly at the oak tree. Theresa had said nothing when she saw the autumn flowers at its base on the way uphill. There were only five people who knew that Magdalena was buried beneath the oak. Sharona, Johnny and she wouldn't have laid flowers on the grave. That left Pense or Daniel to mark the spot. All bets were on Daniel.

Others were interested in the progress that Daniel and Theresa made down Pense's Mountain. Harris's black Buick Imperial was parked at the side of the river road. Three men watched the hill.

"Look at them," Compton said. "Helping each other down the hill like a pair of lovebirds. Why don't you post the property?"

"Too simple, and no one heeds no-trespassing signs," Harris said. "I told you what that old man said to Lillian. He knows too much. Who sent him? What's he up to? Why did he show up now? What's Inachio got to do with him?"

Compton lit a cigarette and, blowing smoke toward Harris, said, "No one knows this Cudzinki fellow. No one saw him come in on the train. Newspaper editor told me that he spent hours looking through old newspapers."

Harris stroked his chin. "What's in the old newspapers? If you have to smoke, Compton, don't do it in my car. Get out."

Blake, the driver, stood a respectful distance away from the Buick. Hearing loud voices and a door open, he turned toward the car. "Trouble, Sir?"

"No Blake. Mr. Compton was just getting out to finish his cigarette. Then you'll drive us past the Wallace property."

Compton got out. Harris followed.

"How's the plan progressing?" Compton asked.

"White, Stewart and O'Donnell were fired in the last two weeks. Johnson, Currie and Lorimer are next to go."

"That'll hurt Inachio's bank account." Compton said.

"My official stand is that those men were fired because they were agitating for unionization, for better wages and work conditions. Some were. What's with them? Who's stirring them up? Have you found anything out yet?"

"Not a thing," said Compton. "How long do you think it'll take?"

"For what?"

"To get your hands on Inachio's land?"

"We've got time." Harris picked lint off his suit jacket. "Patience builds empires. We have to find out more about this Daniel Cudzinki. Let's find his weaknesses. Everyone has weaknesses."

"You should know," muttered Blake.

"What's that?"

"Nothing, Sir."

"What about Wallace?" Compton asked.

Harris laughed. "We'll deal with him when the time comes. He's a little more difficult to handle because he's popular and he doesn't work for me."

"When are you going into Windsor again?"

"Soon. Toss that cigarette," Harris said. "Let's not waste any more time, shall we? Time is money."

"So's Windsor," Blake said.

"I beg your pardon." Harris spun around to face Blake. "You said something?"

"Wind's up, Sir. We should be getting on, wind's up," Blake said.

"When you're in Windsor, ask if a Daniel Cudzinki is representing any corporation." Compton flicked his cigarette into the road and eased his bulk back into the Buick. "He's got that lawyer's look about him. I'll bet he's a legal fellow. He's certainly not your typical labor organizer."

"He just looks like a sacked-out old man," Harris said. "We'll get to the bottom of it before I go to Windsor." Harris called to Blake, "I have a little job for you to do."

The afternoon

Daniel made himself comfortable on a stool at the China Inn's lunch counter, ordered a hamburger with the works and a glass of water. He'd chosen the stool closest to the window so he could monitor Main Street.

The restaurant's interior was more inviting than its exterior. The soda bar, lunch counter, candy stands and a magazine rack lined a wall inside the front door. A half-dozen metal tables with chairs filled the front half of the big room. High-backed wooden booths, their tables personalized by scores of initials carved into their surface, took up the back half. The kitchen, the domain of Mr. Kropolus, was located behind the dining area.

Filthy glass globes hung from the high tin ceiling on long, greasy chains. At least a third of the bulbs were burned out. Mr. Kropolus had suffered a heart attack several years before and refused to climb ladders to change bulbs. The tile floor was clean. Mrs. Kropolus was quick to clear dirty dishes from tables, cleaning up afterwards with a vinegar-soaked cloth.

Cook Kropolus, 'Mr. K,' as he was known, could watch what was happening in the dining area through a large glass window. Carry Kropolus, 'Mrs. K,' as she was called, spent her day coming and going through swinging doors between the dining area and kitchen. When an order was ready, Cook banged on the glass window with a wooden spoon. If he couldn't get anyone's attention, Cook pushed the swinging doors open and shouted for his wife. Because the couple lived on the second floor, they were the eyes and ears of Main Street. There was little went on that they didn't know about.

A radio, tuned to a Toronto station, played behind the counter. Mrs. K hummed a tuneless ditty as she scurried between booths, counter and kitchen. She was a motherly, plump sixty-year-old with thick salt-and-pepper hair that sprung from her head like wire. Locals joked with her, hoping to get free coffee or pie. Women usually sat at front tables where they ate ice cream sundaes, watched Main Street and spread village gossip. Serious village business was conducted in the booths at back.

The China opened at six o'clock in the morning and closed promptly at seven o'clock at night. In defiance of J.P. Harris's decree that everything shut down on Sunday, Mr. and Mrs. K maintained the same hours seven days a week.

Daniel saw Blake cross the street and heard the bell on The

China's door as it swung open. He watched the driver's progress in the soda bar's mirror. Blake hesitated, got his bearing then headed straight toward the counter. He sat on the stool next to Daniel who acknowledged his presence by nodding and saying, "Fine day, isn't it?"

"If you say so," was the response. "Hey, you!" Blake yelled at Mrs. K, "A coffee and a ham sandwich. Pour a coffee for Mr. Cudzinki, too."

"That's kind of you," said Daniel. "You even know my name."

Blake shrugged. "You're new in the village, and you're the one staying at Inachio's. Everyone knows your name."

"I'm boarding with Miss Inachio."

"You come from Toronto?"

"I'm . . . from Europe."

"Served in the underground, I heard."

In the silence that followed, Daniel kept one eye on Blake while he monitored the restaurant's comings and goings in the mirror. Mrs. K. put a plate of food in front of Blake.

"Good-looking sandwich," Daniel said.

Blake didn't answer but took a huge bite of bread and meat.

May as well get straight to the point, Daniel thought. He isn't seated beside me to play footsies. "You drive for Harris, don't you? I've seen you in his car. I saw you today on the road below the hill near Miss Inachio's. You play poker at the Old Boys Club, too. I've seen you go in."

"You know a lot for a stranger," answered Blake, taking a gulp of coffee. "Damn! Cold coffee. Hey, dump this hogwash and give me hot coffee."

Obviously there was no love lost between Blake and Mrs. K, who took her time coming back to the counter.

"I'm on holiday," Daniel said. "I've lots of time to observe people."

"This's a stupid place for a stranger to be takin' a holiday."

"Why? It's pretty, peaceful, miles away from a dirty city. People are pleasant. The place has a certain charm to it."

"Humph," snorted Blake. "It wouldn't be my choice. Besides, most people who come snooping around here, and say they are on holiday, are really looking for cheap land."

"You travel a lot – Toronto, Windsor, Detroit. So does Mr. Harris, I gather."

Blake gave Daniel a long, hard stare. "What makes you say that?"

"It's common knowledge if one pays attention to the local paper. Harris is always mentioned for being away. I just read and make a few deductions. As I've told people, being an old military man, I see patterns in behavior."

"Harris goes away on business."

"Yes, business," Daniel said. "You like your job? It pays well?"

"Why the hell do you want to know?"

"Just asked," said Daniel, changing his tactics. "A man plays poker for fun or money. I gather the stakes are high at the Old Boys Club. Thought perhaps you played because you needed money."

Blake pursed his lips. He was the one supposed to ask the questions. He was the one sent to get information. "You play poker, Cudzinki?"

"A little." Daniel added sugar to his coffee. "I learned to play in the army."

"Good at it?"

"I've won a few. I can't find a decent game around here." Daniel glanced out the window and grinned. "Mrs. K, two slices of apple pie. With ice cream?" When Blake nodded Daniel said, "Pile some on, if you please, Mrs. K."

The door opened and Johnny entered. Before heading for a booth, he made eye contact which Daniel acknowledged by nodding slightly to the mirror.

"So," said Daniel. "Does the job pay well?"

"I get a car, a uniform. I get to travel. I get meals. There are benefits in driving the Harris family around."

"Ah, but the pay isn't so good, then," Daniel said.

"I didn't say that. What about you? What do you do for a living?"

"Speculate," said Daniel. "I like watching people and looking around the territory."

"I noticed," Blake said. "I also know that wolves hide in sheep's clothing."

"The world isn't perfect." Daniel nodded to Mrs. K and dug into his ice cream. "No one can mold it to meet their needs for perfection. That doesn't happen."

"Some can try," muttered Blake. He finished his coffee. "How long will you be staying in the area?"

"No longer than I have to," Daniel said. He smiled at Blake. "Not long."

"Is Big Johnny Wallace a friend of yours?"

"As you know, he boards at Inachio's and has been kind enough to befriend me. I can't fault a man for that."

"Know much about him?"

"No."

"He's an agitator, gets people all worked up about conditions and wages. Some people say he's a Communist. He's one to talk, you know. He should be jailed for murder. Heard he killed a man, one of our guys, with his bare hands . . . in Africa. Says he didn't know what he was doing but it was one of his best friends."

"God bless!" exclaimed Daniel. "The circumstances?"

"Don't know," Blake said. "I heard it from Harris."

"I see." So, that was the way Harris would strike at Johnny, Daniel thought. The bastard had no idea what soldiers went through in the trenches. He never fought in a war. "Blake? You fought in the war?"

"Harris got me off. He needed a driver. The Factory had to keep operating . . .ammo cases, trigger mechanisms, you know."

"Ever feel you should have gone overseas?" asked Daniel.

Blake didn't answer. Stabbing at the pie, he abruptly changed the subject. "Are you married?"

"I was engaged, but the wedding never took place."

"She died?"

"No," Daniel said. "A difference of opinion."

"A fight?"

"Not really." Best I get off this tack, Daniel thought. Turning the subject back to Blake, Daniel said, "You married?"

"I have a couple of friends. I'm on the road so much it wouldn't be fair to a wife."

"And your wages won't keep two."

"I didn't say that."

"You didn't have to," Daniel said. "I'm familiar with Harris's pay scale."

Blake lowered his voice, an edge of anger punctuated his words."You're one of those labor men, aren't you? You've come to agitate, haven't you? Johnny Wallace asked you to come. Otherwise, why would you be interested in Harris – and my pay?"

"My dear man." Daniel laid a hand on Blake's arm. "I've

worked for men like Harris. None of them pay a decent wage. Look at me. I'm an old man. Do I honestly resemble a cigar-smoking Communist, a fire-eyed agitator? Be honest now. I'm closer to death than life. I'm here for a bit of peace and quiet."

Constable Keough came through the door, glanced around then straddled a stool. "How are you, Blake?" He tipped his hat to Daniel.

"What're you up to?" Blake spoke to Keough. "I saw you head out early this morning."

"Got word that the Gypsies are down by Fergus, should be in the village the day after tomorrow. I went to see for myself. Coffee, when you have time, Mrs. K."

Mr. Kropolus, who'd brought two fresh apple pies from the kitchen and hung around to listen, scurried for the pot.

"Heard there were a lot of them." Constable Keough ladled sugar into his cup. "Sure enough, there are close to fifty and more joining all the time along the way. Even found some of those signs they put up to show the route."

"There's normally only a dozen or so," Blake said.

"I know,"said Keough. "And the old woman, Zizou, is back. You know, the old bag that used to drive the covered wagon and tell fortunes. They're taking their time because she's in the horse-drawn wagon, driving the team herself. She's got to be over a hundred years old."

Johnny and several other men had come to the front. Johnny stood directly behind Daniel, hand on the old man's shoulder. "How many did you say?" he asked.

"Forty-nine and more joining at every major crossroads. It's like a reunion of some sort. I'm off to Inachio's next to tell her they can't stay on her property. There're too many of them this time."

"I don't believe you can stop her from welcoming the Kumpania," Daniel said quietly, looking at no one in particular. "Miss Inachio's property lies outside village limits. You have no jurisdiction over whom she allows on her land, Constable."

The room went silent.

Daniel was unperturbed. "It might come as a surprise to some people, but in reading old land documents, I found that Miss Inachio's property is not officially part of the village's responsibility regarding taxation and policing."

Johnny nudged Daniel in the ribs, a signal for him to shut up.

Daniel smiled and raised his hands. "I apologize. I'm a

stranger here. I shouldn't have spoken out. But the Roma can camp on Miss Inachio's land without harassment from the Constable or from Harris."

Johnny gave Daniel another sharp nudge.

"Just lock up your wives and kids," Keough said. "And gather your leaky pots and dull knives. I'll see to Inachio and the Gypsy camp when the time's right."

His remarks seemed to defuse the situation a bit. Several men ordered a refill of coffee and turned back to the counter.

"Put your foot in it, didn't you?" Johnny whispered hoarsely to Daniel.

"Told the truth," said Daniel.

"Yeah, well sometimes it's best to keep quiet."

Daniel shrugged.

"Are you finished?" Johnny said.

"I have to pay my bill."

"Blake won't mind treating you," Johnny said, raising his voice so people at the counter could hear him. "Blake can pay for the privilege of bending your ear for nearly an hour. Can't you, Blake?"

Blake looked from Johnny to Daniel.

"Please," said Daniel. "I insist on paying my bill." He reached into his pocket while Blake looked down the counter, then back at Daniel.

"We wouldn't hear of letting a war veteran pay his own bill." Johnny slapped Daniel on the back. "Mr. K, give Blake the bill."

Cook Kropolus plunked the bill on the counter in front of Blake.

"Thanks," Daniel said. "Blake? What is your first name?"

"Robert." Blake gave Johnny a drop-dead glare and dug for his wallet. Johnny prudently took Daniel by the elbow and steered him toward the door.

"Wait!" Keough said. "Mind if I walk with you two?"

"Please do," said Daniel.

Outside, Keough asked, "Is it right that the Inachio property is outside village jurisdiction?"

"It's true. I spent a rainy morning in her library looking through old documents. And furthermore, her property is not included in the village's up-to-date plans that I saw at the newspaper office."

"I never knew that," Keough said. "That makes my job easier for the next few days. I always figured it was my responsibility to police the Gypsies. No one told me differently."

"Consider who pays your salary," Daniel said. "It wouldn't be in his best interests to tell the truth, would it?"

"Harris pays me. I'm the village constable but Harris pays me, gives me and the wife a house to live in."

"I didn't know that!" Johnny said.

"It's in the records, in the old newspapers." Daniel addressed Keough again. "Don't you have a problem being village constable and a Harris employee?"

"Only if I don't do his . . ." Keough colored. "I don't see anything wrong with the arrangement. The village gets policing free of charge and the peace is kept."

"The peace, as written by Harris," Johnny said.

"No doubt," Daniel said. "Sir, if you've finished with us, we'll be on our way. We have to start collecting our pots and pans." Daniel turned his back on Keough and marched along the street, Johnny trailing in his wake.

"I'll be damned," said Johnny. "You're something else, Daniel."

"Just stick with me," replied Daniel. "I'm not finished yet. I've a lot more up my sleeve."

Knightswood - supper

"I can't understand why so many are traveling this time," Theresa said as she sat down at the table. She was answered only by munching sounds. Even Daniel and Johnny's usual banter surrendered to Theresa's boiled tongue with spicy raisin sauce. "Why's Zizou coming? She hasn't been here in years. And to think she's driving that old wagon."

"The last time Zizou came was in the spring of 1936." Sharona passed around hot rolls and joined them at the table. "And the wagon hasn't been used since 1914. Zizou rode in Tamas's car for the last few years she traveled with the Kumpania. I wonder what's up."

"You're very quiet tonight, Pense." Johnny elbowed Pense who was seated beside him. "Cat got your tongue?"

Pense only shrugged and pushed the food around on her plate, too excited to talk or eat.

"I guess we'll all have to wait until they arrive for answers." Daniel made an effort to rise from the table.

"Not so fast." Johnny put his hand on Daniel's arm."You're going with me tonight. Dress warm and don't ask questions."

"Where am I going?"

"Don't ask. Wear my old leather jacket. It's hanging in the carriage house. The roads are dry so we'll take the motorcycle. I'll meet you at the barn in fifteen minutes. Pense, I'm leaving Loco tied in the barn so he won't run after me. I don't want the dog around the farm tonight."

"The motorcycle?" Sharona said. "Johnny, he's an old man. Take the car."

"Nope, the bike," Johnny said as he left the room.

Johnny's Farm

Uncomfortable, were yuh?" Johnny laughed as he threw his leg over the bike. "You don't ride motorcycles often, do you? I was wearin' you like honey."

"If God wanted us to ride like bats out of Hell, he would have built us with wings, wheels and a motor already attached," said Daniel, dismounting stiffly. "I am an old man, as people insist on reminding me."

The pair arrived at Johnny's farm and Daniel could see they were not alone. A half-dozen cars lined the drive near the barn and a light shone through the boards of the upper level that housed the threshing floor, granary and hay mow.

"There's a meeting I thought you'd be interested in attending," Johnny explained. He opened the door and stepped inside. The smell of fresh hay mingled with that of manure and motor oil. Walking around a threshing machine, Johnny was greeted heartily by a group of men. Everyone went silent when Daniel appeared.

"Why's he with you?" asked one.

"Believe me," Johnny said, "he's on our side. Did anyone check for spies?"

"Gord's down by the road. He should be here any minute."

"Harris employees," Johnny said to Daniel. "I'll introduce yuh." Johnny took Daniel around to meet each of the eighteen men in the barn, giving running commentary about each while at the same time taking great pains to explain that Daniel had served in the underground during the war. "Harry's got a wife and seven kids. George's a veteran, has a wife and one child. Bill's a veteran, newly married." Hands were shaken, heads nodded. A bottle was passed. Gord slipped in to join the gang.

"So, what do we know?" Johnny asked. "George. You were going ask about a raise."

"Nothin'! Frickin' nothin'!" George said. "There's no raise. Five damn hellish years an' no more money in our pockets than 'fore the war. Made a killin' off the war and put the whole damn works into his own pocket, he did."

"Harry. You were responsible for asking Harris about insurance."

"He just laughed. I was told I'd be out the door if I persisted about insurance. White's been fired. Harris said that I was lucky to have a job at all if I didn't shut up."

"Are you comfortable pushing Harris a bit on this point?"

"Sure," Harry said. "I've been thinking of moving to Hamilton anyway. Wife's got relatives down that way. If I'm fired, we'll move a little sooner."

Johnny nodded toward Bill. "You were goin' to ask about a shorter work week? What flak did you get?"

"'Twas a warnin' I got," said Bill. "As I dinna' have a family, I pushed hard. Ma wee wifie and me can pack a kit and find better awa'."

The bottle made the rounds again, each man wiping the neck with a sleeve before taking a drink.

"Are you all still willing to meet, considering the firings that have taken place lately?" asked Johnny.

"Aye, aw doot," responded Bill. "We took a vote 'afore ye came. We canna' stop now."

"Good. The question is how to proceed."

Silence hung heavy as the wind whistled through cracks in the wood siding, skipping dust along the floor near the steps to the stables.

"What are your concerns?" Daniel asked, looking sympathetically at the work-weary men lounging around him.

"A forty-three-hour week, $.25 cents more an hour, an insurance plan to cover our families, safe working conditions, a guarantee that Harris can't fire without just cause." Johnny ticked each demand off on a finger.

"You're forming a union?"

"We don't want to go that far. We're not in the majority, yet."

"There's more wants tae kiss his arse than kick his butt," Gord said.

Everyone laughed and the bottle went round again.

"Secrecy is what we need. If someone rats, we can be fired for meeting like this," Harry said. "We can be fired for drinking. Hell, we could be fired for having kids. I mean kids mean sex." Harry looked around the loft to see if he had everyone's attention. "Booze and sex. Two of Harris's pet vices. Not that he didn't partake of at least one. He has a daughter."

Everyone roared. The thought of Harris being sexy was funny.

Daniel smiled and said, "What've you done so far?"

"Frickin' asked," George said. "More'n once too."

Johnny explained. "They've all taken turns asking about changes. Every time they put their hand out for the pittance they get each week, they ask about a raise, insurance, hours."

"How many of you are there in total? I count eighteen here."

"What you see are the ones who feel strongly enough to risk holding meetings," Johnny said. "There are others, maybe twenty-five. We haven't been organized that long."

"Thought conditions might improve after the war," Harry said. "When they didn't, we all felt it was time to do something. Johnny lent his barn so we wouldn't have to meet in the village."

"Thar's fifty percent if we could get organized." Charlie spoke for the first time. "We have to prove we're serious. God, if we could win one demand, small as it might be."

"Is fifty percent of the work force good enough to ensure that changes will be made?" asked Daniel.

"It's the best we can hope for," Johnny said. "You see, no one wants to be branded a Communist, and some people worship the ground Harris walks on. Their families have worked for The Factory for two or three generations. They don't see anything wrong with Harris's brand of dictatorship."

Bill took up the story. "They've inherited a cradle-tae-grave-mentality sae Harris be the ticket tae heaven. They canna think past their noses. They canna think there's better tae be had. Lacka God's-given eyes they need tae use tae peek roun'."

"We amount to nothing more than a mosquito in the face of a cow," a fellow by the name of Mike said. "We buzz around and annoy but unless there's a hundred of us, the cow won't move. And we occasionally get slapped out of the sky for trying to jump over the moon."

Eddie came to the front of the group to speak. "We're damn well too few to walk out, but that's what it'll take. We're nuthin' to Harris but a body at a machine, and bodies come cheap. Everyone's looking for work. Men're standin' in line lookin' for work. We'd damn well be replaced in a minute, and I need the job."

"Can't defeat Harris," Mike agreed.

"You can," Daniel said. "Harris has his soft side, an underbelly to expose."

"If he has, we haven't found it yet," Gord said.

A door blew open causing nervous fellows to jump. An owl swooped from the rafters, glided silently over the lights and flapped its way out the open door. Johnny's horses stomped restlessly in their stalls on the lower level.

"I'll take a look downstairs and quiet the horses," Johnny said, moving away from a post.

"I'll take a tour around outside." Gord went toward the upper door.

"Bring another bottle back with you," Mike said. "There's one under the rug in the back of my car."

Nothing was said until Johnny and Gord returned.

"I didn't see anyone but the horses are skittish. Best keep our voices down. Explain about this underbelly," Johnny said. "Gather in close, guys. Gord, pass another bottle."

"Harris's underbelly is lined with money," Daniel explained. "Hit him in the money. Ask yourselves. Where does he make his money? He makes it through the sale of products. No sales – no revenue. Slow sales – slow revenue. If he manufactures a poor product, there're no sales. A breakdown of equipment means nothing manufactured. Nothing manufactured means no sales. No sales, no revenue."

"Got ya!" exclaimed Harry. "There's a hell-of-a-push next week to fill a huge order for Saskatchewan and Alberta. Stores need it by the end of month. Put a clinker in the line."

"The time to act is when he's under pressure to get products off the lines and shipped quickly," Daniel said. "Lines stop. Things break down. Presses can't be repaired quickly."

"Tools go missing." Charlie was warming to the issue.

"We gotta be careful," interjected Mike. "We can't afford to lose a couple days' pay if a line's shut down."

"Little acts add up to big effects," said Daniel. "And nothing should be strung together to look like sabotage. Random acts of disruption. Stupid little things that usually go wrong at one time or another, now all go wrong together."

"Johnny, the man's a frickin' genius," George said, passing the bottle round one final time.

"Don't tell anyone what you're up to," Daniel cautioned. "Keep your little *accidents* to yourself. That way you protect the others from dismissal if you're caught. And don't do anything that will lead to the injury or death of a worker."

"Shake on that," Johnny said, holding his hand out to George. Everyone shook hands, sealing trust among friends.

"We'll meet here again, one week from tonight," Harry said.

"Don't be predictable," Daniel counseled. "Make it another night, another place."

"Where might you suggest we meet that we won't be seen?" Mike asked.

"I was thinkin'." Johnny stretched his long legs as he stood. "Why hide? Why not be seen? We could meet right under Harris's nose at The China. Meet after-hours and call ourselves something educational like 'The Stamp Club'. The Kropoluses will cooperate and won't give away our real purpose."

"Good idea," Daniel said. "What better ruse than a Stamp Club? If you're a little bolder about your activities, more people might look at your group in a more serious way."

"Done!" Mike said. A murmur of approval went through the group."You call the meeting, Johnny. We'll all be there."

"You might want to test the waters by scheduling your next meeting when Harris, and his nose Blake, are away from Millbrook," Daniel said. "They'll leave when the Gypsies arrive, if not before."

"It could backfire," Johnny warned.

"We're with you," said Harry. "I've a friend who knows a lawyer. I'll get in touch with him about the question of wrongful dismissal if there is such a thing."

"Agreed then?" Johnny said.

"Aye" . . . "Yes"

"Meeting's over."

The group dispersed in twos and threes while Johnny and Harry checked for live cigarette butts and gathered the empty bottles.

"Good meeting." Harry shook Daniel's hand. "I'm going to dump the bottles at the foot of Harris's driveway."

"No," Johnny said. "Let them be part of the first sabotage attempt. See if you can sneak them into his office. Let his secretary see them on his desk, in his file cabinet or waste basket."

"That might be a bit risky," Daniel said. "There'd be some pointed questions asked if you were caught. It would be easier to dump them in a waste basket in the executive washroom. That'll cast suspicion on a number of J.P.'s yes-men, henchmen."

"What a man!" Harry said, slapping Daniel on the back.

"That he is," Johnny said. "Daniel, you want a ride back in Harry's car or want to make like a monkey with me again?"

"I'll trust you not to lay us down on the road," said Daniel. "But you'll be held so tight you'll figure you're wearing a shadow."

"How do you know Harris'll leave the village when the Gypsy caravan arrives?" Johnny pulled his heavy leather jacket over his flannel shirt.

"I read it in the papers," said Daniel, struggling into his jacket. "He usually leaves just before the Kumpania arrives. The paper doesn't say this in so many words, but the information's there if you read between the lines."

"I'll be damned!" exclaimed Johnny.

"You will if your ruse about a Stamp Club doesn't work out." Daniel smiled. "Tell me, Johnny, why are you helping these people?"

"On account of my father, my mother and my sisters. I owe them one."

"You're leaving yourself wide open, Johnny. Harris plays dirty pool."

"I know what he's up to," said Johnny. "I'll handle it. I have to face it up sooner or later."

"You were sucking pretty heavily on the bottle tonight. That's not the way to handle it," cautioned Daniel.

"I've got a few things to sort out. Drinkin's one of them," Johnny said.

"You've got people that love you and are counting on you, Johnny, me included."

"What do you mean by that remark, old man?"

Daniel shrugged. "You know, if people keep calling me 'old man' I might begin to believe I am. Let's go while I have some nerve left and a bit of life in these weary bones. Sleep awaits."

Chapter 7

Knightswood - October 1, 1947: morning

Theresa's bedroom wasn't the largest suite at Knightswood – nor was it the most pretentious, but it was her sanctuary. Until she had a wall removed, her comfortable chamber had been two rooms, a sewing room and a tiny sunroom. Combined, they made a comfortable boudoir with large windows that faced east for the first rays of the sun, and south for views of her gardens, meadows and Pense's Mountain.

Theresa was a creature of habit. She had an early morning routine that varied little from day to day, year to year. Morning prayers were said while seated by the east window to catch the sun as it began its journey over her valley. Today a full palette of color spread before her as the huge golden globe turned the pale grey sky into ribbons of pink, yellow, mauve and bird's egg blue. High clouds slipped through, diffusing the colors in the east, intensifying them in the southern sky.

She was not one to close any doors that might lead to heaven, so she thanked anyone who might be listening for the life she led and the people who shared it with her. She gave thanks for plentiful food and the means to grow it. For several days she had included Daniel in her prayers because she sensed that problems lay under his confident exterior. For the last week or so, she gave special attention to Pense and her problems. Theresa felt it was best to keep uneasy spirits happy, so always ended her prayers with a mention of Magdalena.

When the sun shone through sifting drifts of mist to dance around the oval-framed portrait of her parents, Theresa finished her prayers and moved to the south window to watch for deer in the meadow and the fox on the hills. This morning a huge buck drank from the spring while two timid does held back.

"No one will hurt you, my beauties, drink," Theresa said, watching for the albino doe that came last to drink. Her heart ached for the little white deer. If Johnny had found it as a baby, it would be a pet, not fodder for the hunters' rifles. He'd put signs up all round Knightswood and his farm telling hunters that the area was off-limits. But signs don't stop deer from traveling past the boundaries. There was no sign of the albino this morning, neither did the fox run over the hill. Perhaps she was at the chicken house, looking for breakfast. Maybe she was in the orchard waiting for her half-grown kit to finish playing round the trees.

When the sun shone higher in her south window, Theresa turned to the task of making her bed. She usually worked around the cats, reaching to pet them once in awhile. After Daniel arrived, the cats began the night sleeping on her bed and ended it in Daniel's room. The man was obliging enough to leave his door open, just a crack, so they could come and go during the night. Theresa had justified this break in her routine as a good omen. If the cats accepted Daniel with no hesitation, she could too.

After making the bed, Theresa dressed, then straightened scatter rugs and pictures. Like other walls in the house, Theresa's were hung with favorite paintings. These pictures were her escape from the mundane world of Millbrook. She strolled among sheep in the English Cotswolds, purchased fruit at a stall in Venice, Italy, or sat by the Shenandoah River in Virginia.

Theresa sat at her dressing table, working the silver strands of her hip-length hair from its braid. When arthritic arms could no longer reach to do the job, Pense enthusiastically took on the responsibility of brushing and fixing Theresa's hair. Kenneth had liked her hair long, so she'd never had it cut. It was the only physical thing she had kept to remind her of the man she'd loved so many years ago. Theresa closed her eyes, once again feeling the sensation of Kenneth's fingers running through her long, black locks.

Pense knocked, then came in without waiting for an invitation. "How're you this morning, Grandma? Are you daydreaming again?"

"Oh, my child. You frightened me."

"Sorry," Pense said. She chose a brush from the dressing table and ran a comb through it to clean the bristles. Pense tucked the stray strands into an ornate handmade wooden hair-saver. "Did you enjoy your walk with Mr. Cudzinki yesterday?"

"Daniel's a good companion. He makes poetry of conversation."

"It's been a long time since you've climbed to the pinnacle."

"And I'm feeling that climb this morning," Theresa said. "That and our little midnight cavort. I'm much too old to be dancing in the rain. I should have known better. That was foolishness."

"That was fun," Pense said. She began to brush from top to bottom, holding the long fall of hair in her left hand. Pense hummed as she worked.

Theresa enjoyed having her hair brushed. Like many old people, she ached for physical contact . . . a hug . . . a kiss . . . a touch. Pense had always been a happy child, she thought, listening to the tune the girl was humming. When Pense picked the tune out on the piano's keyboard after the birthday supper, Theresa had experienced a glimmer of recognition. Now the song preyed on her mind.

"That tune you're humming. It's the same one that Daniel was talking about?"

"It is," Pense said. "Mr. Cudzinki found the complete poem and gave it me to read. Grandma, it's hard to explain but I knew that poem although I'd never read it before he gave me the book. And the music . . ."

"I've heard it too." Theresa pursed her lips and tried to tap into old memories where familiarity lay at the edge of consciousness. "It's terrible when you get old, Pense. You forget so much."

"You're not old, Grandma." Pense bent and kissed the wrinkled brow then fell silent again as she brushed the hair gently.

"You've been looking in the wrong mirror, child. I'm well past three score and ten."

"Grandmother! Don't say such things."

Theresa watched Pense's reflection in the mirror for several minutes. In the past several weeks there'd been a noticeable change in the girl's personality. Perhaps she had taken the first steps toward a womanly maturation.

"Mirrors don't lie," Pense said. "They tell the tale, just like our eyes."

"That's true," Theresa said. "I know what you're thinking. I can see it in your eyes."

Their eyes met in the mirror image, age acknowledging youth, as woman to a child, wisdom to the unschooled.

"You're free to go," Theresa said. "I won't stop you. You're thirteen years old. You've a right to be with your family. I'm sure that your mother goes through the same struggle every time the Kumpania arrives. You're both free to leave."

Pense lowered her head, breaking eye contact."Grandma, I—"

"Hush child. Just listen to me for a minute." Theresa glanced into the mirror again, wanting to catch Pense's reaction to what she was about to say. "Please, think hard before you make any decision. And talk with your mother. Don't shut one door, just for the experience you might gain by opening another. Make sure something good waits past that new opening. Pense, my girl, don't do anything rash."

"You can read my mind." Pense methodically began to plait Theresa's hair.

"I've always known that the time would come when you'd have to wrestle with the choice of whether to stay or to leave. I knew the day that you were born you'd be faced with the decision. Mind, you have the maturity to handle the situation, but I think you're a little young to leave your mother."

"Grandma, I yearn to be free. I have this feeling that I need to leave . . . . "

"Free from what, dear child? To go away, and not know why you left, is not to leave at all."

"Maybe *free* is the wrong word," Pense said.

"There are a lot of *maybes* in life. Maybe your mother should never have left the Kumpania. We've tried to raise you as a free spirit but maybe we didn't try hard enough. Maybe you're tired of being restricted by walls and rules. I know that walls can be oppressive."

"I love Knightswood," Pense said. "I'm not sure why I want to leave. I'm not sure of anything anymore." Pense reached for hair pins and began to wind the braid around Theresa's head. "Whatever I do, I have to make my mind up soon."

A lump rose in Theresa's throat. The thought of losing Pense was too much for her to accept.

The two exchanged a brief glance in the mirror. Pense said, "Why don't I just fold your braid several times so that it doesn't fall into the soup pot and keep it in place with some ribbons? You need pretty ribbons in your hair today. Ribbons always make you feel better. What color? Gold for autumn?"

"Yes, gold and red." Theresa leapt on the opportunity to change the subject. She opened a small wooden chest and chose two ribbons. Kenneth always said a woman was never too old to wear ribbons in her hair.

"There you are, Grandma." Pense held a hand mirror up behind Theresa's head so that she could admire the completed hairdo in the reflection of the larger looking glass.

"That's lovely, Pense. You go down for breakfast. I'll be along shortly."

Pense had her hand on the doorknob and turned wistfully back to search Theresa's eyes. "What has mother said to you about her feelings toward the Kumpania?"

"Nothing. Away you go. I'll be down shortly."

Theresa closed her eyes and leaned back in her chair. Why must Pense make a decision now? She's too young. She doesn't know what she's leaping into. Sharona's a different story. She knows the situation. What decision will she make this visit?

When Theresa glanced in the mirror again, she saw the face of an old woman fraught with troubles. "Foolish," she said aloud. "You can't hold either back. Your days on earth are nearing an end. Their journeys through life have only begun. Part of their journey lies with the Gypsies." The other part? That, Sharona would have to deal with – and very soon.

Theresa stood, bowed under what seemed to be the weight of the world. And there was Daniel. As each day dawned, she thought more about Daniel. He reminded her so of her beloved Kenneth.

"Silly woman!" she said. "You're too old to fall in love and he's too old to reciprocate. You can't love a man that entered your life one week ago." Theresa's heart skipped a beat when she remembered that the moment she had laid eyes on Kenneth years before, she had fallen in love with him. "You're feeling sorry for an old man," she spoke to the image in the mirror. "You're feeling nothing more than sorrow."

Theresa sat again at the south window. The view over Pense's Mountain had a calming effect. What about Daniel? Her mother would say that he wore like an old glove. He's comfortable around her and she responded. He's familiar – his mannerism, his lips, his eyes. Theresa turned to look at the photograph of her parents. Go easy, the images in the picture whispered. Take your time, daughter.

Lust? Love? Pity? Theresa thought. I mustn't confuse the three. Were her emotions simply compassion for an old warrior? Did she need a companion's love? Was it lust from a body never fulfilled? A snippet of music came from the other side of Theresa's bedroom door. Who was singing that song now? Why does that music keep surfacing?

As her fingers beat a rhythm on the window sill, Theresa thought back to the dinner conversation. Daniel said music had been written for the poem. Magdalena loved to play the piano and had a large collection of books and sheet music. Had she played the song?

Theresa hurried downstairs to the parlor. Pulling a leather-bound volume of handwritten music from the piano bench, she sat leafing through its musty pages. "That's it!" Turning to the keyboard, Theresa began to play, slowly at first, reading notes that had been written in Magdalena's precise style. As Theresa played, she began to sing, *Oh hush thee my babie the time will soon come, When thy sleep shall be broken by trumpet and drum; Then hush thee my darling, Take rest while you may, For strife comes with manhood, and waking with day.*

Hearing the music, Daniel finished dressing and descended the stairs to the first floor. As had become his daily routine, he glanced in the mirror at the foot of the stairs then blanched at what he saw. Daniel's hands flew to his face, his hair, his neck. They felt solid under his touch. Daniel rubbed his eyes then peered intently into the mirror again. The grey haze was quite apparent. Were his eyes deceiving him or was he fading away?

"Spiffin' up for a woman, are ya?" Johnny said, coming through the hall from the direction of the kitchen.

Daniel covered his confusion by saying, "Couldn't remember if I'd shaved this morning. Do I look different to you?"

"Nope." Johnny looked at Daniel, then into the mirror. "Mirror needs cleaning," he said. "Looks like it's got a scum on it, or somethin'."

Daniel, touching his face again, said "You look okay in the mirror?"

Johnny glanced into the mirror. "Yep," he said, rubbing the

mirror with his shirt sleeve, "Breakfast's on the table. Sharona sent me to round everyone up."

"Oh. Sorry, forgot all about breakfast," Daniel said. "Came down when I heard the music. Who's playing the piano?"

"It has to be Theresa," Johnny said. "Pense is helping Sharona in the kitchen. Funny thing, it's the first time I've heard Theresa play the piano since I got home from the war. Somethin' must have inspired her."

Glancing into the parlor, both men saw Theresa hunched over the keyboard.

"Don't disturb her, Johnny. She's sorting through a problem." Daniel said. "Would you do me a favor? Tell Sharona I won't be eating breakfast this morning. Time's wasting. There's things need doing that can't wait any longer."

"Yuh'll make yourself sick by skipping a good breakfast."

"I'll be all right, Johnny. Don't worry about me."

Daniel left the house and walked with determination toward the river path and the Harris estate. The morning sun highlighted the riot of colors surrounding him. Leaves clung tenaciously to branches, ready for another few days of glorious display before succumbing to October's windy assault. A sad time of the year, Daniel thought. Autumn was summer's funeral, spring was her birth.

If habit held true, Daniel's quarry would be found somewhere along the footpath at this time of the day. A dog barked close by, but Sebastian hadn't mentioned a watchdog in his notes. Daniel smiled when he spotted Lillian Harris by the Cascade.

He doffed his hat and said, "Good morning, Miss Harris. Or as the Irish would say, 'Top 'o the day'."

"You were told never to use this path again," Lillian said, keeping her distance.

"And you were told that it belongs to the village, public land, I believe it's called," Daniel replied. "I came to see you, Lillian. As I gather that the welcome mat wouldn't be out at your house, I stand before you now asking for an audience, several moments of your time."

"And if I don't feel like hearing you out?"

"You will," said Daniel. "If only because you're curious about why I'd seek you out."

Lillian's lips curled in a hint of a smile. "You do pique my interest."

"Good!" Daniel said. "It makes my job easier. Shall we walk to the gazebo?"

Lillian didn't accept the offer of Daniel's arm. They walked side by side in silence until they reached the wooden gazebo tucked into a copse of cedar trees.

"This is quite nice," Daniel said. "I have to admit that it was kind of Harris to give the village a present like this that doesn't have his name all over it."

"He wouldn't see it that way," Lillian said. "As far as he's concerned the gazebo is on his private property. He called you a stupid old man when I brought up your claim about the land."

Daniel cleared leaves and twigs from a bench, then offered it to Lillian. "There's an old saying where I come from, 'Stupid one may think me, but clever I am'." Daniel sat down beside her, hat in hand. "Miss Harris. Does the name Kenneth Walker mean anything to you?"

"No."

"J.P. has never mentioned him?"

"No."

"Come now, Miss Harris. You can tell me the truth. J.P. isn't here, looking over your shoulder. Blake drove him to Windsor late last night. For all intent and purpose, it appears that he's at the factory. In reality, he's not in Millbrook."

"How do you know?"

"A little bird told me. He can leave. His henchmen won't let the village go to hell in a handbasket while he's away. He's trained them well. They'll rat on anyone that steps out of line."

"Mr. Cudzinki. You're despicable."

"That I may be," Daniel said. "But I'm right, am I not?"

Lillian nodded. "He received a note that the Gypsy caravan, including the woman Zizou, was due in today. He never stays around when they come."

"Why? Does he hate them so much that he can't stand the sight of them?"

"He claims they're a pack of lying, thieving heathens. Rather than confront them, he leaves."

"He can't control them, so he runs."

Lillian gave Daniel a scathing look. "Who are you to judge my father? What are you up to? Blake says . . ." When she stopped short, almost as if she gave away a secret, Daniel continued.

"Ah, yes, Blake. We had a long chat yesterday, Blake and I. You're his special friend, are you not? That's one relationship Harris and your mother would be furious about, if they knew."

"They don't know."

"Of course not! And I'm not going to tell them."

"Father wouldn't understand. He'd fire Blake if he found out we were seeing each other." Lillian pulled her jacket more tightly around her waist then tucked her hands up its sleeves for warmth.

"I understand," Daniel said. "Even if love does enter the picture, such relationships aren't often given family blessings among the wealthy."

"I'll marry whom I want to as long as I love him," Lillian said. "I just don't want Blake to lose his job."

"So love doesn't enter into the relationship with Blake?"

"Not particularly."

"These new relationships confound me." Turning his hat in his hand, Daniel looked upriver, toward the mill. "Lillian, how do you feel about Gypsies?"

"I couldn't care one way or the other. I like having my fortune read. I love their music. But they come for such a short period of time that no one ever gets to know them well."

"Pity," Daniel said."They're nice people. They lead interesting lives."

"No doubt. They're supposed to arrive today?"

"Tomorrow," Daniel said. "The note that was given to your father was misleading. The Roma are arriving tomorrow."

"Why are you showing so much interest in me and the Gypsies?"

"A private reason," Daniel said. "And I'm amused at your father's reaction to them."

"It's a deep-seated prejudice. He's reacted the same way for years."

"More's the pity." Daniel reached into a pocket. "Would you read this, Lillian? At your convenience, of course. We'll talk again very soon."

Lillian glanced at the handwritten page."Why do I want to read Kenneth Walker's biography?"

"In time, I'll explain and you'll understand his importance," Daniel said. "Now, if you'll excuse me, I'll be off to my next appointment. By the way, are you seeing Sebastian Temple?"

"The man who works for my father? The one who's in charge of the turbines at High Falls Dam?"

"Yes," Daniel said as he stroked his chin, a smile on his face."Have you known him long?"

"I know him well enough. He's a friend."

"As in a Blake type of friendship?"

"That, Mr. Cudzinki, is none of your business." Lillian searched her pockets for cigarettes.

"Allow me," Daniel said, taking a pack from his pocket and offering Lillian a smoke. "A physical relationship with a man like Sebastian Temple is understandable. He's handsome, pleasant and very capable. But you must be careful. You might get hurt."

"You know Sebastian?"

"Yes," Daniel said. "I know of him. I'll take my leave, Lillian. Until tomorrow?"

Main Street - morning

Daniel's next stop was Adamo's. Not eating breakfast had been a mistake. He was hungry. Franco Adamo's was the place to get date turnovers and good information on the village.

Adamo's General Store on the square was a holdover from a time when crackers, pickles and apples came in barrels. It smelled of coal oil, hemp rope, soap, smoked ham, vinegar and spices. Pine floors creaked beneath his steps. Wood shelving stretched from floor to ceiling. One section was packed with bolts of cloth, another jammed with tinned goods. A wall of small drawers held items such as screws, nuts, bolts, bone stays and knitting needles. Glass-fronted oak counters, full of china and glassware, ran the length of the store. Display cases burst with thread, buttons, tooth powder and soap.

At the back of the store, a rope strung from one side to the other displayed samples from the latest shipment of shirts, pants and overcoats. A ball of string hung from the ceiling above a roller of brown wrapping paper bolted to the counter's top. Sales were rung up on an ornate cash register. Franco had no intentions of replacing it or any other fixture in the store.

Although Franco Adamo, Jr. had inherited the business from his father, he wasn't enjoying much prosperity. When Adamo refused to give the Harris family a twenty-five percent discount, Harris purchased a building on Main Street and opened a grocery store of his own. Chapman's – what became the China Inn – went under almost immediately. Adamo hung on to serve those few people who hated Harris's guts and the farmers who came into Millbrook every Saturday night. Any Harris employees who wanted to keep their jobs shopped at J.P.'s store. Franco appreciated any business that came his way, even if it was for a half-dozen date turnovers and a bottle of chocolate milk.

Adamo was busy weighing cinnamon sticks for an old woman. "How's Mr. Cudzinki today?" he asked, looking up when he heard the bell on the door. "You can't ask for a better beginning to October, can you, Sir?"

"It's a fine day," Daniel said, eyeing an old man dozing in a chair that was tipped up on its back legs by the pot-bellied stove. Next to him a checker game was set up on an upturned barrel waiting for players.

"He can rock like that in his sleep." Adamo laughed. "I'll be with you in a minute. I'm helping Granny Smith."

Daniel stared at the elderly woman by the counter, then turned away, but not quickly enough.

"Don't think that I don't know you." Granny Smith pointed a gnarled finger at Daniel. "You're . . . you're . . . older, mind you. Darn, the name won't come." She stared hard at Daniel.

"Granny, your sight's deceiving you. Mr. Cudzinki is a stranger in the village. He's visiting from Europe. Isn't that right, Mr. Cudzinki?"

"Indeed," Daniel said, meeting the situation head-on. He took one of Granny's gnarled hands, bowed low and kissed it. *"The Count Daniel Cudzinki,"* he said, staying low enough that she could only see the top of his head.

"*The Count Daniel Cudzinki,* you say?" Adamo asked.

"You don't fool me," Granny Smith said. "I'm old but I rarely forget faces."

"I can't say that I remember faces." Daniel laughed to hide his lie then turned to a pocket knife display, giving Granny no opportunity for another close look. "Finish Mrs. Smith's order. I'm in no hurry."

Adamo took Granny's money and promised to have the order delivered within the hour. Granny, cane tapping a rhythm on the floor, gave Daniel another stern look on her way out.

Franco held the door for her, then turned to Daniel. "Apologies, Mr. Cudzinki. She is more than ninety years old and does get a little confused at times."

"No harm done." Daniel smiled. "I've heard the same said about myself. Mistakes are easy made. I'll have my usual order, if you don't mind – six date turnovers and a bottle of chocolate milk."

"So you're a real European Count, castle and everything. On an important visit, are you?" Adamo put an extra date pastry in the bag. "You going to settle down here? A lot of people are coming through these days you know, after the war and all. A true Count, eh?"

"Figuratively speaking," said Daniel. "I'm not here to buy a grocery store if that's what you're aiming at."

"A lotta factories got bombed out in Europe. Some companies are thinking of starting up again in Canada," Adamo said. "Land! Land's a good buy around these parts. Did you say chocolate or plain milk, *Count Cudzinki*?"

Daniel seized the opportunity, said in a loud voice, "Chocolate please. *Land* around here is a good buy. If I were setting up a business, say a *factory*, I'd *buy* right here now."

Over by the stove, a chair hit the floor and the words *Count Cudzinki - factory - buy - land* stuck in the old man's sleepy brain.

Knightswood - afternoon

At the kitchen table, Sharona viciously kneaded dough on a wooden bread board. With each turn she slapped the dough then punched it into shape. She looked up briefly when Theresa walked into the kitchen then went back to her assault.

Theresa sat at the table and went through the motions of greasing bread pans. When she finally spoke, she said, "Can you stop beating the daylights out of that dough for just a minute to listen to me?"

Sharona glanced up then rubbed her hands together over a bowl of chicken scraps. "Something eating you too?" she asked.

"I just had the strangest conversation with Franco Adamo." Theresa wiped her hands on a tea towel. "I was placing my weekly order and got to bananas before he interrupted to ask if I knew what property The Count Daniel Cudzinki was planning to purchase. I told him that he must be mistaken. Adamo went on taking my order as though he hadn't asked the question."

"I wouldn't know anything about Daniel and property. I've enough problems around here without getting involved in his schemes."

"You're really angry this morning," Theresa said. "You're killing that dough."

Sharona looked at the dough and then at her hands. She shrugged. "There's a few things bothering me these days."

"You and Pense are suffering from the same thing – wanderlust," Theresa said. "I'll tell you what I told her. You're free to go. I love you both with all my heart but I've no hold on you. You can leave at any time. You know that."

"You're wrong," Sharona said. "Your hold on us is your love. It's the strongest emotion man has – love and hate. There's a fine line between the two." Sharona rubbed her hands on her apron then gently laid a hand on Theresa's arm."Theresa, I'll not lie to you. The pull of the Kumpania this autumn is stronger than it's ever been. It's tugging at my heart." She smiled wanly. "I'd almost forgotten my Gypsy heart."

"And Pense has inherited it."

"Pense spoke to you about leaving?"

"Pense said nothing but I know what's bothering her. Her heart's an open book."

"This is our home," Sharona said. "And we should stay, if only for her father's sake." Sharona went back to mauling the dough. "What's in one's heart is not always the truth, is it?"

"I'm not a good person to answer that question. Heart's desire has a strong pull. The choice is yours. You know what's best, what's right for you. We each have a different journey."

Theresa got up to check the pork roast in the oven then sat down again to mull over Adamo's strange question. Daniel would be interested in old deeds if he were going to purchase land. Was he lying to her? Who was he working for? He didn't appear to be wealthy, but looks could be deceiving, a pauper can be a prince in disguise.

Theresa's musings were interrupted by Pense and Loco coming in the back door. "I met Mr. Cudzinki, Daniel, downtown. He said to tell you not to hold supper for him. He'll be visiting an old friend."

"I didn't know he had any old friends around here." Johnny had come in behind Pense with an armful of firewood. "Strange, when I was down in the pasture cleaning out the spring, I could have sworn he was sitting under the oak tree. I recognized the long white hair." Wood clattered into the box behind the stove. "He looked like he was in trouble, knees up, arms around them, head down. I was going to call to him but thought better of it. I figured, by the way he looked, he needed privacy."

"Has he introduced himself as *The Count Daniel Cudzinki* around the village?" Theresa asked.

"He makes a point of not saying *Count*," Johnny said. "He introduces himself as Daniel and hardly ever mentions the word *Count*."

Knightswood - evening

Daniel found Theresa dozing in front of the hearth in the library, a blanket over her knees. Her right hand lay across the cats sleeping on her lap. A book had dropped from her left hand onto the floor. Playful shadows from the hearth's fire danced around the room and softly illuminated her face. Daniel sat opposite Theresa and waited. When she moved, he coughed conspicuously, and again louder when he saw she was waking from her light sleep.

Theresa opened her eyes, gazed at the ceiling and then at the hearth. She looked around then realized that she wasn't alone. "Goodness. It's dark outside. I've slept a long time."

"Perhaps you needed the rest."

"I don't recall that you were here before I dozed off."

"I wasn't," Daniel said. "I slipped in twenty minutes ago."

"For what purpose? To watch an old woman sleep?" Theresa moved to get up then realized that her lap was full of small warm bodies.

"A hearth fire's comforting on a cold night," Daniel said. "I had some thinking to do and decided to find a quiet place. The parlor's far too noisy with that silly radio on all the time. You beat me to the library so I decided to share it with you. You're lovely to look at when you sleep, Theresa Inachio. All your worry lines vanish from your face."

"Posh!" said Theresa, stroking one of the cats. "You've a silver tongue, Daniel Cudzinki." She rubbed the side of her neck. "I must have been snoring. My neck's sore. That's an embarrassing thought."

Daniel smiled, got up and put another log on the fire then made himself comfortable again. "Are you fully awake? I'd like to have a chat."

"I'm awake." Theresa pulled herself up in the chair, easing the cats to the floor, and rearranged the blanket. "I think it's high-time we got a few things straight," she said. "If you're going to continue to be a boarder here, we've got to clear a few things up."

"Perhaps you'd like to go first?" Daniel said.

"Fine with me. What about this heart problem you say you have? Apparently, you told Pense yesterday that you suffered regularly from heart problems. She missed you at supper. She was worried."

"I sustained a severe . . . wound in the general area of my heart that's . . . painful." One of the cats jumped to Daniel's lap and curled around twice before settling in. "And I didn't come home for supper because it was a gorgeous day and I wanted to enjoy every minute of it. After all, it could have been my last . . . on earth . . . had my heart given out." Daniel gently stroked the cat's round frame.

"Franco Adamo asked the strangest question this afternoon. He has the impression that you're a wealthy Count from Europe who's going to purchase property in the area."

Daniel smiled. "As soon as I introduced myself to Granny Smith and let *The Count Daniel Cudzinki* slip out, I knew I'd erred," he said. "Franco picked up on it immediately and assumed that I own a castle and have lots of money. He suggested that industrial land was cheap in the area. As it is to my advantage to let certain people think that I'm going to purchase land, I didn't correct him."

"Adamo jumped to an erroneous conclusion?"

"I'd say to several of them. But it wasn't Franco Adamo I wanted to have the information. It was old man Compton who was having a nap by the stove."

"Why do you want anyone to have the information?"

"It furthers my cause that they do," Daniel said.

"And Granny Smith was in the store too?"

"Yes," Daniel said.

"Well, Granny Smith won't say much," Theresa said. "But that old devil Compton will tattle around. By tomorrow morning you'll be a millionaire wanting to buy The Factory. He's Compton's father, you know. Hangs around Adamo's store to find out as much as he can for that no-good son of his."

"I know. I'm counting on his gossiping ways." As for Granny Smith, Daniel thought, she could prove his undoing if he wasn't careful.

"You're giving Harris some rhetorical competition!" Theresa saw the humor in the situation and laughed. "Talking in front of old man Compton is like shouting the information from a church steeple. Silas Compton's mouth runs like a motor. When are you going to let the truth be known?"

Daniel thought for a moment. "I'm not going to be too hasty at relieving my shadowy coffers of millions of dollars. All will be revealed when I've finished my mission."

"A mission, is it?" Theresa played with the blanket's fringe. "Daniel, why did you choose to come here, to Knightswood? You say that it's not the property you want to lay claim to?"

"My dear Theresa. As I've told you, I'd never relieve you of this property. I don't want or need land." Placing the sleeping cat on a footstool, Daniel got up to check the fire."You've been very accepting of me and my mysterious ways. I've tried to be honest with you. I don't want to jeopardize my welcome."

"I'm twisted enough to like a mystery and anyone who appreciates cats has to be a good person," Theresa said. "As long as you pay board and are no threat you're welcome to stay, but I do expect honest answers. I've sent other boarders packing quick enough when they lied to me. I'll toss you out if I have to."

"You know, you're the second person that has threatened to send me packing from Millbrook. You, I take seriously." Daniel retrieved the cat and returned to his chair. He laid the animal on his chest with its head tucked under his chin. The cat's purring soothed the rhythm of his heart. "Is it my turn to ask questions?"

Theresa nodded. "Go ahead."

"What do you know about Kenneth Walker?"

The question startled Theresa. She never for one moment thought that the name of her long lost love would be uttered by Daniel. "Kenneth Walker! Why are you asking about him?"

"We shared the same house in England," Daniel said, patting the cat. "He mentioned your name many times. He's part of the reason I'm here."

"Kenneth Walker. Sweet memories take me back a few years." Theresa closed her eyes, the better to remember.

"Tell me about him."

"I can do better. I can show you pictures of him. The albums are upstairs, in my room. I'll be right back."

Theresa hurried from the room. Five minutes later she was back with photo albums and a tray of milk and cookies.

"Eat." She set the tray by Daniel and settled herself on the ottoman. Opening an album, Theresa turned the pages and pointed out various photographs. "Here Kenneth is with some young people at the river. In this one he's standing in the parlor by our Christmas tree. Look, in this one he's seated at his desk in the bank."

"Yes," Daniel said. "That's him! Tell me all you know about Ken."

"*Kenneth,*" Theresa said. "He always wanted me to call him *Kenneth.*" Theresa passed the albums to Daniel, stirred the fire then took her seat opposite him.

"What can I tell you about Kenneth? It was in the spring of 1904 when he arrived at Knightswood with a letter of introduction for Magdalena. He had a job with the bank. Maggie wouldn't hear of him staying anywhere but here at Knightswood."

"Did she let you read the letter?"

"She never did. But after Kenneth arrived, this house came alive with music and song. He cajoled Maggie into inviting people for dinners and entertainment. Oh, she never participated in these evenings. She hovered in the background to enjoy the antics of the young people. Kenneth could twist Maggie around his little finger. Why, he even talked her into hosting a number of events to raise money for fatherless children and orphans of wars. At Kenneth's insistence, she put J.P. Harris the third on her invitations list. Kenneth had to work with the Harris accounts at the bank and, I suppose, wanted to get to know the family socially. J.P. the third was around Kenneth's age."

Theresa smiled at the memories of Kenneth -- playing tennis, sitting in the library, sharing a meal. "He was a wonderful, talented man and popular, especially with the women. In January 1911 when he received word that his aunt had passed away, he left for England to clear her estate. He had all intentions of coming back."

All the sad memories Theresa had kept to herself for years flooded to the surface. She groped for a handkerchief. Tears welled up in her eyes and her voice cracked. "I never saw him again. " She sniffed, sighed, and continued. "We had grown very close, you see. It was the Christmas of 1909 . . . we were planning . . . we intended to . . ."

"I'm sorry to ask you to dredge up old memories," Daniel said. "But they are important."

Theresa wiped her eyes. "Kenneth wrote regularly, said the estate was such that he had to stay in Britain for a while. Then he penned that he'd accepted a job which meant a lot traveling through Europe. But he always wrote that he would come back to Canada. We didn't hear from him after July, 1914. I was devastated that things didn't work out between us. He was my only love. Magdalena was inconsolable that he didn't come back. She had no desire to live after he stopped writing. I never really understood their relationship, but her ties seemed as close as mine."

"Yes," Daniel said tenderly, running his fingers over the image in the photograph."Well, you see, he worked for British Government's Intelligence Service, you know. He was fluent in a number of languages so was useful to the War Department. He undertook very dangerous jobs, long before war was actually declared." Daniel's hand rested gently over Theresa's. "Kenneth was shot in France in early 1915."

Theresa's hand flew to her heart. "Died," she whispered. "Oh my! I wondered. It had crossed my mind he might have joined the forces. But my letters of inquiry to his address went unanswered. When we wrote the British War Office to find out if he'd enlisted, we received no answer. Oh dear! Oh my dear sweet Kenneth." Theresa couldn't check her tears. They ran down both cheeks and fell to her lap.

Daniel couldn't bear to see Theresa cry. He found his handkerchief and handed it across to her. "He couldn't always tell the truth in his letters, Theresa my dear." Could it be my fault they weren't told Kenneth had died, Daniel thought, closing his eyes. Was I to have done that? But this time as his memory churned through the years, instead of bloody scenes from a field in France, he was lying in a kraal near a kopje in South Africa, blood spurting from a hole near his heart.

Daniel shivered, shook the dream away, willing himself into the present. "And Magdalena," he said with difficulty, "tell me more about Magdalena."

Theresa struggled to contain her emotions. "Yes. Maggie. If you look at the first page in the album, you'll find a good photo of Maggie."

Daniel touched the photograph with so much gentleness that Theresa had to look away. There was poetry in his touch, music in the motion. "What about Magdalena, Theresa?"

Theresa dabbed at her eyes, snuffed and said, "Maggie was a beautiful woman. She had alabaster skin, golden hair and brilliant blue-green Celtic eyes. Even in old age her beauty shone like a diamond. Plus, she had a quick wit and a gentle nature." Theresa wiped the tears from her cheeks and continued, "Maggie painted well, played the piano and sang like a bird. Her voice was as good in her fifties as it had been in her twenties. She could have performed on the stage but her father wouldn't allow it. She was eccentric, as many creative, intelligent people are."

Theresa stopped talking as memories of Magdalena Anderson bubbled to the surface. There were so many, both good and bad. Thinking of Magdalena seemed to bring the woman to life, seemed to physically put her in the library.

"Go on," Daniel said in a whisper.

"People said that when she was young, Maggie was full of fun and loved to dance. Although she never had a bad word to say about anyone, during her last years she had few visitors. There were just we two. For the most part she lived in her mind. Sometimes we weren't much company for each other. It seemed some days that this house was her prison, and mine too. The best thing that ever happened to her was when Kenneth stayed with us."

"Beautiful," Daniel said with welling emotion, eyes on the photograph.

"There are other pictures. Maggie was so distinctive-looking that you can easily pick her out of a group."

Daniel leaned forward. "Did she talk about a beau?"

"She didn't say much," Theresa said. "I know that she made plans to marry him. You found her trousseau. She did say that her family was overbearing and too protective."

A blast of cold Arctic air seemed to come from the ceiling and swirl to the floor. Theresa shivered and drew the blanket around her. Daniel gasped at the stabbing pain in his chest, then covered it by coughing.

"There it is again," Theresa said. "That ungodly cold. What is that?"

"Mysterious things happen during our special time on this

earth. I don't question. I only accept." As the cold shot through him from head to toe, Daniel's heart beat erratically. He coughed again. "Please go on."

Theresa pulled the blanket up to her chest but couldn't rid herself of the icy blast. Even as the fire blazed hot on the hearth, the cold seemed to funnel down the chimney. "Apparently at one point, Maggie suffered a terrible trauma that put her to bed for weeks. During that time her father treated her like a delicate flower. Maggie's mental and physical state were a problem, no doubt. She did have a weak constitution. And she was unpredictable."

Talking about Magdalena aggravated the cold. Theresa glanced at Daniel. He was pale, drawn, shivering. "You need a throw. There's one on the love seat. I'll get it."

"No, I'm all right," Daniel said. "Please. Please continue."

"Magdalena's spirit soared well beyond her frail body and troubled mind. I was like her younger sister. Oh, we had good times together when Kenneth lived here. And she loved it when the Kumpania arrived. Why, she'd go stand for hours at her window waiting for them. My God," Theresa exclaimed. "That's why Pense reminds me of Maggie! Pense's life revolves around the Kumpania's twice-yearly visits."

"There is a definite resemblance."

Theresa continued, "That wait for the Kumpania contributed to her death. She contracted pneumonia after standing out in the cold and rain on the pinnacle, watching for it to arrive. Daniel? Daniel!"

The cat leapt to the floor. Daniel's face was death-grey. One hand gripped his chest, the other lay on Magdalena's photograph. "A little spell," he gasped. "It's the wound. It'll pass quickly."

"I'll call the doctor. I'm worried about you."

"No! No doctor! It's the wound. Worrying about death is part of living. No one lives forever. Some wine . . . wine will help."

"Plum wine. In the dining room!" Theresa ran from the room, colliding with Sharona in the hall. Her face was red. Eyes were puffy. She'd obviously been crying. "Sharona, Daniel's not well. He's in the library. I'm going for the wine."

Sharona crying? Theresa hurried around, gathering glasses and wine. What's happened that Sharona's shedding tears? My Sharona never cries. Theresa had the distinct feeling that her secure little world was collapsing around her.

Chapter 8

Johnny's Farm - October 2, 1947: morning

Why had he gotten himself so involved that he was now behind the wheel of a car bouncing along the river road toward Johnny's farm? Daniel had been reading old letters when Sharona came rushing into his room. "You've got to go to Johnny," Sharona had said. "There's something wrong. He was drinking heavily last night. His bed wasn't slept in."

"Why me?" Daniel had asked. "How do you know there's something wrong?"

Sharona burst into tears and sobbed that after Johnny had come in from the farm they had a terrible fight. She added that it wasn't like him to leave in anger then stay out all night.

"I told her," Daniel said to himself, gripping the steering wheel, "I told her that I didn't drive. I told her I'd never been behind the wheel of a car. But that didn't seem to bother her."

Sharona begged again saying that Theresa had walked to the village to find Johnny but she knew he'd be at the farm. Sharona went on to say that Johnny would listen to Daniel. He respected age, she said.

When Daniel reluctantly agreed to go to Johnny's farm, Sharona insisted that he take the car and she gave him a fast driving lesson – steering, brake and clutch. She said the gears and pedals would come naturally. He'd learn by the noise the car made while he was driving.

Daniel was making noise all right, grinding gears as he lurched along at what he felt was a dizzying rate. At least there were no other vehicles on the road. Someone, recognizing the car, waved from a field but Daniel was afraid to take his hands off the wheel to acknowledge the greeting.

"Confounded contraption," he muttered as the car climbed the hill. A left turn at the top demanded a stop and a change of gears which he managed to do, badly. Another turn into Johnny's laneway caused Daniel's teeth to grind along with the gears.

"Whoa! Damn you! Whoa!" Daniel shouted. Then he remembered that a car had brakes and that he had to push a pedal. The car skidded to a halt three feet from a rail fence. It didn't help that Johnny was leaning over the fence watching the entire show, a bottle in his hand.

"Hey," Johnny shouted. "Watch my fence! I heard yuh comin' a mile away. Thought at first it was Sharona, but she's a good driver."

"She sent me," Daniel said, remembering to turn off the ill-tempered machine before his feet found terra firma again..

"She did, did she? Afraid to come herself?" Johnny held the gate open for Daniel.

"I'd say she was afraid of your drinking."

"She doesn't need to be. She knows that."

"Maybe she does. Maybe she doesn't," said Daniel, keeping his distance while he assessed the situation. He had a deep respect for Johnny's ham-sized fists. Johnny didn't appear drunk and they were alone, so now was as good a time as any, Daniel thought. Shock has its value. "Were you drinking before you strangled the fellow in Africa?"

The bottle stopped before it reached Johnny's lips. "What do you know about that?"

"Very little," Daniel said. "That's why I asked you."

"No," Johnny said, taking a swig from the bottle. "I started in earnest after it happened."

"Trying to drown the memory?" Daniel asked. "It won't work, Johnny. They don't make enough liquor to drown a memory like that."

"How would you know?"

"I tried it once."

"Sit down." Johnny threw the empty bottle over his shoulder. "Memory has nothing to do with this black mood."

"Sharona does, though, doesn't she, and Pense too. "Daniel seated himself on a stone, an arm's length from Johnny. "Pense is your daughter, isn't she?"

"Aye, she is," said Johnny. "I suppose Theresa told you."

"Theresa said nothing. It was a simple deduction. I could've been as wrong as I'm right."

"Well, I take responsibility for Pense. I always have, always will."

"And what about responsibility for Sharona?"

Johnny sniffed and wiped his nose on a sleeve."I sowed some wild oats in my youth. Sharona traveled with her people. She was looking for a permanent home and I was looking for a good time. We were together in May and she stayed in October when it was obvious she was pregnant. She was carrying my child." Johnny paused, waiting for some remark from Count. When it wasn't forthcoming, he continued."Theresa took her in, no questions asked. When I saw that child, I knew," Johnny said. "I knew I'd have to be part of her life. I stuck around. When I went overseas, I signed everything over to Sharona. Never thought I'd come back. After the war, I moved into Theresa's, to be near them."

"I asked specifically about your feelings for, and responsibility to, Sharona now."

Johnny paced in front of Daniel. Instead of answering the question, he asked one. "You know what? She has this urge to leave, not Sharona, but Pense! She wants to leave Theresa, to desert Sharona, to abandon me."

"She has a right to."

"She's my daughter."

"Her grandparents are arriving today," Daniel said.

"Whose side are you on?"

"There are no sides in this situation. Let's talk about Sharona. What if she decides to leave too?" Daniel asked.

Johnny stopped pacing. "Sharona? Leave? I don't think so."

"Why not? Aren't you taking her for granted? Just because she hasn't gone before, doesn't mean she won't leave this time. She loves you, Johnny, but she needs love in return from you. If she doesn't get it, she may well leave."

Johnny, hands deep in pants' pockets, walked to the fence to gaze over his land. In the distance the maples marched in golden fury toward Pense's Mountain. A huge flock of migrating birds, a skein of beating wings a thousand strong, rode a black wave over his fields. Swooping, curving, soaring, the undulating mass of energy moved to their own rhythm, painting an invisible mural in the sky with the movement of their wings. He watched until the mass disappeared above the Long Swamp then turned his attention back to Daniel.

"Why am I trying to save all this if she's going to leave?" He swung his arms around to indicate his land holdings. "This is for Pense."

"Perhaps not," Daniel said. "Perhaps it's for you, Sharona and Theresa, and Magdalena Anderson."

"To hell with Magdalena. She can't leave, Daniel."

"Who? Pense? Sharona?"

"Both," Johnny said.

"Do you love Sharona?"

"Yes, damn it!"

"Have you told her so? You're the only one that can keep her here. She wants to hear you say that you *love* her. She could have taken Pense away years ago. She didn't because she loves you. She's always loved you. And she knew your child needed a permanent home, needed to have a father. Both are looking for your love, Johnny."

"How would you know?"

"I made the mistake of leaving a woman once." Daniel got up, walked to Johnny and put his arm around a broad shoulder. "Life deals some ugly cards, Johnny. You have to play them as they come. You win a few, lose a few. You've been dealt a couple of bad hands but you're still in the game."

"You seem to know a lot about cards."

"It's a vice," Daniel said. "Like booze."

"Look. I can't marry Sharona. I'm afraid I'll . . . kill her."

"Tell me about it, Johnny."

Johnny shook his head.

"Come on, Johnny Get it out. There's no one here but me. And I'm an old soldier. I'll understand."

Johnny turned back to the fence and his land. "In the desert," he finally began, "you never knew. I always slept with a knife in my hand. You know how it was, Daniel. The bastards crept up on you and slit your throat while you slept." Johnny scuffed his boots in the dirt. "Archie and me were out," he said. "We'd little water, little food left. We were on the move all the time, trying to figure the enemy out and keep clear of 'em at the same time. Hardly slept at all and when we did, it was one slept and one watched. The last night out, when it was my turn to sleep I fell into a deep stupor."

Johnny hesitated, then lowered his head. Daniel tightened his grip on Johnny's shoulder. Johnny began again, voice strained.

"When Archie woke me for my watch, he must have . . . he must have touched me. Survival tactics kicked in. I did what we were trained to do. I didn't stab him. I strangled him." Johnny stopped talking and looked at his hands. "I killed him with these hands. He didn't make a sound. He couldn't. I woke up with my hands around his neck."

Johnny stared into space.

"Johnny! Johnny!" Daniel's voice seemed disconnected and far away.

Johnny sobbed. "Archie was my best friend, my pal. I killed him!"

Daniel had stepped a respectful distance away. Johnny's eyes were haunting, blank. His hands trembled.

"Keep talking, Johnny. Don't quit now. Tell me all of it."

"They said it was an accident. We'd all been under pressure. They said it was regrettable and I should forget it. They sent me to England. They sent a letter to his parents. *In the line of duty*, they wrote. *Archibald Cochrane died in the line of duty.* When I got back, I went to their house. I got as far as their door before I turned and ran. I ran away and I've been running ever since."

"You stopped here. You stopped running at Theresa Inachio's."

"It was Sharona that made me see that I needed to quit running. And there was Pense. When she kissed me the first time after I got home, it was like an angel had brushed my cheek. I'd die for that girl. And now she wants to leave me. They can't leave. Without them this place wouldn't be home – it would be my prison."

"There are words like '*love*' and '*marriage*'. There are separate beds if you're worried about harming Sharona. There's '*duty*'. What are you really afraid of? What're you still running from?"

Johnny stared at Daniel. "Don't you understand? I killed a friend."

"Don't use that as an excuse. I killed too."

"You didn't kill your best friend."

"No, I didn't," Daniel said. "Look Johnny. If you don't get your life together, you're going to lose everything, everyone you love and care for."

Johnny rounded on Daniel. "Who are you that you can walk into my life and tell me what to do?"

"I'm not telling you what to do. And I can walk out of your life as quickly as I dropped into it."

Daniel turned on his heel to walk toward the car. He couldn't leave Johnny now, not in this state. He had to think of something. He wheeled around again. "I can't leave," he said. "I can't drive that confounded car." He smiled benignly, laughed, breaking the tension.

"You idiot! You fool!" Johnny said. "You could have killed someone."

"Yes," Daniel said. "I could have killed someone. But I was trying to reach you before you killed yourself."

Johnny shook his head and started pacing again. "I wouldn't kill myself."

"Not with a gun, perhaps, but the bottle can kill too. Why are you keeping this mess balled up inside? Why don't you tell the guys," Daniel said. "They'll support you." Daniel put his arm around Johnny's shoulder again. "Look, Johnny. They're soldiers. They'll understand if you tell them. Then you wouldn't have to carry the burden alone. You would have people to talk to when the going gets rough. You might find out that they have difficult times too."

"Maybe you're right," Johnny said.

"Take my advice. Take them into your confidence before Harris uses the information against you. What's worth fighting for, Johnny? Are you going to turn your back on your friends, your family, your true love? Or are you going to stand and fight for everything you believe in?"

Johnny looked at Daniel, then turned toward the barn. "Give me some time to work things through," he said. "Would yuh help me finish the chores, and then I'll drive us home."

"Home's good," said Daniel, following behind Johnny. "You okay, Johnny?"

"Yeah," Johnny said. "I guess I'd better get down to some serious thinking."

"You'll handle it." Daniel slapped Johnny on the back. "It'll all come out right for you, with the help of your family and friends."

Knightswood - afternoon

Sharona was hanging laundry when Johnny drove in. As he came around the side of the house their eyes met. "You're back then?" she said.

Johnny smiled. "Thanks. I acted badly, didn't I?"

"You did. You're forgiven."

"We're back. Daniel and me are in need of a change of clothes. We're going to The China for lunch."

"If you see Theresa, will you give her a ride home. She shouldn't walk to the village and back at her age."

"Don't let her hear you say that."

Rubbing her hands together and blowing on her fingers, Sharona went back to her steaming laundry. The difficulties of her first sixteen years had given her an early case of arthritis. When she stooped to get one of Daniel's shirts, a label on the inside left cuff caught her eye. Sharona fingered it as she read the name. She bent for another and examined both cuffs and the neck. A noise overhead distracted her. Someone seemed to be tapping on the attic window. Can't be, she thought. There's no one in the attic. Sharona turned her attention once more to the unusual markings on Daniel's shirts.

The tapping became incessant, a vicious sharp sound that couldn't be ignored. Puzzled, Sharona stepped away from the basket and looked up toward the gable window. There were no branches near the roof, no dangling eavestrough. A white dove suddenly swooped to the window and began to beat its wings and beak against the glass.

"Stupid bird," Sharona called. "Pense isn't up there. She went to school." Sharona found a pebble and aimed it at the wall thinking a noise would distract the winged fury. "Go away with you," she said, lobbing another stone."You'll break your neck."

An earsplitting whistle at her side caused Sharona to jump, but it had the desired effect on the dove. Daniel whistled again and the bird swooped toward his outstretched hand. From the hillside another whistle rent the air. The dove turned away from Daniel and flew low toward Pense's Mountain.

"I heard him from the bathroom," Daniel said. "He must see his reflection in the glass."

"That's a mating response," Sharona said. "He's either a late starter or stupid. Who whistled from the hill?"

"I imagine it's Pense. She was on the mountain when we passed by."

Sharona sighed. "I actually thought she'd gone to school."

"Not today, I'm afraid. She's waiting until the Kumpania arrives." Daniel smiled. "Aren't we all? If I'm going with Johnny, I'd better finish washing up."

"She's isn't dressed warm enough to sit up there for hours," Sharona said.

"I would imagine that detail is irrelevant to a child like Pense."

Sharona finished hanging the laundry. She found a heavy sweater for Pense, made a lunch and left a note for Theresa. Leaving the kitchen door unlocked just in case Theresa forgot a key, Sharona walked through the pasture to the oak tree where she found fresh flowers in a jam jar and a rough stone-and-wood bench. Who had been decorating Magdalena's grave?

Sharona's attention was caught by the haunting call of Canada geese. The sky was heavy with them. Formation after formation, two hundred each, flew south, down the river valley. For Sharona the massive flypast marked the end of autumn, and years ago the end of her nomadic wanderings. It was on such a day when the geese were winging south that she'd flown home to Knightswood.

Pense waved from the pinnacle and ran to meet her mother. "Did you see them?" Her eyes sparkled. Her hair flew behind her, brown tendrils caught by the autumn wind like angel wings. "Aren't they majestic?"

"I never cease to be amazed at their show."

"They're free to fly wherever they want."

"Listen." Sharona stopped and raised her hand. "Freedom has its drawbacks."

Far down the valley, near the Long Swamp, the crack of shots rang out from hunters eager to end some goose's flight.

Pense covered her ears. "Poor geese," she said. "They're too beautiful to kill."

On the pinnacle both sat, backs to the granite absorbing its heat. The village and valley, glorious under autumn's vibrant mantle, lay below them. Scudding clouds painted moving, abstract patterns across the landscape.

"If you'd gone to school you would have missed this," Sharona said. "But you should have told me you'd be on the mountain. I wouldn't have disapproved."

"I'm sorry. I started for school and got as far as the river before turning back. Mom, I really tried this time to do what you asked."

Sharona stroked Pense's dark hair. "I know you did. It's the time of year for that wanderlust to take hold of both of us. We both have Gypsy hearts."

"I wanted to see them arrive. It's so romantic to see them pull into camp."

"Romantic it may look, but there's nothing glamorous about the way they live. It's a hard life."

"They enjoy it," Pense said defensively.

"I'm sure some do or they wouldn't still be at it," Sharona said. "But during the winter most live in apartments or houses with central heat."

"They don't."

"They do. They don't live in tents all winter. They live in Hamilton, Detroit, Toronto. Others live in shacks in the Northern Ontario bush. This is Canada. Now their children go to school during the winter. They didn't when I was a child. And there were several winters when I lived in a tar paper shack with seven other people."

"Mom!"

"It's the truth. I lived the life. I know." Sharona put her arm around Pense. "I'm sure you could handle it. You're a sturdy one. You've a perfect right to go with your grandparents. You should ask them first if they want to be bothered with you. They live near Peterborough so you can go to high school."

Sharona hugged Pense to her, savoring every precious moment of her girl's fleeting childhood. "Are you really listening to me? Or are you listening to your heart? Have you somehow romanticized the Gypsy way of life? Can I tell you a story?"

"I'm listening." Pense turned her gaze to Sharona.

"When I was your age, I was young and foolish. I was tired of poverty. I wanted to know how the other half lived. I wanted a nice home, a better life. I hated traveling from place to place. I hated the way we were treated by others. I hated the fact that there was never enough food for the table or wood for the stove. Us kids went without clothing."

Sharona closed her eyes and hugged Pense again. "When I was fourteen I met your father for the first time. He was handsome, wild, full of life. Each spring and autumn we got to know each other better. During the Kumpania's spring visit in 1933, when I was sixteen, just after Johnny's father was killed at the factory, one thing led to another and the friendship became more than that. By the time the fall visit came round it was obvious I was expecting. I didn't tell anyone Johnny was the father. When my parents began looking for a Roma to marry me under the very obvious circumstances, I decided to make a life for myself and my child in Johnny's world."

Pense moved closer to her mother and clasped her hand.

"Johnny talked to Theresa and she took me in. She didn't chastise me. She gave me a home, motherly love. We became her family, you and me. She has nurtured us for a long time. I'm grateful to her for a new life and I'm grateful that she helped raise you. Theresa's care allowed us to be near your father."

Pense reached to hug her mother.

Sharona pulled Pense's hat tight on her head and hugged her daughter. "Johnny said he'd marry me but I refused. I felt that I'd trapped him. I knew there had to be *love* for a marriage to work and I didn't feel I loved Johnny – or that he loved me."

"But he does love you, Mom."

"Does he? My parents are coming today, and I'd be lying if I said I didn't miss them. Sometimes my heart aches for them and for the road. But another part of me says that my home is now with Theresa and your father."

"I get teased because the kids think I don't know my father," Pense said. "I haven't told anyone who he is."

"That's a problem for you," Sharona admitted. "And you're a good girl not to tell anyone that Johnny's your dad. I know it's hard but until he acknowledges you publicly, you can't say anything."

"But he should marry you."

"Your father's a good man, Pense. I love him. I've told him so. But love has to come from his heart. He can't marry me out of duty. Love's an overwhelming emotion, just like those we get when thinking of our people. He's got to feel that."

"I can't remember him hugging me and I can't remember sitting on his knee."

"He did both when you were a baby. Then he worked away for several years and the war chopped another six years out of our lives. We've not seen much of him. He missed your very early years and that's a pity. But every child whose father was in the war has the same trouble. Theresa and I gave you hugs and love enough to make up for it. Is that why you want to leave? You think your grandparents will give you the family you believe you've missed here?"

"It's not that I want to leave Knightswood. I have this urge to go – somewhere – a need to see what it's like away from here. It's like there's something waiting for me – somewhere. I love you. I love Grandma. I love my father."

"You're too clever for your age," Sharona said. "You've always been grown-up. You've a different view of life. That's partially our fault. We didn't harness your mind. We let you grow up too soon, think for yourself. Maybe it was the wrong thing to do."

"I'm not a child anymore."

"No, you're not. No other thirteen-year-old would build a memorial under a tree for a woman she didn't know."

"I didn't do it."

"You didn't build the bench or leave the flowers?"

"Daniel did that. He said he didn't need any help. He said he wanted to do it alone, which was just as well. He needed something to do and he seems terribly sad when he's near the tree."

"Daniel?" Sharona said, tucking her feet up and wrapping her arms around her knees. "Has he told you anything about himself?"

"He told me he had a terrible wound near his heart," Pense said. "He asked me about the song, if I remembered anything about the song and I told him I didn't. He asked if I'd seen him before and I told him that *Yes, I thought I had.*"

"You saw Daniel before he came to board with Theresa?"

Pense turned from her mother to look toward Millbrook nestled along the Saugeen. Church spires stood tall against a sea-blue sky. The factory's tall brick chimney broke the horizon on the north hill. The river showed as a dark, tree-lined slash through the middle of the valley. Even from the pinnacle, a faint roar from the high dam could be heard. All this is important to Daniel, Pense thought. If it's important for him, it has to be important to me. The situation between Daniel and herself made little sense but she felt a connection.

"Did you see him before?" Sharona broke into Pense's thoughts.

"Yes, Mom. He's so sad. I know I shouldn't encourage him but I want to hug him. I want to touch him. I feel sorry for him. When I look at him, I know I've seen him somewhere. I remember him. He's familiar . . . but he . . . it's so vague."

"He's touched you!"

"Oh, no. No!" Pense shook her head. "I say the stupidest things around him. They just come out. I do the stupidest things too. I gave him the penny. I know it was his. I'm like a different person around him."

"Perhaps you feel sorry for him."

"Maybe," Pense's voice trailed off.

Sharona leapt to her feet. "Look, look! They've come. There's Zizou's wagon. Isn't it beautiful? Tamas's car is right behind it." Sharona waved and in response a half-dozen horns blew. "My goodness. There are so many vehicles this time. The meadow will be full. Quick, let's meet them in the back lane."

Pense and Sharona, hand in hand, hurried down the hill.

The China Inn - afternoon

"They're here," Johnny called, stepping in the door at The China, Daniel behind him. A colorful procession of cars and trucks, led by Zizou's wagon, slowly made its way along Main Street. Zizou held the reins of the horses while a young man sat beside her. The restaurant emptied.

"So many!" Carry Kropolus exclaimed. "It's nice to see so many this time."

"How many do you figure?" Johnny asked Daniel.

"There must be more than seventy. Constable Keough will be in a sweat. Pense'll be on her mountain."

"Yeah, for now," Johnny said.

Harris Estate - afternoon

Lillian paced in a circle, from the parlor to the garden room then into the dining room, down the hall and back to the parlor. She paced mindlessly, snapping anyone's head off who crossed her path. In exasperation Charlotte, her mother, took her sewing to a quieter part of the house, saying as she left that if Lillian was bored, she could find a job. In fact, Lillian would love to find a job but her father wouldn't hear of it. She'd love to do anything that would take her away from the confines of the village.

On one of her rounds, Nellie hovered near the parlor door, a small package in hand.

"This was delivered, Ma'am."

"By whom?"

"I didn't recognize him, Ma'am."

Lillian retreated to the garden room where among the potted palms, she examined the packet.

"No name," she muttered, breaking the string and unfolding the brown paper wrap. Looks like a grocery bag to me, she thought. Smells like date pastries. It's the photograph of a young man in tennis whites on a court. She flipped the photo and read, 'Kenneth Walker, 1907'.

The biography! She had stuffed the paper in a pocket meaning to toss it away. She was wearing the same jacket and rummaged through its pockets to find the note. She looked at the photo again then read the paper. "So what?" she addressed the photograph of Kenneth Walker. Behind him stood a man that looked like her father. Could it be that Walker was a friend of her father? Her parents were married in 1910.

Lillian flicked a finger at the photograph. "So you knew my father. Am I to care?" She stared at Kenneth Walker and he stared back at her with bright, deep-set eyes. He was taller than her father, had dark hair, a pencil-thin mustache, high forehead and a square, handsome face.

Lillian read the biography. "What does this matter to me?" she said, rubbing the picture. "You died in 1915. I don't know you. That old man must be responsible for sending this."

Lillian wrapped the paper around the picture and put both in her pocket. When he got back, she'd send Blake with a message for the old idiot. It would be interesting to know what he was up to. Lillian started pacing again, the image of Kenneth Walker on her mind. She pulled the packet from her pocket and looked at the photo again. If you were a friend of Father's, Lillian thought, you'll be in some of his pictures. Lillian slipped into J.P.'s library to search her mother's photograph albums.

The Meadow - evening

Daniel took his time crossing the meadow wanting to avoid any curious villagers. He had waited for Sharona to come in before he left the house. Pense and Theresa were already in bed. Johnny had walked out to his farm to bring the horses into the barn. Daniel circled the camp once to make sure no one was hanging around in the shadows. Then he came up beside Zizou's wagon. Her horses whinnied softly when they saw him. He whistled. Zizou, standing by the fire with several men, turned her head.

"*Palumb Furtuna.* If it is you, make yourself known to us."

Daniel moved toward the light, his eyes on Zizou. She had changed. Her once-willowy figure had expanded, then shrunk. White hair was braided and hung to her waist. Her face was leathery from pipe smoke and wrinkled with age. How old was she? By his estimation, Zizou had seen more than ninety years. She wore the traditional long skirts but was layered in heavy sweaters to combat the cold that ate into her brittle bones.

"You must have expected what you now see," Zizou said, feeling his intense scrutiny. "You must accept what you now see. We all age, Palumb Furtuna. It is you, isn't it? You've returned."

Daniel walked closer to the fire. Zizou gasped then stepped back. The men muttered among themselves and moved into the shadows, away from the fire – away from Daniel.

"It appears I've returned. But I do not bear the beauty of age as you do. You are beautiful, Zizou."

Zizou cautiously moved toward him, then reached out to pinch his hand. Gathering courage, she slowly ran her fingers over his face. " Frozen in time. Flesh and blood," she whispered. "You it is. Truth we heard. What we knew stands here now."

"I stand solidly before you," Daniel said. "How this came about I do not know. How long I am here is also in question."

"Come. Sit you down." Zizou took Daniel by the arm and led him to the fire, her eyes searching his face, her fingers unconsciously pinching his hand. "In fear don't shrink away," she admonished the men. "Flesh and blood he is. *Palumb Furtuna, Dove Storm,* has flown back to us, feathers with him."

"You got my message?"

"The note received," Zizou said. "And the word spread. We are eighty strong. They said for you to return was impossible but come to see, they did . . . those that remember . . . those that are left . . . those that are curious."

Daniel lowered his aching bones onto a stool by the fire.

"I'd have to admit it seemed impossible too, but I'm seated before you tonight."

The men filtered back and squatted nearby, staring at Daniel. "How do we know it's really Palumb Furtuna?" asked one. "We've seen no pictures of him. This man could be an impostor."

Daniel looked from Zizou to the encircled group.

"Bring the violin, Tamas," Zizou instructed.

Tamas obeyed and gave the instrument to his mother.

"Only Palumb Furtuna can make the stars dance in the sky. Only Palumb Furtuna can make the moon laugh." She turned to Daniel. "Play and they will know it is you. The violin will tell them so. The music will speak."

She reverently handed Daniel an ancient violin, so polished it shimmered in the firelight. He caressed it and said, "I laid this down so long ago."

"Make it talk," Zizou said. "It is waiting for you."

Daniel smiled, put the bow to strings and played, quietly and slowly at first to 'read' his *lavuta* . . . to communicate . . . to let it be known that he was back and in command. He hadn't felt this instrument against his cheek, or the bow in his hand, for many years.

Closing his eyes, Daniel played and his music soared through the valley on the crisp night air. It pealed off Pense's Mountain and crossed the river, sweeping church steeples with its melodies before rousing villagers from their sleep to wonder where the sweet sound originated.

Theresa woke, rose and went to her window. Opening it wide, she sat, closed her eyes and swayed to the cadence. She was transported thousands of miles away to unfamiliar shores where worries were few and pleasures many.

Sharona moved restlessly around her room until the music changed to lilting Gypsy dances. Crying, she whirled and hummed the familiar tunes, putting her frustration into wild gyrations.

Pense's bed was empty, her door wide open.

At the farm, Johnny, a smile on his lips, burrowed deeper into his pile of blankets, Loco at his side. For the first time ever he let the dog sleep with him. Johnny rolled to his back, hands behind his head. Relaxed, he enjoyed the music and, for a little while, pushed the nightmare to the back of his mind.

Lillian stirred and thinking she heard the wind, got up and shut her window. She hated the wind. Ten minutes later, unable to sleep, she dressed warmly and sneaked down the servants' stairway.

The Kropoluses smiled at each other as they held hands on their back porch.

Daniel played, eyes closed, body swaying – remembering the music he'd known and translating it once again to bow on dancing strings. When he opened his eyes, the entire camp stood mesmerized before him. Pense stood by her grandparents.

"It is Palumb Furtuna." The whispers rushed like wildfire through his people.

Daniel's eyes met Pense's. They held the gaze. They knew. . . they knew! Pense whirled and ran across the meadow toward Knightswood.

Too late, Daniel realized that the last melody which found his fingers and bow was the music Magdalena had written so many years before to accompany 'Lullaby of An Infant Chief'.

Knightswood - midnight

Daniel knew where he'd find Pense. He was drawn to the dining room like his bow was drawn to the strings. She was standing in front of the marriage board, her back to the door, stroking its surface with her hands. The only light in the room came from candles, whose flames shone bright in the wood's patina.

Daniel closed the door and crossed the room, hesitating only when he'd reached a chair a few feet away from Pense. He stood behind the chair, common sense telling him to put a barrier between them.

Pense heard Daniel enter but she didn't turn to address him until he'd stopped walking. Light from the candles danced through her dark hair and electrified Pense's expressive eyes. Looking directly at him, she said. "You are of the *tumnimos,* aren't you?"

"I was, a very long time ago."

"You shouldn't have come back."

"I didn't come by choice," Daniel said. "Pense. Please listen to me. You brought me back. You've seen me before, haven't you?"

Pense stroked the marriage board with her right hand, while intently watching Daniel.

"Haven't you?" he persisted. "Tell me, Pense. I have to know."

"Yes."

"Where?"

Pense hesitated, turned her back to Daniel and began stroking again with both hands.

"You must tell me."

"In the barn," she whispered.

That wasn't the answer Daniel wanted to hear. "Yes, the barn," he insisted. "But before the barn, long before the barn?"

"I can't remember, Mr. Cud – Daniel."

Daniel slipped around the chair and sat down, feeling suddenly very old and tired. His right hand automatically went to his heart and the coin that lay on his chest.

"You must remember, Pense. You must."

"Why did you come back to Knightswood?" Pense's voice was low. "What did the old woman call you?"

"Zizou called me by my Roma name, *'Palumb Furtuna'*, which means *Dove Storm.* I was known as *O Palumb.* I was good at quelling arguments, settling disputes. But mainly I was known as Palumb because my bow appears to hover over the violin's strings, like the dove hovers above your hand. I was their *Baro Shera,* the Elder, *their Head.* But you know that already, don't you Pense?"

Daniel talked quietly, watching Pense for any reaction to his answers.

"Why did you leave them?" Pense turned again to face him.

Daniel looked to the floor. He could no longer stand the penetrating eyes.

"The love of a woman is powerful enough to unseat a king," he said.

"How did you get here this time?"

"I can't answer that. I thought perhaps you could. I'm here, Pense, in flesh and blood. But we haven't much time. There's unfinished business that I must tend to before I . . . leave. It has to do with Magdalena, with you and me. Tell me what happened in the barn when you saw me. Pense! Think! It's important. I must know. What was I wearing in the barn?"

Pense bit her lower lip. "I was in the barn, at the sideboard. Grandmother said it could be moved to the dining room so I cleaned it and was rubbing it with oil. I had the penny in my left hand, and the cloth in my right." Pense acted out the scene as she remembered it. "I began to hum that song. It just came to me. I suddenly knew that I wasn't alone. Someone was behind me, humming along. I turned around and saw you. You were in a . . . uniform."

Daniel rose from the chair and took a step. "And then what happened?"

"You were staring at me. I didn't know you, but you were as close to me as you are now. I didn't hear you come in. The horses didn't whinny. Loco didn't bark. He backed off and whined. I was cold, so cold. . . . "

"And what did you do?"

"You didn't frighten me. I put my left hand out, the hand with the coin. I reached toward you and you did the same thing."

Daniel's right hand went up.

"The coin seemed to slip right through your fingers like they weren't there. But when our palms touched I felt so warm and I could feel your . . . skin. And when I looked at you I realized, I knew . . . "

Pense stopped talking. Their palms had met and Daniel's fingers closed around hers.

"You knew," he breathed heavily, the coin hot against his chest, his voice choked with emotion.

"You are him. And I am her," Pense whispered. Her eyes met his. "You should not have come back, Daniel." The voice was a woman's, not Pense's. The touch was a woman's, not a child's.

"It wasn't my choice," whispered Daniel. "It was yours. You brought me back, Magdalena."

The moment was shattered by the slamming of a door. A voice shouted in Daniel's ear. "Pense Magdalena Aventi! What are you doing? Daniel Cudzinki! Get your hands off that child!" Theresa had entered the room.

Daniel dropped his arms and sat heavily on the chair, a spent man, all emotions wrung from him. Pense wrapped her arms tightly around her chest.

"I will insist, Mr. Cudzinki, that you cease this charade immediately. You do not thrust yourself upon a child in my house."

"Grandmother," Pense said in a strong voice, covering for Daniel. "Dan . . . Mr. Cudzinki and I were talking, about the marriage board and his music. It was Mr. Cudzinki that played the violin tonight. He's responsible for the beautiful music."

"No matter! Daniel should not be sneaking around this house. He should not be touching you. I must have an explanation now. Pense, go to bed."

Pense glanced furtively toward Daniel. When he nodded in her direction, she ran from the room.

Daniel roused himself enough to focus on the conversation. How much longer could he hide the situation? "I was walking past the door on my way to bed when I saw light in here. I thought I should investigate. After all, there are strangers in the area and you have good silver in your cabinets."

He found his legs and stood to face Theresa. "Pense was at the marriage board. She'd lit the candles. I didn't think she should be up at such an hour and went to speak to her. I thought she might be distressed. She was at the camp very late. We talked about the marriage board, and about me because she saw me play the violin tonight."

Theresa stood close to Daniel, listening intently to his explanation. "Why were you holding hands?" she asked.

"It may have looked as though we were holding hands, but we weren't. I put my hand out to make a point and she reached to touch it. It was . . . spontaneous."

"It was stupid. Toying with a thirteen-year-old's feelings is dangerous. Pense is mature for her age and she's also enamored with the Gypsy way of life at the moment. She may be attracted to you for that reason. You are after all a Gypsy."

"I've never denied that I was born a Gypsy," said Daniel. "Does that information now color your attitude toward me?"

"No," Theresa said. "I've still got an open mind. It's just that I found out today that you haven't been honest with me, Daniel. I asked a few questions around the village. You didn't arrive by train last week. No one saw you disembark, although they do recall you hanging around the station. Sharona says that you're wearing shirts with someone else's initial in them, as though they have been . . . borrowed. Granny Smith swears that she's seen you before. There are many questions, Daniel, and you have expected me to ignore them and accept you as family."

Daniel leaned forward and reached for one of Theresa's hands then pulled away knowing contact was dangerous at the point they'd reached in the argument. "I apologize," he said. "Things aren't as they appear. Believe me. I'm a little confused myself. Before you toss me out, would you read some letters? They're in my room. Theresa, under the circumstances this request might sound ridiculous, but you must trust me. I know what you're thinking. . . . " Daniel now touched Theresa's arm to make his point. "No one else trusts a Gypsy, so why should you? You must believe me, Theresa. It's for the good of Knightswood, and Pense, that you read the letters and that you trust me."

"I've nothing against your people," Theresa said. "I do have difficulty with anyone who lies to me."

"I didn't lie. I was never directly asked how I liked the train ride."

Theresa, head down, went silent. When she did speak, her voice had a hard edge to it. "You're splitting hairs, Daniel. Stay away from Pense. If you break one more house rule, I'll have Johnny help you pack."

"Thanks. I need to stay just a little longer, another three or four days. I promise you don't have to worry about me after that. I have a job to finish. And Theresa, I'm too old to be thrown out in the cold."

"Don't hand me that rubbish. I'm an old woman too, but I don't take nonsense from boarders, whoever they may be. I respect your age, but that doesn't give you the leeway to cheat, lie or steal. Go get the letters. I'll have more to say to you after I read them."

Daniel responded by following Theresa out of the library. He didn't have the courage to look in the mirror before he started to climb the stairs. He was afraid of what he'd see.

Theresa followed behind and had to stop often to wait. "You can't be that tired, Daniel."

"Let me assure you that this is the tiredness of the dead that carries the weight of years of trials and tribulations. I'll be much better in the morning, if I don't die in my sleep from a broken heart."

"There'll be none of that talk around here," Theresa said, "and I assume you mean a weak heart."

Daniel stopped to catch his breath. "This might seem like a very personal question, Theresa. Was there really no man, after Kenneth?"

"I was so in love with Kenneth. After we spoke of an engagement, I started my trousseau and waited for the ring Kenneth promised. He was going to give me one when he returned from England for the wedding." Theresa fingered the wooden railing, studying her gnarled hands. "I never let myself love a man again. But that's history, Daniel. That's in the past. I was so busy caring for Magdalena that I didn't have much time to socialize. I've managed for a long time without a man in my life."

"Lonely existence, wasn't it?" Daniel reached to touch Theresa's hand and she didn't withdraw it. He squeezed a little to let her know that he felt for her. "He would've come back to you if he hadn't died. He loved you very much. Don't judge the man too harshly."

"I still love Kenneth Walker. But it's been lonely, especially after Maggie died. You know. Sharona and Pense filled a huge void in my life."

"What did you call Pense in the dining room?"

"Pense Magdalena Aventi. She has never been formally adopted by her father. You've figured out that Johnny is her father. We felt that if she was going to inherit Knightswood, she should carry the name Magdalena."

"Yes," Daniel said. "That should be so."

Chapter 9

Knightswood - October 3, 1947: early morning

Theresa's morning routine was completely shattered. She'd read the letters Daniel had given her until two in the morning then endured a brief and restless sleep. Awake again by four she got up and sat at her dressing table to read once more.

As people began to move around the upper floor, Theresa made a mental note of who was up. Shortly after six, Sharona went downstairs. At six-thirty, Daniel made his way along the corridor. Around seven o'clock, Pense bounced down the hall without coming in to brush her hair. By eight-thirty, Theresa felt an overwhelming urge to explore the back attic.

The attic was not one of Theresa's favorite places. A fear of bats kept her trips up the stairs alone to a minimum. With a flashlight in one hand, and the broomstick that she kept handy at the foot of the steps in the other, Theresa climbed the stairs. As she didn't have Daniel to go first, Theresa waved the broom around and warily watched for bats while making her way toward the back attic.

At Maggie's trunks Theresa spread a horse blanket on the floor and sat down. She sneezed as dust and the smell of musty clothing and rotten wood enveloped her. Opening the first trunk, Theresa went through its contents methodically, placing the articles on the blanket beside her. She set aside several packets of greeting cards, some pretty buckles and a pair of brocade slippers. The second trunk yielded a satin bag with a dozen handkerchiefs embroidered with the monogram *MC* and an autograph book.

Time passed quickly and Theresa realized she'd been sitting much too long. She realized how cold she was. Her spine felt frozen. Her fingers were blocks of ice. Shivering, Theresa took an old carriage robe from a rocking chair and shook it, coughing as clouds of dust rose around her. Wrapping herself in the smelly robe, Theresa picked up the bundle of cards and worked at untying the blue ribbon. She hadn't gotten far when her attention was taken by the white dove, beating its wings against the window's glass panes.

"Shoo! Be gone with you!" Theresa waved her hands but the dove beat harder. Wiping the filth off the pitted, distorted panes with an arm of her sweater, Theresa banged on the glass. The dove banked away from the window and flew over the pasture toward Pense's Mountain where mists rose through gilded trees, and the oak slowly emerged from a gauze-thin mantle of haze. From her vantage point Theresa could see the Kumpania. Women stirred cook pots hung over smoky camp fires. People scurried around vehicles. Zizou's wagon rose like an island of color from a grey sea. Horses grazed with Betsy. Someone was milking the cow, crouched beside the Jersey, bucket in hand.

"Lots of activity today," Theresa muttered. Facing the window her face felt the heat of the morning sun but her back was freezing. Theresa felt the hair on the back of her head rise. She had the feeling that she was not alone. Turning slowly Theresa peered into the dark recess of the main attic, gasped then giggled nervously. "Be still, you foolish heart. It's a dressmaker's form."

Theresa swung the flashlight to and fro, from floor to ceiling, all the while talking to herself. "Why did you come up here, Magdalena Anderson? What did you do? You wanted to be alone, didn't you? Away from your father . . . then away from me. This was your escape – this horrible musty attic. What little secrets did you have?"

With the broomstick and flashlight, Theresa began a thorough inspection of the back attic. Under the dust was a cozy nook with a chair drawn up by the window and apple crates overturned for tables. An easel stood in one corner. There was an oil lamp ready for use and stacks of books, some tubes of paint and brushes. "Maggie, what were you hiding?"

As though in answer, Theresa felt a shaft of cold go through her back to front, like a sharp knife. The cold was so tangible it shimmered in the window's light. Theresa's heart fluttered. Her breath came in gasps. "So horribly cold," she muttered, as she scoured the wooden walls with the flashlight's beam. "Well, you've scribbled nothing on the walls or floor, Maggie."

Theresa left a trail of dust and dirt as she poked the broomstick into crevices and joinings. She screamed and ducked as a bat dropped off a joist and flapped away, inches from her hair.

"Enough is enough!" Whacking her stick in a crevice below the window, Theresa hit an obstacle. She whacked again and a small black diary fell to the floor. Another swipe brought two more slender notebooks to light.

"Bingo!" Theresa exclaimed, bending to retrieve the books. Another shaft of cold penetrated her body, front to back. Shivering, she backed away from the window.

"Theresa. Theresa?" An ethereal voice echoed through the attic.

Theresa, heart pounding, peered through the gloom, afraid to reply lest something answer back.

"Theresa?" the voice said again and a figure manifested itself at the head of the stairs.

Theresa pulled the robe tight around her, gathered her courage and stepped toward the figure. At the same time the apparition moved from the head of the stairs toward her. Both ducked and screamed as the bat swiped past again.

"Theresa," the voice said again. "Are you up here?"

"Sharona! For a moment I thought you were Magdalena. I thought I saw her."

"And so did I," Sharona said. "I could have sworn it was her over by the window looking just like she does in her photographs. Look, behind you."

Theresa turned toward the back attic just in time to see a shimmering light float past the window.

"I've had enough," Theresa said. "Let me gather these few things and we'll leave." With trepidation she returned to the back attic to retrieve her treasures.

"Whatever possessed you to explore this place today?"

"I wanted to look through Maggie's things myself," Theresa said, letting the carriage robe fall to the floor. "I thought Daniel might have missed something."

"Constable Keough's downstairs on his semiannual crusade," Sharona explained as they descended the attic steps."That's why I came looking for you. He wants permission to go to the meadow."

"I thought Johnny said he wouldn't bother me again." Theresa sniffed her hands. "I smell like horse and attic, don't I? I'll have to wash and change. There's plenty for him to look at in the front hall. Have him wait there."

When Theresa came down the stairs, Constable Keough was looking closely at a large painting hung by the parlor door. "Morning, Miss Inachio," he said. "Nice statue. Nice picture too," he said pointing to one opposite the mirror. "Looks like our valley."

"That it does," Theresa said. "It's a George Henry Durrie, painted in 1853." She smiled at Keough and thought, I'll go easy on him this time. He's a pleasant enough young man. Johnny likes him. "I apologize for keeping you waiting, Constable."

Keough stood with his hat in his hand. "It's kind of you to see me. I realize your land's outta' my area but I thought a little visit wouldn't hurt."

"I know you've no jurisdiction. You know you've no jurisdiction but they don't. So it wouldn't hurt to make your presence known. I don't want trouble any more than you do. They know they won't be welcome on my land if they break any laws. I don't expect trouble. But there are so many new ones come this time. I'll go with you so they know I mean business too."

"Why do you allow them to camp? You know how Harris feels about it."

"I couldn't care less about what Harris's feelings are toward them. Pardon my language but I don't give a damn what he feels about me either. The Gypsies have been coming for a long time. It's a tradition I'm not about to break because of someone else's intolerant attitude. I know that they're good people, despite what some others seem to think."

"Well then, we'll be off," Keough said. "I've got to get back to investigate the rumor about some big meeting on Sunday night, a labor group that's disguising themselves as a stamp club. You haven't heard anything about it, have you?"

"Why would I hear anything? Aren't meetings allowed? Isn't this a free country? Isn't that what the boys fought for – freedom to express themselves and their views?"

"Johnny's mixed up in it," Keough said.

"Johnny's a grown man. He can take care of himself. What he does is his business. He knows his rights."

Later, Theresa sat in the warm kitchen mending socks by the stove, mulling over the day's events with Sharona. "You say Daniel didn't stay for breakfast. And he told you he'd be away for several days."

"That's right," Sharona said, chopping eggs. "He had a change of clothes under his arm. He paid me for next week's room and board and said if you wanted him for anything, you could leave a message with Zizou or Johnny."

"And Pense is at the camp? I didn't see her when I was there with Keough."

"I had a word with my parents last night about her romantic view of their life. They'll put her to rights but they won't stop her if she wants to join them. I couldn't persuade them to turn her down if she asked."

Theresa put her darning aside and pushed her glasses up the bridge of her nose. "We knew the choice would have to be made at some point. We thought we were prepared for it. We aren't. I've been afraid you'd leave me ever since you came. The urge to wander is inherited. Gypsy blood runs strong through your veins."

Sharona took the bowl of egg salad to the ice box on the back porch and came back with a basket of pears. She sat down and began to peel vigorously. "If only Johnny would adopt Pense, make her feel his own flesh and blood. I think that would help."

"It would be public knowledge then that Pense was his child."

"Not that there isn't already talk," Sharona said. "Don't think you're not judged for accepting a 'live-in' relationship. You're a fool if you believe there aren't rumors and talk."

Theresa tucked a cat in beside her and stroked his shiny fur. "The answer is that Johnny must marry you, but we both know the one big stumbling block he's raised to that issue. Some men will use any excuse to get out of a commitment. But Johnny's not like that. You'll have to have more patience, Sharona."

"I'm running low on patience."

"Don't we all at some point?" Theresa said. The rocking motion of the chair was making it difficult for her to keep her eyes open. "Keough says Johnny's up to something."

"No doubt. He's got his nose in a lot of things around the village."

"You know what it might be?"

"Whatever it is, the factory's involved," Sharona said. "I think that he and Daniel are plotting something."

"Ah, Daniel," said Theresa, her mind full of letters and diaries. "What do you now make of our friend, The Count Daniel Cudzinki?"

"He's a clever man," Sharona said. "I don't think he's a threat to us. He's the only one that can silence Pense, merely by being in the same room with her."

"He's certainly not what he appears to be," Theresa said, making room for the second cat on her knee. "He knows that simplicity is often viewed as stupidity. He's hoping that some will think him simple, but he's far from that and definitely not stupid."

"Don't take him for granted," Sharona said. "I'm sure that he's responsible for all the men arriving with the Kumpania. They call him *the ancient one*, say no one can destroy him. And none in the Kumpania will confide in me. I think that they feel I've been apart from them for so long that I'm no longer one of them. My parents kept the fact he was going to join them secret from me. Mom didn't mention him in her letter."

Sharona measured sugar, cinnamon, flour and eggs into the pears, stirred and poured the mixture into a bake pan. "I heard the legend around the campfire when I was a child. It meant nothing to me. I can't even remember what it was all about."

"Whatever the situation, it's very mysterious," Theresa said. "Zizou wouldn't tell me anything, said that it was Palumb Furtuna's life and he'd have to finish the story."

Sharona removed her apron and hung it behind the door. "I'm going to see my parents. Will you put the cobbler in the oven for thirty minutes, Theresa? Johnny's horse-trading at the camp so you'll be alone for lunch."

"Will you give Zizou a message?" Theresa asked. "Tell her that Constable Keough is asking about Johnny and some sort of stamp club. Enjoy your visit. I'll take care of the baking."

Theresa managed to stay awake until she'd removed the cobbler from the oven, after which she covered herself with a blanket and fell asleep. She was roused some time later by incessant knocking. Struggling to waken, Theresa looked around bewildered, wondering where she was. The noise came from the front hall. By the time she reached the front door, a figure was retreating down the verandah's steps.

"Can I help you?" Theresa called, desperately trying to tidy her hair. The figure turned. "Why Miss Harris, Lillian, isn't it? Are you in trouble? Has your car broken down?" That was the only thing that Theresa could think of to say, so surprised was she to see Lillian Harris on her verandah.

"I'm looking for Mr. Cudzinki. Is he here? I'd like to talk with him."

"He's away, Miss Harris, but do come in. Maybe I can be of assistance. It's lunch time and I'd enjoy company if you feel so inclined. I apologize for my appearance. I didn't sleep very well last night and dozed in front of the stove. Sharona's made an egg salad and pear cobbler."

Lillian pursed her lips and sniffed. "Why not?" she muttered. She was hungry.

Theresa held the door wide then led the way through the hall. "Come through to the kitchen, Lillian. This is a pleasure. I remember you as a child."

Lillian walked slowly behind Theresa, taking in everything. She stopped to examine the bronze nude gracing the newel post. "I'd no idea this house was so large and pretentious. It's quite sumptuous as a matter of fact. Such gorgeous artwork and statuary."

"Of course, you've never been here before," Theresa said. "The Anderson family appreciated fine things – statuary, ceramic, artwork. I inherited the hallmark of good Victorian taste. The house lacks nothing. As Johnny says, we've nude statuary, a ghost or two, skeletons in closets and a tennis court too."

"Well, I'm impressed."

I'll bet eating in a kitchen will be a new experience for this one, Theresa thought as she cleared the table and laid her best kitchen dishes. "I'll just go get the egg salad," she said, leaving Lillian to stare at the paintings on the wall. "That colorful picture's called *Silhouette*, just in case you were wondering."

"An appropriate name for an unusual picture," Lillian said.

Theresa was back in short order with the egg salad and a crock of cook cheese. "I'm sorry you missed Daniel. He left early this morning. You can leave a message for him."

"Maybe I'll do that," Lillian said, still looking around the kitchen."How many servants do you have, besides Sharona?"

Theresa laughed. "Sharona's no servant. She's a partner in the business. We share responsibilities, although I'm slowing down in my old age. I understand that Mr. Anderson had at least six people working for him." Theresa cut thick slices of white bread and put them on a plate beside a crock of butter. She sat down opposite Lillian. "I've updated the kitchen a bit. There's an electric ice box in the pantry. But of course, as long as we can buy ice we'll never get rid of the box on the porch. It's handy for large quantities of milk, eggs and cheeses. We prefer to keep the wood stove because it throws a comfortable heat and we do have a woodlot."

"Seems like a lot of work to me," Lillian said. "Doesn't make sense when you can just turn a knob and have heat for cooking."

"It's a link to the past," Theresa said. "People have gathered around this table for nearly one hundred years to eat and talk. The room has a nice feel about it, don't you agree? Eat, Lillian. Make yourself at home."

Lillian made herself a sandwich, taking great care to cut the crusts from the bread.

Easy to see she didn't suffer through the depression, thought Theresa. Why on earth is the daughter of J.P. Harris looking for Daniel Cudzinki? I may as well ask. "You know Mr. Cudzinki?"

"Not really, " answered Lillian. "He made himself known and left some information for me to read. You've lived here for a long time, haven't you?"

"I've been here forever," Theresa said, buttering a slice of bread.

"Did you ever meet a man by the name of Kenneth Walker?"

Theresa's knife stopped midair. Her heart gave a flip. "It's strange that you should mention that name. You're the second person that wants information on Kenneth. Daniel was the first to ask."

Lillian reached into her purse. "Read this." She handed the biography and a photograph to Theresa. "Mr. Cudzinki left it with me."

"That's Kenneth," Theresa said, pointing to the figures in the photo."That's your mother and I. It was taken at a garden party, here – at Knightswood. The fete was to raise funds for local orphans. It was held just after Kenneth arrived. Magdalena organized the event."

Theresa read the paper that was written in elaborate longhand. Why would Daniel give Lillian the history of Kenneth Walker including the places he had lived in England? Why would he provide her with the date and battle in which he had been killed and where he was buried in France?

"It's an incomplete biography," Theresa finally said. "When was he born? Where was he born? This information begins in England when he was four years of age. Daniel gave you this? For what reason?"

"I've no idea. I was curious enough that I found several photos of Kenneth Walker in father's albums based on a photograph Mr. Cudzinki provided." Lillian handed another photo across the table, one Theresa recognized immediately as having come from her album.

What sort of skullduggery is that man up to now, Theresa thought, comparing the photos. "There's no mistake. Both photos are of Kenneth. This one," Theresa indicated the last photograph, "was taken here, on the tennis court. Your father's standing behind Kenneth. Your father did try to enjoy life, you know. But he had his father's ways about him which ultimately ruled his attitudes and decisions."

"How well did you know Kenneth Walker?"

Theresa took a deep breath trying to decide how to answer this latest breach of her privacy. Truth will be told, she thought. "Well enough that I thought we were going to be married. . . . We discussed marriage. Kenneth returned to England before he gave me a ring and he never came back."

Lillian wanted to hear the whole story, so she poured a cup of tea for both, hoping the action would encourage Theresa to continue.

Theresa acknowledged the gesture with a smile and said, "Of course, now I know that Kenneth died during the War. I'll be honest with you, Lillian. Most people, including your parents, felt I wasn't good enough for Kenneth. With their smug village meanness, they put me in the role of servant after I became Miss Anderson's companion. Your mother was one of the worst to categorize people."

"I won't make excuses for Mother," Lillian said. "She's capable of making an apology when necessary."

"I don't expect an apology," Theresa said. "Your mother may have been jealous of Kenneth and me. She was smitten with him but he paid her no mind. Have you shown her these photographs?"

Lillian laughed. "Mother and I don't speak much these days. She's not impressed with my friends, not that I have many. If it's any consolation, there are very few people around here that bother with me."

"Touche!" Theresa said without a touch of remorse. "Why do you stay in Millbrook if you can't stand the place?"

"I've no means of financial support. I'm totally reliant on father's generosity. He'll cut my inheritance if I fly the coop."

"To tell you the truth," Theresa said, "I wouldn't use J.P. Harris and the word *generous* in the same sentence. Don't let feeble excuses stop you from having a life. You don't need his money. Stand on your own two feet, my lady! This is the twentieth century."

Lillian pushed her plate away. "I didn't come for a lecture," she said."I was looking for more information on Kenneth Walker. I wanted to upbraid Mr. Cudzinki for involving me in the man's life."

"What makes you think you have anything to do with Kenneth's life?"

"It's a hunch, I suppose. Why else would the man bother me?"

"I don't try to second guess Daniel Cudzinki." Theresa stood to clear the table. "Help me do the dishes Lillian. Then I'll show you around Knightswood. I can even show you more photographs of Kenneth. Then we'll walk to the camp and have our fortunes told." She stopped short of saying it was there that they could leave a message for Daniel.

Lillian, who had never cleared a table, found herself puttering around the kitchen of a woman she hardly knew, in a home far superior to any she'd lived in. She found the experience enjoyable.

The China Inn - breakfast

After Daniel left Sharona, he deposited his pack with Zizou and set out for the village in pursuit of the Buzzard. Crossing the bridge, he rounded the corner by Memorial Church and found his quarry smoking a cigar, one foot propped against a wall at the post office. A frontal assault was always best for men like Compton, Daniel thought. "Can I offer you breakfast at The China?" Daniel stood solid in Buzzard's only line of escape.

Compton, always game for a free meal, nodded. Fancy that, he thought. The man he was looking for stood right in front of him. What luck! The China Inn was not his first choice for a chat. He would have preferred his car. But the bait can't choose the fish and fools are easily parted of their money.

Daniel waved to Cook Kropolus and chose a booth at the back, partially obscured by several large ferns, a huge dieffenbachia and aggressive potted mission fig. When he suggested to Carry Kropolus that he needed some privacy, Daniel didn't expect to have a jungle appear around his favorite booth. She'd obliged but told him that if he wanted a bush lot, he'd have to keep the plants watered. Daniel slid in opposite Buzzard and signaled to Carry who brought a jug of water and two menus.

"Good morning, Mrs. K," Daniel said. "No need for menus. Two Saugeen specials please; double the back bacon, easy on the tomatoes, throw a couple of farm sausages on the platter too." Daniel poured a glass of water for himself, one for Buzzard and one for the fig.

Compton made small talk, mostly slurs about the Gypsies, until the food was delivered, then he ate heartily, waving his knife each time he spoke to emphasize his point. "I understand that you're a Count."

"The title is part of my name."

"I hear you're looking for land."

"From whom?" Daniel let the conversation flow. He ate slowly, playing the man like a fish, waiting to see in which direction Buzzard would take the questioning. He couldn't underestimate the man. Harris surrounded himself with intelligent but devious people.

"Everyone's talking about you and your land deals."

"What am I building on this land I'm going to purchase?"

"You're building?" Compton's knife and fork stopped in midair.

"Did I say that?" Daniel smiled and salted his eggs.

"You just did."

Mrs. K, hovering nearby, rushed over. "More toast," she said, putting another stack on the table. "I'll be right back with coffee."

"Thank you. And a bowl of strawberry jam, if you please." Daniel wiped his mouth with a napkin and helped himself to toast. "If I were building, I'd need three or four hundred acres. I wouldn't be interested in a small property, you understand."

"That much land?" Compton ate the bacon with his fingers, licking them afterwards. "You couldn't buy that much land around here without suspicion."

"That's true. There would be a land rush, wouldn't there? That's why people try to keep things like this quiet. It keeps the price down, doesn't it?"

"What're you manufacturing?"

"Did I say anything about manufacturing?"

"I heard you were into radios and that newfangled thing everyone's talking about, television. I heard you were bombed during the war, factory destroyed – that sort of thing. I heard you were looking to restart in North America."

Daniel coughed, his napkin covering his mouth, "Hmm. Yes, well rumors certainly do get around, don't they?"

"I heard you were even interested in Harris's land, and if the price was right you might buy *The Factory*."

Daniel gave Buzzard a disgusted look. "I wouldn't buy that pile of rubbish. Harris hasn't put money into the buildings or machinery for years."

"You've thought about it, then?"

"Of course." Daniel warmed to the conversation, liking the direction it was taking. "As I see it, I'd have one problem. Harris would have several big ones."

"What might they be?" Compton helped himself to sausages.

"Hypothetically speaking, say that I have the land but I need workers. I'll woo Harris employees because I'll offer more money and benefits." Count waited for Buzzard to absorb his information then said, "Oh yes, I'll definitely offer more money and the best benefits."

"All you're talking about is spending money like water," Compton said. "How're you going to make money is more the question."

"Harris's former workers will need a place to live because he'll throw them out of his company houses. Harris now has to find new workers from outside the area. They won't settle for living in company hovels. They'll want new homes."

"I get the picture," Compton said. "And where might these homes be built?"

"The only land available to build two or three hundred houses lies back of the factory on the North Hill."

Compton dropped his fork. "Let me get this straight. You have the land for your factory?"

"Let's just say that land won't be a problem."

"Where?" Compton's eyes bulged, his jaw hung open. No one beat him at his own game.

Daniel smiled at Buzzard. "Think now, Mr. Compton. Other than Harris, who owns that much acreage in the village?"

"Theresa Inachio."

Daniel winked. "And we are forgetting the North Hill. Who owns that land?"

"A couple of stupid foreigners bought the land from Henderson, an old bachelor who tried for years to foist it onto some unsuspecting person. It's bog, slurry clay and quicksand. No man in his right mind would attempt to farm it. It's swallowed enough animals and machinery to stock ten farms."

"With the technology that came out of the war, swamps can be drained. I'll say no more. I've already talked too much. You draw your own conclusions to what we've discussed. You're an astute man Compton, and trustworthy." Daniel enjoyed reeling in the fish. "I wouldn't have spoken with you but I feel you can be trusted. Perhaps my partners and I can do business someday."

Daniel waved to Carry. "I'll just pay the bill."

Mrs. K hurried over.

"The bill, if you please," Daniel said.

"Breakfast is on the house, Count Cudzinki. And thank you for your patronage. It's always a pleasure to serve *The Count*."

Compton looked from Daniel to Mrs. K. No one got a free meal from the Kropoluses. "I'll leave the tip," he said, feeling generous. Compton threw a quarter on the table. "If you'll excuse me, I've a busy day ahead of me."

"See you around," Daniel said to Buzzard's retreating back. He winked at Mrs. K and said, "I can't understand how a man that Cave Bat thinks is so clever, can be so gullible. In order to control the world, Buzzard has to learn how to control himself, wouldn't you agree, Mrs. K?"

"I'd say that greed is blind, but it's also a generous tipper," Carry said. "As my son Sebastian would say, he belongs to the kiss-a-butt race. He is always racing around and always kissing – "

Daniel laughed. "Greed is going to provide a windfall for your two friends on North Hill."

"They're all the same, these land sharks." Carry scooped the dollar and cleared the table. "They're grasping, greedy buggers who have never in their lives done an honest day's work for an honest day's pay."

Compton wasted no time walking to his car. Harris was away but he had to beat Cudzinki at his own game. If the man didn't know who owned the North Hill, he hadn't approached them about selling. Compton drove to North Hill Farm, introduced himself to the Silver brothers and was invited in for coffee. In one hour,

Compton had persuaded the two fellows to sell the farm for cash. They agreed, with one stipulation. All papers had to be signed and money handed over by ten o'clock on Monday morning.

Stephen and Michael Silver, better known to the Kropoluses as Stefan and Mitko Sliven, shook hands on the deal. As soon as they had Compton's cash, the Slivens would leave as quickly as they'd come. As a water-witcher, Stefan knew the ebb and flow of the area's water sources. On the north side of the river valley, the flow was directly connected to the underground supply of J.P. Harris's factory. If Compton and his cohorts drained the swamp, Harris's industrial water source would dry up.

The Mountain - morning

Pense had climbed to her pinnacle to watch the sun rise over the camp but she was deriving no pleasure from the show. She felt as broody as her mountain. Grandmother Aventi had said that she was at that in-between age when all young girls experience a restlessness of mind. They were ready to divest themselves of the shackles of girlhood, but hadn't yet accepted the responsibilities that came with being a woman.

Pense could no longer trust her feelings. Crying was unheard of for the child known as Pense Aventi. But last night as the woman called Magdalena, she'd cried herself to sleep. During the bit of tormented sleep that she managed to get, Daniel as a much younger man, had appeared to her. He came and she gave him the answers he so desperately sought. But, when she woke, the answers were as elusive as the albino doe.

Noise from the camp reminded Pense where she needed to go. She left the hill to walk through the makeshift stock fair. Ropes, tied from truck bumpers to trees, corralled horses that waited for the practiced eye of a buyer. Grandpa Aventi said that with a little touch of oil and a few strokes of the tar brush, some of their defects wouldn't be noticed.

Pense was aware of the young fellows who followed her through the camp but she paid them no attention until she stood by her grandparents' fire. Then she relied on her grandmother who was stirring a pot of stewed chicken and vegetables, to tell them to find something better to do with their time. "They're wife hunting," Grandmother said. "You're old enough. You're fair game."

Yesterday Pense asked her grandparents if she might travel with the Kumpania next spring. Her question caused such a commotion that the neighboring family got involved. Each point, pro and con, was digested, discussed and given full measure, with no regard for Pense or for an answer. Then her mother, Sharona, arrived and got into the fray, arguing strongly that Pense must stay at Knightswood. Pense found solace at Zizou's fire.

"Can they do nothing without arguing?"

"It's not arguing," Zizou said. "Options. Consequences with questions travel. Answers hard come or not at all. It's the way we live. No answer your choice means, not theirs." Zizou patted Pense on her cheek. "Fetch a bucket of *paanii.* That's our way too. Young girls all the work do."

Pense, returning from the spring with the full bucket, had to admit that the best part of the camp was Zizou wearing her colorful skirts, chains of *galbi* and baubles.

"Gypsy look fortunes sell," Zizou had said. She went on to explain that the jewelry was her talisman and all she had left to remind her of her mother and grandmother. She said that it was the Roma custom to burn the clothing of female relatives when they died. She related that the *galbi* is passed from one female relative to another. Pense had turned several of the coins between her fingers then asked if they were really gold. Zizou said that some were and that she had sold a few pieces over the years so that she could live comfortably in her old age.

Pense set the bucket by Zizou's wagon then went to sit by her at the fire. The elder was twisting a *dicklo* to cover her hair, her tiny hands working slowly at the task. "Were you born in Canada?"

"Zizou am I and ninety and two. Europe was my home until my familia fled. At thirteen there came the *mule-vi.* Look," Zizou swung her arms slowly and painfully around to encompass the camp. "Nice *atchin tan,* is Theresa's." She went back to knotting the *dicklo* at the side of her neck. "The way vanishes, *schej. Gadje* jobs some do have. Towns and cities call us home. We be the last Kumpania to take the *lungo drom.* The life is over. But for Palumb Furtuna's promise, the Kumpania would have died years ago."

"What was that promise?"

"That he would come back," said Zizou, straightening her long skirts.

"From where?"

"Child, that question, you must answer. You be born there to answer it when he came." Zizou rose and drew a large shawl around her shoulders. Pulling her *kesht* from the back of the wagon Zizou said, "Show me your land. My age to respect and slow to walk. Lead to the seat under the oak and tell all."

Soon the two were seated on Daniel's bench.

"Look." Pense pointed toward the house. "The dove's at the attic window again." She stepped away from the bench and whistled several times. The dove broke off its frantic beating and flew to her. Pense came to sit beside Zizou again, the dove on her hand.

"Like the one before, birds greet you," Zizou said, patting Pense on the head.

"Could I be like you, Zizou? Am I *mule-vi?* Could I be a *drabarni*?" Pense raised her hand and the dove flew away, toward the pinnacle.

"The *dook* you must have to tell fortunes. And the third eye is to see beyond." Zizou pulled a scarf-wrapped packet from a concealed skirt pocket. "Red cloth binds the power." She undid the knot, laid the red material on the bench and shuffled the cards. Then she laid them out, one by one on the cloth and leaned over to see them, her braids touching the bench.

"These talk for you," she said, tapping each card with a dirty fingernail. Then she began to speak with slow and deliberate intent. "You will live long and with hard work, prosper. You will eat well. Your life will be shared. You will walk the earth."

Zizou hesitated, then looked into the timorous eyes of the child-woman beside her. "I speak what *gadje* want to hear. Now, I tell what is true, hurtful or happy may it be."

Pense, her heart pounding, looked into Zizou's watery, beadlike eyes. "I'd like to hear it," she said, thinking that the piercing eyes were familiar.

"Hear it, you must. Give right hand." Zizou stroked the small, cold hand then traced the lines with a thin bony finger. "These hands, they help people. *Chavi*, there be many sides. Young body and old mind, you have. Young spirit and old soul live as sisters. Woman is trapped in body of child. Restless heart makes sadness."

Pense swallowed and nodded.

"There be divide. One goes; one comes. Long road to go before end. One stands on journey; one waits at end. Come again you will, you came before."

Zizou stopped abruptly, dropped Pense's hand and turned away. She gathered her cards, tied them in the scarf and tried to rise from the bench. "You be frightened?"

"Yes," Pense was truthful. "I read once that truth is sour, and lies are sweet."

"Take all as spoonfuls of sweet," Zizou said gruffly. "Give me hand. Look! The *gadje* come for the *ofisa*." Zizou took a careful step forward, her ancient bones protesting every move she made. "I have not traveled the Kumpania in years. A child grows into a beautiful woman."

"Why did you come this time?"

"Long time ago, promise was made with Palumb Furtuna." Zizou lifted her arms and pointing to the four winds, said, "Listen. Eat with your eyes. You give all this to run with us? Why? Easy is not the life we have."

Pense stood beside the elderly woman, respectful of her age, listening to her advice.

Zizou chose her words with care. She wanted Pense to fully understand the consequences of leaving Knightswood. "Some believe no schooling, and early wed for girls. Want you marriage without love? Want you many children?"

Zizou looked to the winter horizon for inspiration. Instead of advice, she sensed *Mamioro* waiting to visit her with the illness. She had to impress upon this girl what was at stake. She had to make Pense understand that her place was at Knightswood. "Hear me, child. It is stigma to be different. The Roma be not accepted. If you have not lived the Kumpania, you won't understand. People run to us. They run back home. Many Roma turn their back on familia. Few return."

Zizou turned and squeezed Pense's shoulder with her thin, strong fingers. "Once before you had the same decision. You walk in old footprints. The question. Are you her? If yes, you stay with Theresa. *Schej*, I talk much. It is for Palumb Furtuna to now explain."

"You call me a Gypsy girl, yet say I should stay at Knightswood." Pense steadied Zizou as they stepped over a tree root.

"There be two living in the same shell. You speak with Palumb Furtuna. He shares the journey with you," Zizou said. "Child-woman, we are the old and the young speaking secrets of years past and beyond."

Pense stopped walking, gazed at Zizou and said. "You say that I was born after you stopped coming with the Kumpania. But I've seen you before. My memory says that I was old at the time and you were young. I dreamed that last night."

"Live the dreams," Zizou said. "Now listen. The *lavuta* of Palumb Furtuna will sing again tonight, after the *gadje* sleep. Come with Theresa and Sharona for the *Pakiv.* Speaks the music all languages. *I phuv kleldias,* the earth danced last night. It will again. Let his music talk to you."

Main Street - afternoon

Hands in pockets, Daniel lounged against the south wall of Murray's Drug Store, a cigarette dangling from the corner of his mouth. He pulled his hat a little lower on his forehead, smiled and kicked a stone with his left foot. It spun into the street and stopped by the right back tire on Harris's car. Blake had left the vehicle ten minutes before and disappeared into Ham's barbershop, which doubled as the shoe repair.

Daniel smiled when he looked around. It was apparent that some villagers believed the stories circulating about his people. Mothers, who usually left their precious infants outside while shopping, wheeled their carriages inside. Merchants hadn't bothered putting displays out on the sidewalk. Doors normally thrown open for fresh air were kept closed. Grandparents walked small children to school.

Daniel had, in a very short period of time, managed to establish credibility, but only because no one but those at Knightswood connected him to the Kumpania. He had to keep the information secret just a little longer. He didn't want prejudices interrupting his unfinished business. Daniel hadn't been to the camp since sunrise, relying on one of the urchins to get messages from Zizou. That was how he'd heard about Constable Keough.

Daniel began his stakeout after breakfast when he came to the conclusion that the Old Boys' Club was not his target. Regulars at the Club were a group of older residents who liked to play nickel poker. With the exception of Blake or Compton, who played on a regular basis to clean them out of change, no one worthwhile belonged. Keen observations of Main Street told him the action was elsewhere and close by.

Crushing his cigarette underfoot, Daniel crossed the street, waving to Johnny as he drove through, his wagon loaded with grain sacks. "See you at The China at five," he shouted. Johnny tipped his hat to acknowledge he'd be there.

Daniel opened the barbershop's heavy door, removed his hat and stepped inside. He reached to silence the brass bell. He didn't need to be announced. As his eyes adjusted to the dim interior, Daniel sized up the small room that reeked of shaving cream, after-shave lotion, leather and shoe polish. The area on his left was set up for shoe repair with lasts and sewing machines, visible by the light of a filthy front window.

On the right, the barber sat alone on one of four wooden benches. His barber's chair faced a huge dirty mirror and dresser covered with bottles of lotions, jars of combs, brushes and other hair paraphernalia. A soiled, white cape hung over the black leather back of the chair. Two green metal light fixtures and a window with cracked glass panes lit the area. Ahead of him, at the far end of the shop, a heavy curtain hid a narrow, high doorway, the entrance to the living quarters at the back of the long, one-story wooden building.

"Cut and shave?" Ticky Ham asked.

"Trim," said Daniel. He walked across the hair-strewn, linoleum floor to the chair. "Just a trim. I keep it long, a little past the neck."

"Never saw a man before with such long hair, except one they dragged out of the bush upriver who'd been hiding from the draft. Must be a European thing?"

"It is," Daniel said. "I got used to wearing it this way during the war. It keeps the back of my neck warm."

"Sounds like you weren't near a barber too much during the war."

"I was . . . underground."

Daniel found himself facing the mirror. Although it was filthy, one quick look told Daniel that although he was still flesh and blood, the fuzzy haze was creeping down from his hair and up from his neck. He couldn't see his ears. Life was being squeezed out of him from all sides. His forehead, eyes, nose and mouth were still clearly defined. The eyes stared back at him but they seemed less clear. Time, Daniel thought, was running out.

Ticky looked at Daniel's reflection in the mirror. "In this light," he said, "you look half there. I ain't got the energy to clean the mirror or light fixtures. I'm hoping to get a new shop soon."

"Half of me is better than none," Daniel said. "So you served in the war?"

Ticky trimmed, careful not to cut an ear. He pursed his lips as he worked, tongue in the side of his cheek. "I was in England most of the war," he said.

"Good man," Daniel said, trying not to look in the mirror. Instead he listened for various sounds in the building and stayed alert to odd smells.

"Saw some long hair on those Gypsies that came through yesterday," Ticky said. "Don't expect to do business with any of them." Ticky worked slowly around the right ear, swinging the chair as he clipped, giving Daniel a good view of the curtained doorway. "Are you really a European *Count*?"

"Hmm? Ah, yes. I'm known as *The Count Daniel Cudzinki* where I come from."

"Never met a *Count* before," said Ticky. "It's a pleasure. You were in the underground, you say? Where?"

"Europe," Daniel said. "Really, I went where I was needed. I speak five languages. I was in Africa – France – Ro . . . Russia."

"Decorated?"

"There was no official acknowledgment. I don't keep an association with anyone but those I helped."

"Isn't that always the way?" Ticky combed, snipped and brushed. "Weren't you a bit old to serve?"

"Knowledge overrides age. Who worries about age when lives are being saved?" Daniel said. "Have you been around here long?"

"Lived nearby all my life. Went to school here. Apprenticed under my father. I was too old for the front lines but served four years overseas, cutting hair. I moved into the business when I got back seventeen months ago."

"So," Daniel said, pulling a wad of bills from his jacket pocket. "You know all the doings around the village."

Ticky shrugged, his eyes on the money roll. "Some."

"I'm looking for a little action," Daniel said. "The Yanks taught me how to play poker. It's a vice of mine. I can't find a good game. I haven't played for three weeks. My fingers are getting itchy for the cards. If you know of anyone who wants a game, tell me. I win a few – lose a few. What's money when you're a *Count*? How much did you say I owed you?"

"One buck," Ticky said, "includes tip."

"Take two." Daniel peeled back two ones to expose a one-hundred-dollar bill.

"You shouldn't carry all that money with the Gypsies hanging around."

"Thanks for the warning," Daniel said. "By the way, have you seen J.P. Harris's driver, Blake? I saw him come in."

"No. No I haven't," Ticky lied.

"If you do, would you tell him that I hear he's a good player. I'd like to sit in on a game or two. Are you sure you haven't seen him? He didn't leave. Is there a back door?" Daniel stepped toward the curtained doorway.

Ticky jumped in front of him, eyes darting from the roll of money to the curtain. "Will you excuse me a minute?" he said.

"Certainly," Daniel said. "Works every time," he muttered as Ticky slithered behind the curtain. After several minutes he returned, followed by Blake, a thunderous look on his face. His eyes went automatically to the roll of bills still in Daniel's hand.

Daniel smiled and turned the wad slowly. "You're back from the city, alone."

"I just got in," Blake answered. "What do you want?"

"To get in on your game," Daniel said. "I understand this is the place to be for high stakes."

"Says who?"

"Says the Editor of the paper who'd love to write it up," Daniel lied.

"As if he'd know." Blake sneered.

"I'm not here to argue. I came in for a trim and smelled cigar smoke. I heard the cards hit the table. My money's as good as yours."

Blake leaned against the door frame. "How good are you?"

"Win a few – lose a few," Daniel repeated, playing with the roll. "You afraid of competition or something?"

Blake stroked his chin, his eyes on the money. "Come on then," he finally said. "There are rules, the first being that you don't tell anyone who's in here playing the game."

"Fair enough."

Daniel followed Blake through the curtain and down three

steps to a large, windowless room that appeared to be a dining room. Bottles of liquor and glasses were lined up on a cheap walnut-veneered bookcase. A sideboard, whose top was buried under newspapers, hugged the north wall, its dirty mirror reflecting the bare light bulb that hung over a wooden gaming table. A round black stove with pipes running the length of the room overhead gave off heat. Dense smoke swirled from expensive cigars in the mouths of players who turned to see who Blake had brought with him. Daniel recognized everyone.

One rose and said, "Take my seat. My congregation awaits."

Daniel put the roll of bills in an inner pocket and sat down. An afternoon's work lay ahead of him.

The Camp - afternoon

Johnny rose from examining a horse's fetlock as he caught sight of Theresa, Sharona and Lillian Harris. "Holy jeez!" he said, rubbing his hands on his pants and then running them through his hair. "That's an unusual trio."

When all three came within hearing distance, he stepped away from the horse and stood in front of Lillian, legs apart, arms crossed, a smile on his face. "Fancy meeting you here, Miss Harris. Aren't you a bit out of your element?"

"We had lunch after Lillian came to the house looking for Daniel," Theresa said as if there were nothing unusual in the situation. "Then we came down to the camp to have our fortunes told."

"Miss Harris? Looking for Daniel?"

"It's a rather complicated affair," Theresa said.

"An interesting one, I'll bet you,"Johnny muttered, wiping his hands on his pants again. "So, did Zizou tell you anything you didn't already know?" He spoke to Sharona.

"Nothing I'd believe," she said. "Have you seen Pense this afternoon?"

"Not recently," Johnny said. "Just after I got here, I saw her at the oak tree with Zizou."

"If you're talking about that wild child, I saw her in the fortune teller's wagon," Lillian said. "She was trying on the old woman's clothes."

"She'll be all right then," Theresa said. "If you're not busy Johnny, could you give Miss Harris a ride home? You can take the car."

"I'll be free in an hour or so. I want to take the team and another couple of horses out to the farm first. You'll have to ride in the wagon, Miss Harris."

"I'd prefer to walk. That might constitute the long journey the old woman spoke of."

Johnny shrugged. "Sharona can drive you home if she's not busy."

Sharona gave Johnny a drop-dead look. He knew how she detested Lillian Harris. She'd made a point of ignoring Lillian for years.

"Perhaps Miss Harris should take the car and you can pick it up later," Sharona said, eyes flashing.

"I can't drive," Lillian said. "I've never had to learn. We've always had a driver."

"I'll drive," Sharona conceded with reluctance. "I'll drop her off on my way to the shoe repair shop and the butcher."

When Tamas approached, the ladies decided it was time to leave.

Johnny waited until they'd turned their backs to him then approached Tamas. "Nice crowd, Tamas. Good selection of horses brought in for trade today too."

"Found some good ones, did you?"

"Not from your ragtag lot." Johnny laughed. "I bought a couple off MacDougall."

Tamas shrugged. "Want a glass of wine?"

"Sure," Johnny said. They walked to Tamas's tent which had been erected in the middle of the camp. Sitting, backs against the truck's running board, the pair watched the action.

"We don't have to go find business," Tamas said. "It comes to us. We just sit here and let it roll in. They can't stand us walking their streets but they don't mind walking ours."

Johnny stretched his legs and made himself comfortable. He'd made a few observations during the time he'd been in the camp and he wanted to run them past Tamas when they were alone so he'd get a reasonable answer. "There are a lot of men that came this time."

"They came for the *ancient one.*"

"Who?"

"Palumb Furtuna."

"You don't say." Johnny scratched his chin.

"So this Pal . . . whoever. He's here?"

"Yes," Tamas answered cautiously, not knowing how much Daniel had told Johnny, or how much Johnny knew. "But he doesn't travel with us. He's returned to us, after a number of years."

"And who might he be?"

"Daniel Cudzinki."

"My friend The Count!"

"The one and the same."

Johnny held his cup out for a refill. "I'll be damned," he muttered. "This wine comes from Theresa's cellar, doesn't it?"

"Sure does, just like the *kanny* in the stew pot came from her hen house."

Johnny settled back against the running board. "So, Daniel asked these men to come?"

"No. He left word he would be at Knightswood this autumn, and they came of their own accord."

"He's got that much pull?"

"He was well respected and . . . we knew he'd be back."

"I don't follow," Johnny said, thinking his mind was becoming fuzzy with the effects of the plum wine. Tamas was talking in circles.

"You don't need to," Tamas said. "Do you know him well, Big Johnny?"

"Apparently not well enough," Johnny said.

"Don't underestimate Daniel. He's our Head . . . Our leader."

Johnny shook his head then closed his eyes and stuck his glass out for another shot of wine. "Tamas," he said, "would yuh do me a favor?"

"If I can," Tamas said.

"Pense, my daughter is thinking of joining the Kumpania. She can't leave us, Tamas. We must think of something to stop her."

"You're her father?" Tamas sat up, surprised at the revelation.

"Did yuh not know?" Johnny asked.

"No one knew," Tamas said. "Sharona didn't tell us. Either her parents don't know who the father is or they've chosen not to say."

"I'm sure they know. It's a long story, Tamas. Have you got time to hear it?"

"Now you've started, and you'd better finish."

Johnny nodded agreement. It was time that he got the whole business off his chest. Who better to tell, especially the part about Daniel in the desert; the part he had remembered last night after hearing the music. "You realize that now I mean to make it right. I love Sharona and I mean to marry her," Johnny began.

The China Inn - evening

Johnny's motorcycle stood outside the China Inn, keys dangling in the ignition. Daniel removed them and put them on the table when he sat down in the booth. Johnny winced. "Wouldn't leave them in the bike, Johnny. That's an open invitation for someone to steal it."

"Let 'em take it." Johnny nursed his head between both hands.

"What's wrong with you?"

"Plum wine and Tamas."

Daniel chuckled. "Serves you right, you souse. He can drink anyone under the table."

"Shh! Not so loud."

Cook Kropolus appeared round the ferns. "Drink this," he said plunking a large glass of tomato juice in front of Johnny, followed by a jug of water. "You have to dilute the stuff in your system. You been drinking too?" Cook addressed Daniel.

"Yes," said Daniel. "But I can handle it and I wasn't drinking Theresa's potent brew. Are you coherent, Johnny?"

"Sure," Johnny said. "It's the headache that's bothering me but I'm listening."

"Are you going to eat or are we going to talk first?"

"We'll talk," Johnny said. "Let's get things sorted out before this place gets really busy."

Cook Kropolus said. "I don't expect it to be full tonight. It's not pay day, and most farmers won't be back until tomorrow to check out the livestock at the camp."

"It won't do them any good. All the good horses are taken," Johnny said.

"Don't bet on it," Daniel said. "They're pasturing a few good ones at Silvers and the farmers always bring animals along to trade."

"Jeez! That's hard on the pocket book. I buy today and they bring better ones in tomorrow," Johnny said, pouring himself a glass of water. "So, you owe me one, Daniel. I knew you were Roma but why didn't you tell me you were their big fat head?"

"Would it have mattered, Johnny? Does it matter that the Kropoluses belong to the same familia too?"

Johnny took a big drink and looked from Daniel to Cook Kropolus. "You really a Gypsy?"

Cook Kropolus nodded and smiled. "We achieved a measure of domesticity some years ago when we realized we didn't want to be on the road. We bought this place on one of our spring visits. We're saving up to go live in Greece."

"I suppose it doesn't make a bit of difference," Johnny said. "I just didn't like to hear the news from Tamas when I should have heard it from you, Daniel."

"What else did you hear at the Kumpania?"

"Nothing," Johnny said. "I told Tamas more than he told me."

Johnny watched as two women came through the front door and looked around. They chose a seat by the front window. Mrs. K. hurried over with menus under her arm. She gave their table a quick wipe then went back to the counter for cutlery and glasses of water.

Johnny's stomach rumbled, then heaved. "Maybe I will eat. Bring me a juicy steak and double mashed, hold the parsnips."

"I'll have the same, with carrots," Daniel said. "Does Theresa know we're not eating there tonight?"

"I told her." Johnny made himself more comfortable by stretching his lanky frame under the table. His blond hair stood in rows where he'd run his dirty fingers through it. His plaid shirt was filthy. "What are you damn well looking at?"

Daniel smiled and patted Johnny's arm. "A hard-working man. I was thinking that I'd never survive a hard day's work now. You're lucky to be young, Big Johnny Wallace."

"I'll change clothes and have a bath when I get back to Theresa's. It's been a long day."

"Tell me about it."

Johnny finished the juice and poured himself another drink of water to which he added a shake of salt and a dash of Worchestershire sauce, his own prescription for a hangover. He kept his eyes on Daniel. "It appears Keough knows somethin' about the meeting. Someone's told him. And Blake's back."

"But as we haven't set a time or day for the meeting, and if it's here after hours, neither can interfere."

"The point is, who told them? There must be someone in our group that's talking out of line."

Mrs. K appeared around the plants and put two huge plates of food on the table. "I'll be back with the coffee pot," she said.

"Mrs. K, has Constable Keough asked you about the Stamp Club?" Johnny asked.

"He has. I told him it was a bunch of men discussing a boring subject and they met at night. I told him it was none of his business. I'll be right back."

Daniel put three spoonfuls of sugar in his empty cup. Deep in thought, he stroked his chin and pursed his lips. "Johnny. How soon can you call a meeting? Is tomorrow morning too quick?"

"I can get hold of everyone. What do yuh have in mind?"

"Keough's on call twenty-four hours a day, isn't he? But he only comes on full duty at seven in the morning."

"I think so," Johnny said.

"We meet here at six in the morning. That all right with you, Mrs. K.? You keep the door locked. If Keough shows up, he can plaster himself against the window."

"What about Blake?" Johnny asked.

"I'll get one of the camp girls to tend to Blake. That'll keep him out of the way."

"Shame!" Mrs. K said, wiping a spill with her apron. Then with coffee pot poised over Daniel's cup, she said. "You're going to die using that much sugar."

"I'm going to die anyway," Daniel said. "And sooner than you might think."

Both gave Daniel an odd look.

"I'm staying out of that one." Carry Kropolus retreated to her front counter from where she could survey her culinary kingdom.

"They say one knows when death comes calling," Daniel said. "I have that feeling."

"You've been sitting at Zizou's table too often," Johnny retorted. "So, Mrs. K?" he called across the room. "Is it a deal?"

"Anything you say," she called back.

"Set up the meeting," Daniel said. "And we'll tell the fellows to carry on with their campaign of small disruptions. We'll tell them that there's nothing new to report, but that they should, under all circumstances, stick to their routine. Only you and I will be party to a plan I have in mind. We don't have jobs to lose." Daniel added another spoon of sugar to his coffee.

"We can organize a little disturbance without any of them knowing about it. I don't want any hot heads jumping into the fray, so we'll have to be careful. But I do want it to look like they're organized and have the potential to strike. We might have to lie a little, to gain a lot."

"What do yuh have in mind?"

Daniel looked around the restaurant. "Not here," he said. "Give me a ride to the camp and we'll talk."

Johnny ate ravenously, slicing his steak and sopping the juice with chunks of bread. "Why are you so angry with Harris?" he asked, his mouth full.

Daniel speared a carrot with his fork. "In confidence?" he asked Johnny.

Johnny nodded.

"Swear on your mother's grave."

"On my mother's grave and my father's too."

"The Harrises have interfered with my family a couple of times. Both were a long time ago."

"Well, start talking," Johnny said. "I'm game for a fairy tale today."

"I lived here once and tried to make a civilized man of myself," Daniel said. "To do that I needed a job but the Harris family made it plain that they didn't hire Gypsies. The situation took a turn for the worst and I had to run for my life. I was blamed for the rape of a woman. I didn't do it but I know who did. And he made sure I was accused of the crime. Because I was a Gypsy, I was made his scapegoat. That man was a member of the Harris family."

Johnny's fork stopped short of his mouth."You're a man on the run?"

"I was a younger man at the time. Only Granny Smith can recognize me."

"I'll be damned."

"You will if you breathe a word of this to anyone, dead too."

Johnny put his fork on his plate and looked Daniel straight in the eye. "You're here for revenge."

"That's part of the story," Daniel said.

"You sure it was Harris? Are you positive that he did it?"

"I said, a member of the Harris family. Let's leave it at that for now. Look. I've not got much time. I don't think Keough's clever enough to piece my story together. He's younger than you and I.

Even if he did know the story, there's nothing to connect me, as I appear now."

"What about Harris?"

"He's the loose cannon."

Johnny resumed eating, all the while watching Daniel. "You swear you didn't do it?"

"I swear."

"The woman. Who was she?"

"I can't tell you, Johnny."

"What about the second tale? You said they interfered a couple of times."

"Just leave it, Johnny. I'm not at liberty to tell you that story at the moment."

By the tone of Daniel's voice, Johnny knew not to push the issue. "You'd better eat before your supper gets cold."

"You believe me?"

"Yeah," said Johnny. "I have to after what you did for me in the desert."

Daniel put his knife and fork down. Careful, he thought, we're on thin ground now. Picking up his coffee cup, he said. "Tell me what I did."

"You remember, don't yuh?" Johnny said. "After I killed that fellow, I panicked and ran into the desert. I don't know how far I went. How far can a crazy man run? Eventually, I lay down. I wanted to die. I wanted the enemy to find me. Instead, you found me and your group alerted my unit. You stayed with me until rescue was at hand."

"You saw my face. You know for sure it was me," Daniel said, voice steady.

"Goddamn it! It was you. I don't know where you came from or what group you were attached to. I was in and out of consciousness all the time. But I remember you were holding me, cradling me in your arms. There you were, an old man, shielding me from the sun like a baby, talking to me."

"An old man, "Daniel said. "Didn't you question why an old man was in the desert?"

"In the hospital, when I asked about you, the doctors thought I suffered a breakdown. No one would talk -- no one! There was so much secrecy. I wanted to know about the dove. There was this white bird, a beautiful white dove that came to me." Johnny's voice rose. "They were sure I was hallucinating when I talked about the white dove."

"Johnny," Daniel said. "Get a grip on yourself."

"Last night," Johnny continued, "I slept well for the first time in three years. The dog slept beside me. I've never let him do that before. It was the music that did it, the music that came from the camp. After I fell asleep, I remembered . . . . "

Johnny turned piercing blue eyes in Daniel's direction. "Now I don't know for sure if I killed the man. I remember him lying on top of me. I recall rolling out from underneath him and running. Maybe I wasn't running because I killed him. Maybe I was running from the enemy. What if someone sneaked up behind and stabbed him. Maybe he was trying to warn me and was killed and fell on top of me. Whatever the answer, I cracked and ran. That's why they sent me back to England. I cracked under pressure."

Daniel reached across to grip Johnny's wrists. "Lower your voice, Johnny," he cautioned. "The ladies are looking this way."

"Sorry," Johnny said. "I forgot where we were. You should've told me as soon as you arrived in Millbrook that you were the guy that saved me."

"You're one of the reasons for my being here. You couldn't die in the desert. Something led me to . . ." Daniel struggled with an answer. "Look, a lot of good men cracked during the war. People can only be pushed so far, take so much, before they lose it."

Johnny slid his hands up to grip Daniel's. "I know," he said. "I've gotten over the crackin' part. How can I say thanks? How can I repay you? I would have died and never seen Pense or Sharona again."

"Your thanks is enough. It's for their sake you had to live. You had to come back. You had unfinished business."

"What I can't understand is why you were in the desert. You're too old to be in military service."

Daniel coughed. "I go where I'm needed. Age is irrelevant when lives are at stake."

"I guess," Johnny said. "You were wearing a uniform and all. Someone must have figured you were valuable and able to do the job."

Daniel dug around in his pockets for a cigarette. Johnny was leading him into dangerous seas, waters he'd been trying to avoid until he'd spoken to Pense. "Did the uniform give you an idea about what country I was working for? What did it look like to you?"

"Cheez Christ! I was too far gone to think of uniforms," Johnny said.

"You must remember something."

"You looked ragged," Johnny said. "Yuh held my head on your lap. I remember looking up and seeing a huge dark stain on your jacket, and a big hole. There was a hole," Johnny pointed toward Daniel's heart then frowned.

"Go on."

"Can't," Johnny said, shaking his head. "Gotta think this one through. Can't remember anything more. It's confusing . . ."

"That's okay, Johnny. But if you want to talk, I'll like to hear the details. An old man's mind gets muddled, you know."

Johnny pushed his plate back. "Let's go. It's getting dark. You ready to play monkey on my back again? There's one thing I don't understand. If you've never driven a motorcycle or car, how on earth did you survive in the desert? They were the only way of life for us out there, in the middle of nowhere."

"I managed." Daniel smiled. "Have you heard of camels or angel's wings?" He quickly changed the subject by pulling a fat wad of bills from his pocket. "Supper's my treat."

"Where'd you get that from?" Johnny's eyes mirrored his surprise at seeing the roll.

Daniel took a ten off the roll before putting it back in his pocket. "The product of this," he said, retrieving another roll and putting it on the table. Unrolling a one-hundred-dollar bill, Daniel revealed a stack of carefully cut newspaper.

"God!" exclaimed Johnny. "The oldest trick in the book."

"I spent the afternoon playing poker with some of the village elite," laughed Daniel. "I wiped their slate."

"That won't go down too well."

"I threw caution to the wind," Daniel said. "There are bigger fish in the sea that I want to catch. I dropped the hint I was looking for real poker players."

"Holy torpedoes!" Johnny said. "I wouldn't want to be in your shoes."

"What are they going to do? They can't tell anyone they lost at poker. They're going to want the opportunity to win back their money. They'll find someone they think will clean my clock. They'll find a worthy opponent, Johnny. I know who he'll be. too. And as I'm not going to be here much longer, short memories take a long recess."

"How good are you?"

"Very good."

"Well, then you have a point. Did you cheat?"

"Come on, Johnny. You know me better than that."

Knightswood - supper

"Are you sure?" Theresa said, her arms up to the elbows in soapy dishwater. Because she was concentrating on watching the sunset, she thought she hadn't heard Sharona correctly.

"I'm sure," Sharona said, drying a plate. "I was in Ticky Ham's when I heard loud voices. They were coming from the back, behind the curtain. Then Harris's driver came through, mad as a wet hen. Ticky went behind the curtain and everything settled down. "Trouble?" I asked when he came back. He didn't answer, just took my money and showed me to the door."

"I don't trust that weasel of a man," Theresa said. "I hear he allows gambling in his living quarters. But what's new about that? Like father, like son."

"I'd bet they were gambling," Sharona said. "Ticky certainly didn't want me around."

"You heard Daniel's voice but you didn't see him?"

"I'm sure it was his voice. The accent gave him away. Where's he now?"

"I don't know." Theresa scrubbed the roasting pan. "Perhaps he's at Zizou's. I've learned in one short week never to assume anything as far as our star boarder is concerned. Whatever possessed us to open our door to him?"

Sharona hung her wet dish towel over the handle of the oven door and got another from the drawer. "We've done it before. There's been far worse stay here until they got on their feet. I'm sure Daniel's being here has a lot to do with him writing that he was connected in some way to the Anderson family. Are you going to the camp to hear him play tonight?"

"I'll leave my window open so that I can hear the music. I'm going to have an early night. I found some more things in the attic that I want to take a closer look at. I've not finished the letters either. They're difficult to read." Theresa shivered. "Honestly, Sharona. It's as though someone's been peering over my shoulder for the past several days."

"Are they letters that Maggie wrote?"

"No, they're letters she received, from someone with the initials *YLD*. It's strange that only initials were used. Were they from a friend, a school chum? I can't even tell if they were written by a man or woman, although an educated guess would be a man. The letters are about people they knew, places in North America and Europe that one had visited." Theresa tipped the dishwater down the drain, then wiped the pan and tucked it under the sink. "Whoever it was wrote about gifts – a book, a hair saver, fishing rod."

"Fishing rod?" Sharona said. "Hair saver? *YLD*?"

"I still have a bundle to go through," Theresa said."Why Daniel thought they are important is beyond me, but I'm fascinated enough to want to finish them."

"You'll be alone tonight," Sharona said. "Pense won't disturb your train of thought. She's with Zizou. She's taken a great liking to the old woman."

"You make sure she comes home with you. I don't like her staying in camp overnight."

"She'd be fine but I'll bring her back with me. Really, Theresa, when the Kumpania leaves, we must try to keep Pense in school more regularly. She's getting a bit out of hand."

"If she stays. If you stay," Theresa said, "you and Johnny must make a few rules and stick by them. Pense'll understand that parents need to make rules. She's on the brink of womanhood. Pense doesn't recognize that although she's been mature and responsible for a long time, she still needs to cross that invisible barrier that changes a girl into a woman."

"You expect Johnny to make rules when he's never lived by one in his entire life?" Sharona laughed."The day I see that, Betsy will be able to fly."

The Harris Estate - supper

Blake's vicious mood carried over the supper hour. When Lillian found him in his apartment over the garage, he was in a temper and playing it out by slamming cupboard doors and throwing dishes on the table. She stood well back from him.

"I expected you home this morning. I could have used your services."

"Anytime," Blake snarled, waving his free arm toward his bedroom.

"I mean," said Lillian, "I needed a driver."

Blake opened a can of soup and dumped it in a pot on the hot plate.

"Why don't you eat in the house with the servants?"

"I'm not in the mood." He scraped a chair across the floor to the table. "Sit down."

"No thanks. Mother's expecting me for supper. Why are you angry this time? It seems to be a regular habit with you these days."

"The old man, the *Count*, cleaned me out at poker. He won every cent I had on me."

"Maybe now you'll stop gambling?"

"Over my dead body. It's not as simple as laying the cards down, Lillian. What did you need me to do?"

"Compton says you should get in touch with my father and bring him back as soon as possible. He says there are important things happening that J.P. should know about. Compton was babbling on about some land deal he'd made. "

"I'm driving to Windsor on Saturday afternoon and I'll bring him back on Sunday morning, if he's ready to return."

"Why not sooner?" asked Lillian. "Where is he anyway? You tell me where he's staying on this holiday and I'll give him the message."

"Nope," said Blake. "I won't rat on your father. He's my bread and butter. His private dealings are none of your business."

"I'm his daughter. I have my suspicions."

"Keep them to yourself if you want to live the good life."

"Speaking of the good life," Lillian said. "It's over, Blake. It's over between you and me."

"At your convenience, our little dalliance is over?" Blake came round the table. "You're calling it off, just like that?" He snapped his fingers in Lillian's face.

"Yes," Lillian said, backing toward the door. "It was never anything but physical. And if you don't keep your distance, you'll be out a job. I'll cry rape."

"You dirty little whore!" Blake spat toward Lillian then reached for her.

"Lay a hand on me and I'll scream," Lillian said. "You know I will."

Blake's arms fell to his side. "Get out of here," he snarled.

"Get out of my life. You're not worth the hassle."

Lillian ran down the stairs and through the courtyard to the main house. Blake had a vicious streak. She should have terminated the relationship weeks ago, but beggars couldn't be choosers. He was the only man that paid her any attention. "Not entirely true,"she muttered, slamming the back screen door. "Sebastian Temple can't keep his eyes off me. He said I was all he thought about during the past five months. He's worth ten of Blake."

The Camp - midnight

When Daniel was sure the villagers had all left the Kumpania, he climbed to the top of Pense's Mountain with his violin. He played, passionately, vigorously, putting his heart to the bow, his soul to the strings. As the music soared so did he, beyond *Silhouette*, beyond his age, beyond the village, to an enchanted place where all was light and beauty and peace – a place he'd been before. His heart throbbed with pain but he kept playing. The valley resounded again with sweet music that spread like leaves on the winds of an autumn day, leaving a pile here, a leaf there, a gentle swirl that touched the hearts of everyone who chose to listen.

Daniel finished by playing *Magdalena's Song* once again. Sensing he was not alone, Daniel opened his eyes. Pense stood before him with tears coursing down her cheeks. Daniel set his violin down and reached to cradle her sweet young face in his old-man hands. He gently wiped the tears away, the touch of his weathered fingers like silk on her skin.

"Hush, hush," he whispered, leaning forward to kiss her forehead.

"Palumb Furtuna, why have you come back?" she cried, "My love. My life. My agony!"

Daniel's hands trembled, his face twisting in pain as her words struck his heart. "I had to explain to you. I had to come for you," he said. "I begged to come back for you. You must come with me this time."

Pense closed her eyes and reached to touch a weathered cheek. "You shouldn't be here, on my mountain, with me."

Reality cut through Daniel like a knife. He gasped and stepped back, hands dropping to his sides. "We must leave the mountain," he managed to stammer. "I'll walk you home."

"No," said Pense. "Let me stay with Zizou."

"You mustn't!" Daniel said, his voice gaining strength as he spoke. "It's too dangerous for you in the Kumpania, Pense Magdalena. You made the decision to stay once before and paid dearly for that decision. You must go home to Knightswood and sleep in your own bed."

Pense nodded in silent understanding and wiped tears away in a familiar gesture that wrenched a gasp of pain and recognition from Daniel's lips but only strengthened his resolve to protect her this time.

Carrying his violin, Daniel let Pense go first down the steepest part of the path and allowed himself to put a hand on her shoulder to steady his walk. As they passed near a car in the darkness, Daniel recognized it as Sebastian Temple's. He could vaguely discern two shadowy figures in the back seat. Tightening his grip on Pense's shoulder, Daniel was comforted that she was with him and not at camp where her inexperience around young men might be taken advantage of.

Unseen by anyone in camp, Lillian had sought the company of Sebastian Temple Kropolus. Under the spell of Daniel's music, she had succumbed to her emotional hunger and given herself over, wholly and completely to him. In her need for compassionate intimacy Lillian never gave thought to what the consequences of such a liaison might be.

Chapter 10

The Harris Estate - October 4, 1947: morning

Unlike the bountiful presence of Theresa's Knightswood, the Harris residence was a two-story square brick building, utilitarian in its overstated frugality. The house was surrounded by an acre of lawn that was kept trimmed by a gardener but there were no flower and vegetable gardens or orchard. The building's front entrance faced Broad Street and its back butted onto the river's public land.

After J.P. inherited the property from his father, he began adding to its boundaries, though added real estate did little to enhance the place. The fact that the disputed quarter-mile piece of land, the property of the village, lay between J.P. and the river was no deterrent. Harris claimed possession with no resistance from village fathers, since J.P. sat on the Board of Ethics. Board members were all well aware of who really controlled the village's finances.

Very few people visited the Harris home and none arrived without an invitation. It was of great interest to the servants, therefore, when an elderly gentleman appeared at the front door and asked to see Lillian. He was ushered into the parlor and Nellie ran to summon Lillian.

Lillian, asserting her authority, took her time getting to the parlour. To get the upper hand, Daniel, seated on a comfortable chesterfield with a book in his hand, ignored her for several minutes. Lillian lit a cigarette, took several puffs, flicked ashes into an empty flower vase and stood in front of Daniel.

When she didn't speak, Daniel looked up. "Have you finished your cigarette? Are you ready to talk? We'll both be more relaxed if you just sit down, Lillian."

Lillian threw the butt into the vase then sat opposite Daniel, keeping a low table between them. Pulling several photographs from a pocket, she laid them on the table. "You piqued my curiosity about Kenneth Walker so I went looking for you. I guess it doesn't matter what house we meet in, Theresa's or mine."

"I should hope that you have some curiosity for Kenneth," Daniel said, coming right to the point of his visit. "You see, Lillian, he is your father."

Lillian's hand stopped midair and her eyes narrowed. "I beg your pardon?"

Daniel reached into an inner pocket then handed Lillian another handwritten sheet. "It's true. Kenneth Walker is your father. He told me so. He had the proof. I can't show you documents but I can show you dates." Daniel leaned back and waited for her reaction. It wasn't long coming.

"This is preposterous!"

"It isn't. When your parents visited England in 1912-13, your mother made a point of contacting Kenneth. J.P. left to spend two months in Germany. Citing illness, Charlotte didn't travel with him. Instead she spent time around Chelfont St. Peter. While J.P. was away, as the old saying goes, the mice did play. Kenneth left here with all good intentions of cleaning up an estate and coming back to . . . " Daniel hesitated, then restructured his sentence, " . . . returning to Canada."

Lillian kept silent and looked from Daniel to the paper waiting for him to resume his narrative.

"Your mother had a crush on Kenneth when he lived in Millbrook and was most persuasive in England. I believe that she told a few lies, enough to plant seeds of doubt in his mind that Theresa was waiting for him in Canada. Charlotte was a beguiling woman. Kenneth wasn't totally innocent. They had a brief liaison."

"My mother isn't that kind of a woman," Lillian said. "She's a mouse who hides from people. She wouldn't have been so bold."

"She was," Daniel said. "By the time J.P. returned, your mother was pregnant. We could assume that she told J.P. it was his child. But Kenneth was thrown aside as soon as your mother knew she was pregnant, an action that led to a more substantial theory about your conception."

Lillian made to speak but Daniel raised his hand. "Let me continue. Each story has two sides. The story is even less savory when examining the second theory. Kenneth did a few calculations and knew for certain that Lillian had to be aware she was carrying his child. That's when strong suspicions that he had been used by your mother developed. Kenneth was frustrated and embarrassed by his own weakness. He continued to write Theresa but couldn't bring himself to tell her what he'd done. So, he buried himself in some very dangerous work."

"And Theresa Inachio suffered because of a stupid act on the part of both of them."

"That's right." Daniel said. "They are both to blame. Perhaps time would have healed wounds had a confession been made. But Kenneth was killed in France before he could be reconciled with the woman he really loved. All might have worked out. Theresa has a generous, forgiving heart."

Lillian's hand trembled as she reached for a picture. Ever since she'd found the photographs, she had detected an uncanny likeness, especially around the eyes and mouth. "Am I truly to believe this is my father?"

"The interesting fact is that J.P. took Charlotte to Ireland for her confinement," Daniel said. "So you were born in Dublin, away from Kenneth. This makes me think that J.P. knew the circumstances and purposefully kept her away from Kenneth. When you were three months old, the happy family sailed for home."

"What you're telling me is hard to believe."

"It's from the messenger's mouth to your ears," Count said. "If you take time to read old newspapers and other documents, you can piece the story together. It's all there, in bits and pieces. One of the things Kenneth made me promise to do if he didn't come back from the war was to find his child. It was a promise that had to be kept."

"You knew Kenneth well?"

"Yes," Daniel said. "I spent a lot of time with Kenneth." He stopped short of giving dates, times and places. "On the paper, I've written several addresses in Ireland that have information. There's also an address for England, a church office that holds documents you might be interested in. Your mother's a foolish woman. She left a paper trail that's easy to follow. A number of people were paid to keep quiet about the delivery of a healthy full-term baby, but they're still alive."

"And if fa . . . J.P. was involved?"

"I'm sure he was part of the conspiracy," Daniel said. "J.P. came home and threw himself into the factory. Your mother perpetuated the Harris myth, her happy little family being the example set for their workers – all church and no play."

Lillian began to pace again. "And what am I to do with this information?"

"First I suggest that you make sure you've accepted the fact that Kenneth is your father. Then do with the information what you must. There is one thing I ask. I took a calculated risk approaching you. The last thing I want is for Theresa Inachio to be hurt. She must never hear from you that you're the daughter of her former fiancé.

"But I mentioned his name when I visited her yesterday," Lillian said. "Won't she wonder why?"

"It's up to your mother to talk with Theresa. Your mother must offer the olive branch. She must make amends. Theresa's a wonderful woman. I had hoped the situation wouldn't arise when her love for Kenneth would be shaken."

Lillian nodded. Since her visit to Knightswood, she'd developed respect and admiration for Theresa. "I won't do anything to hurt her," she said.

"I have to believe you, Lillian Walker. I've given you freedom. You're not adopted by J.P. Your only ties to the Harris family are emotional. You can marry whom you like, make a life for yourself elsewhere. Life is now yours to grasp and to run with. If you choose not to act, you'll inherit J.P.'s wealth. But is that what you really want? Don't you want to know more about Kenneth – your father? Don't you want to know what sort of man he was? Don't you want to make a life for yourself far from Millbrook?"

"If I believe you." Lillian said, although she felt a sudden surge of freedom, a feeling that Daniel had lifted a huge burden from her shoulders.

"You'll believe," said Daniel, struggling to his feet. Hat in hand, he glanced around the sparse parlor, a far cry from Theresa's cozy room, "If you'll show me to the door, please, I've a great deal to do today."

"And if I want to talk to you?"

Daniel looked to the floor, then at Lillian. His smile was sad.

"I won't be in the village much longer. I have to leave soon. But if you feel that we must talk again, leave word at the China Inn."

"Should I be thanking you for this information?"

"That's up to you, Lillian. Kenneth left nothing in way of an estate. You have only a few photographs of him, Theresa's reminiscences, your mother's memories and his biography."

"That might be enough," Lillian said. "You must be a marvelous poker player, Count Daniel Cudzinki. You make all the right moves whether talking to me or playing the game."

"Just luck. Everyone has good and bad days with people and at the table. And, dear Lillian, I've had years of experience in handling people. May I kiss your cheek? You look a little flustered and an old man doesn't get to kiss a beautiful young woman often."

Lillian wondered at the odd request, but bent toward Daniel who gently kissed her cheek. On a sudden impulse, she threw her arms around him. Neither spoke until she let go and stepped back, embarrassed by her action. Lillian had tears in her eyes.

Daniel struggled for control. "You are not so crusty a woman, Lillian Walker," he said, his voice cracking with emotion. "You need only to break free of this gilded prison to find out what kind of person you really are, and you've already taken the first step." Daniel steadied himself on her arm as she led him toward the door.

Johnny's Farm - morning

One could tell where Johnny had been by the prints of his rubber boots in the heavy ground frost. He walked, Plumb Loco by his side, along the fence line at the road then up the stream to its south fork. He paused to repair the fence, then followed along the line of burnished beech trees to the back of Pense's Mountain. Cutting across the brow of the hill, he stopped several times to look over the valley and his property. His steps came back along the pasture fence. Loco barked as the albino doe broke from the bush twenty feet away.

"Heel!" Johnny commanded as the deer leapt across the south field and disappeared into the alders by the stream. "Weather's changing," he mused aloud, watching the sky. "Midweek we'll have snow." Johnny was ready for it. The house finally had a roof. Next spring it would be his permanent home – his and Sharona's if she was willing. He walked in silence back to the barn, Loco trotting by his side.

After he opened the stable door, Johnny whistled to the horses who responded with heads up. "Go! Get 'em!" Loco leapt the fence and bounded into the north pasture.

Inside the barn, Johnny busied himself by laying fresh bedding in two new stalls. "Damn it," he said aloud. "Plan's the work of a genius. We can't fail and no one'll get hurt. The part about church is a stroke of brilliance. It's guaranteed to raise the hackles on Harris's head. I wish I'd thought of it."

Hearing Loco and the horses, Johnny went outside to close the gate between the pasture and barn yard. The Clydesdales followed him back into the barn. Talking in a quiet voice, Johnny moved between them, patting muzzles and checking hooves. Loco lay inside the door, alert, patient. "It's Sharona I have to think about," Johnny said, slapping a rump. "I've got to do right by her after all these years. I've been a real jerk. She's the one who's suffered."

Loco snapped to attention, ears up, warning growl in his throat.

"Company?" Johnny said.

In response the dog barked viciously. Teeth bared, he lunged toward the door ready to sink teeth into flesh.

"Call him off," a voice shouted.

"Heel, Loco! Heel!" Still growling, Loco backed to Johnny's side, eye on the figure, muscles taut. "Compton? Stay where you are. Don't come any closer. I can't guarantee the dog won't turn you into mincemeat. What's a scumbag like you doing here? Let me guess. You don't go anywhere that there isn't a buck to be made. You're here about my land."

"You'd do well to treat me right," said Compton. "We can work together. There's lots of money to be made, Johnny. You're sitting on a gold mine."

"I'd ask you in," Johnny said, stepping into the bright sunshine, both hands on Loco's collar. "But I don't want to pollute my barn and this dog's got a long memory. He hates your guts."

"Your mouth is going to get you into big trouble, Johnny Wallace."

"You threatening me?"

Compton looked at the blond giant of a man and muscular, snarling dog then backed off. "There's no need to," he said, trying not to make any sudden moves. "I've time to wait you out. You'll sell sooner or later. You've not stuck to anything in your life."

Johnny was ready, coached by Daniel. "I'll not sell to you," he said. "I've already promised the land to The Count Daniel Cudzinki."

Compton's jaw dropped. "You don't say. For how much?"

"I just did say, and the amount is none of your business. The man has bettered yuh at your own game. Just think. All this land will be in the Count's hands. What do you think he'll do with it? He's now got access for a south railway spur, to acres of gravel. He'll squeeze Harris's scrawny little neck just like I'd wring a chicken's."

Johnny demonstrated with a big, dirty right hand, his left still holding the dog's collar. "Now get out of here, Compton. I've got work to do." Loco took the one-handed opportunity to lunge for Compton, pulling Johnny along with him. "Loco. Heel!"

Compton backed across the barnyard toward the gate and his car. "That dog's going to kill someone," he said. "You should've let it die."

"He's sure got a hate on for you," Johnny said. "Get outta here. Close the gate behind you. You're leaving just in time. I've got more company coming."

Constable Keough's beaten-up '39 Dodge pulled into the lane while Compton's '47 Buick pulled out. Johnny kept his hand on Loco's collar while Keough got out, stretched and looked around.

"Down, Loco. It's okay, boy. This one's not going to hurt us." Loco's nose picked up Keough's scent as soon as he'd stepped from the car. His low, measured growl was one of warning, not attack.

"Rein in the pooch," Keough said.

"He's reined." Johnny held Loco's collar until the dog stopped growling. "If he'd any intentions of attacking, your family jewels would be history by now."

"Ouch!" Keough said, looking around. "Nice place. Gave up my dad's farm and now I'm thinkin' I should've kept it."

"Yeah, well, I don't think Harris would swing for one," Johnny let go of Loco's collar. Dog and man walked toward Keough. "What brings you out here?"

"You were in the village early this morning, meeting at the China Inn."

"The Stamp Club held a meeting."

"Stamp Club, be damned. You're forming a union, aren't you?" Keough leaned against the barnyard fence. "That Count fellow has something to do with it too."

"He's the biggest stamp collector in the group because he's traveled so much."

"Look," Keough said. "I can't do anything about you organizing a union. But if you're not working for Harris, why're you getting involved?"

Johnny didn't answer. He looked over the pasture to the smokestack and water tower on the horizon, to the place his father died young.

Keough interrupted his thoughts. "I said I can't do anything about people organizing a union. That's a right in this country. I can step in if there's civil disobedience – trouble – a threat to the general public."

"Stamp Club members don't make trouble," Johnny said. "They're all church-going, Harris-kissing, God-fearing men – with the exception of me, of course."

"Johnny, will you never learn?" Keough slapped Johnny on the shoulder. Loco jumped and snarled. Keough removed his hand. "Touchy dog! You don't have a cup of coffee in that shell of a house, do you?"

"Good dog," Johnny said. "I've a big thermos of coffee and some of Theresa's apple cinnamon muffins. Come on. It's time for my break. Tell me about your dreams of owning a farm. Did you ever think of splitting away from Harris? You must hate bein' his toadie. Have yuh ever thought of being your own boss? You weren't always a policeman. You were a farm boy."

"I was in the military police. When I returned, I didn't want to go back to Dad's farm. I wanted to try something else."

Johnny put his arm around Keough's shoulder and led him toward the half-built house, a smile on his face. Loco followed at Johnny's heels.

When the men sat on the temporary wooden steps that led to the roughed-in front doorway, one-eyed Loco lay beside Johnny, close enough to touch. Loco's nose made up for what his eye couldn't see. The images and smell of the black-booted men who'd tried to kick the life out of him were imprinted in Loco's memory. The only person he'd allow near Johnny without hesitation was the old one who had no scent. Loco kept an honorable distance from the ancient who by his presence on earth demanded respect.

Knightswood - morning

Theresa walked away from her cluttered desk, reasoning that if she sought the sanctuary of the reading nook in the upper hall, she'd be able to sit quietly and think. But the nook held no solace because its windows overlooked the barn and Pense's Mountain. Theresa didn't need to be reminded of Pense when her heart was burdened with Magdalena. Theresa had read half the night, then forced herself to rest. Up again at five, she sat at the desk, wrestling with words on paper. Things didn't add up. Dates seemed off. People mentioned were nonexistent in the village she knew so well. Theresa had begun with the first diary, a journal with a series of jottings and some missing pages.

Theresa sighed. There was nothing to do but go back to the attic. She tied a kerchief around her head and pulled on a heavy sweater. Before she climbed the stairs, Theresa looked in Pense's room and was pleased to see the girl was sleeping. Much to Theresa's relief, Pense had come home from the camp last night.

An hour later, Theresa reappeared at the foot of the steps, papers in hand. "Who would have thought you'd be so crafty, Maggie. Really, under a floorboard was a bit extreme," Theresa muttered as she dusted herself off. After making tea and toast, Theresa retreated back to her room and went to work again, going patiently from letters to notebooks to scraps of paper.

After nine o'clock, Theresa left her bedroom and wandered aimlessly through the house, from floor to floor, room to room, article to article. She talked with quiet reserve as she walked, a habit she learned from Magdalena who always spoke to the house spirits when she was upset.

"My dear Magdalena, Knightswood was both your prison and your sanctuary. You lacked no amenities, yet you had nothing. You were mistress of your destiny, your own worst enemy."

Theresa stood in the middle of the parlor, addressing a portrait of Magdalena as a child that hung over the fireplace. "You shut yourself away in this home. You lost the man you loved here. You suffered here. I was your friend and compatriot yet I never really knew you. The side you showed to me must have been the person you wished to be, not the woman who lived inside your shell. My dear Magdalena, who is he? Who is *YLD* ? You've given me everything but his name. Why are you still keeping secrets? Why didn't you go with him?"

As if in answer, the door to the parlor slammed shut and sheet music rustled on the piano. "So that's the way of it, is it?" Theresa said. "You're being silly, Maggie. On the other hand there'd be people say I'm being stupid talking to a ghost." Theresa sat on the bench and began to play *Magdalena's Song*. "What is this all about, Maggie? Why is this music stuck in Pense's mind? Why does Daniel play it on the violin?"

Not expecting an answer, not getting another sign, Theresa left the parlor and banged around in the kitchen until she could no longer tolerate her own company. "Ghosts make difficult companions. I have to get out of here for a while." Theresa donned her coat and tied a scarf around her head. It took fifteen minutes to walk to the newspaper office. As the press was on the main floor, the building resounded with the noise of machinery. Its floor shook as the big press went through a production run. Everything reeked of ink, sweat and old building. When Theresa opened the front door, bells jingled and Jim Ball, the editor, came to the front counter.

"I'm here to look at your old papers," Theresa said, "anything prior to 1880."

With an ink-stained hand, Jim opened a wooden gate between the counter and press room.

"They're back here," he shouted above the noise. "This is certainly a popular place. Lillian Harris was in, and Granny Smith dropped by, too."

"Do tell," said Theresa, putting a scribbler and pencils on a reading table.

"The papers are bound and stored by year. Just dig around for what you want and I'll lift them down for you. They're very heavy."

When Jim came through again, he had two cups of coffee in his hand. Smelling of ink and cleaning fluid, he sat down next to Theresa. The press had stopped and the building ceased its constant shaking. "What exactly are you looking for?"

"Well, whatever it is, I haven't found it yet. What did Granny Smith ask for?"

"She puttered and muttered and concentrated on my file of photographs."

"And Lillian Harris?"

"She wanted to see the papers for 1900 and later. She got me up at seven this morning and left about fifteen minutes before you arrived. Look. I'm leaving for lunch. I can lock you in. You can let yourself out."

"If it's all right with you, I'd like to stay another hour or so."

"If you don't mind my saying so," said Jim,"you look tired."

Theresa was exhausted. She was drained of energy, her eyes sore from reading. "I've got a bit more to look up. Then I'll go home and rest."

"You know," Jim said, standing by the table, "Count Cudzinki spent hours in here. Is this all connected?"

"What was he looking for?"

"He was most interested in the papers for the 1870's and those for around 1900. He's a nice fellow. He didn't bother me and I didn't bother him too much. I think he hung out here for the free coffee and the view of Main Street from the window."

When Jim didn't return an hour later, Theresa let herself out. Her next stop was Granny Smith's cottage on Queen Street. She found Granny seated at her kitchen table, photographs spread out in front of her. Granny had a large magnifying glass in her hand.

"Darn it, I'll find him," she said. "My eyesight tain't so good, but I'll find him."

"Who're you looking for?"

"That Count fella. I know him from somewhere. When I was a girl, I worked for Harris's. Bought myself a camera with the money I earned. Took pictures all round the village and sold them for pocket money. If my photo had Harrises or Andersons in it, they usually bought it. Sold some to the newspaper. If I took that man's picture, it'll be in this pile. I kept the originals."

Granny insisted on making tea. While she puttered around the kitchen, Theresa thumbed through the stacks of photographs. She picked up a small, faded picture, frowned and reached for the magnifying glass. Peering intently, she finally called Granny over, "What do you think?"

Granny looked through the magnifying glass. "It's so faded," Granny said, "I can't make either out. I'd have to say no."

Feeling guilty, Teresa sneaked the photo into her purse. "Well, if you find anything, would you let me know right away?"

"That I will," Granny said, lowering herself into her chair with care. "I wish my mind wasn't so bad and my bones not so weak. I'm having difficulty remembering things these days."

Theresa smiled. "Do you want some tea? You left the pot on the stove."

"You see?" said Granny. "I'd forget my head if it wasn't attached to my body."

"I'll write down my telephone number and leave it on the bake cabinet. You call me before anyone else if you remember anything about the Count."

"I'd call sooner if I had a telephone," Granny Smith said. "Adamo will let me use his. Why the interest in him?"

"I like to know all about the people that are staying in my house."

Theresa ended her day at three o'clock, when she arrived back in her kitchen. She could hardly put one foot in front of the other.

Johnny was snacking at the table when Theresa came in. "Sit down, Theresa." Johnny jumped to his feet and held a chair for her. She looked awful.

"Where's Daniel?"

"Darned if I know." Johnny had a suspicion where the fellow was but he wasn't going to share it with Theresa.

"I'm too old to be playing detective. If you see him, tell him that I'm looking for him."

Johnny stopped eating. "Are you in a temper?" he asked.

"Let's just say that I'm disturbed and want to talk to him."

"Can I tell you something about him?" Johnny said. "Can I tell you what he did for me?"

"Go ahead," Theresa said, "then help me up the stairs."

"Are you feeling all right, Theresa?" Johnny's love and concern for his chosen mother overwhelmed him and he reached for one of her hands, then looked intently at her face. Theresa was his rock, his sheltered cove. He never thought of her as old and frail.

"I'm a silly fool to be troubling myself with Daniel and his problems or Magdalena and her past. I've my own life to live. And the way I'm burning the candle at both ends, I won't have much time left to enjoy it."

"Now you're talking like Daniel. He told me he had a feeling he wasn't long for this world. You don't believe in feelings like that, do you, Theresa?"

"No," Theresa said, patting Johnny's hand. "Interesting that Daniel feels he's on his way out. What date is this, Johnny?"

Johnny glanced at the calendar hanging by the clock. "October 4," he said. "It is Saturday, October 4."

The Camp - noon hour

Sharona had tossed and turned for hours then wakened with the feeling that a fragment of her past, something associated with childhood, was trying to float to the surface. She tried recalling bits of her youth with the Kumpania but nothing seemed relevant. She lay awake until daylight wondering what it was that had caused this illusive insight. Finally, Sharona got up, dressed and walked to the camp. Sitting by her parents' fire, Sharona realized the answer wasn't at the Kumpania.

Sharona watched as the smoke rose to canopy level, then angled south, down the valley on the freshening wind. She threw more logs on the camp fire, then pulled her hat lower on the back of her neck and buttoned her jacket. Above her, the wind taunted the maples and played around the oak. Leaves, answering the call, released their hold to join the colorful cascade for a wild ride to the ground. Winter's calling card, the north wind, had descended on the valley.

The familiar activities of the camp were comforting yet distressing – as always, pulling and pushing her desires. A few menfolk were off around the countryside collecting pots, rags and anything else they could find to their liking. Others were horse trading. Zizou had a steady line of women waiting their turn at her table. Several women stirred pots of stew for a communal meal. The few young mothers in camp looked like old women as they tended the fires.

This was a scene that Sharona remembered well. It was such a setting that she abandoned fourteen years before. As Zizou said, life with the Kumpania is bred in the spirit, leaving the *lungo drom* does not lie easy on the heart. With the arrival of each Kumpania Sharona felt the tug of her heart which ached to embrace her old life once again. Like all Gypsies who turn their back on the vagabond way, she yearned for it when she was visually reminded of it. But, to join would bring many regrets. Twice a year, Sharona agonized whether she should stay or go. Sharona knew that part of her restlessness stemmed from the lack of the close ties of the familia, that overwhelming sense of tribal community that replaced both education and religion. It was a Gypsy-hood, not well understood by outsiders. This time her decision would be difficult because her Gypsy blood, pumped by Palumb Furtuna's music, coursed strong through her veins.

"The music of decision," Zizou said of his haunting melodies. "Palumb Furtuna's music touches the heart. And it is the heart which must decide the path the body takes. The soul follows whatever decision the heart makes."

Sharona had put down comfortable roots in Millbrook. She was sensible enough to know that if she left Theresa, another yearning would begin to gnaw at her, an urge to return to Knightswood. And there was Pense and Johnny to consider. As Zizou had explained, she was torn between two worlds, that of the known past and that of the uncertain future.

The Kumpania would leave soon, Sharona thought, looking at the sky. Her people would break camp and spread to the four winds for the winter. Whatever she decided, Theresa would understand. She was a wise woman and the one person who would understand her decision, be it to stay or to go. Sharona looked toward the oak where Pense sat looking over Knightswood. "Pense, baxtalo ghel," Sharone said. "We must make the right decision. . . ."

Ever since Palumb Furtuna had escorted her down her mountain, Pense had spent as many daytime hours as she could under the oak. With her back against the tree, she listened to a squirrel's chatter, and watched the undulating masses of birds winging their way south above the river valley. Winter would soon lay a mantle of white on her mountain. Nature's autumn music would be silenced. With winter came the confining walls of school.

Pense was now obsessed by Magdalena. She had wakened during the night, found the photo albums and sat at the dining room table by the marriage board studying pictures of the woman. Pense's mind was now a prison for the song. There was one subtle change. She no longer wished to be free of the song or of thoughts of the *Lady of Knightswood.* She was, as Zizou said, 'comfortable in another's skin.' Pense's gaze fell on her mother seated by the fire. Why was it that when her mother visited camp, she looked like a different person?

"You're all so ragged-looking," Pense said to Zizou.

"Beggars everyone thinks. No need comes to mend or stitch." Zizou answered. "No use for needles and thread, means rags to look the part. Beggars don't hand in tuxedos."

Zizou had a point, Pense thought. But there was pride in appearance and cleanliness. There was beauty in the seasons, too.

Yet Zizou hadn't recognized autumn as beauty, only as the beginning of their second season, winter. Summer was when they traveled, and winter was when they settled to work, Zizou said. She too had danced in the rain on the eve of September 30, hoping for a chance to see one hundred winters.

When Pense noticed her mother and grandmother heading for the meadow, bucket in hand, she smiled. Not to repeat the past few days when the cow 'went dry', Pense had milked Betsy early so Theresa would have milk for the baking and the table.

When Pense asked her grandmother what decision they had come to about her joining the Kumpania, she had been sent to Tamas. The Elder had said that freedom brings a high price.

"Are you willing to pay the price of happiness and security for the price of uncertainty?" Tamas had asked. "Are you willing to fight for a life that you now enjoy? Are you ready to accept the responsibility of new relationships when you are now surrounded by loving family?"

"Am I?" Pense talked to the wind. Her question went unanswered.

Tamas was seated by his fire, too old to travel around the countryside looking for rags, too tired to sell horses. He alternately sucked on the pipe in his hand and the wine bottle by his side. Tamas read the wind like a book. He wasn't looking forward to this winter. In the past, he'd cut wood on the Bruce for a living and, surrounded by books, survived in a tarpaper shack. By doing so he remained independent of his mother. There were family members to care for her in her meager city apartment. Tamas was of two temperaments – a loner in winter when he read and wrote; a leader in the summer when he wisely governed his tribe and freely gave advice. Until this year, it was the life he chose. His was a life that was getting increasingly more difficult to lead. Years in the bush took their toll on his health. Yet, he had no skills that could make enough money to spend winters in a warm boarding house.

Tamas had, at the request of Zizou, spread word that Palumb Furtuna had returned. Tamas's mind told him it was an impossibility, yet when he heard the music, Tamas's heart told him it had to be true. If Palumb Furtuna was an impostor, he was a good one.

Tamas sucked on the bottle, then let the sweet wine lie on his tongue. Religion lay on Tamas like oil did on water. It didn't mix with his Roma ways but he kept an open mind. If he believed that no one could beat the Divine plan laid out by God himself, Daniel had to be an impostor. If on the other hand, this flesh-and-blood man was indeed the ancient one, Palumb Furtuna returned from the dead, a much higher being had to exist who had control over souls. If he held to the belief that mortal man could return, it meant he'd have to return to his books during the winter, to examine and to expand on other beliefs.

Daniel Cudzinki made the right moves, spoke the right language, said the right things and played the violin magnificently. His people accepted the man for what he was. They pinched and poked then whispered among themselves. The attention given Dove Storm amounted to hero worship.

Palumb Furtuna requested they tell no one his secret. "It is," he said, "My story to tell." His wishes were respected, as were his latest requests, odd that they were. One sent the camp's women stealthily through the village to check clotheslines. And every day Niki made a run to the train station to pick up sealed cardboard boxes.

Every year Tamas's one hope was that when the Kumpania left the village, they'd receive an invitation to return. He had no doubts that Theresa Inachio would withdraw her support if his tribe overstepped the boundaries of common sense and decency. Theresa was tolerant but tough. Tamas had admired her for years. He and she were the same age. He should have made his move thirty years ago and told her how he felt about her.

With the arrival of both Dove Storm and the north wind came the realization that Tamas would never be able to enjoy Theresa's library, her good food and fine company. Tamas knew that mistakes must not be repeated. Palumb Furtuna, according to Zizou, had made the first mistake. It was not, from his example, a mistake that Tamas wanted to repeat. He glanced toward his mother's wagon. The frail one was seated at her table, gathering her cards. His grandson Niki hovered close by, always ready to assist the elderly seer.

Zizou glanced up and realized there was no one in line. She gathered the cards into their red cloth, tucked them in the inner pocket and turned her back to the table. Ever vigilant, Niki stood by her wagon. Leaning on his arm, Zizou laboriously climbed up into the box. From her high vantage point Zizou turned, looked over the camp and saw all – Tamas the thinker, Sharona of the decision, Magdalena Pense at the oak tree.

Down in the meadow Zizou saw Lillian leaving the camp. If that woman had listened, Zizou thought, she wouldn't have committed the ultimate mistake with Sebastian Temple Kropolus. Now she must live with the consequences. History was repeating itself. When the woman asked again where her future lay she was told with a child, and far away.

Zizou shrugged. She didn't really know now what was rhetoric and what was reality, what was fantasy and what was fact, what the cards truly told her and what she told the *gadje*. Some people never heard the truth. They couldn't handle it.

Zizou lived in the future so much she longed for the past. She had lived to see Palumb Furtuna return. With his return the future now became the present. Dove Storm was flesh and blood alive. The past was now also the present. The cycle was complete. Zizou rubbed her eyes. "Go find a pencil and paper," she said to Niki. "I'm going to lie down. Tell Alana to come sit with me. Bring the paper then go find some man-things to do. Keep warm. The north wind blows no good. *Mamioro* nips at its heels."

In answer the wind blew around the wagon, whipping dust into her eyes, swirling heavy skirts around her swollen ankles.

The Barber Shop - afternoon

Daniel studied the angry, defiant faces on the men seated around the table in the smoky room.

"Really gentlemen, you must do better than this." Daniel drew a pile of bills toward his end of the table."There must be someone who can really play poker? Shall we say here, tomorrow morning?"

"Monday morning," someone growled. "Tomorrow's Sunday."

"Right. I forgot there's no gambling on Sunday. Well, if you want a game tomorrow, leave word at the China Inn. Sunday's my lucky day."

Daniel pocketed his winnings, rose and backed to the curtained door. He learned a long time ago never to turn his back on an angry table.

"Until Monday, then," Daniel said, tipping his hat.

The players waited until they heard the front door close then erupted into a barrage of insults and swearing.

"He's cheating," one said.

"I don't think so," said another. "He's a city card-shark. We're too stupid for him because we don't take chances."

"Well, I'm out," said the third. "I can't afford him."

"There's one that will take him on," Blake said, stepping from a dark corner.

"Who?"

"It's none of your business."

Knightswood - evening

Sharona came home to a dark house. She turned on lights as she hurried through the first floor and climbed the stairs to the second. It was so unlike Theresa to be away at supper time. Where was she? Sharona opened Theresa's bedroom door and glanced in. Theresa lay asleep on her side, fully clothed. Sharona tiptoed in and drew a blanket over the tiny figure, checking first for a pulse. Lately she had the morbid thought she'd find Theresa dead in bed. Sharona shivered, touched a wrinkled cheek and left the darkened room.

Hurrying back downstairs, Sharona shook up the coals then added wood to the fire. She sliced potatoes into one frying pan and onions into another, then floured a plate of raw liver. A jar of peaches would do for dessert.

Sharona didn't have long to wait. Johnny burst in the back door, rushed across the kitchen and hugged her.

"What's this all about?" Sharona asked.

"Just thought you needed a hug," Johnny said. "Well, maybe I needed a hug. Is there anything I can do for yuh? Daniel won't be in for supper. Pense is at the camp with her grandparents. So it's just you and me. Exciting, huh?"

"Stop groping," Sharona said, hitting Johnny's wandering right hand. "Set the table. There's only two of us. Theresa's sleeping."

Johnny set the table and opened the jar of fruit while Sharona finished cooking the liver.

"Maybe I should start the furnace after supper," Johnny said. "Now the north wind's arrived, the house'll get cold and we gotta keep Theresa warm. She was bushed today, poor soul." Johnny tipped the peaches into a bowl.

"I'm not going to wake her for supper." Sharona dished potatoes, liver and onions onto two plates. "She needs the sleep. Ouch! Stop that."

Johnny had reached around to pinch Sharona's backside. "Just wanted you to know I was thinkin' about yuh."

"Sit down and eat your supper before it gets cold," Sharona said, amused by his antics.

Johnny did as he was told. "I've brought the motorbike into the barn. The Clydesdales are there too," Johnny said, cutting his liver. "Loco has to stay on the porch. I'm going to be around the house for a couple of days."

"In your mood, that should be interesting for both of us," Sharona said. "Who's checking the farm?"

"Keough says he'll swing by and check the new horses for a couple of mornings."

"Keough?" Sharona asked, giving Johnny a curious look.

"He wants a farm so I'm giving him the opportunity to do a little farming. Got any more of that shoe-leather liver?"

Sharona passed a piece off her plate. "Isn't the farm a bit out of Keough's way?"

"Sure it is. But Keough says he gets up early and Harris is away at the moment."

"How much did this cost you?" Sharona said.

"Nothing. Honest. He came out to the farm this morning and we had a little chat."

"I saw you at the camp," Sharona said.

"I was there to get Tamas. He's more than seventy, you know. Intelligent fella. Took him out to the farm. I wanted him to drive the Clydesdales in while I rode the motorbike.

"The barn'll be full tonight," Sharona said. "I told Zizou that she could sleep there if she got cold in her wagon. She said that Daniel has been sleeping in the barn and that she would stay in her wagon. If that's true, why isn't Daniel sleeping in the house? He's paid his room and board for a week." Sharona got up to clear the table.

"Don't ask me," Johnny said, reaching around her waist.

"And," Sharona said, waving her fork at Johnny, "I hear that the camp men are meeting in the barn tonight. Father told me that much."

"You don't say." Johnny acted surprised.

"Johnny Wallace! Don't lie to me." Sharona's eyes flashed. "What's going on?"

"All right. All right. They're having a meeting and it doesn't concern you – but I do."

"But it does include you."

"Yeah," Johnny said, winking at Sharona then doing a Charlie Chaplin imitation with his eyebrows. "You feel like a little hoochie-coochie tonight?"

"Johnny!"

"I'm asking you to go to bed with me," Johnny said. "Maybe I should have brought flowers and candy, wooed yuh a little?"

"Maybe you'd better slow down, think about the last time we did that."

An awkward silence fell over the kitchen and when they spoke again, it was together.

"You go first," Johnny said.

"This is all a little sudden," Sharona said. "You've been home for two years, but you hardly notice I'm in the house most of the time. Now you can't keep your hands off. You've not so much as said to my face that you love me, and now you're asking me to climb into bed with you."

"Aw, Sharona. I just thought it was about time we consummated this live-in relationship everyone figures we're having. I wrote *I love you.* I wrote it in every letter I sent during the war," Johnny said. "And I meant it."

"Writing is one thing. Saying is another. Showing is something else. What are you aiming for, Johnny?"

"I love you, God damn it!" Johnny raised his voice. "I love you. Do you hear me? *I love you.*" His arms found their way around her for the first time in years. He had forgotten the softness of her, the heady fragrance of her hair.

"I hear you, Johnny." She gazed into his eyes, questioning.

"Now, tell me that you love me."

"I've loved you a long time, Johnny. You just haven't noticed."

Johnny kissed her, hard on the lips. He whispered hoarsely, "I've been doin' a lot of talkin'. I may as well get down to the point. I've done some really stupid things. I've ignored you. I've not given you one reason to love me." Johnny turned from Sharona to pace in front of the sink.

"I can't argue those points," Sharona said. To avoid Johnny's pacing she sat at the table again. "There's one thing for sure, Johnny Wallace. You never do things halfway."

"Sharona?" Johnny was now practically dancing around the table. "Sharona?"

"Stand still, Johnny."

"Listen to me. Hear me out. I wasn't shirkin' my duty by not marrying yuh. I didn't wanna tie you down. You missed the Kumpania and I figured if we tied the knot you'd not be happy. You'd feel trapped and you'd resent me for reining yuh in. You turned me down once. That's hard on the ego, yuh know. And then I went off to war. That solved a coupla problems but caused a couple more."

"All I needed was for you to settle down, say that you loved me, and mean it. I didn't want to tie you down either. There's only one Johnny Wallace and you're not easy to corner. No, wait a minute," Sharona said, hands up to halt Johnny's pacing. "Look at me. There's blame on both sides. I'm not the easiest person to live with. I'm moody and expect too much from relationships. They can't all be as unconditional as Theresa's"

"Sharona?" Three times round the table and Johnny slipped down on one knee in front of her. Reaching for her hands, he said, "I love you. Despite all my faults, marry me." He fumbled in a pocket and withdrew a small box that he pressed into Sharona's right hand. "It was my mother's. Be my wife, Sharona, please. I should'a done this a long time ago."

Sharona stared blankly at the ring in the box then at Johnny. This was the one thing she wanted Johnny to ask but the last thing she wanted to hear tonight.

"Johnny, Johnny, Johnny! Why now?"she cried, before running from the room.

Bewildered, Johnny heard a door slam upstairs."What did I do wrong now?" He sat dumbly, then climbed the stairs and stopped at Theresa's door. He listened before opening it. Stepping into the room, Johnny hurried across to the bed and stood for a moment before touching his fingers to a thin-veined wrist.

"You okay, my girl?"

Theresa, the cats curled against her side, stirred but didn't waken. One cat acknowledged his presence by touching his hand gently with an outstretched paw.

Johnny slipped from the room and went down the hall to Sharona's door. He had his hand up to knock when he heard the sobbing. Johnny listened for several minutes then decided against interrupting. He went downstairs to the kitchen and wrote a note to Pense, *'Check Grandma Inachio before you go to bed, and don't disturb your mother.'* Finding a grocery bag and a thumb tack Johnny wrote another note and hurried upstairs to tack it on Sharona's door.

'I love you,' the note read. *'Marry me, please.'* Hat in hand, Johnny retreated to the barn with Loco.

Pense arrived fifteen minutes later. She stood in the kitchen with a milk pitcher in hand. The house had never been so quiet. Pense read the note and made hot cocoa, Teresa's favorite. If she's been asleep, Pense reasoned, her grandmother would want something to eat and drink.

Taking the tray of cocoa and cookies, Pense climbed the stairs and tapped on Theresa's door. Getting no response, she opened the door and heard the cats hit the floor. They scurried out as she went in.

"Grandmother?" Pense put the tray on the dressing table and turned on a small bed lamp. Theresa lay on her side, one hand tucked under her pillow. Pense stood at the side of the bed and bent to kiss a weathered cheek. She stroked the wrinkled brow then the silver hair. "I've made hot chocolate," she whispered. Theresa's eyelids fluttered. She groaned.

Pense knelt by the side of the bed. The eyelids opened. Her mouth curled into a smile of recognition. A thin hand then reached to touch a cheek.

Her reward was Theresa saying, "My goodness, the sleep of the dead," as she blinked and tried to focus on Pense's face.

"You've wakened just in time to change into your nightie to go back to sleep. It's nine o'clock." Pense adjusted the pillows. "I made some cocoa. It might be cold by now, though."

Theresa wasn't yet a member of the living world. She focused on the windows, then the hands of a clock on her night table. "I've slept nearly six hours. Why didn't someone wake me?"

"I imagine they felt that you needed the sleep."

"Pense, what would I do without you?"

Pense smiled then noticed the cluttered desk. "Do you want

the drink?" When Theresa nodded, Pense gave her the cup then went to the desk. "What have you been doing?"

"Reading, playing detective. Look at the photo on top. What do you see?"

Turning the switch on the desk lamp, Pense found the photo, two in fact, one a larger copy of the other, both in terrible condition. A jolt of recognition coursed through Pense. Under the light she recognized the marriage board. Magdalena Anderson stood beside it with a man, who had a hand on her shoulder. Although the figure of the man was faded Pense knew immediately who it was.

"Who's the man? I can't even make him out under a magnifying glass," Theresa said.

Pense drew her fingers across the larger photo as though the action would remove the curtain of uncertainty. Shivers of recognition ran through her. "I can't . . . say," she murmured.

"That woman has to be Maggie in the 1870's."

"So very long ago." Pense touched the photo gently.

"The clothing dates the picture," Theresa said. "If you look at one of the other pictures of Maggie dated 1874, you'll see she's wearing the same dress. Go downstairs and see if the marriage board doesn't match too."

Pense left the room and was back a short time later, much subdued. Theresa was seated on the edge of her bed.

"It's the same piece of furniture with the exception that in the photo it appears complete. The rosette is in place but I can't make out the details." Pense rubbed the photo and felt a warm rush of love in her heart. She tried hard to mentally push aside the veil of grey that hid details of the crestboard. "Where did you get these pictures?"

"The smallest one had been tucked into a notebook I found in the attic. I'd rather not say where the other one came from."

"Can I keep the small one for a while?"

"Certainly. If you look through all the albums, you might recognize the man." When Pense didn't answer, Theresa said, "Would you make me a peanut butter sandwich? I'm starved. Where's everyone?"

"Dad's in the barn with Daniel and I think that mother's in her room."

"It's *Dad* now, is it?"

"He said that I should call him Dad from now on."

"My goodness," Theresa smiled. "Interesting things happen when one sleeps for a few hours during the day. Are you pleased with the change?"

"Yes," Pense said. "I'm happy. I'll go wake Mother and make a sandwich for both of you."

"Good girl. I'll be right down. What are Johnny and Daniel doing in the barn?"

"They're holding a meeting of some sort with the fellows from the camp. They made it plain that women were not allowed."

"Did that ever stop you?"

"No," Pense said. "But tonight Dad really meant it. There are guards on the door. We'd best stay inside. He said he's planning to be at home for a while. He brought Loco in from the farm."

Theresa laughed. "Plumb will give the cats a run for their money."

Sharona heard Theresa's door open and then steps in the hall but she didn't respond to the knocking at her door. She sat by the window in her dark room, fingering the delicate band of gold and rubies she had slipped onto her finger.

"Damn you, Johnny Wallace!" she said, "You've complicated my life again. Everything was so cut and dried, until tonight. The puzzle was nearly complete. I was going to walk out of your life."

Sharona was aware of light from the hall as her door was partially opened and what appeared to be a grocery bag dropped on the floor inside. Then she heard running footsteps down the hall and Pense calling excitedly to Theresa.

Chapter 11

The Village - October 5, 1947: morning

Tense was the only word that described the atmosphere around Theresa's breakfast table. When Johnny asked Sharona if she had an answer for him, she said *maybe*, to which he snapped, "There are a lot of *maybes* in this house these days." Theresa announced she wasn't going to church which was the first time she had missed Mass in years. Pense declared she was locking herself in the dining room and didn't want to be disturbed. Sharona stated she was taking the car for a run and if she got back in time, they'd have lunch. If not, they could all fend for themselves. Eventually everyone went their own way, relieved to be alone and away from the bickering.

Church bells pealed over the valley, mingling with the sounds of car engines on the highway and people arriving for church. It was cold enough that no one lingered long on the steps. They hurried to their respective pews, men with hats in hand, women with children in tow.

Reverend Sneed looked down on his expanded congregation and wondered what had brought them all out on this particular autumn Sunday. Charlie, Bill and Gord sat noticeably close to the front. At Christ Church, Father Thomas was surprised to see people who hadn't attended since Christmas, sitting in his pews. He scratched his head, adjusted his collar and looked with approval at George, Tom and Mike. These were brave lads who took their chances by being J.P. Harris employees and Catholics too.

Theresa, seated at the south window, noticed extraordinary activity in the camp. Men were covering stake trucks with tarps. Women scurried to and fro, from Zizou's wagon to Tamas's tent. People were packing things away as though preparing to break camp. There were no villagers around the camp that Theresa could see. When the trucks drove off, Theresa hurried from her room to the reading nook to watch their progress along the back lane. They stopped at her barn and backed up to the granary door on the far side of the building. What are they loading, Theresa wondered. It wasn't long before the trucks pulled away and drove toward the highway that led toward the village.

Sharona made her escape right after breakfast. She nosed the car along the North Valley Road, east of the village, eventually pulling into a lookout on a high, wooded hill. Sharona was desperate for privacy. Perhaps she would find it here, surrounded by autumn's beauty. The river valley spread below her, a patchwork of trees, fields and farms. Smoke rose from the chimneys. Cattle grazed meadows. Church bells rang up and down the valley.

Johnny sat in The China playing with his watch. His motorcycle was parked on the street in front of the restaurant where he could see it from the booth. At ten o'clock, when a man leapt onto the bike and roared away, Johnny jumped into action.

"My bike's been stolen," he shouted. "Call Keough. Someone stole my motorbike."

Down the street, Ed MacTavish was shouting his own lament. "I've been robbed," he shouted at the top of his lungs. "Someone broke into the garage last night and cleaned me out."

Constable Keough was shaken from his comfortable pew by Cook Kropolus, who whispered hoarsely in his ear. Keough in turn whispered to his wife, then ran out, leaving a string of curious worshipers to watch his retreating back. They were immediately brought back to full attention by the raised voice of Reverend Sneed, angry at being disturbed in the middle of his sermon.

By the time Keough reached the China Inn, he had reasoned that the robbery and stolen motorcycle were done by the same fellow. When Keough walked in the front door at The China, Daniel nodded to Johnny then left by the kitchen door and waved to Tamas who was parked in the back laneway.

Tamas drove quickly to The Factory where the covered stake

trucks were hidden behind a storage building. A word from Tamas and scores of people climbed out of the back of the trucks, all wearing bed sheets over their heads. They carried placards which denounced Harris for a variety of reasons – poor wages – no insurance – dangerous working conditions. Sixty-three agitators marched back and forth in front of the factory's main door, chanting, whistling and causing a general ruckus. The watchmen, skeleton boiler room and maintenance crews left their posts to stare in disbelief at the first protest they had ever seen in Millbrook.

Jim Ball, acting on the advice in an anonymous note, showed up with his camera, as did Tubby Propp, a reporter from one of the larger Toronto newspapers. He had received a note giving details of a strike in Millbrook and had driven three hours to get to the village. Any demonstration was news, but J.P. Harris, Ltd., was a large manufacturer and had never had a strike. When Ball and Propp cornered the agitator who appeared to be the head man, he said nothing but handed over unsigned, handwritten sheets of grievances.

"I called the Constable," one watchman said. "But his wife told me he was called out of church. There's been trouble on Main Street."

Harry, the second watchman, smiled. "Well, there's nothing to do then but listen. There's no one to stop them."

"I'll call the Ontario Provincial Police."

Harry stopped his companion with a hand on a shoulder. "I wouldn't for a little while. Give them their dues. Let them get it out of their system."

Suddenly the lights in the main entry went dead and there was silence from the plant.

"I'll be damned," Harry said. "The power's gone down."

On Main Street, Johnny followed Keough to Ed MacTavish's garage where it was obvious a window had been broken to gain entry to the building. Keough questioned Ed as Johnny poked around the building.

Back in the car, Keough headed for the Gypsy camp figuring that all problems stemmed from that particular group. He explained that Ed had come to the garage to get some tools to fix the Kropoluses' furnace when he noticed a window had been broken. Ed knew that there was more than one hundred dollars in cash left in the till, so he checked around. Sure enough the money was gone. Keough stopped the car at the edge of the meadow. "The camp's quiet," he said. "I don't see any motorbike from here. I don't see many other vehicles either."

"It's better if I look," Johnny said, jumping from the car. "You'll only get their backs up." Johnny was back in a few minutes. "Luck. One of the kids saw someone riding my bike on the River Road, going east."

"Well, let's drive out the road to see if we can spot it. If these two incidents are connected, the thief has got a good head start. Did I tell you there has been a rash of things stolen off clotheslines in the past few days?"

"Nope, yuh didn't," Johnny said, trying not to look at Keough.

From her high vantage point, Sharona noticed unusual activity in the valley. Someone was on the catwalk near the sluiceway gates at the head of the overflow channel. The gates were rising slowly. Water began to pour from the river into the channel. The higher the gates rose, the more water was diverted. When the gates were at their highest, water thundered through the narrow channel and over low-lying ground nearby.

Sharona couldn't believe what she was seeing. Now, a man was dismounting Johnny's motorcycle. He pulled it into dense bush by the river and walked away from it toward the catwalk. There was no doubt it was Johnny's bike because it had distinctive red and white markings on the fuel tank, but the man was small – clearly not Johnny.

Sharona got out of the car to take a closer look. Now, both men were on high ground, east of the overflow channel and getting into a beat-up 1933 Ford, a car that looked vaguely familiar. The car went east, away from the channel and the flooding. They had no sooner left than she saw Constable Keough's police car race along the road. Keough drove right past the bike, not seeing it in the thicket. The police car stopped at the area where water flooded the road.

Lillian was out for a walk when she noticed water rising in the overflow channel, turning the once dry Cascade into a waterfall. She watched in fascination as the Cascade grew from a trickle to a thirty-foot wide torrent of dirty water. As the Cascade grew, noise from the High Dam diminished until there was just a murmur from the big falls.

Back at The Factory, Ball and Propp, the Toronto reporter, snapped pictures.

"I've never seen anything like this!" exclaimed Ball. "If Harris was here, they'd all be fired."

"Is that so?" Propp said. "You telling me that they don't have the right to complain, off Factory property, on their day off?"

"Not bloody likely," Ball said. "They'd be out a job and kicked out of the village too. That's why they've hidden their faces with bed sheets. No one can recognize them when they're disguised."

"Sounds like a dictatorship to me."

"I suppose, in a sense, it is. I've got all the pictures I need. Paper's printed tonight. It'll hit the street at five tomorrow morning."

"Well, I'm outta here too," said Propp. "It's a long drive back to Toronto and I've got to make the deadline. My paper's printed tonight too. Where's the nearest pay phone?"

"Give me a ride to Main Street. I'll put the coffee pot on. You can place your call from my office. I'll fill you in on some village details."

Tamas, ever observant, saw Ball and his friend leave. He then noticed that Compton had pushed Harry aside and was running into the factory. Time to go, he thought. Compton's going to call for reinforcements. Tamas gave a sharp, high whistle that was picked up by others in the crowd, until it became an ear-piercing sound. As quickly as they had formed, the protestors filtered back to the hidden vehicles. When they climbed into the trucks, they left piles of sheets and protest signs behind.

By the time Keough and Johnny arrived back at the police station, located in the Constable's home, the village was buzzing with news of the protest and the flooded channel. Word spread as men streamed from church. Not knowing where else to go, everyone congregated at The Factory, filling the parking lot with cars, men, wives and children. When George found the pile of sheets and signs, the women began to dig for their stolen property, recognizing some by monogrammed corners. While Mrs. Keough told her husband about the protest and flooding, Johnny called The China Inn.

"You don't know anything about this, do you?" Keough said as he got behind the wheel of his car again.

"I was with you," Johnny said.

"That doesn't exactly answer my question."

"Why do you think I'm behind everything that goes wrong around here? Would you drop me off at The China?"

A few minutes later, Johnny joined Daniel and Niki in the booth, behind the hedge of plants. Not a word was said about the protest or flood. Mrs. K. poured coffee and winked.

"You're a good sport, Mrs. K." Johnny said.

"It might not be over yet," Daniel warned. "We're going to sit tight and see what develops next."

Keough drove quickly to the factory, nudging his car into the crowd to get to the front entrance. Strange, he thought. The Factory is ominously quiet and dark.

"Okay," he shouted. "Fess up! Who's responsible?"

"We were in church," a chorus of voices shouted back.

"Someone has to know," Keough roared. "Come clean, one of you!"

Charlie and Bill dumped some of the sheets at Keough's feet.

"What's this?"

"Cover-up. You'll never know who it was."

"All of you, go home. And don't get any more ideas about another protest. It won't happen. This'll probably blow over. You've had your day. I didn't see the protest. I won't make too damning a report if you leave now. Don't make matters worse by hanging around."

"Matters are worse," shouted someone. "The power's off. Water can't be fed to the boilers so The Factory's down. Looks good on Harris, doesn't it?"

That's why it's so quiet! Keough thought. The sluiceway was opened. That accounted for the flood upriver. Water has been diverted into the overflow, an action that shut the turbines down.

"Patsy," someone shouted.

"Yeah . . . Patsy . . . Patsy . . . Patsy!" The cry went up around the parking lot and men began pressing around Keough's car.

Keough, startled by the sheer mass of the crowd, backed off. He jumped into his car and backed with care out of the crowd while a few men beat on the hood. A farm was looking better by the hour. As Keough drove away, a cheer went through the crowd who had suddenly realized they did have a voice and it did count if they all stuck together.

Keough took the back streets down to the old mill complex. The building, normally shaking with the momentum of machinery, was still and quiet. He found Sebastian working around the turbines, sweat staining his shirt.

"What happened?" Keough asked.

"I don't know," Sebastian said. "The water began to drop and I had to get these babies shut down before there was serious damage done."

"You didn't see anyone near the sluiceway?"

"It's a mile upriver," Sebastian said, wiping his brow. "I'd have to have God's vision to see anything from here, wouldn't I?"

Keough took a few minutes to look around the complex. Everything seemed in order but the silence was ominous. Keough was leaning against his vehicle writing on a notepad when Sharona stopped her car and waved out the window.

"What's up?" Keough said, walking over to her car.

"Johnny's motorcycle's been stolen," she blurted out. "It's near Barr's Line on the River Road, in the bush by the bend in the river. Someone probably took it for a joyride, I guess Niki was waiting for him."

"Let me guess," Keough said. "I'll bet he is one of the Gypsies. He probably stole the one hundred dollars from the garage too. I know they're your friends, but you've got to draw the line at robbery."

Sharona realized her mistake as soon as she'd opened her mouth. She'd broken the Roma code. She knew how much Johnny's motorbike meant to him and had opted for *him* rather than *them.* Sharona had put an outsider before her tribe. She'd ratted on one of her own people.

"Miss Aventi, Sharona. Tell me about this Niki fellow?" Keough stood by the window, ready to take notes.

She didn't have to tell the entire truth, did she? Obviously the gates were opened for a reason. If Niki was involved, the Gypsy camp was involved. If the camp was involved then Daniel was involved. From Daniel the line led to Johnny.

"Sharona, look, I'm dealing with four separate issues. There's been a disturbance at the factory. The machinery's down because water's been diverted into the overflow channel. Ed MacTavish's garage was robbed and Johnny's bike was stolen. If you can help me, I'd appreciate it."

That's what this is all about, Sharona thought. Damn Johnny and Daniel. The bike was meant to be stolen, the channel was meant to be flooded. Everything had been planned except the fact she'd seen them. "Maybe it wasn't Niki's car that was waiting."

"And what was the make of the car?"

"It appeared to be a Ford, from the 1930's." How stupid had she been? How stupid could she be? How *gadje* had she really become?

"You're a decent, honest woman," Keough said. "Go home now. I won't tell where I got the information. The guy who pulled the robbery is probably miles away by now with his accomplice, the person who drove the car."

Was Johnny in the car, Sharona wondered. It couldn't be Daniel because he doesn't know how to drive.

Keough backtracked and found Johnny at the China Inn, seated in the booth with the Count and another young man.

"I know where your bike is, Johnny. Let's go get it."

"You do?" Johnny said, a little surprised at the speed with which Keough had found it.

"Yep, and I'm looking for Niki of the Gypsies. I'm going to put a bulletin out on him."

"Niki," said Daniel. "It couldn't have been Niki. He's right here." He pointed at the young man seated beside him. "He's been here all morning. Cook Kropolus can vouch for that. Mr. K. had him changing light bulbs. And I bought him breakfast. We have a lot in common, you know."

"You? Niki? A lot in common?" Keough looked around the restaurant. Sure enough, all the lights were clean and working properly.

The young man put out his hand for the Constable to shake. "I'm Niki," he said.

"Where's your car?"

"It's parked on the street."

"Let's go take a look at it."

Niki slid from the booth. The two were gone for several minutes.

"I'll be damned," said Keough when they returned. "It appears that someone has stolen this fellow's car."

"You sure have your hands full today," Johnny said.

Keough agreed then said, "You come with me, Niki, and we'll see if your car's parked close-by. If we can't find it, I'll do a report. By the way, has anyone seen Jim Ball? He's the only one that's got a printing press. I'd like to know what he has to say about all the signs used in the demonstration."

When Sharona parked the car next to the carriage house,

she heard Loco in the barn and went to quiet him. Plumb Loco was howling his own protest at being tied up. Sharona was surprised to find Niki's 1933 Ford parked in the granary, the engine still warm from a run, its back seat full of cardboard signs. "That Johnny Wallace has got a lot of explaining to do," Sharona said, rubbing Loco's ears.

J.P. Harris heard about the protest and flood on the car radio just outside Windsor city limits. He'd been dozing when he thought he heard his name mentioned. Harris ordered Blake to turn the radio up, then to pull off the road. It was a phoned-in news item, the announcer said, confirmed by the local police force, that there has been a riot at the factory of J.P. Harris, Ltd., in Millbrook over better working conditions and wages. Constable Edwin Keough said that more than sixty people had taken part and that they were an ugly group. Indeed they threatened him.

"To add to Mr. Harris's woes," the announcer said. "Sluiceway gates have been opened which caused the loss of power to the factory. Some local flooding has occurred but was held to a minimum by an overflow channel that was built specifically to divert water around a dam owned by the Harris family. The incident has effectively shut down J.P. Harris, Ltd."

Knightswood - afternoon

Theresa, seated at a card table next to a hot air register in the parlor, rubbed her eyes then shook her head in disbelief. Despite the furnace's warmth, she was chilled to the bone, more from what she had learned than from the cold. Letters, photographs and cards were spread on the table in front of her. Pense sat opposite, open photo albums on the floor beside her.

"You always said it was possible, Grandmother. You said that the past couldn't just vanish, that it left something of itself in the present. You said you believed the house was occupied by more than us. You said Knightswood was comfortable because we were living with the ghosts of the people who loved it as much as us."

"I know I said that. But I don't think we can stretch it to such an extreme. What you're saying goes against everything we were taught in the Catholic Church."

"It's him in the picture," Pense said.

"It can't be. It's a look-alike? Is it his father?"

"It's him!" Pense said passionately.

"Pense," Theresa pleaded. "If it is, do you know what you're telling me?"

"Yes."

"Once again. How did you meet him? When?"

Pense sighed. She'd been over this so many times. She'd spent the morning in the dining room at the marriage board reconstructing the scenario over and over again in her mind.

"I was upstairs in the barn working on the marriage board. I was rubbing oil in with one hand. The penny was in the other. I sensed I wasn't alone. I turned. Daniel was standing behind me. I don't know where he came from. He just stood with his hands out and stared at me." Pense extended her hands to show how Daniel stood. "I stared back at him and didn't say a word. He didn't speak either. As he moved toward me I felt heat, like he was warming me with his body. His hands touched mine. Then he turned and walked away. He disappeared down the stairs."

"You mean he vanished?"

"I mean he walked away. But when I went to look for him, he'd vanished. He wasn't on the lower level. Loco and me checked. Strange thing is that Loco didn't smell Daniel. And the dog backed off whimpering when he finally saw him."

"When was this?" Theresa asked.

"It was in April of this year."

"Perhaps he'd been sleeping in the barn and you disturbed him. You said he wore a uniform. You know that there are a lot of displaced, mixed-up veterans on the road these days. And they've been sleeping in the barn on their way through the area."

"Grandmother," Pense said. "Daniel's uniform was odd looking. It was dirty and had a hole with a dark stain . . . here." Pense put her hand up to her left breast. Her voice became a whisper. "It looked like Daniel had been shot or stabbed and had bled a lot."

"The barn was dark."

"It wasn't that dark. I know what I saw, Grandmother."

"When did you see him again?"

"When he was standing in your kitchen. The day he arrived at Knightswood."

Theresa closed her eyes. Her fingers drummed the table, giving away her agitation.

"Your mother found strange initials in Daniel's shirts. He

could be a vagabond soldier who stole a wardrobe off a few clotheslines. He could have heard part of our story from people like Johnny whom he helped in the desert." Theresa recounted Johnny's story of the desert rescue.

"Maybe," Pense said softly. "Maybe he wasn't a soldier. Maybe he was the dove. He is Dove Storm. What if he wasn't in the desert? Maybe Dad dreamed the story up."

"It does seem a little far-fetched in view of the fact Daniel is so old," Theresa said.

"In April the dove began to hang around, to fly at the attic window and to come to me."

"That's true," Theresa said. "It came from nowhere, didn't it?"

"There's something else too," Pense said, "and you must accept what I'm going to tell you. I believe that I'm her . . . that I'm Magdalena Anderson."

"No. No!" Theresa looked sharply at Pense. "No. You've too active a mind, Pense. You're impressionable and overreacting to a charming stranger."

"Please listen to me," Pense pleaded, sitting on a footstool by Theresa. "I've been doing the strangest things since April. I've always thought and acted differently but these are unusual things. You knew Magdalena and her ways. I love sitting on the barn roof. Did she?"

"Yes," Theresa said. "She went to the roof to watch for the Kumpania. When she got too old to climb up on the roof, she stood in the back attic window or on her mountain."

"I love this house but have had the feeling lately that I have to escape from it."

"She loved it too, until *YLD* left her. Then she became a recluse and viewed it as her prison. When I became her companion, she settled down a bit. After Kenneth arrived, she was the happiest woman on earth, opened the home to everyone, held parties. When he left she refused to leave the house, even to shop, for fear he'd come back and not find her here."

"She looked like me. Grandma, look at my forehead, around my eyes and mouth, my build."

"There's a resemblance."

"I see a great deal of resemblance," Pense said. "And there's the dove. She loved birds."

"She had a pet dove when she was a young woman. It was

given to her by *YLD*." Theresa acknowledged the truth with a growing sense of apprehension.

"You see, Grandmother. There are big similarities."

"Pense, she loved the man. He was Roma," Theresa said. "She was to marry him. He left and never came back. She waited for him. Maggie loved *YLD* enough to never marry another and there was at least one other suitor."

"I love him too," Pense said.

"Pense!" Theresa exclaimed. "I'll have no more of that sort of talk. There's no way Daniel is the man who jilted Magdalena."

"Most of the time it's not passion as a woman would love," Pense said. "But when Daniel touches me, I change. I know that I'm Magdalena Anderson and he's my lover."

"Daniel touches you?"

"Gently. On the hand – the face – the shoulder."

"Pense, this has to stop."

"It won't if he's *YLD* and I'm Magdalena. I think he's come back to finish what he started, to end what he left," Pense said.

Theresa rose and moved around the parlor, from fireplace to piano – to her favorite painting. What am I to do, she thought? Pense is fixated by the man.

"And there's the song," Pense said. "What about the song?"

"Maggie never dwelt on the song," Theresa said. "I never heard her play it."

"But she wrote the music. How do I know the music for the song if I've never heard it before? How can Daniel play it on the violin?" Pense said.

Theresa couldn't answer. She walked to and fro, deep in thought, a hand to her forehead. When she spoke again, it was to try to impress Pense with the gravity of the situation. "You must stay away from Daniel. He poses a danger to you. What if he's an impostor and up to no good?"

"Daniel would never harm me."

Theresa paused by the window overlooking the front lawn and driveway. Good Lord, she thought. I was stupid enough to let him board here. I let him see my personal papers. He knows a lot about us, about the house, about the property, about Pense. He's talking to Lillian Harris whose father collects land like we do pennies.

"Adamo tells me he heard that Daniel has bought my property and Johnny's too." Theresa turned to look at Pense.

"Grandmother, you can't believe Franco Adamo," Pense said. "If Daniel is Magdalena's lover, he's not here to harm anyone. Didn't he help Dad? Has he harassed me? He hasn't bought property. He doesn't need land. Adamo's lying or spreading village gossip."

"Well, Daniel hasn't harmed you yet," Theresa said. "And I'm going to make sure he doesn't get the chance. I'll not have him in the house."

"Grandmother. Daniel's a ghost. *YLD* died. He was shot to death. He couldn't be alive now."

"How do you know *YLD* was shot to death? We don't know what happened to the man."

"The uniform, the hole, the stain," Pense said. "And can we be positive that ghosts can't take a flesh and blood human form? I believe they can because I truly believe that Daniel is *YLD*."

Theresa put her arms around Pense, desperate to give her reassurances that all would be okay. "Daniel's not the man," she said, stroking Pense's dark hair. "We have nothing to connect Daniel to *YLD*."

"Yes, we do," Pense said. "*YLD* means *'Your Lover, Danny.'*"

A shiver went through Theresa. Out of the mouths of babes came truth. "Danny?

"Danny," Pense said. "Magdalena called him Danny."

"I think it's time you knew more about Maggie. What do you really know about her?" Theresa led Pense to the chesterfield and sat her down.

"Precious little and yet a great deal," Pense said. "I know that her dad was a founding father and owned a lot of property in the village. There was an unwritten partnership between Harris and him. Both came as young men from the British Isles. Harris had a son, and Anderson had a daughter. Magdalena was born in1846."

"That's right," Theresa said. "After an argument with Harris, Joseph Anderson sold most of his village property. He retreated to Knightswood and invested his money elsewhere. I believe that the argument was about the children. Harris wanted Maggie to marry his son, so that they could keep their money in a tight family compact."

Pense took up the story. "She refused because she didn't love Harris's son. She had only one man in mind for marriage, a man she'd seen with the Kumpania."

"He arrived each spring and autumn with the Kumpania,"

Theresa said. "She was twenty-seven and *YLD* was thirty years old when they realized there was a strong bond between them. I gather from the letters that he eventually decided to leave the Kumpania, to make a life for himself in the village."

"That's when they became engaged and Daniel built the marriage board," Pense said. "That was important to Magdalena. When I started to clean up the marriage board, that's when I began to feel different, like I was Magdalena."

"We don't know that they were formally engaged," Theresa said. "*YLD* mentioned a gold locket in his letters, but didn't say anything about a ring."

"Daniel built the marriage board because they were going to wed," Pense said."The board is the engagement ring. It's proof they were planning to marry."

"Magdalena was quite ill for a while. She took to her bed shortly after *YLD* vanished from her life."

"He loved her. He would have stayed but he had to go," Pense said. "He was forced to leave."

Theresa pushed stray hair off her face. "They kept in touch. Maggie devised the most elaborate codes so that they could write. One of the notebooks is nothing but codes. When the codes are used to decipher the letters, *YLD* is the writer of all of them. He wrote beautiful letters, gave dates, details of travels, little bits of other information."

"Daniel was always good about writing," Pense said.

"The letters are fascinating. He mentions gifts that she gave him including a fishing pole and tackle box, for instance."

"The same ones that I gave Daniel to use," Pense said. "He recognized them. The initials *YLD* are carved into the grip on the pole."

My Lord, Theresa thought. She reached for Pense's hand then continued, "They used codes so her parents wouldn't know he wrote, which leads me to believe her parents didn't approve the match. Magdalena told me that she received letters from pen pals. The letters stopped abruptly in 1901. I know, even I was party to the ruse, delivering letters to her."

"They used codes because Daniel didn't want anyone but Magdalena to know he was alive or where he was," Pense said. "Magdalena's father hated him. Tell me again when the last letter was written."

"The last letter was dated Fort Itala, September 4, 1901."

"Then Danny died in South Africa in 1901," Pense said. "But that's where pieces of the puzzle don't fit. South Africa is nowhere near where Dad was during the war. And there's no physical connection between 1901 and the 1940's. It has to be a spiritual bond that holds everything together."

"Daniel was reading one of my library books on the Boer War," Theresa said. "The book was one that Magdalena purchased. She must have known that he signed up for the Boer War. He was reading old newspapers too. Maybe he was reading about the war, looking for his name."

"Daniel knows when he died," Pense said. "He was looking for other information. Did the book have pictures?"

"Yes. Go get it. It's lying open, on the desk in the library."

Pense soon returned with the book. While leafing through the pages, she stopped to read several times. A page with several illustrations brought her up short. "This is all the proof we need. Daniel's uniform looked just like this and there was a battle at Fort Itala."

"No. No!" Theresa said. "It's ludicrous that we'd entertain these ridiculous ideas. I refuse to believe that Daniel is *YLD* and that he was killed in South Africa in 1901. Let's try down-to- earth reasoning."

"We must believe Daniel is *YLD*," Pense said. "What other logical explanation do you have?"

"Pense! When Daniel comes back today, I'll expose him to you for what he really is, an impostor."

"If he comes back," Pense said, grasping Theresa's cold hand. "He might not return to Knightswood."

The Factory - afternoon

Harris's office was as sparse as the man. Furnishings consisted of one desk, four chairs, two wilted plants and a bookcase. Three curtainless windows faced the street. Harris sat at his desk in the dark, cold room. Compton stood on one side, Blake on the other. Constable Keough stood, ramrod straight, hat in hand on the other side of the desk.

Three quarters of an hour before, Harris had stormed through the back door, pushed a watchman aside and slammed into his office, shouting for Keough. Blake found the Constable at the China Inn and strong-armed him into the car.

Word spread quickly that Harris was back. A curious crowd gathered on the street below his windows. Proud of their newfound voices, they had booed both Keough and Blake as the two pushed their way to the main door.

"I want to know who the protesters were. And I want to know now!" Harris said through clenched teeth.

"I don't know who they were," Keough said. "All the members of the Stamp Club were in church. I checked with the preachers. Anyone suspect was in church. Johnny Wallace was with me. We were looking for his stolen motorbike, and dealing with a robbery."

"They had to leave some identification. Someone had to see them arrive."

"No one saw them come or go. They did leave a pile of bed sheets and signs. The signs have been lined up along the public sidewalk for your benefit."

"They're where?"

"The signs are posted on public property, outside the factory, Sir." Keough clipped the word, 'Sir'.

"Blake, get rid of the signs."

"Me?" Blake said. "That's a hostile crowd out front. I'm not going to remove any of their signs."

"Do you value your job?"

"Before he leaves," Keough said, "you should know that it's legal for those signs to be on public property. The sidewalk's not your property."

"To hell with whose property it is. Blake, get rid of those signs."

Harris waited until the door closed before rounding on Keough. "So you were investigating a robbery and a stolen vehicle when the agitators arrived at the factory. How did they get here?"

"I don't know. I questioned the watchmen and they don't know either. They didn't see or hear anything. The protesters walked from the old warehouse area. That's far enough away from the factory building that the watchmen wouldn't hear vehicles pull in."

"How long did they stay?"

"Just over an hour," Compton said. "I was inside when they dispersed. They left as quickly as they came."

"What were you doing inside? What were the watchmen doing during the protest?"

"I was on the fringe assessing the situation and keeping an eye on Ball and the other reporter. I managed to push my way through to the front doors. There were too many people for the watchmen to control, so I thought I'd better get inside and try to round up some backup. I was going to call the O.P.P. but the factory's phone lines were down."

"Reporter?" A vein bulged in Harris's neck.

"There were two," Compton said. "One was Jim Ball from the local paper. The other was a slick city fellow. I spoke with the stranger, asked what it would take to suppress the story."

Harris pounded a fist onto his desk. "Stupidity and incompetence," he shouted. "A huge protest has taken place that had to be carefully planned, and neither of you knew anything about it. You, Compton, tried to bribe a reporter. What am I paying you both to do? What do you have to say for yourself, Keough?"

Keough drew himself up to his fullest, lankiest height. Now's as good a time as any, he thought. "I've a lot to say, but I'll hold my tongue for all but the important thing. I'm giving you notice now. I quit. I'll be out of this uniform in fifteen minutes and out of the house by midnight. I want to live in this village. I don't want to be associated with a person like you any longer."

Harris snorted. "Where're you going, fool? What're you going to do?"

"I'm going into farming." Keough turned on his heel showing his back to Harris. He turned once and said, "You know, I fought in the war to rid the world of dictators like you." Keough, head high, walked out leaving the door open behind him. Victory was sweet. Freedom never felt so good.

"Good riddance," Compton said. "There's better than him can be bought."

"How would you know?" Harris said. "You were stupid enough to buy six hundred acres of swamp and bog with my money."

"I told you that Count fellow's going to build a huge factory to manufacture radios and televisions. He's got dibs on the Inachio and Wallace properties. He needs workers, and workers need housing."

"Who says?" snapped Harris.

"He said."

"Look, goon. I asked around and no one's heard of him in Windsor or Toronto. I don't know what his game is but he's not what he appears to be. He's an impostor."

"If he is, he's a good one," Compton said.

Blake, arms full of signs, stood in the open door. "What do you want done with these?"

"Take them to the boiler room. Tell the men to make sure that they're burned. When you've finished, I want you to drive me to the mill to see Sebastian Temple. He's the only one I can trust to get the turbines up, and operational again before the midnight shift comes in."

"You'll need a crew to close the sluiceway gates," Compton said.

"Blake has already delivered a note to the shop manager's home that we need a crew upriver, immediately."

"Yeah," Blake said, "And he told me to stick it. He said that but for the usual skeleton crew his men don't work on Sunday. Your own rule apparently. They're not going to work. They're all supposed to be in church again tonight."

The Camp - afternoon

Daniel sat on a small stool by Zizou's cot while anxious women lingered outside the wagon. Zizou lay with her thin face on a red pillow, hair falling onto the bearskin rug that covered her frail figure. Zizou clutched Daniel's hand, her grasp remarkably strong for a dying woman.

"Zizou, you didn't tell me." Daniel wiped his eyes.

"You couldn't have done anything," Zizou said. "And you will follow soon."

"I know. I know. But maybe this time I'll beat the odds and complete the journey."

Zizou sighed. "Always flying, Palumb Furtuna. You might not, just to build the legend."

Daniel kissed a cold hand. "Just like you, I'm prepared to die. Whichever way the wind chooses to blow, I'm at rest. Tamas knows what to do with both of us?"

"Yes," Zizou said, squeezing Daniel's hands. "The cards I believed. That you would come back, I believed. I held life for the day when I would see you again. My wagon was not destroyed because I wanted to meet you as I was years ago."

"Answer me, Zizou. Did Palumb Furtuna return? Am I he? Or am I someone else who fell into his shoes? Did I know him? Or somewhere, at sometime, did he tell me about himself and Magdalena, about you and the prophecy? Am I a stranger who has assumed an identity?"

"You doubt yourself," Zizou said. "Never did you doubt."

"I must doubt," Daniel said. "I can't explain my sudden appearance in the village. Had I been mindlessly wandering for years? Zizou, war is such a terrible thing. Did I suffer amnesia during the war? Am I just a very old man who lost his memory?"

"Listen to me," Zizou said. She tried to raise herself to look at Daniel but fell back and coughed. Daniel held her head and gave her a sip of wine. "You are he. You have returned as I foretold. I said you would leave, would flounder, would fall and then return to right the wrong. Have I ever lied to you?"

"Zizou, I have gone over this a hundred times. There are so many questions. Was I mortally wounded? Did the dove take me only to have something interrupt my flight to the afterworld? Did I not fall back to earth? Am I a ghost? Did Pense call me back?"

"You be Dove Storm, Palumb Furtuna," Zizou said.

"I remember South Africa and war," Daniel said. "I remember a searing pain, a primeval scream. I remember a white dove. I remember a field in France. I remember holding Kenneth to my heart. I remember what he told me. I remember the desert and Johnny."

"You hold many secrets in your heart." Zizou coughed again. A feeble hand reached to touch Daniel. "You came as the dove, Palumb Furtuna."

"If I am flesh and blood, what have I been doing for the past forty-six years?" Daniel said. "Where've I been? If I'm not, how did I materialize into this form? Am I of this world? My most vivid recollection is standing whole and alive before Pense in the barn. Until then, was I like the wind?"

"The answer," Zizou said, "is in your heart, your Roma heart. You speak the language, play the cards. You embrace the violin. But like me you are fading, Dove Storm. You wait again for the beat of the Dove's wings."

"I could have traveled with a *didikai* and he could have taught me. But, were our wanderings of a spiritual or physical nature?"

"You question too much," Zizou said, looking gravely into Daniel's eyes. "Listen to me. Only Palumb Furtuna can make the violin dance. With my dying breath I tell you that you are Palumb Furtuna. You are Daniel Cudzinki. You are Magdalena's Danny. In what form it matters not. From spirit you are flesh and blood."

Daniel kissed Zizou's hand.

Zizou smiled and reached to touch his cheek. "You are named right, Dove Storm. Wherever you walk there be peace amid chaos, and chaos amid peace. You bring the wind with you."

Zizou lay back on the pillow, her breathing shallow. "Remember you my wishes?" Her voice became a whisper. Her hands trembled.

"I promise to carry them through," Daniel said.

Zizou gasped for air. "Never forget who you are. To forget is to die forever. You will never leave forever, Palumb Furtuna. A child's laugh will always interrupt your journey, my manus. But I must go far away. *Mamioro* is at the door with *mulo* in his hand. The dove! The dove is here. I will ride its wings to the stars." Zizou lifted her arms to heaven. "Believe, Schav. Believe."

"No! Zizou, don't leave. For God's sake, don't leave." Daniel waved his left hand valiantly over Zizou's body to try to capture her soul, to pin it to earth. But his words and actions were too late. Zizou's spirit had begun its final long journey home.

An unearthly wail swept through the camp, carried on a wind that suddenly blew over the meadow and whistled around the wagon. The wind too was crying for the old woman, Zizou.

Sharona, a sudden pain near her heart, glanced up from peeling potatoes. "Why's Loco howling so?"

"I'll go see," Pense said, feeling suddenly very cold.

"Not to worry." Theresa was stirring a pot of soup. "Loco smells Johnny nearby. It's gotten cold in here, hasn't it? Must be that the north wind blew a basement window open."

The telephone interrupted the conversation. Theresa wiped her hands and went into the hall to answer it. Granny Smith was on the line.

"Terrible wind,"Granny shouted into the receiver.

"That it is."

"I'm calling from the Adamo house," Granny said. "I remembered. That picture you were looking at, it's him. I was looking for the old man, the Count. The picture's of him, the same man but younger. It's the one that . . . you know, assaulted the woman at the factory. Maybe you were too young to remember the crime. She was a sweet young thing and worked in the office at J.P. Harris, Ltd. The fellow hung around the village doing carpentry. Called himself Danny Cudney. But he was really a Gypsy. He raped her, they say. Miss Inachio? Theresa, are you there?"

Theresa found her voice. "It can't be," she said. "Daniel's only past seventy years of age. I read about the Cudney case. That happened in1876, Granny. Your story would make the Count more than one hundred years old."

"I'm more than ninety," Granny snapped. "It's possible."

"I don't think so."

"Well, I already talked to Constable Keough."

"You did?"

"Mr. Keough told me that I was wrong and shouldn't spread any information like that around the village," Granny said. "He also told me he quit so I shouldn't call him again."

"Look, Granny Smith. Daniel Cudzinki is not Danny Cudney. He's not the 1876 rapist." Even as she said it, Theresa thought of the similarities between the names *Cudney* and *Cudzinki.*

There was silence on the other end of the phone.

"Granny?"

"Maybe I shouldn't trust my eyes. Maybe you're right."

"That's right," Theresa said. "You've confused the Count with someone else. You said that your mind isn't as good as it used to be. The accusation would be a terrible thing to say about a man if it wasn't true. You know what the village's like. You know what they'd do to the man if they thought it was true. Thank you for calling. I'll come have tea with you and we'll discuss this further. Please, Granny Smith. Don't tell anyone. They'd laugh at you and think you'd really lost your mind."

Theresa listened as Granny assured her she wouldn't talk to anyone else, then hung up and hurried back to the kitchen.

"What's up?" Sharona asked.

"It was just Granny Smith," Theresa said. "And a case of mistaken identity."

"She's quite an old lady," Sharona said, glancing at Theresa, who although not so young still had a sound mind. "Do you think I can have some privacy tonight? Johnny and me have a few things that we need to discuss."

"Of course you can. Pense and I are going to spend some time in my bedroom. We've got a bit of work to do before we sleep." Theresa reached for Sharona's hand. "Sharona, Johnny's ring? Why aren't you wearing it?"

Pense stopped setting the table. Her gaze went to her mother's hand.

"Don't get excited," Sharona cautioned both. "There's a lot to talk about before a marriage takes place. But I realized today that I really do belong by Johnny's side, wherever his life may take us. Pense, I'm not forgetting who we are. Not at all. But we both belong here now with Johnny and Theresa. I want Johnny to slip the ring on my finger. I want him to truly understand his actions."

The Harris Estate - evening

J.P. detested dinner parties. He had little in common with people in the community and hated small talk. Each February he hosted a meal for his henchmen. During the rest of the year his most frequent dinner guest was Stanley Compton.

Compton was an enigma. The son of the village undertaker, he left for Toronto after high school and no one heard from him for ten years. He returned with talents that included gambling, womanizing and making money. Compton joined his father in the funeral business but it wasn't long before the pair had a parting of the ways. Stanley realized there was more money to be made from the ground in which he buried people, than from the estates of individuals he was burying.

Compton began buying land around the village. The Depression had left many farmers land-rich and cash-poor. Some were only too happy to sell the family home or the farm, and to rent back. Others jumped at the opportunity of a five-year mortgage, believing that in two or three years their financial situation would improve. In ten years Compton's land holdings rivaled Harris's. He was never known to give fair market value, or a decent shake when conditions didn't improve. He was a bastard for foreclosing on mortgages.

Because Compton and Harris had similar interests, they gravitated to each other. Opposite poles attract. Compton was Harris's alter ego. It was a partnership of convenience and strategy.

Four people were seated at the square mahogany dining room table. As a result of the turbines' shut down, the group was having a cold meal by candlelight. J.P. dominated the head of the table, scowling at family and growling at staff. His day hadn't gone well. The ride from Windsor was overshadowed by the radio broadcast. The afternoon at the factory was a pot boiler. The situation with the gates and overflow channel was costing him money and lost production. J.P.'s mood matched the main course, fowl. J.P. glared around the table, wondering what happiness he ever derived from keeping women around. They didn't do anything but complain and spend money, his money.

Compton sat opposite J.P. Lillian was to his left. Charlotte Harris sat to his right. Charlotte, a mouse of a woman, kept her mouth shut and her head low, as if ducking the verbal abuse which spewed from J.P. constantly.

Lillian sat singularly defiant, her head held high. All afternoon she'd built her confidence, ready to confront J.P. and her mother about Kenneth Walker. Of course, with Compton present, she had to hold her tongue. Lillian viewed the balding fifty-four-year-old Stanley Compton as an ingratiating flatworm. His clever, tricky land deals intrigued her but she couldn't get past his shifty eyes, false smile, swaggering walk and know-it-all attitude. No one knew more than Stanley Compton. He was never wrong, at least in his own mind.

J.P. made his usual long-winded grace last even longer, knowing that it irritated the women. After the blessing he launched into a tirade about unions and unreasonable demands. Harris was fixated with the idea that he would fire everyone involved with the protest including the members of the so-called Stamp Club. The only one he trusted was Sebastian Temple who was, at the moment, working hard at the mill to get the water level up in the dam and the turbines operational again.

Compton had the nerve to remind him that no one knew precisely who was involved. He also brought up the subject of the city reporter. What was going to happen after the Labor protest was written up in large-circulation newspapers? Like it or not, unions were a strong brotherhood. Harris workers would get a lot of sympathy. If the big organized unions decided to get involved, there would be trouble. Things could get rough.

J.P. waved his knife while speaking, to emphasize that he

wasn't about to let anyone push him around. He wasn't going to negotiate with any union.

Lillian managed to carry on small talk with her mother until Compton mentioned Count Daniel Cudzinki. She then gave her full attention to what was being said. He was wealthy, he was a manufacturer, he was receiving boxes at the train station, he was rather mysterious but that was in keeping with the business of huge land purchases.

"He's a fraud," J.P. said. "No one's heard of him. I tell you that he's got some sort of scam going on."

Compton insisted that he had dibs on the Inachio and Wallace properties. Johnny Wallace said as much. The man couldn't be discounted so lightly. "I tell you, some sort of factory's going in on the south side of the river."

"The man's a fool," Harris said. "He can't just walk into a community, take over, push people around. The village Council won't allow it."

"Why not?" Lillian asked. "If he has money to throw around why won't they cooperate? His money's as good as yours. Maybe he has more of it."

"You forgot who owns this village," J.P. said, "Who pays the bills?"

"If a big corporation wants to bring a factory to Millbrook, the Council won't turn them down," Lillian said. "They need new industry."

"Lillian has a point," said Compton. "It might become a battle of the banks and big corporation against local industry. You're a little fish in a big sea. You can't keep the village in the palm of your hand forever. This is the twentieth century. The strategy may have worked for your parents and grandparents but it might not for you much longer. People are going to rebel against tyranny and the family compound. The writing's on the wall."

"And you're just waiting for that day, aren't you?" Harris said. "You'll be the only one that stands to come out the winner with the amount of land you've stolen around here."

"Both of us stand to make money," Compton said. "I've made some shrewd deals for you, too."

"At the expense of a few poor families that couldn't keep up with their mortgage payments," muttered Charlotte.

"It was theirs to lose," snapped Compton. "And mine to receive."

"They have a heart and soul and dreams," Charlotte said, eyes to the table. "They're human beings."

"Since when have you worried about human beings?" J.P. eyed his wife suspiciously. "Since when did you begin to care about the rabble in the village?"

"If the villagers knew what you dally in during your frequent trips, they might change their allegiances," Lillian said, taking up her mother's tack. "Oh, I've an idea what you're up to. You're going to be found out."

J.P. looked surprised, then said, "No matter. Money talks. People need jobs. They do what I tell them. They mew around my feet. They're loyal to the Harris name. Look what I've given them – parks, paved streets, a Christmas party for their children, jobs for their sons. The only thing I demand is loyalty."

"Think what you've taken away," Charlotte said, more to her chicken salad than to her husband.

"Inbreeding," Compton said. "Your father exercised the same control. I can only put it down to inbreeding and stupidity in the village. There's little new blood that would know better than to follow the Harris creed. But that can't last."

Lillian normally would have found such banter enjoyable, but tonight it seemed repugnant. She glanced from her mother to J.P., then said, "If Count Cudzinki does build a factory, people won't need you. They'll have a choice. Your loyal followers will abandon your leaky ship. You'll own the factory but your influence around the village will drop to zero." She wiped her mouth with a napkin. "Could you ring for dessert, Mother? The sooner I leave this room, the better I'll feel."

After Charlotte rang the bell, Nellie scurried to clean the table, backing into the butler's pantry each time she had to leave the room, then served dessert.

"You've got your staff scared out of their wits!" Compton said.

"That's the way I like it," Harris said.

Over dessert, J.P. changed the subject. Smiling secretively at Compton, he addressed Lillian. "I'm going to present you with a little business proposition, Lillian. I assume, however stupid it may be, that you, being the only heir, will step into my shoes and run the company after I die."

Lillian was quick with a response. "I wasn't responsible for your having only one child. Why didn't you have two or three? You would have produced a son sooner or later. Heaven knows, you can afford a large family."

Charlotte cleared her throat and gave J.P. a furtive glance.

J.P. raised his hands. "As I was saying, you should have married a long time ago and produced an heir. Is it your intention to remain an old maid?"

"I'm only thirty-three," Lillian snapped.

"As I said, are you not planning to marry?"

"Maybe you haven't noticed but men aren't exactly lining up to date me," Lillian said. "You wouldn't allow me to live in Toronto to meet people, to pursue a career. What did you expect?"

"An heir, sooner or later. So I've taken matters into my own hands. Stanley has agreed to marry you."

"You can't be serious about Stanley." Lillian said, giving Compton a scathing look.

"He kids you not," Compton said. "There's only twenty-one-years' difference in our ages. I'm healthy, wealthy. What else could you ask for?"

"I think love enters the picture at some stage," Lillian said.

"It's a perfect match," J.P. said. "With his money and my wealth we'd own everything. We could expand the factory."

"I'm better than others you've chosen to play with," Compton muttered into his napkin.

"What's that?" Lillian rounded on Compton. "I wouldn't be casting stones if I were you, Stanley." She looked from Compton to J.P. "So I'm the pawn in a marriage of convenience that's all about money."

"I'd be a good husband," Compton said. "I have some winning ways."

"So does a moose," Lillian snorted. "What says I wouldn't take your money and run?"

"Our lawyers would arrange everything," J.P. said.

"In other words, this repulsive man would be paid to marry me."

"I wouldn't put it that way."

"I think it was very aptly put," Charlotte whispered.

"Let me put it my way," J.P. interrupted. "If you don't agree, you won't inherit much, Lillian. I'll write you out of my will if you don't produce an heir."

"Oh," said Lillian. "That's the tack you are taking, is it? How many times have I been threatened with this?"

"I'll do it. I mean it this time. You know the options. It's your choice."

Lillian placed her napkin on the table, rose and ignoring the men, spoke directly to her mother. "I wash my hands of this entire family. It's an insult to have a husband chosen as a stud, isn't it Mother?" When Charlotte lowered her eyes, Lillian continued. "Have you ever heard such nonsense? I'll not be part of any of it."

"Don't slam the door," Compton said. "The offer's a standing one. You won't be given better."

"I might decide to choose worse." Lillian turned from the table.

"She'd be a handful," Compton observed after Lillian had left the room.

"She'll come around. She knows where her bread and butter comes from. She'll change her mind before I leave."

"You're going away again, so soon?" Charlotte said. "Where?"

"It's none of your business what my plans are," snapped J.P. "Are you coming with me tonight, Compton? I want to go back to the factory to make sure those signs are gone and everything has settled down."

Both men rose, leaving Charlotte a dejected little woman seated at the table. "And may the devil find you in a cozy corner," she muttered twisting her napkin into a noose. Charlotte rang for the maid, then went to find her daughter.

Lillian was curled in a wicker lounge at her bedroom window.

"You don't have to marry him." Charlotte came to stand beside the lounge. "You don't have to marry anyone. You don't have to give him an heir. It might be better if you didn't. The company will survive."

"Sit down." Lillian moved her legs, then waited until her mother was seated before speaking.

"Am I the daughter of Kenneth Walker?"

The startled look on Charlotte's face was all that Lillian needed to confirm that J.P. Harris was no flesh and blood relative.

"Who? How did you find out? Charlotte asked. "Who told you?"

"That's not important. I want to know why."

Charlotte wrung her hands in her lap like a chastised child.

Lillian reached to quiet them. "I haven't told J.P.," she said. "It's our secret. I'm not going to confront him."

"He knows," Charlotte said. "He was the one that thought it up. He was the one that suggested a relationship and pressured me into it. He chose Kenneth from a number of young men. Kenneth was going to marry Theresa Inachio. I did have a crush on him, no doubt. The trip to England was partially for me to pursue Kenneth. I trapped Kenneth at a vulnerable time. J.P. needed an heir.

"He needed an heir!" exclaimed Lillian. "He's a man. He could have done the job himself."

"J.P. can't," Charlotte hesitated, then said. "He can perform but he can't produce. It's not in him to produce children. He's sterile. Oh dear . . . ." Charlotte burst into tears.

"Why didn't you just say no? You ruined a wonderful relationship so that bastard could have an heir."

"Lillian, I couldn't say no to J.P. I made my bed by marrying him. I had to live with him. I thought, give him a child and he'll leave me alone. Involving Kenneth Walker was a mistake I'll have to live with for the rest of my life, but I never regretted having you. You're the only bright light in this sham of a marriage."

"What about Theresa Inachio? How did you feel after destroying her relationship with Kenneth?"

"I can't look her in the eye. I can't be in the same room with her. I ruined her life," Charlotte said. "Kenneth was a wonderful man. He was gentle, kind, sensitive, and too much a gentleman of the old-school to return to Theresa after our liaison. So many times I wanted to say something to her. So many times I walked half way to Knightswood, thinking I had to talk with her. And always the thought of my husband stopped me. I'm afraid of him, Lillian."

"Why don't you leave him now?"

"Look at me. When my parents died they made sure the inheritance money was given to J.P. to manage. They felt I couldn't manage an estate. With the exception of the Conservatory, I haven't seen a cent of my parents' money. Some days, when I think about things, I get so angry I'd like to throw rocks through its windows. I'm trapped. You don't need to follow in my footsteps. You've an independent streak. Whatever you do, never marry a man you don't love – like I did."

"Why?"

"Remember how terribly your grandparents in Toronto treated you? When I became pregnant they knew I'd slept with someone other than J.P. And before you ask, I slept with no other men but J.P. and Kenneth Walker. You are Kenneth's child."

"For all that Grandfather was a doctor," Lillian said, "He had a mean streak to him and a miserable bedside manner."

"J.P. was Father's patient. Venereal disease made him sterile. Father never kept secrets from Mother, especially when an eligible young man was available for their backward daughter. During their negotiations with J.P. they didn't give thought to what would happen after the marriage. Of course, when you arrived, it was all my fault until J.P. explained he needed an heir."

"How disgusting that a doctor would break a patient's confidence," Lillian said. "It's even more disgusting they'd arrange a marriage and you'd go along with it."

"I was not a pretty, outgoing socialite. I was the little mousy-looking daughter who lived in my mother's shadow and she was a domineering social butterfly. J.P. was an excellent choice, according to my parents."

"Why didn't you say no?"

"Different times make for different choices. You wouldn't understand what it was like to live in the shadow of a mother like mine. Nothing I did suited them. No man I liked suited them."

"But didn't you want children?"

"At the time, marrying J.P. looked like my answer to escape the stifling confines of a lonely, miserable existence. So I abided their wishes, but will forever regret it. J.P. had another side few knew about. I didn't realize how dreadful he was until after we were married. We live a lie. You live a lie."

"Did you ever try to see Kenneth again?" Lillian asked.

"I'm sure he wanted to do the right thing, to take responsibility for the child until he thought things through and realized he had been used. I sent a letter and pictures when you were one year old."

"Why?" Lillian asked.

"It was the one time in my life when I thought seriously about leaving J.P.," Charlotte said. "Perhaps I was hoping that Kenneth would tell me to come to England. Maybe I wanted something to come of the liaison. I wanted to get out of this house, out of this marriage. That's when my parents built the Conservatory, thinking it would appease me, make me a happy woman in this trap of a house."

"Did Kenneth answer your letter?" Lillian asked.

"It came back, unopened, with return-to-sender written across it. My spirit died along with my plans to leave. In a way I didn't expect an answer. I also understood why Kenneth never came back to resume the relationship with Theresa. He couldn't live a lie either. And he couldn't reside in the same village as his daughter without acknowledging her."

"Kenneth was killed in 1915," Lillian said.

Charlotte gripped her daughter's hands. "I've ruined your life, too. No one should be forced to live under J.P. Harris's tyranny. But don't be hasty about doing anything. There may be a way to salvage our lives without sacrificing too much. Let's put our heads together, Lillian."

Lillian put an arm around her mother, something she hadn't done for a long time.

"I'm glad you know about your father," Charlotte said. "I didn't have the courage to tell you, but I'm glad the truth is out now."

"Let's make this situation work to our advantage," Lillian said, feeling for the first time in her life, she had established a common bond with her mother. She drew Charlotte to her and allowed the curly white head to rest on a shoulder while the wind played an ungodly lament around the eaves.

Theresa's Barn - evening

Johnny searched everywhere for Count Daniel Cudzinki. He checked the camp and found it abnormally quiet and subdued. He checked with the Kropoluses who were worried because they hadn't seen Daniel since midmorning. Johnny looked in the windows of the Barber Shop. He checked at the mill and the garage. Daniel was nowhere to be found. Neither was Sebastian Temple, according to Blake who was searching the mill for the man. In the end, Count turned up of his own accord in Theresa's barn.

Johnny was pulling his motorbike up beside Sharona's car in the carriage house when he heard Loco's howling lament. Running to the barn, Johnny took the stairs to the granary two at a time. Plumb sounded like he was dying.

"What's bothering you, Loco?" Johnny knelt to pat the dog. His presence seemed to calm Plumb Loco who put his head down and whimpered. "What's the matter, boy?" Johnny lifted one paw then the other, looking for imbedded objects.

"Loco's mourning a friend," a voice said, causing Johnny to jump to his feet. The dog whimpered.

Johnny turned to see Daniel, standing at the far end of the threshing floor, a lantern in his hand.

"Good Lord! You can give a man a heart attack by doing that. Where've yuh been? Theresa's looking for you. I've been all over the place on my bike. The Kropoluses are worried too."

"No one should be concerned about me." Daniel came to stand beside Johnny. He held the lamp in one hand, a uniform in the other.

"You look ill." Johnny reached to support Daniel.

"I'm fine," Daniel said.

"You shouldn't be sleeping out here when there is a perfectly good bed for you in a warm house. Are yuh trying to kill yourself old man?"

"There's no need for that." Daniel set the lamp on the floor and sat on a bale of hay, the uniform on his lap.

"You'd better tell me what's up, Daniel." Johnny eased himself down onto the floor by Loco. "It's okay, boy. I'll take you into the house with me tonight."

"Well, we were successful with the protest," Daniel said.

"That we were. The fellows tacked signs on the factory ceiling for everyone to see tomorrow morning. Signs were left for burning but that didn't happen because the boilers are shut down. Harris thought they'd been destroyed. It was too dark in the factory for him to see what was up in the rafters. No one has a clue who the protesters really were. That's good."

"The city reporter came. Jim Ball covered it, too. I don't know if the radio used the information, though." Daniel coughed and rubbed his chest.

"Blake says that Harris heard it. By the way, everything's set for early tomorrow morning – in the barn at my place."

"Will you drive me out?"

"I will, at six o'clock in the morning."

"Thanks, Johnny."

The wind shook the door, rattled the eaves and moaned through holes in the barn's siding. Something flew from one rafter to another. Daniel looked up to confirm that it was the dove, then glanced at the uniform in his lap. "I was wearing this when I arrived," he said, holding up a jacket for Johnny to see.

"I don't think so. Yuh weren't wearing a uniform when I first saw you. I'm sure Theresa would've said something about a uniform if you were wearin' one when you arrived."

"Before you saw me at the mill. Before I showed up at Theresa's door," Daniel said.

Johnny reached for the jacket.

"Whoever wore this suffered a severe injury around his heart." Johnny looked toward Daniel but couldn't read his face in the lantern's light. "What're you trying to tell me, old man?"

"This is my uniform."

"This is the same type of uniform my uncle wore in the Boer War. You told me that you fought in the First and Second World Wars."

Daniel coughed again and clutched his left side. "I told you I fought in a war and that I was underground. I didn't specify what war." Daniel stood and, coming closer to Johnny, whispered, "I was on reconnaissance. I was shot, a bullet through the heart, in 1901."

"Now you're hallucinating," Johnny said. "You must be running a fever. You're standing in front of me, flesh and blood, telling me you're dead. I was thinking about you last night, you know. I figure you lost everything in this war, your home, your way of life – maybe bits of your mind. It happens. As a child, you might have traveled in this area with your parents and the Kumpania. You've returned to something you remember. Look. I'll help you piece everything together. Sharona and Theresa will help. You're not alone. You have me and Theresa, Sharona, Pense."

"Thanks, Johnny. But I won't be staying long."

Johnny turned the jacket slowly in his hands.

"Does it look familiar, Johnny? Is this the jacket I was wearing in the desert when I came to you?"

Johnny frowned then gave the jacket over to Daniel. He stood quickly, emotions in check.

"Is it?" Daniel asked again.

To cover his confusion, Johnny leaned down to untie Loco. When he rose, Johnny looked directly at Daniel. "It has to be. The hole and stain are in the same place," he said quietly. "Look, Daniel. Come to the house with me. You're rasping like you have pneumonia. That would explain your cough."

"No," Daniel said. "I want time to say my goodbyes to a few old friends."

"Are you going to be all right?"

"Yes, Johnny." Daniel coughed again and kept his hand over his heart. "Tell Theresa to leave the back door open. I'll come to her. I'll see her in the library sometime after midnight."

"Okay, after midnight," Johnny said. "Since I saw you last, there's been a few things happen. Keough's quit. He's going to finish my house and rent the farm for a while. Keough says I should tell you that Granny Smith is stark raving mad. She found him on the street today and tried to tell him that you were a man named Danny Cudney and that you committed a heinous crime and that you were much older than you look."

"What did he say to her?"

"That she was a crazy old woman, or something to that effect. That this Cudney fellow was accused of raping a woman in the 1870's. And that if you were him, you would be more than one hundred years old."

"Dead or live count?"

Johnny laughed but his mind was brought back to a conversation with Daniel at The China. He bit his lower lip and looked closer at Daniel. Could it be, Johnny thought? Can he be that old?

"If Keough's going to live at the farm," Daniel said, "where are you going to be?"

"I'm marrying Sharona. We're going to live at Knightswood," Johnny said. "You made me see the light, Daniel. I asked Sharona to marry me and she said *yes*. Well, she said *maybe*, but that's the same as *yes*."

Daniel smiled. "Told you so, Johnny."

When Johnny gave the jacket back to Daniel he let his hand rest momentarily on the older man's arm. "You promise. You'll keep your word? You will come after midnight to see Theresa?"

"I will. And Johnny. Thanks for everything. I might forget to thank you properly tomorrow."

"I should thank you," Johnny said. "We couldn't have gotten under Harris's skin without your help. You came at the right time. Just take good care of yourself, old man." Johnny called to Loco. "Come on, dog. Let's go into the warm house."

Daniel coughed and again clutched his chest. “I won’t see you at midnight Johnny?” It was more a statement than a question. He needed time alone with Theresa.

Johnny got the hint. “I’ll be asleep,” Johnny said. “Six in the morning comes early.”

“If I’m hitching a ride with you tomorrow, I’ll sleep inside tonight. Look for me in the library before you leave.”

Chapter 12

The Camp - October 6, 1947: after midnight

The moon rose and Martiya, the spirit of the night, whispered in the trees at Knightswood. Tamas and Daniel made the rounds of the camp, speaking with all members of the familia, supporting the *romipen* of the group before the Kumpania left Theresa's meadow for the last time. Whispers that he was the *mulani* of the *trito ursitori*, the triple spirit, gave Daniel further respect as he gave out bags of sweets and small bundles of *drab* to be used for the *pomano*, the funeral feast. Whether they had traveled the Kumpania out of curiosity or respect for Palumb Furtuna, each member expressed genuine sorrow when saying their goodbyes. All listened carefully to what he said, as the visit of *o zhuvindo*, the storm dove, would be added to the traditional lore.

Kumpania travelers were subdued about the ancient seer, Zizou, who had been correct about her own death. Their hearts were heavy with her loss. Many wept at the mention of her name. Some refused to speak about her for fear of interrupting her journey. Out of respect, Palumb Furtuna's violin remained silent. Instead, he let the north wind sing the lament for the dead.

Cars and trucks pulled away from the meadow one by one, until only Tamas, Sebastian, Niki and several other *terno shav* remained with their vehicles.

"Niki, we'll leave my truck in the meadow and I'll take your car," Tamas said. "You drive Zizou's *vurdon*. Sebastian, you follow Niki to help with the horses. You men, finish what you have to do, then bring my car to the meeting point to wait for Palumb Furtuna.

Drive carefully. We don't want to draw attention to ourselves. My friend, do you have everything you need?"

"It's all in the grain sack," Daniel said, pointing toward his feet.

"We'll meet tomorrow, then?"

"I sincerely hope so. Could I ask one more thing, Tamas? *Te prakhon man pasho o Magdalena."*

Tamas put a hand on Daniel's shoulder. *"Na daren, Palumb Furtuna, vi ame sam Rom chache."*

"*Nais tuke*, my friend."

After the last vehicle pulled away from the meadow, the men drove round Millbrook in Tamas's car. Working quickly, and quietly, they tacked large signs on telephone and hydro poles, trees and fences. With the exception of the West River Road and the hill leading to Johnny's farm, they posted every street with signs demanding better wages and working conditions. And for the first time, the words attacked J.P. Harris personally for contributing to local government corruption. When the job was finished, the Roma drove toward the bowels of the Long Swamp.

Knightswood - after midnight

No weight is heavier than that of love surrendered. By the time Daniel slipped into the house, the grain sack felt as though it weighed two hundred pounds. His body was tired, his heart weak. Daniel checked the dining room, thinking Pense might be at the marriage board. The room was dark and empty. He next opened the library door and found Theresa sitting before the fire, a blanket around her knees.

When Theresa heard the door, she looked up. She was stunned by what she saw. Pain etched Daniel's face. Sadness lay in his eyes. The speech she had rehearsed was swallowed by compassion for an old man. She rose, to meet him on common ground.

"Daniel. Sit by the fire. Take my blanket. Johnny's left some whiskey, saying you deserved it and would need a drink."

Daniel lowered his weary body into a chair, putting the grain sack beside it. The fire felt good after his nights in the cold barn. He allowed Theresa to cover him and accepted a glass of single malt. "I do apologize, Theresa. I've been going out of my way to avoid you. There were so many questions I wanted you to answer by reading the letters before I spoke with you."

"And so many that have been raised by the letters."

As the whiskey warmed his throat and stomach, Daniel closed his eyes.

"Have you eaten?" she asked.

"Don't fuss, Theresa. I'm here to talk, not eat. You're one of the kindest, most caring people I've known. No wonder Kenneth loved you. What have you ascertained, Theresa? What questions must you ask?"

"I don't know where to begin."

"Begin with Kenneth Walker. That's the logical place and something that was never explained in the letters, but he's relevant to Magdalena."

"What about Kenneth?"

"I'll try to speak in the first person so as not to confuse you. Kenneth was Magdalena's out-of-wedlock son, our child."

"Her son!" Theresa exclaimed, stunned by the information. Never would she have guessed that Magdalena had been a mother. "Magdalena had a lover? She gave birth to a child!"

"According to her mother and father our love was an infatuation. They thought she'd get over it and did everything they could to break us up. They didn't realize the depth of our feeling and understanding for each other. I built the marriage board as a token of that love, as an engagement present. At first I felt we could conquer all odds and wed. Then when permission to marry was refused, I tried to persuade Magdalena to leave. She refused to let go the safety of what she knew."

"Why?"

"Elizabeth and Joseph Anderson felt so responsible for this less-than-perfect daughter they wrapped her in the cocoon of this house. Knightswood held her like a vise."

"When she refused to leave with you?"

"I gave up the *lungo drom* and adopted the *gadje* life. The obvious happened as always does when two people are very much in love. We . . . Daniel and Magdalena, took to-bed and she became pregnant. We considered ourselves married in the Gypsy way."

"What did the Andersons think of that delicate situation?"

"We were honest. As soon as Magdalena knew for sure, we told them. They were furious. Before they had the opportunity to think the situation through, to come to their senses, I was accused of a rape. That accusation came within a week of our telling them about the pregnancy. As you can well imagine, I had to leave the village quickly, in less than pleasant circumstances."

"Poor Magdalena," Theresa said. "What happened next?"

"Magdalena, in a highly emotional state, took to her bed. I understand that she was quite out of her mind at times. Your mother was hired to take care of her."

"I do remember mother telling me that there was a time when Magdalena rarely left her room," Theresa said, "except to play the piano. And she hid in the attic to paint."

"Your mother wouldn't have told you all the circumstances. As it was deemed in the best interests of both Magdalena and the child that she not keep our baby, I devised a plan. After Kenneth was birthed, I'd take him to England."

"Why such a plan?" Theresa asked.

"You knew Magdalena. You can answer that. Was she capable of raising a child? Then too, I thought that when Magdalena found the babe was being taken from her, she'd come with it and I'd have both with me. I know now it was the wrong decision."

"How did you get Kenneth?"

"To their credit, Elizabeth and Joseph went along with the plan. They knew Magdalena's limitations. They'd seen her through her dark moments. Joseph Anderson, accompanied by your mother, brought the baby to me in Montreal."

"Mother took the secret to her grave," Theresa said.

"For fear he'd change his mind about giving the baby over, I left immediately with Kenneth for Britain. We lived near Chelfont St. Peter with relatives of my mother's by the name of Walker. I stayed close to my son when I wasn't on the road and raised him to know his Roma heritage. He was also told of his mother and her situation. It was Kenneth's choice not to travel the open road, to lead a traditional *gadje* life."

"Did Magdalena realize Kenneth was her son when he lived here?" Theresa asked.

"Dear lady, I can't answer that. I was long dead by that time. It's possible from what you've told me of his visit. Kenneth certainly knew where his mother lived." Helping himself to another glass of whiskey, Daniel leaned toward Theresa. "Let me explain.

Twice a year Magdalena watched for me to arrive from the barn's roof or the attic window." Daniel closed his eyes, trying to visualize Magdalena on the roof. "At her best, she was an amazing, creative, loving woman. She made me feel as though I was a god. She was that elusive bird, that rare gem that all men want to possess. She alone had the ability to turn me into a *gadje.* I was her knight come to rescue her. Yet, when I offered my horse to carry her off, she refused."

"At times Maggie had considerable charm," Theresa said."There were also occasions when she was an out-of-control misery."

"I chose to dwell on Magdalena's best attributes. She couldn't help herself during those turbulent times. Even Zizou couldn't understand my infatuation with this rare bird. She saw what would happen and predicted I'd return to make things right. You do understand what I gave up when I left?"

"I understand you were held in high regard among the Roma and that you sacrificed a lot for Magdalena. In doing so you must have loved her very much. What happened after you left the Kumpania?"

"No one in Millbrook would give me a room so I slept in the carriage house. I changed my last name to Cudney and tried to get a job. I gave Magdalena a locket as an engagement gift. It didn't bother her that I couldn't find work. In her strange way she believed that as long as we were together, I'd be satisfied to shut myself away in this house."

"That must have been a stifling thought, Daniel. You strike me as someone who needs freedom."

"It was, but I was willing to try because with heart and soul, I loved this wild creature that was Magdalena. I was infatuated by her."

"Why did the Andersons oppose your love so vehemently?"

"Joseph Anderson was tolerant to the point of letting the Kumpania use his land but didn't appreciate more intimate contact with his family. It was one thing to share his field, another to share his daughter and home. His excuse was that I needed to acquire Victorian respectability." Daniel looked at his hands. "The fact that I was well educated – that I was the head of my tribe – that I played the violin beautifully – that I was a leader of people – that I could work with my hands, that wasn't relevant."

"Surely time would have changed Joseph's attitude?"

"Perhaps," Daniel said.

"And Elizabeth Innes Anderson? How did she treat you?"

"She had no use for me. She believed that I was an opportunist, taking advantage of Magdalena's fragile emotional state to gain land, money, respectability."

"What happened after the charge was laid?"

"No official charge was laid. I knew the girl but didn't lay a hand on her. When Johnny's grandfather came to warn me that I was the prime suspect in the rape, I wasted no time leaving the village. Because I'd never been accepted in the area, the first person they'd accuse was me, the misfit, the scapegoat. I lay low in Montreal while waiting for the child to be born."

"I assume that's when the coded letters started to arrive for Maggie."

"Magdalena and I kept in touch. If there was one thing that remained constant in this crisis, it was our love for each other. We quickly realized there was no way to fight the charges, not with a Harris involved."

"To Joseph Anderson's credit, he had to know where you were hiding but didn't tell. Perhaps he believed you. Did he offer assistance?"

"Only to the point of partially fulfilling our pact about the baby. Elizabeth and Joseph put a twist in the tale. As they didn't want Magdalena to follow the child, they told her that it had been born dead. I was not a party to that horrible deed."

"And after the birth?"

"No letters came from her – perhaps the Andersons intercepted them – but when writing I always mentioned our child. Four years after the birth, she began to write again – to my address in England. She never acknowledged the baby, never asked about Kenneth. It was as though that part of her life hadn't happened or she'd blocked it from her mind. And I stopped asking her to join me."

"Maggie's physical and mental condition changed day to day, week to week. Mental instability is a dreadful thing," Theresa said. "She was an emotional teeter-totter, swinging from high euphoria to deep despair. She never made mention of a child to me."

"I'm certain that while I was telling her our child lived, her parents were saying he'd died. As long as J.P. Harris II was alive, I was on the run for a crime I didn't commit, so I couldn't come back with Kenneth."

"And the crime . . . the rape?"

"The girl worked in the factory office. She was the first woman hired by Harris II. He had his eye on her, curried her favor with a job then raped her. The girl said as much before she changed her story. It wouldn't do to have the man who controlled the village, accused of such a crime, would it? Who better to blame than *the Gypsy?*"

"And what happened to the girl?"

"I'd left the village but understand that she disappeared shortly after the accusation was made. Some months later, her body was found in the Sydenham River near Owen Sound. The verdict was suicide but there were circumstances which led some to believe it was murder."

"What happened to the baby?"

"The baby's dead body wasn't found," Daniel said.

"What a horrible family! Treachery and deceit run through their veins."

"It seems all of the Harrises sanction extramarital dalliances."

"Daniel, what a tragic story."

"There's more." Count closed his eyes, drawing on an inner strength to continue. "I'm the physical proof of a clandestine love affair between my mother, an eastern European Countess and a Roma manus. I was raised by the Count and given all the benefits of being his son. I doubt that the man was any the wiser that I was a bastard child. It was only after the Count died, and I inherited his title, that I was told my true paternal heritage." Memories of his eclectic early life put a smile on Daniel's tired face. It was several minutes before he continued with the story. "After my mother died, I was able to delve more fully into my father's heritage. After realizing that I had to be part of the *lungo drom*, I quickly divested myself of most *gadje* trappings. When a branch of the familia escaped persecution by coming to Canada, I joined them. Like my father, I was chosen the *Rom Baro*."

"Just like Sharona and Pense, the wanderer in you craved the open road. "

"Interesting, but I never felt out of place in either culture. On one hand I was surrounded by old wealth, art, music. I lacked nothing, including a good education. On the other hand my heritage was that of eastern European Gypsies with little to their name but pride and joy of living. Which decision would you make if given the choice? You know mine and must have realized by now that Danny Cudney's name was *The Count Daniel Vincent Cudzinki.* Daniel Cudzinki's Gypsy name is Palumb Furtuna, Dove Storm, given to me by my father at my birth."

Theresa had to ask the question. "You believe that you are *YLD*?"

"I do believe. From my options and the evidence that has been presented, I believe that I am Danny Cudney," Daniel said, his eyes searching Theresa's face for compassion and understanding. "I also believe that all the threads of my life have now been gathered and that I'm here because this is where I was meant to be at this time in my existence- - be that existence one of spirit or flesh and blood man. My life unfolded as it did, because I was meant to be here at this particular point in time, to spend this very moment with you. The questions are why, and from what, did I evolve to be here? Where, and into what, do I now go? Can you answer those questions?"

"No, I can't," Theresa said. "I don't know how you got here. I don't know why you're here. You can be one of three things: an imposter who knew Kenneth Walker, Daniel Cudzinki and more than one hundred years of age or a spirit, the ghost of Palumb Furtuna who has come back to life as a flesh and blood person."

"It took a long time for me to accept that I'm a solid presence," Count said. "I've been whispers in the wind. I've been mist in the meadows. I've guarded Magdalena. I've guarded the people she loved. She once wrote that she would find a way to bring me back. Before I left I promised her that I would return if a way could be found to enter *gadje* time again."

"She was in Danny's heart and the heart is strong. It conquers all."

"That's true," Count said. "I know now that I was brought back by Magdalena. She's using Pense."

"You're confusing me, Daniel."

"At the beginning I was confused too," Daniel said. "But I believe that my time on earth was unfinished - - that I was not taken up to the heavens. Neither did I fall back to earth. I hovered between the two until Pense called me here."

"Can that be?" Theresa said. "Can a ghost become real? Can

a spirit take on physical form? Can a soul be called back to earth?"

"Flesh and blood I now am as Palumb Furtuna, father of Kenneth Walker."

"But what made you finally believe that you are a ghost?"

"Danny was shot through the heart on October 6, 1901, at 5:03 p.m. while on a reconnaissance mission in South Africa during the Boer War. His group was looking for Botha and rode into an ambush. His obituary was written up in several papers and there is a death certificate in England that confirms the date."

"Daniel!" The conversation she'd had with Pense came flooding back to Theresa. "Daniel, think logically. What you're thinking can't happen."

"It can," Daniel said. "And if I am Danny and have come back to life, I have to assume that I'll disappear again today, on the anniversary of his . . . my death."

"How did you arrive? Appear? Manifest?"

"My theory is that it took someone Magdalena could influence to bring me back, to make me whole. Pense was that person, an impressionable, open-minded young girl. I was hoping Pense could tell me how she accomplished the feat. I'd like to know where she called me from. It's a place I have to return to." Daniel managed a smile. "After all, a man needs to know if he's going to heaven or hell."

"Where were you between April and September of this year?"

Butterflies fluttered through Daniel's chest. His heart skipped once then settled into a light, rapid, erratic beating. Rubbing his chest, Daniel waited for it to resume a normal rhythm before speaking. "I was in Windsor, Detroit, Toronto, Montreal, collecting information, gathering an appropriate wardrobe, scheming against Harris. You see, when I stepped into life again, I knew everything that went on before 1901, but was shy on some of the details for certain periods of time afterward."

"Poor man," Theresa said. "And you've vowed vengeance on Harris."

"I want an apology from Harris for the accusation his father made about me – Danny Cudney – and for the grief he caused Magdalena."

"You're after justice."

"I deserve an apology."

"But it was J.P.'s father that was responsible," Theresa said.

"J.P. Harris III will do." Daniel made no mention of his second reason for extracting an apology from J.P., that being the situation that led to the termination of Kenneth's relationship with Theresa.

Theresa, rubbing her neck, leaned back in her chair to think. What to believe? What to do? Theresa's logical mind told her that what she was thinking was impossible. Her illogical heart told a different story.

"Daniel, could you be more than one hundred years old? What if you sustained serious injuries in South Africa and lost your memory for a number of years?"

"It's possible," Daniel said. "I knew the risks when I signed up. But I felt the bullet strike. I saw my heart's blood spurt. I felt the pain of death. I heard myself scream."

"On the other hand, if you're an impostor, someone must have taught you how to play the violin – and told you everything about Magdalena and Kenneth and Knightswood."

"Who knew the entire story but Danny? I'm not an impostor. I knew when the violin was handed to me by Zizou that I had returned. It was mine. I made it sing. I knew I could make the earth dance. The ability is in these hands." Daniel looked at his hands. "I've never taken lessons. The music comes from my heart."

"How do you explain Johnny's experience in the desert?" Theresa asked. "Were you with him?"

"My spirit has been guarding the people that mattered in Magdalena's life. I can tell you that there was a man in a desert and I remember holding him until someone appeared on the horizon. I've left Johnny with his own explanation. It's eased his mind. I can tell you that there was a battlefield in France. I can remember holding Kenneth. That's when he told me about you, about his love for you. You see, Theresa, if he hadn't told me, I would never have known. I died in South Africa before he came to Canada to be with his mother."

Daniel's words stunned Theresa. There had to be another explanation as to how Daniel knew about the relationship. And what about Johnny? Why would a spirit be connected with Johnny? He's too young to have known Danny Cudney or Kenneth Walker.

"Why would you . . .your spirit . . . get involved with Johnny?"

"The only explanation I have is that I owed his grandfather a favor. Johnny was connected to you and he talked about Sharona and Pense when I was holding him in the desert. Daniel shook his head, a sob in his throat. "Zizou, who was my first love before I met Magdalena, said that I'd guard those who cared, that I'd leave but return years later to right a wrong. She said that I might not recognize Magdalena but she would be here when I returned. She didn't question when I contacted her this April through Tamas with some unusual requests."

"My dear Daniel. Pense believes she's Magdalena reincarnated."

Daniel's eyes brightened. His hands gripped the chair.

"She knows, then."

"She's a young girl, Daniel, an impressionable child with a vivid imagination."

"May I see her?" Daniel opened the sack and withdrew his violin which he placed on the footstool. He then took Zizou's strings of golden coins, several books and three decks of cards wrapped in red scarves from the bag. "I must give these to her."

"Zizou's things?" Theresa said.

"She wanted Pense to have them."

"That must mean that Zizou's – "

"She's gone. The camp's broken up. They've all left."

"Sharona? Pense?" Theresa's hands flew to her chest, fear in her heart that she'd lost her precious family.

"Sharona and Pense didn't leave with the Kumpania, Theresa. They stayed at Knightswood. Your love was strong enough that it surmounted their Gypsy blood."

"Daniel. What are you going to do next?"

"I'm going to see Pense, then I'm going to rest."

Theresa didn't really want Pense involved. Yet, it was unfair, if she believed that Daniel was the father of her beloved Kenneth, and Magdalena's lover, that he not see the girl. No matter how Theresa feared for Pense, she couldn't deprive Daniel of the opportunity for one last meeting. "Play the lullaby, Daniel. Play it softly." Theresa knew that Pense would come when she heard the music.

Daniel stood, raised the violin to his shoulder and began to play the compelling strains of Magdalena's song. The soulful music bound Theresa to her chair and brought Pense to the library within moments. Standing before Daniel, her eyes spoke volumes, her voice nothing.

Daniel stopped playing and said softly, "My job is almost

done. I'm leaving my violin in your keeping, Pense Magdalena. The strings will dance again some day in the hands of another. You'll know to whom you should entrust the instrument." Daniel sat down, put the instrument on the footstool and reached for Pense's hands.

"I'll keep it until I know who must play it," Pense said.

Daniel drew Pense slowly to him. "You believe you are Magdalena?" When Pense nodded Daniel continued, "I believe it too. Listen, my dearest. The marriage board was mine to give and it's the one thing you have left of my love, incomplete as it is. I built it not realizing that our marriage was never to be."

"I understand." Pense's eyes never left Daniel's face.

"Somehow, rubbing that board completed the cycle," Daniel said. "We've come together again one last time."

"The marriage board was the means that brought you to Knightswood," Pense said.

Daniel let go of Pense's hands and reached for the coins. "These were Zizou's. She wanted you to have them, along with her books and her cards."

Pense reached for the coins. "Zizou's dead, isn't she? She wouldn't give these to me if she was alive."

"Zizou was a young spirit in an old body."

Pense raised her hands to touch Daniel's face. As she ran her fingers over his craggy features, the room seemed to lack air. Nothing moved. Time stood still. Pense's fingers stopped at his lips.

Daniel's heavy breathing broke the silence. "Thank you for bringing me back, Magdalena. I had to return to close gates, finish business. I had to make you understand that our son lived. I'm so sorry, my darling. What your parents and I did was wrong. Kenneth should have stayed with you, at Knightswood."

Pense silenced Daniel by bending forward and gently kissing him on the lips. Tears coursed down her cheeks and in a voice that was mature and loving, she said, "It was you that sent him back to me. I knew as soon as I saw Kenneth that our child had lived and come home to me, that you hadn't lied in your letters. You can rest in peace, Palumb Furtuna. You're forgiven." Pense dropped to her knees at Daniel's feet. "You mustn't leave without me, Palumb Furtuna. I have to go with you this time. Don't leave me here again."

"I won't," Daniel said, tears running down his cheeks. He

bent to kiss Pense on the cheeks, the hair, the forehead. "You've got to heed the dove, Magdalena. Only then will your spirit be rejoined with mine, my love."

Theresa, startled by Daniel's actions and fearful of what Pense's next move might be, acted to break the spell, to get the girl away from Daniel. Taking Pense under the arms, she struggled to help her to her feet. Not daring to look directly at Daniel, Theresa said, "Pense, listen to me. Daniel's too upset to realize you're not Magdalena. I think you should go to your room."

"And if I'm Magdalena, as I believe," Pense said, "I must leave when the dove comes. But what will happen to Pense Aventi?" She looked imploringly from Theresa to Daniel.

Daniel put his hand on Pense's shoulder. "It's difficult to separate spirit from life but Magdalena must leave, only Magdalena. Nothing must happen to Pense the young woman."

Saying nothing, Pense reached to touch Daniel's face, his hair, his cheeks, his lips. Then turning from him, and without glancing back, she left the library

Daniel bent his head so that Theresa wouldn't see his anguish, then touching her arm said, "I have something for you. Kenneth loved you, my dear Theresa, and was planning to marry you. Each week while he lived here, he put some of his pay on this." Daniel took a small velvet box from his pocket and gave it to Theresa. "When Kenneth didn't return from England, the jeweler put the box away and forgot about it. On my insistence, his son, the present owner, searched and found it. Please wear it in remembrance of Kenneth."

Opening the box, Theresa found a ring of gold imbedded with diamonds. She recognized it immediately as the one that she and Kenneth had chosen years before. "Would you do the honor, Daniel?"

"My pleasure." Daniel took the ring and slid it on the appropriate finger. "Shh, don't say anything," he bent toward Theresa. "May I be so bold as to ask for a kiss. I shall carry it with me to Kenneth."

Theresa put her hands up to Daniel's face. She leaned toward him and kissed him gently on the forehead . . . on the lips. "It was a pleasure knowing you, Palumb Furtuna. I know we won't see each other again on this earth. Wherever you go, whatever you do, our thoughts will be with you, always. Take care, my friend. Tell

Kenneth I'll love him forever." She lovingly wiped Daniel's tears with her fingers and kissed him again on the forehead.

"Theresa," Daniel said, his heart ravaged with the anguish of a second separation, "Magdalena's going to need your guidance. You'll understand what I mean."

"Pense and I have talked about this a great deal during the past several days. I'll handle whatever comes along." At the door of the library Theresa turned and said, "Daniel, Godspeed. May you truly rest in peace this time. I'll pray your journey isn't interrupted and that the winds carry you as far as you wish to go."

Daniel sat for a long time, thinking, recuperating. When he finally moved, it was to climb the stairs to his room. He sorted his possessions into three piles on the bed – one for Johnny, one for Sharona, one for Pense Magdalena – then placed a note on each. In a last gesture, he removed the handkerchief from the back of the drawer and put it in a pants pocket.

At the foot of the stairs Daniel forced himself to look in the mirror. The reflection that looked back at him confirmed his innermost fear. Life was leaving his body. His image was so faint that all he could discern were his eyes, nose and mouth. His life hung on foresight, the smell of success and the ability to talk his way to victory. That's all Daniel had, all he needed during the next twelve hours.

Memories flowed as Danny Cudney wandered from room to room, looking, touching, remembering. The last room he visited was the dining room. Danny closed the door behind him. When he appeared again, he went to the library to wait for Johnny's six o'clock call. Miraculously he managed to fall asleep, a much needed rest if he was to fight, and win his biggest battle

Johnny's Farm - early morning

Johnny found Daniel sleeping in the library, a blanket tucked around him, cats on his knee. He looked so pale and quiet, Johnny feared he was dead. One gentle touch to a warm hand, and Daniel's eyes opened. What his body lacked in energy, Daniel's eyes made up for in brilliance. Unlike most old eyes, his were bright and sharp as though they belonged to a forty-year-old rather than a man who could be more than one hundred. "Give me a few minutes," Daniel had said. So Johnny left for the barn.

Fearing a motorbike ride would be too strenuous, Johnny hitched the team to the wagon and made the seat comfortable with an old buffalo robe. After helping Daniel into the conveyance, Johnny untied Loco expecting him to jump into the back of the wagon. Loco instead jumped into the front and laid his big head on Daniel's knee.

"That dog has a mind of his own today," Johnny said, slapping the reins over the backs of the horses. "I had to tie him in the barn last night. He was heading back to the farm but I wanted him here at the house. The albino's been hanging around the barn. I didn't want that deer run into the ground. He'll do it and have venison for lunch if I'm not there."

"Poor Loco," Daniel said, stroking the big head. "You're a real rogue, aren't you boy, just like the guy that saved you."

Avoiding deep holes and corduruoy rills, Johnny drove along the West River Road and up the hill beyond Pense's Mountain. At Daniel's request Johnny stopped at the crest of the hill.

The valley was a study in grey and white. At some point during the night winds had died and a heavy mantle of icing-sugar hoarfrost coated everything. Mists that rose from fields and glens were tinted by the thin rays of the rising sun. The eastern horizon blazed red to orange. While delicate tints of pink streaked toward the southern skyline, tendrils of yellow blushed through the grey north sky.

Johnny concentrated for several minutes on the western horizon where a deep red glow came from the direction of the Long Swamp.

"What do you make of that?" he asked Daniel, pointing in the direction of the phenomenon. "I'd say it was someone's barn in flames. But I know there's no farm that deep into the swamp. There's no one lives within ten miles of that area of the bog. The hunters don't even travel through there."

"Swamp gas," Daniel said. "It's rising through the frost from the swamp muck."

"I've seen will-o'-the-wisps and swamp gas and they've never been red colored. That's so high in the sky too. I can't figure it. The light's bouncing like fire. I can't tell whether it's in the middle of the swamp, or way over on the other side."

"As long as it's not your barn, I wouldn't worry, Johnny. Strange things happen that we aren't meant to know about," Daniel said, his mind on more pressing issues. "Do you think they've arrived?"

"A truck's been along the road, but there aren't any car tire tracks. I'd say we're the first."

"Good. I want the upper hand."

"Are yuh sure that you're up to this? You don't look well. Didn't sleep well last night, did you?"

"It's my heart that's acting up. This is a now-or-never situation, Johnny. It won't take long and I won't have another opportunity."

"If you look sharp," Johnny said, "our lucky token's standing in the field by the cedar copse. She's been to the spring to drink. She's a beauty."

The doe, made almost invisible by white frost on trees and ground, picked her way toward the cedars and disappeared into the thick underbrush.

"Your luck's going to hold," Johnny said. "Well, looky here." He pointed at the track leading to the south pasture gate. "It looks like a truck backed right up to the gate. I've either lost or gained horses. I'll let you off at the barn and go check."

While Johnny was away, Daniel busied himself in the barn's upper level where a temporary area had been set up in a corner of the granary. Daniel pulled two chairs up to an old pine table. He lit three barn lanterns and hung them from nails in the beams, then methodically searched the area for holes and cracks where a card could be hidden. When he found one, Daniel stuffed it with straw. The setting was definitely to Daniel's advantage. The sounds and smells of the barn were familiar and calming to him. His heart warned Daniel again and again of what was to come, but he willed the pain to be gone. When it stubbornly remained, Daniel tried to ignore it.

Johnny, blowing on his hands, appeared from the stable area. "Loco'll let us know when they arrive. I've fed all the horses, includin' the two that pulled Zizou's wagon. What are they doing in my pasture?"

"Zizou wanted you to care for them. She's no use for them now. She left money for feed. It's on my bed at the house."

Johnny rubbed his hands together to warm them, then shoved them into his pants pockets. "She won't need them again?"

"No," Daniel said. "Not where she's going."

Johnny looked over the arrangements. He used this corner of the barn as a makeshift shelter while building his house. "Are you positive yuh want me to stay?"

"You're the one who has to make sure he never goes back on his word. Don't say anything. Just listen. I've all the information here." Daniel patted the breast pocket of his suit. "I'll make him sign and then everything is yours for safekeeping."

"What direction is the chit-chat going to take?"

"I don't know. Just listen."

Outside, Loco barked. "They're here. Are yuh ready?"

Count sat down, adjusted his jacket and straightened his tie.

"I've never seen the like," Johnny said. "It's seven in the morning and you're seated at a table in my barn dressed in suit and tie like you're going to a dance."

"I'm going out in style." Daniel smiled. "This time I have a choice."

Plumb Loco's welcome alternated between frenzied barking and vicious snarling.

"Damn!" Johnny exclaimed. "The dog's gone into overdrive." Johnny ran across the threshing floor. "Loco! Plumb Loco," he called. "Heel, boy!"

He disappeared out the door and returned with Loco in tow.

"Everything all right?" Daniel asked.

"Don't know what's got into the dog. He won't let them out of the car."

"I'd think that Loco's found one of the men that abused him," Daniel said. "Give him to me. I'll hold him." Daniel put his hand through Loco's collar and talked in a quiet voice, commanding the dog to sit. Loco obeyed, eyes on the door, a threatening growl in his throat. "It's okay, boy. Let it be for now. We'll get the man together."

"This way, gentlemen." Johnny came through the door, Blake behind him, followed by J.P. Harris. Johnny gave a toothy grin, bowed and gave a flourish of his arms as though he were greeting royalty. "Welcome. This isn't what you're used to, but I hear the competition can't be beat."

"We'll see," Harris said, his eyes adjusting to the dim interior. He focused on Daniel seated at the gaming table, Plumb Loco at his side. "Get that goddamn dog out of here."

"He stays," Johnny said. "I gather you two knew each other in less than pleasant circumstances. I'd say Loco hates your guts."

"Come in," Daniel said. "Sit down. Make yourself comfortable. This won't take long."

His words were accentuated by Loco's deep-throated snarling.

"Cocky, aren't you?" Harris said.

"I'm sure of my talent," Daniel answered. "Shall we start? I'd like to be away from here soon."

"Does he have to be here?" Blake jabbed a finger toward Johnny.

"Yes. Johnny owns the barn. Are we going to play cards or personalities?"

Harris walked toward the table. "You're in my seat," he said. "I always sit facing west."

Johnny had taken hold of Loco's collar and moved to squat, his back against a barn beam to Daniel's right.

Daniel acquiesced to Harris. "Whatever you wish. I don't have any preferences or superstitions." He got up stiffly and walked around the table while Harris slid into the vacated seat and drew an unopened deck of cards from his pocket. Round one is mine, Daniel thought as he sat in the chair he preferred and set a sealed deck on the table.

"You'd better be good, Cudzinki." Harris motioned that Blake should stand directly behind his chair. "I hate someone wasting my time."

"I don't think so." Daniel motioned Blake to the side. "No one sees the cards but you and me, Harris."

Blake moved away, careful to keep a distance between himself and Loco.

"Shall we check the cards?" Daniel reached for Harris's deck, broke the seal, then sorted through them. Harris did the same to Daniel's. They exchanged decks and checked again.

"I'm satisfied," Harris said.

"Then don't stand on ceremony. Standard rules. Five games. Five card stud. Two card draw. Money on the table."

The Village - early morning

A village of one thousand souls is quick to rise and as quick to comprehend that something important has happened in their midst. Workers were the first to see the barrage of signs and posters when they arrived at the factory for their Monday-morning shift. The next were the shopkeepers who found their weekly paper full of photos of bed-sheeted protesters and a well-written story of the event.

By eight o'clock in the morning, every telephone in the area was busy, as word spread throughout the countryside that someone had taken on J.P. Harris. The factory's office and Harris's home were inundated with long-distance calls from city newspapers and radio stations wanting to speak with J.P. He was nowhere to be found. The village, like a crock of sauerkraut, was in full ferment.

Knightswood - early morning

Sharona entered Pense's bedroom and touched Theresa's shoulder to wake her.

"I'll sit for awhile," she whispered when Theresa roused enough to understand. "You try to get some proper sleep."

"She hasn't moved, hasn't opened her eyes," Theresa said.

"The poor child." Sharona stroked a pale cheek. "She isn't running a fever. This isn't at all like our Pense."

"We can only wait. We'll keep a vigil and hope for the best. She's just physically and emotionally exhausted."

Sharona made herself comfortable in the chair and reached for Pense's hand.

"What time is it?" Theresa asked.

"Eight o'clock. We talked until three and then you fell asleep. I had a horrible thought. Suppose that Daniel really is the ghost of Danny Cudney. If Danny died today, shouldn't he consider the difference in time? Five o'clock our time is not 5:00 p.m. South African time. Daniel might die five-six hours earlier than he anticipates."

"That would put his demise around the noon hour today! This situation is so surreal, Sharona. Think of this. What if Daniel *is* the real flesh-and-blood Danny Cudney and has got it in his head that he has to die today? He'll die by hook or by crook. Where did Daniel go?"

"I don't know," Sharona said. "Johnny wouldn't say what they're up to. He only said it was a most important meeting for Daniel."

Theresa tucked the covers around Pense and gently stroked her hair. The girl stirred but didn't open her eyes. "I saw this once," Theresa said. "Magdalena did this when Kenneth left. She opted out of life, slept as much as she could for several months, wouldn't come out of her room, didn't eat much. It was her way of grieving. She came around eventually, then wouldn't allow talk about Kenneth."

"But Pense is mourning an old man she hardly knew."

"In her mind she's Magdalena. And the mind is a powerful thing. So's love if we're to believe that Daniel is Danny Cudney."

"Who knows what we're to believe? I'm just worried about Pense. Let's hope she snaps out of this soon," Sharona said.

Theresa turned away from the bed to look out the window toward the hill and the oak tree. Something had to be done, but what? "I'm going to the kitchen. What I need is a cup of strong coffee. I need a clear head now."

Johnny's Barn - 8:00 a.m.

In the heat of competition no one complained about the cold or the smell in the barn. Harris lost the first game to a Royal flush – won the second with four of a kind – lost the third to four of a kind and won the fourth with a straight flush. A substantial pile of money lay on his side of the table. Harris was gloating over his good luck. "I think I'll quit now," he said. "I don't take IOU's from people like you."

"We said five games," Daniel reminded him. "I'm looking forward to the opportunity of wiping your slate." Daniel's right hand was inside his jacket massaging his heart. There was something very wrong. He had been expecting the pain, but it was coming too soon.

"One more game," Daniel said. "But we don't play for money. I've no need for your money. We play for land and an apology."

"An apology? Land?" Harris, busy sorting the bills on the table, laughed.

"Given by you, if you lose," Daniel said.

"And if I win?" Harris asked.

"Information from me." Daniel replied.

"What sort of information?"

"About developments, factories, televisions," Daniel said.

"No money. Just information from you or an apology and some land from me. What land?" Harris was interested enough to stop counting his money.

"The hill. Put your portion of Pense's Mountain on the table."

Harris laughed and slapped the table. "With odds like that, what do I have to lose? Words are useless, you crazy old man."

Daniel shrugged, then smiled, knowing that he was both crazy and old. "Your deal," he said. "Keep your hands where I can see them, Harris."

"Same applies to you, fraud. What've you got in that inside pocket that your hand keeps going in there?"

"Nothing," Daniel said opening his jacket.

"Blake," Harris commanded. "Check the pocket."

When Blake put his hand into Daniel's pocket, Loco went wild. It was all Johnny could do to restrain the dog.

"There's nothing in there, boss."

As the two card sharks went head-to-head again, Johnny and Blake were silent. The only sounds were the cards hitting the table, Loco's constant growl and the horses moving in their stalls on the lower level. Despite the cold, Daniel loosened his tie and unbuttoned his collar. Harris wiped his brow with the sleeve of his sweater.

Harris, confident that he was going to win, leaned back in his chair. "Gimme two."

Daniel wiped the back of his hand over his mouth, then ran it through his hair. "One for me."

Harris fiddled with his sweater, pulling the right sleeve down then diddling with the left one.

Daniel folded then fanned his cards several times before saying, "Okay Let's see what you've got."

Harris placed four-of-a-kind on the table.

Daniel smiled and spread a Royal Flush in front of him. "Silly man."

"You cheated," Harris accused.

"I wouldn't accuse him of cheating," Blake said.

"You're right, of course, Blake," Daniel said. "Johnny, would you be so kind as to check the left sleeve of Cave Bat's sweater. If anyone's cheated, it's him."

Smiling, Johnny and Loco walked toward Harris.

Harris gripped his left sleeve with his right hand. "Just try to check it," he taunted.

"Take the sweater off, Harris." Johnny stood over the man, with one hand still on Loco's collar.

"Johnny," Daniel said. "Under the circumstances it's better that Blake helps his boss remove the sweater."

Blake, leery of the dog, didn't move.

Loco bared his teeth and lunged toward Harris. Johnny's strong arm held him back.

"All right," Harris said. "Back off with the dog. So I have a card or two up my sleeve. You won, so what?"

Daniel coughed. His hand went into his jacket to his heart.

"Could we get on with the apology? I really have little time to hang around."

"I'm not apologizing for anything. I'm leaving. I've got a factory to run." Harris gathered his money.

"Not so fast," Johnny said, helping himself to a fistful of the money. "If you cheated once, you cheated before. I say most of this loot belongs to Daniel."

Harris grabbed Johnny's arm. "It's mine," he said. "Keep your goddamned hands off it."

Loco twisted from Johnny's grasp and leapt. His jaw snapped around Harris's left wrist. Bones cracked. Blood spurted.

Harris screamed. "Get him off me! Get him off me!"

Blake made his move. Loco turned and lunged for Blake's knee, dropping him to the ground. Blake howled in pain.

Johnny grabbed Loco's collar and pulled him back.

"Down, Loco. Down, boy!" Daniel's cough was so violent he could hardly get the words out. "As soon as we get rid of these undesirables, Plumb will be okay, Johnny."

"No doubt," Johnny said. "Now that we have your attention, let's get on with business." Johnny put his hand on Daniel's shoulder. "Go ahead, Daniel. What do you want an apology for?"

Daniel's breathing was labored, his speech slow and deliberate. "A long time ago, a man was accused of a crime he didn't commit. He was accused of raping a woman who worked in the office at J.P. Harris, Ltd. The man's name was Danny Cudney. Your father was the guilty man."

Harris, clutching his left wrist with his right hand, laughed. "You stupid fool. You want an apology for something that happened years ago, something my father did?"

"That's right."

"Why should you care?" Harris sneered at Daniel.

"Danny Cudney is a member of the familia. I knew him."

"Well, I didn't and I'm not going to apologize."

"You lost. As per our agreement an apology is due. You may not have known Danny, or been aware of his situation, but I am and I do expect an apology. " Daniel placed three papers on the table.

Harris pushed his chair away from the tableto rise.

Johnny commanded. "Sit down or I'll turn Loco loose on yuh again. He'd love to chew you into dog meat, you arrogant bastard. If you treat humans like you treated this animal, you deserve to die.

You! Blake, stand behind Harris's chair where I can see you, too."

With difficulty Blake got to his feet and hobbled to Harris's chair. "Keep the dog under control, Johnny."

"He'll apologize," Daniel said. "Listen, Harris. You don't want people to know about your little vices, do you? Your apartment in Windsor. Oh, it's under Blake's name, but it's yours. You use it for your little diversions."

"I don't know what you are talking about." Harris said.

"Your preference for blondes, your drinking, your gambling, your marriage of convenience to a wife that could give you respectability, a wife that was willing to bend the rules to give you an heir."

"You're talking nonsense old man."

"There are doctor's records that you're sterile, hotel records that you're wining and dining women, chits for gambling debts."

Harris paled. He looked from Blake to Daniel. "You bastard! You told him," he accused Blake.

"Nobody told me," Daniel said. "And if I can find out, anyone can."

Johnny stood speechless beside Daniel, hoping the man knew what he was saying.

"You're living a lie, Harris. You always have," Daniel continued. "You see, you're the product of that rape. The girl was well paid for her baby. You were raised by the Harris family. Your arrival caused some talk but no one connected the girl to your father. People thought your parents were very clever to hide a pregnancy. After all, Mrs. Harris had been trying for years to have a baby. When all was said and done, your father turned to religion with fervor, trying to make amends."

If he was aware of his parentage Harris never let on. His face was a mask. "You're a vicious, silly old man," he spat at Daniel.

"You'd do well to listen, Harris. You didn't mind inheriting your father's money. You liked the power connected with his name. But you hated his frugal, confining, religious lifestyle." The pain was so great in Daniel's chest, it was all he could do to remain in his chair. "You ran the factory and upheld the Harris tradition of keeping your employees at poverty level and under your thumb. You ran the village. And you cleverly found a way to get around telling the truth about your vices. You became two people . . . the public Harris and the private J.P."

Daniel stopped, expecting a reaction. When Harris didn't speak, he continued. "The *private J.P.* is as devious, slimy and crooked, as the *public Harris* tries to appear straight and honest, isn't he? Both public and private person don't mind using people to get what they want, do they? Does the name Kenneth Walker ring a bell, Harris?"

Harris appeared startled by mention of the name.

"Yes," Daniel said. "I knew Kenneth Walker. Now, to avoid further chit-chat about that situation, I'd suggest you read the papers."

Harris grabbed one of the papers in his right hand and read quickly.

"One paper holds the official apology, the second the information. It's all documented. Johnny will keep a copy. He'll make it public if you ever go back on your word."

"What's to go back on? This is a nothing apology. Nobody'll believe it."

"There are attachments," Daniel said. He handed Johnny a thick notebook. "The facts are all in here – names, addresses, dates. And of course, the last document on the table is the one that gives the hill back to Theresa Inachio."

"You're kidding. That would give you access to more than six hundred acres of prime land on this side of the river for your enterprises."

"You're going back on your word again. But you needn't worry, Harris. There's no factory. I'm not an industrialist, am I Johnny?"

"No," Johnny managed to say. "Keough's renting my farm and Theresa isn't going to sell her land."

"That doesn't surprise me. And I'd be astonished if you weren't involved in the protest too. Aren't you speaking for them? Isn't that what this is really about? You want me to give you some concessions for the men that work for me." Harris addressed Johnny rather than Daniel.

Johnny shrugged. "Of course, that is why I'm here. Let's make some headway with the factory situation while you're caught in a corner."

Daniel, in pain, became impatient. "I'm taking care of personal business. Johnny'll negotiate with you about worker's demands at the appropriate time. The damage is done now. Freedom's out of its cage. Your employees found their voice and you've been forced to negotiate with them. There'll be no more low wages, no more lack of insurance and poor working conditions."

"Damn you!" Harris spat.

"Sign," Daniel said, taking an envelope and fresh copies of the papers from his pocket. "Wipe the blood off your hand first. I don't want it to appear that you signed under duress. Don't take up any more of my time." Handing the envelope to Johnny, Daniel said, "Post this letter, if necessary. It gives my lawyer in Montreal permission to make public everything I've said about Harris, if he backs down on his signature."

Blake made a dive for the envelope. Loco ripped his collar from Johnny's hand and leapt. His teeth sank into an elbow. Blake howled and dropped to the ground, his hands protecting his face.

Johnny dived for Loco's collar again. "You don't learn easily, Blake. Do yuh?"

"Okay." Harris put his hands in the air. "I'll sign. But what assurances do I have that Johnny Wallace won't talk?"

"I can't say we're gentlemen," Daniel said. "We're despicable and disreputable, too. But you have the word of a Rom Baro, and a war veteran, and that's enough. I'd worry more about your driver. Write your name, then print it under the signature on both these papers." Daniel handed the fresh copies and a pen across the table. "Date the papers. Johnny, tie Loco up for a moment."

Johnny, holding tight to the collar, led Loco to the grain room and shut him in. Plumb slammed against the closed door.

Daniel watched Harris sign. "Now, give the papers to Johnny to witness," he said. "He'll keep them. If I were you, I'd start the land proceedings with your lawyer now, so there'll be fewer questions asked. If you don't, my lawyer will contact yours by the end of the week. You'll want to keep those table copies for your records."

Harris handed the paper to Johnny, grabbed the bloodstained copies and ripped them to shreds.

"One more thing," Daniel said, looking at Harris. "Put the money you pocketed back on the table."

"That's robbery," Harris said.

"Could be," Daniel said. "I call it justice."

Harris did as he was told then rose to leave. "Blake, get up off the floor and let's get out of here." Harris scuttled like a rat toward the door, never looking back.

Blake limped behind clutching his elbow. He turned to Daniel just before he stepped through the door. "I've got to hand it to you, old man," he said. "You play a good game of poker."

Johnny waited until he heard the car leave before releasing Loco. "Whoa! That was a revelation. I didn't know about Harris. No one around here knows." Johnny leafed through the incriminating material. "Hell and damnation! With this information he'd be a fool if he didn't agree to everything."

"Keep the papers. And keep my word that you won't talk about this morning's events," Daniel said. "We got what we wanted. The information doesn't go further." Something was very wrong with his heart. He was perspiring profusely and in terrible pain. "What time is it, Johnny?"

"Four minutes past ten," Johnny said, looking at his wrist watch.

It's happening too fast, Daniel thought. I should have more time. This isn't right.

"So, what do yuh want me to do with these papers?" Johnny said.

"Use the information against Cave Bat if you have to. And use the money we took from him to hire a lawyer. There's no address on the envelope I handed you. I don't have one in Montreal."

"How did you know he was cheating?"

"I didn't. I took a chance. He was always fiddling with his sleeve. The gamble paid off. I think he had cards up his sleeve, but I don't think he used them. Another player would have. He was afraid of me. Or maybe he was afraid of you. What time is it? How fast can you get me to Long Swamp crossroads?"

"We'll be there a half hour after I hitch the team. Tell me, Daniel. Did you lose the games on purpose?"

"I had to dangle something to get Cave Bat's attention. There was only one patsy at that table and it wasn't me. If you could hurry with the hitching, Johnny, it would be appreciated."

Johnny worked quickly to harness the team. When he finished, Johnny helped the old man into the high seat. Loco leapt in beside them. Johnny drove out the lane and down the road, stopping at the top of the hill at Daniel's insistence.

Daniel took one last, loving look at Pense's Mountain and Knightswood. The last time he left Millbrook, Danny had the gut-wrenching feelings of a condemned man. This time he could exit with peace in his heart. Below him, where Pense Magdalena slept under the watchful eye of Theresa and Sharona, he had completed his tasks. Now Daniel had to finish his own personal journey.

Daniel searched for the dove. When it didn't fly to him, he whispered softly to the wind, hoping that it would carry his voice to the attic at Knightswood. "Come with me this time, my dearest Magdalena. Follow the dove."

Johnny kept the team at a fast trot, realizing that time was crucial. Plumb Loco sat with his head on Daniel's knee and his rump against Johnny.

Tamas's car was parked at the crossroads, waiting for them. Niki and Tamas stood on the road, watching their approach.

"*Sar San*," Tamas said, coming toward the wagon. "*Rom Baro* is ready?"

"There's something wrong," Johnny said, getting down. Help me get Daniel out of the wagon."

After the three men helped Daniel to the ground, he stood beside Johnny, Loco at his side. "Don't fret, my friend." Daniel put a hand on Johnny's arm. "What matters is that we had good times and accomplished much."

"That we did," Johnny said. "I haven't mentioned it, but the garage robbery was the right touch. Keough wouldn't have taken three hours to investigate a stolen motorcycle. How did you persuade Ed MacTavish to go along with us?"

"I'm afraid the robbery wasn't in the plan," Daniel said. "It was for real - an opportunist who knew our plans."

Tamas shuffled his feet and looked at the ground.

"Johnny. It's time for me to leave," Daniel's hand was still on Johnny's arm. "You will take care of the womenfolk. Love Pense dearly as your daughter, Sharona as your wife, Theresa as a mother and friend."

Johnny threw his arms around Daniel and hugged the frail body. "And you as a father," he said. "Old man, come back if you can."

"I don't wish to come back," Daniel said. "Not as me, not as an old man. I pray nothing interrupts my journey this time." Daniel leaned over a little to meet Loco on common ground. "Thanks, old boy," he said. "You've taken good care of Johnny for me. Continue to do so." The dog licked Daniel's outstretched hand and whined.

Tamas, taking Daniel by the arm, helped him into the car. Johnny wiped tears from his eyes, stayed by the wagon and watched as they drove away, into the Long Swamp. Daniel never looked back. Johnny didn't expect he would.

The Village - mid-morning

West Road wound through bottom-land in the valley, with fields on one side and the waterway on the other. Where the road joined the village, one could drive south and east toward Mount Forest or cross the iron bridge to Main Street and the North Hill. Johnny was torn between heart and humanity. He knew that he should head home but chose to cross the bridge. Curiosity is a strange friend. Johnny wanted to see the results of the final ploy in Count's grand scheme. Johnny heard their success long before he saw any evidence. A swell of shouting, whistling and cheering bounced from north to south hills, filling the valley with its exuberance. People stopped what they were doing to listen, then put down their work to follow the sound. All roads led to the factory.

Johnny pulled his team up at the back of the parking lot, behind a seething mass of humanity, all shouting, singing, jostling for room. He'd never seen anything like it in the village. People were carrying posters that they'd ripped from telephone poles. They wore signs in their hats and had pinned posters to their backs. When Johnny spotted Mike, he leaped from the wagon and into the melee.

"What happened?" Johnny shouted above the din.

"Johnny! We did it! He capitulated. Harris'll talk with us."

"He agreed to everything?" Johnny asked.

"Nah," Mike said. "He's agreed to our demands to talk. Not with him alone but with five people for each side like we discussed at the Stamp Club."

"When did he decide to cooperate?"

"A half hour ago. After the day shift spread word about the posters, the lot started to fill up with workers, their wives and the curious from Main Street. Then the skeleton crew walked out. Everyone started to chant and sing. But no one'd laid eyes on Harris yet. He finally showed up in his car. As soon as Blake saw the protest, he tried to turn around to leave. But the car was surrounded. So he drove slowly through us, right up to the front door."

Johnny and Mike were now surrounded by other members of the Stamp Club. With much comraderie Mike went on to explain that Harris tried to run into the building but was stopped. Blake couldn't protect him because he was limping and couldn't run. Harris was trapped in front of the car door. He and Blake talked, then

Harris climbed on the bumper and sat on the car's hood. That's when everyone noticed that Harris had his wrist wrapped in a chamois and Blake was holding his elbow.

"We figured they were heading for the first-aid station in the factory to bandage their wounds before heading to the hospital in Mount Forest," Charlie said.

"Makes sense," Johnny said. "What happened next?"

"As soon as Harris raised his good arm, the crowd went silent," Mike continued. "Harris said that he would sit down with us but we shouted that wasn't good enough. We told Harris that four people had to sit with him in negotiations and that the workers had to okay who they were."

"Harris agreed," Charlie broke into the conversation. "But only after a few fellows started to rock the car. Then George wrote up the meeting agreement on a piece of paper and it was handed up for Harris to sign. He did! We got it witnessed."

"Great!" Johnny said. "Where's Harris now?"

"We let him go into the factory, him and Blake," Mike said. "He's in there, listening to us out here."

"Frickin' looked like they'd been in a dustup," George said. "Harris was favorin' that limp wrist. Blake was hobblin' and carryin' his elbow. There was blood on both of 'em."

Johnny smiled and thought, if the guys only knew what had gone on in his barn. "Any problems?" he asked.

"Well, there was pushing and shoving. And maybe a punch or two were thrown. Some of the wives are present so the guys behaved themselves. Everyone will go home pretty soon. They're just letting off some steam. Another fifteen minutes and we'll wind up the old manual whistle. They'll obey the whistle. They're used to jumping to its tune."

"Did you ken the gates upriver?" Bill asked. "Harris canna' get anyone tae work on them. Electrics are off and Sebastian Temple is nae tae to be foun'. He's taken his kit and booted."

Johnny shook hands all round. "Good work fellows. I've gotta run. Don't forget to leave a dozen or so protesters here. Tell them to picket on public property. Keep the pressure on Harris. I am happy for all of you."

"They're all asking who the hooded men were," Mike said. "Told them I didn't know and that's God's truth. Where's that Count fellow? You two are the ones that pulled this off, aren't you?"

"It's best that no one knows who planned this. As for *The Count Daniel Cudzinki,* he's gone. In fact, he had to leave rather quickly."

"I'm sorry to hear that," Mike said. "We should've had the opportunity to thank him."

"I was sorry to see him go, too," Johnny said. "He was an extraordinary man. I'll miss him. Look. I've really got to go home. We'll talk later. We'll have another meeting of the Stamp Club. Call them together for next Saturday morning."

"Sure." Mike grinned and waved. "Saturday, at The China."

Knightswood - forenoon

When Theresa heard the Factory whistle, she glanced at the kitchen clock. Odd, she thought, the whistle was thirty minutes early, and it had a strange though familiar sound. She hurried to finish the sandwich tray, then went up to Pense's room.

Sharona was seated in a chair beside Pense's bed, holding the girl's hand.

"I've brought some lunch." Theresa set the tray on the night table. "Has anything changed?"

"No. Pense doesn't appear to be listening."

"Well, I know what has to be done," Theresa said. "You stay here. Don't leave Pense. I'm going to the attic. Now, don't look at me like that. I'm not daft. I know exactly what I'm doing."

Theresa pulled one of Johnny's old sweaters over her head, found the flashlight and climbed the stairs muttering, "You're a crazy old woman, Inachio, but it's worth the chance."

Determined not to be dissuaded by the cold, bugs and bats, Theresa walked with a firm step past furniture and stacks of pictures to the back attic, to Magdalena's corner. Hands trembling, legs numb, she leaned against the sewing table. "Don't lose your nerve now, silly woman."

Bracing herself for 'unusual' occurrences, Theresa spoke to the four walls. "Magdalena, if you're here, you have to listen to me." Theresa glanced around the attic. When nothing seemed out of place or unusual, she relaxed a little. "Magdalena. This is important to me, and to you. It's about Danny Cudney."

What was that rustling in the corner? A mouse? Dirt falling from the ceiling?

"Magdalena. He was here. He came to tell us about Kenneth,

to set the record straight."

Dust seemed to lift from the floor to swirl about Theresa. She gasped as a piercing wall of cold moved through her, back to front. The dust shimmered between her and the window. It seemed to move as though trying to form itself into a mass. Light from the flashlight flickered round the back attic.

"Magdalena." Theresa's voice was not so strong or confident now. "We have a very upset child who believes she's you. If you have anything to do with this, you must cease immediately. You led your life. Let Pense lead hers in peace."

Wood snapped. Theresa's throat constricted in fear. Her left hand flew to her chest. This was too much excitement for an old woman. "Do you hear me?" Theresa said, voice cracking. "There's nothing more that you can do, Magdalena. Danny's gone. He's waiting for you now. He wants you to join him. Magdalena, listen to me. You have to leave Knightswood. You must go to Palumb Furtuna, to Danny Cudney."

Theresa tried to make out what stood between her and the window. Was sun shining on the dust making it look like a wisp of white mist? Was it taking the form of a woman?

"Magdalena, we were close friends. I thought we knew each other. I thought we understood each other. In my years as your companion, I never demanded, never asked, never expected anything from you. I have to demand now that you leave. You must go to Danny. Listen to the grandfather clock. It's chiming the noon hour. In a few minutes, Magdalena, he expects to see you. I demand you go. Go!" Theresa stamped her foot to emphasize her request.

The mass of dust swirled in its private little dervish of wind. It seemed to assume the form of a slender woman dressed in translucent robes of white that flickered with a sensuous, unearthly light.

Mesmerized by the play of light, Theresa glanced from the window and grey day outside to the mass of shimmering mist. She was chilled to the bone, rooted to the floor with fear. The mist swirled toward her. Forgetting she held a flashlight, Theresa instinctively thrust her right hand out to push it away, and the light fell to the floor with a crash. Immediately the spectre changed color and spun away to the window.

"Magdalena, if you're here, I command you to leave. Do you understand what I am saying? You must leave or you'll miss Danny."

The Dove appeared at the window as she spoke. It hovered for a few seconds then began to beat its wings frantically against the glass. On the inside, the gossamer form floated to the window and swirled at the glass.

Theresa reached to the table for support. Her right hand landed on a round covered tin, one of Magdalena's button boxes.

The swirling form scoured the window with its shimmering web of light.

Theresa grabbed the tin and threw it. Glass shattered when the old wood frame broke. As the dove turned away, the surreal misty form seemed to ooze through the broken glass as though following behind. Both of Theresa's hands flew to her breast.

Johnny, heading for the back door, heard glass shatter. He looked up just in time to see a tin flying through the air, scattering its contents. Johnny watched in amazement as a cascade of colorful buttons fell to the ground. One hit him on the shoulder then dropped to the step. Bending over, Johnny picked up a small white button in the shape of a dove.

When buttons rain from the sky, something's very wrong, Johnny thought. "Sharona!" he shouted running through the first floor, then taking the steps two at a time to the second.

"In here," Sharona called. "I'm in Pense's room."

Johnny stuck his head through the door. "Everything okay?"

Sharona nodded. "We're fine," she said. "I'm not so sure about Theresa. She's in the attic. I heard a crash and an ungodly scream."

"Theresa. *Theresa*!" Johnny raced up the attic's steps and found Theresa standing by the broken window. "What happened?"

Theresa put a shaking hand on Johnny's shoulder. "Either I just said goodbye to Magdalena, or I'm experiencing that one moment of insanity that everyone's permitted in their lifetime. You'll have to fix the window, Johnny. I threw a tin of buttons through it."

"The window's no problem," Johnny said, putting his arms around Theresa. "Are you all right?"

"You know, Johnny. I think that everyone's going to feel much better from now on. Did you see Pense?"

"She was crying in Sharona's arms."

"Thank God. Will you help an old woman down the stairs?"

"My pleasure," Johnny said, hugging Theresa to him. "Did I ever tell you how much I love you?"

"Every day. With your smile." Theresa grinned. "I couldn't

ask for a better man to be my chosen son." Johnny kissed Theresa's wrinkled brow and led her down the stairs.

The Long Swamp - afternoon

A light snow began to fall throughout the Saugeen River valley around the noon hour. The first snow of the winter wasn't a heavy fall, but a gentle scattering of flakes, the harbinger of what was to come in the months ahead. Pense's Mountain shouldered its thin white blanket like a regal robe. Autumn's brilliant colors were striking against the pallid landscape. The plaintive call of the wild geese had an urgency to it as they winged their way down the valley.

Activity around Knightswood reflected the onset of an early winter. Theresa and Pense were cleaning storm windows in the carriage shed. Plumb Loco lay near them keeping his one good eye on Pense, hoping that she'd go to the mountain and take him with her.

Sharona and Johnny worked in the henhouse. While Sharona put insulating straw in the laying boxes, Johnny fixed the hole where a mink had sneaked in and killed several of Theresa's best laying hens.

"A *kanny* in the pot has to come from somewhere," Sharona said. "Until I saw the hole, I was blaming the camp for stealing all the chickens that went missing. Tell me again where it was that you saw this red glow?"

"It appeared to come from the bowels of the Long Swamp, somewhere near the bog hole."

Sharona tucked straw into the last box. "Finish up," she said, "then get the motorbike. I'll get the jackets. Let's go see if we can find it before any tracks are covered with snow."

"Why do yuh want to check it out?" Johnny asked.

"It's just a hunch."

The bike roared west along the winding gravel road, on the sort of wild ride that Johnny enjoyed. Sharona was easy on the bike, not at all afraid. Unlike Daniel, she rode well, her arms around Johnny's waist. At the beginning of the Long Swamp, Johnny slowed down and they both watched for unusual tracks on the side of the road.

"Zizou's wagon came through here," Johnny shouted over the motor. "It's the double track with hoof prints between." He stopped four miles in at a narrow dirt path that led north into the heart of the bog. "Vehicles parked at the side of the road and the wagon was driven in here with people walking behind it."

Johnny pulled the bike off the road and parked it behind a

thicket of elderberry bushes. He and Sharona walked hand-in-hand, following the tracks past thick stands of alders, sumac and cedar. As the two pushed deeper into the swamp, birds whistled their disapproval then took off for more secretive roosts. Deer, catching the human scent, turned tail and leapt deeper into the swamp. More than a mile off the secondary track, they found a small trail, just wide enough for the wagon. The horses had been unhitched and it appeared that the wagon had been pulled by hand down this trail. Johnny and Sharona, hand in hand, followed the tracks as they led over a small tamarack-covered hill.

"I'm glad you stayed, Sharona. I thought for sure you'd leave this time." Johnny squeezed Sharona's hand then leaned over and kissed her.

"I made up my mind to leave until I told Keough about your motorbike. At that moment I realized you were the most important thing in my life, you and Pense. I couldn't leave you – no more than Pense could leave Theresa."

"I thought she'd leave also." Johnny bent to look more closely at the tracks.

"At first I did too. But cracks began to appear. Zizou helped us. She tried not to paint too rosy a picture of life in the Kumpania. Pense is clever enough to separate fantasy from the reality of a situation."

"Except when it comes to Count Daniel Cudzinki."

Sharona walked in silence for a while. "I don't know what to make of Pense thinking she was Magdalena. She sure didn't act like herself when Daniel was around. As for Daniel, I choose to believe he was a cunning old Gypsy that took the identity of Danny Cudney. He was probably a member of the Irish travelers who may have had some connection with Kenneth Walker. That would explain Theresa's ring."

Johnny shook his head. "I'm still trying to sort the man out. He was flesh-and-blood solid. He saved my life in Africa. Explain that one. I didn't dream it up, yuh know. He was there and I can't believe it's possible for a soldier to be more than one hundred years old. And where'd the uniform come from? How could he play such music if he wasn't the Gypsy fella? All I know for sure is that he came, and we're all the better for it. I'm leanin' toward him being a ghost."

"Pense believes that he was the ghost of Danny Cudney," Sharona said. "Theresa says that she now thinks that Daniel was really Magdalena's Danny and that he was well over one hundred years old. She thinks that he didn't die in South Africa but was seriously wounded and wandered around for years with no identity. She feels that something triggered his memory and that he came back to Millbrook to see if Magdalena was still alive. But she can't explain how he knew about the ring."

"Theresa believes in ghosts whatever she says now. She went so far as to tell me she was in the attic exorcizing Magdalena Anderson," Johnny said. "Did I tell you that when I saw the buttons flying through the air, I also saw a strange mist leave the attic?"

"No, you didn't," Sharona said.

"I chalked it up to the difference in temperature between the inside and the outside. But it sure had a human shape – head and shoulders. The mist oozed out of the broken window, swirled around the dove, and then disappeared. The dove flew off toward the pinnacle. I didn't tell Theresa or Pense. I didn't want them to read anything into it."

"Chalk that one up to an active mind," Sharona said.

The two had crested the hill and stood looking down into a natural depression about thirty feet in diameter, ringed by cedar, willow and dogwood.

"God!" exclaimed Johnny, hurrying down the hill to a smoldering pile of wood. "It's Zizou's wagon!"

"I thought so," Sharona said, coming up beside him to peer into the ashes. "I figured they'd do something like this. It's a Roma custom. A dead person's personal possessions like clothing are usually burned."

Johnny carefully circled the smoldering pile. Heat from the fire had softened the ground enough that the debris was already sinking into the bog. He bent to pick up a fragment of cardboard, a charred piece of one of the boxes that the protest signs were shipped in. "Well, that's the end of an era. It was a hot fire. They must have dumped gasoline on it. There's nothing much left of the wagon."

"The Roma won't come back, you know," Sharona said. "By burning the wagon they have signaled the end of the Kumpania."

"Sharona? What about Zizou? They wouldn't? She isn't?" Johnny's voice trailed off. He looked with skepticism at the smoldering pile. "That wouldn't be right."

"They could have. It's tradition. It's what she'd have wanted." Sharona shivered.

In the silence that followed both said a little prayer for Zizou.

Johnny finally spoke. "Let's go. We won't tell anyone. We won't do anything about it. Winter and the bog will have their way. If there's anything left for someone to find in the spring, we know nothing. If Zizou was . . . there'd be nothing left but charred bones and the wolves'll take care of them."

"If hunters stumble on it now, they'll think it's an old farm wagon that was burned," Sharona said. "The wide metal rims are the only thing that might give it away. Snow will cover the debris." She shivered again at the thought of Zizou's bones being gnawed by wolves.

Johnny put his arm around her. "Come on. Let's go home." It's good that the falling snow has already covered our tracks into the swamp, Johnny thought, as the two walked out to the main road. If anyone finds the wagon now there'll be embarrassing questions asked. By spring all will be long gone, swallowed by the bog.

"Johnny, but if by chance, Daniel did die around our noon-hour time, what do you think they'd do with his body?"

"I don't want to think about it," Johnny said, fingering the little white dove he'd put in his pocket. The button would be his good luck charm until the day he died. "I'm sure Daniel left instructions. He was a thorough man."

Knightswood - evening

Johnny was the one who discovered the marriage board had been tampered with. He'd gone into the dining room for the carafe of plum wine so that everyone could toast *Silhouette* and *The Count Daniel Vincent Cudzinki* – whoever he was, wherever he had gone.

"You ladies had better take a peek into the dining room," he said when he finally came back to the kitchen. Switching the overhead light on, Johnny led them into the room. He pointed toward the crest-board. The wooden rosette was complete with the insertion of a beautiful gold locket, whose chain lay entwined through the carved leaves. The jewelry obviously belonged, as the rosette had been carved for its oval shape. The locket's cover incorporated a small dove of milky white quartz, carrying a ruby rose in its beak.

"I've never seen the like," Theresa said, looking at the locket.

"It's beautiful." Sharona touched the delicate gold filigree.

"It's her locket." Pense moved in for a closer look.

"Look," said Johnny, reaching to open the locket with a fingernail. "Who do you see?"

Each took a turn looking at the miniature pictures inside the locket. The lid held the photo of a young Magdalena. The interior receptacle held the photo of a man who was without a doubt a youthful Count Daniel Vincent Cudzinki – Danny Cudney. The likenesses were those in Granny Smith's photograph, cut down to fit into the small locket.

"Where did it come from?" Theresa asked. "It wasn't there last night. Who put it in the crestboard?"

"Daniel." Pense was pressed against the marriage board to better see the locket. "He completed his gift for Magdalena. He took the locket when he left. Danny promised to return with it when they could be together again. He brought it back with him this time. That was the reason that kept him earth-bound. He had to come back, to complete the board and to get Magdalena."

"He must have put the locket here before he left." Theresa rubbed her finger over the raised cover. "Pense, how do you know this was Magdalena's?"

"Look on the back," Pense said. You'll find an inscription that reads *To my darling Magdalena - Your Lover Daniel - YLD.*

Johnny raised the locket from its protective cradle high enough to read the back, being very careful not to disturb the chain which was delicately threaded through passages in the carved leaves. He turned the locket to read the inscription. "She's right. Pense, you've never seen this before?"

"Yes, I've seen it," Pense said. "A long time ago I held that locket in my hand, kissed it then gave it to Danny to take as a remembrance of our love." When, she thought, would they believe that she had been the embodiment of Magdalena Anderson? Would any of them ever believe that Daniel Cudzinki was the ghost of *YLD* ?

Theresa put her arm around Pense in a vote of confidence.

"It's a beauty," Johnny said, slipping the locket back into place. "I wonder who kept it for Daniel while he was . . . wherever he was."

Not even Pense could answer that question.

"Do you think we should move the marriage board into the attic?" Sharona asked.

"Oh, no!" Pense said. "Leave it here, Mother. This is where it should be, not in an attic or the barn. You don't have to worry. I don't think that Daniel will return, no matter how hard I polish the marriage board. He'd want the furniture left in the dining room. He went to a great deal of trouble to complete the board for me, for us, for himself." Pense looked imploringly from her mother to Theresa to her father.

"What do you think, Theresa?" Johnny asked. "It's your house."

"I think it has to stay here," Theresa said. "If it doesn't bother Pense, the marriage board doesn't bother me. Like everything else, it belongs in this room, in this house. Just like us, it's part of Magdalena's Knightswood, our home."

Chapter 13

June, 1948

Lillian made arrangements to go to England as soon as she found that she was pregnant with Sebastian Temple Kropolus's child. Charlotte gave Lillian money from her household budget. J.P., who wasn't told what the trip was about, grudgingly paid the ship's ticket.

Before she left, Lillian introduced Charlotte to Theresa Inachio's warm, inviting kitchen. Theresa didn't question but welcomed the woman with open arms and warm heart, as she did all her boarders, as she had Daniel and all the other confused souls who stumbled onto Knightswood.

Neither had Lillian confronted J.P. with her parentage issue. He'd changed. He seemed to lack spirit. Someone or something had a hold on him. He was withdrawn, sullen, unpredictable.

It was easy getting passage to England. Everyone else seemed to be leaving the country. It was more difficult to find accommodation in Chelfont St. Peter, the little village that Kenneth Walker called home in 1912. She eventually found board with a farm family who needed extra cash and a helping hand.

To explain her condition, Lillian told the truth, explaining that the pregnancy was the result of a relationship that didn't work out. This explanation was accepted in a country where many women were left in similar circumstances after the war. If asked about why she decided to live in England, Lillian explained that she didn't feel welcome at home so decided to put an ocean between herself and family. With little money, Lillian learned to live frugally. When not helping on the farm, she walked the countryside, learning as much as possible about her father, the young Mr. Kenneth Walker.

On one of her hikes, Lillian met the Reverend Elisha Horsley, pastor of the church where some members of the Walker family had worshiped. Elisha Horsley was a pleasant fellow and a widower. Over time, Lillian grew to appreciate his hearth-side and companionship.

Although the good Reverend had been a child when Kenneth Walker lived in the village, he assisted Lillian with her research. Indeed, he found Kenneth's death certificate in his old church records. The page in the book had been marked by the insertion of a death certificate for one Daniel Vincent Cudzinki who had been killed in South Africa on October 6, 1901. As Reverend Horsley didn't realize the name *Cudzinki* had a connection to Kenneth Walker, he didn't mention the certificate to Lillian.

Lillian's son, a lusty wee fellow, was born, with the help of the farmer's spouse and a midwife. "He has a musician's hands," the midwife said, looking at the babe's long, slender fingers. "He has violin fingers."

When Lillian held the baby's tiny hands and looked tenderly into his delicate face crowned by a shock of curly, black hair, she knew she must call him Kenneth Daniel. The child was the spit and image of a younger Count Daniel Vincent Cudzinki. Her heart told her that indeed he had a musician's fingers, that he was born *with a violin in his hands.* Lillian also knew that she had to return to Millbrook to introduce him to Theresa Inachio and her mother. Kenneth Daniel Walker's future lay in Canada.

Biographies

Theresa lived at Knightswood until she died at age 94 in 1967. She continued to take in boarders until 1950. Then, fulfilling her desire to travel, and having a companion in Charlotte Harris, Theresa sold a number of pieces of antique furniture and a few oil paintings. The money enabled her to take many pleasant trips to Europe.

Pense finished school and trained as a nurse. She never married. Until she returned to Knightswood in 1986 to care for her mother, Pense nursed in the British Isles, France, Australia and South Africa. Today Pense runs Knightswood as a bed-and-breakfast. Her guests enjoy the eclectic nature of the house. The marriage board, with the locket in place, still stands in the dining room. Theresa's ring is always on Pense's finger. In her will, Pense has left Knightswood to the community to be used for parkland and museum. Should they not want to carry out her wishes, the property must revert to Kenneth Daniel Walker.

Johnny and Sharona were married in December, 1947. They made Knightswood their home, tended its gardens and cared for Theresa in her declining years. Their second daughter Danielle was born in 1949. Johnny died at age 73 in 1987. Sharona lived until age 78 and died in 1996.

J.P. Harris III committed suicide in June 1949, leaving his wife a very wealthy woman. Charlotte and Theresa enjoyed each other's company and took many trips to Europe, especially to England to see Charlotte's grandson. Charlotte died of cancer in 1979.

After J.P.'s death, ***Lillian*** returned to Millbrook with her son Kenneth, but soon realized that her place was at Reverend Horsley's fireside. Lillian married Elisha Horsley in1949 and made her home in England until her death in 2001. She and Kenneth visited Canada often during the ensuing years.

Between visits to Canada and his grandmother's frequent travels to England, ***Kenneth*** got to know his extended family quite well. Kenneth emigrated to Canada, attended university in Toronto then lived in Millbrook to be near his grandmother. ***Kenneth Walker, Jr., and Danielle Wallace*** were married in 1978. Kenneth is the principal violinist with a major symphony orchestra. Danielle is an artist and sculptor. Their three children – two sons and a daughter – are all musically inclined and all share the love of the lungo drom.

Compton died in 1977 leaving a legacy of "Compton's Follies" in his wake, as his strip malls and cheap housing developments are called by the locals. The heart of the village did survive his onslaught, but with the exception of 800 acres, including Pense's Mountain, that belong to Knightswood, the surrounding area is heavily developed.

Mr. & Mrs. *Kropolus* moved to Florida in 1955. Their son Sebastian Temple, the father of Lillian's child, died in an auto accident in 1951.

Keough rented from Johnny until 1950 when he bought a farm east of the village. Johnny's farm then became part of the Knightswood estate.

No trace can be found of ***Blake,*** who left J.P. Harris's employment in January 1948.

Count Daniel Vincent Cudzinki perhaps returned to Knightswood. Someone buried a small, ornate box under the oak beside the remains of Magdalena Anderson. We can only speculate that it contained the ashes of Danny Cudney – Palumb Furtuna. The question is that if Daniel had been a ghost, would there be ash? And if the box didn't contain ash . . . .

As Theresa Inachio would say, dark islands hide strange treasure. The Count Daniel Vincent Cudzinki would put it more clearly – In paradise, who needs *gadje* time?

Glossary: Roma Terms

With thanks to Darnda, who would like readers to understand that spelling varies among different Roma groups. Also note the word 'Gypsy' would not likely have been capitalized in the 1940s. However, we prefer the current usage as more respectful to the Romany people.

atchin tan - stopping ground or place
Baro Shera/shero - Big Head
baxtalo - happy
bengalo - devilish
Bengalo Daj - Devilish Mother!
besh - sit
butji - watch
chavi/chey - girl
Cigany - the Roma, Gypsies
darane svatura - stories of a supernatural nature
dickla/dicklera - neckscarf
didikai - a fellow Gypsy
dook - the second sight
Dordie - an exuberant Gypsy outcry
Dordie miri mort! - Dordie my woman!
drab - herbs
drabarni - fortune teller
drom - road
Eppah! - cry of joy or victory
familia - a group of Gypsies that have family ties
gadje - anyone who is not a Gypsy
galbi - gold coins
ghel - girl
I phuv kheldias - the earth danced
kanny - chicken
kesht - stick
kumpania - bands of Roma familia who travel and live together in a chosen territory
lavuta - violin
Mamioro - the spirit who brings fatal illness
manus - man

Martiya - spirit of the night
miri - my
mort - woman
mule-vi - a medium or person who speaks to the dead
mulani - ghost
mulo - death
Na daren, Palumb Furtuna vi ame sam Rom chache. - Do not fear, Palumb Furtuna, for we too are Gypsies
Nais tuke - Thank you
O Lungo Drom - The Long Road
O Palumb - the Dove
O zhiwindo - "the live one"
ofisa - the fortune telling
paani - water
pakiv - a feast to honor someone special
Palumb Furtuna - Dove Storm
patrin - special signs left along byways to guide the Kumpania
pomano - funeral feast
Rom Baro - the leader of the Kumpania
romipen - Gypsyhood
Sar san? - How are you?
schav - Gypsy boy
schej - Gypsy girl
shon - moon
Te den, xa, te maren, de-nash - When you are given, eat. When you are beaten, run away
Te prakhon man pasho a Magdalena - May I be buried next to Magdalena
treno shav - young men
Trito ursitori - three spirits - one good, one evil and one a mediator
tumnimos - plans for betrothal
vitsa - clan
vurdon - wagon

We invite you to visit Pat Mestern's website, *www.mestern.net* for more about the music that is Magdalena's Song, more about Pat Mestern and her other books and projects.

At the High Country Publishers website, *www.highcountrypublishers.com*, you can read excerpts and reviews of this and other books, visit websites of other authors and find out what's new from High Country Publishers, Ltd.

High Country Publishers, Ltd.

Boone, NC

2002

About the Author

Pat Mattaini Mestern has always called the small town of Fergus, Ontario, home. During her youth, Pat was surrounded by books, stimulating conversation and visual history. This background melded with her love of history to create a writing style that focuses on attractive settings and strong characterizations.

Pat Mestern is the author of four previous works of fiction: *Clara, 1979; Anna, Child of the Poor House 1981; Rachel's Legacy, 1989, The Contract 1991.*

Non-fictional works include *Looking Back, a 2 volume history set, 1983; Fergus, a Scottish Town By Birthright,1995, So You Want to Hold a Festival, A-Z of Festival & Special Event Organization. 2002.*

Mestern's books have been chosen for newspaper serialization, considered for movie production and nominated for awards. When she's not penning book length works, Pat writes travel, life style and local history columns for a variety of national and international publications.

Pat is the mother of four children: Andrew, Celeste, Julia and Cecile, and shares her life with husband Ted and ten grandchildren.